Up, Up, and Aw[...]

Tres Leches Cupcakes

"**A delicious concoction of suspense and surprise** baked in the warm New Mexico sun. You'll enjoy every bite of *Tres Leches Cupcakes!*"

> —Tristi Pinkston, author of the Secret Sisters Mysteries, reviewer for AML

"Kilpack is a capable writer whose works have grown and taken on a life of their own. ***Tres Leches Cupcakes* is an amusing and captivating addition to her creative compilations.**"

> —Mike Whitmer, *Deseret News*

Banana Split

"In *Banana Split*, Josi Kilpack has turned a character that we've come to love as an overzealous snoop and given her the breath of someone real so we can love her even more. **This is a story with an ocean's depth's worth of awesome!**"

> —Julie Wright, author of the Hazardous Universe series

"Josi Kilpack does an excellent job with the setting and creating a believable plot with *Banana Split*. The Sadie Hoffmiller series continues to be **one of my favorites.**"

> —Heather Moore, author of *Daughters of Jared*

Pumpkin Roll

"*Pumpkin Roll* is different from the other books in the series, and while the others have their tense moments, **this had me downright nervous and spooked.** During the climax, I kept shaking my head, saying, 'No way this is happening.' Five out of five stars for this one. I could not stop reading."

—Mindy Holt, www.ldswomensbookreview.com

"*Pumpkin Roll* is tightly plotted, with twists, turns, and pinches in just the right places, and it's obvious Josi takes the recipes just as seriously as she does the story. Complete with expert character development, unique premise, and polished voice, *Pumpkin Roll* is a thumping good read!"

—Luisa Perkins, author of *The Book of Jer3miah* and *Despirited*

Blackberry Crumble

"Josi Kilpack is an absolute master at leading you to believe you have everything figured out, only to have the rug pulled out from under you with the turn of a page. *Blackberry Crumble* is a delightful mystery with wonderful characters and a white-knuckle ending that'll leave you begging for more."

—Gregg Luck, author of *Blink of an Eye*

"*Blackberry Crumble* offers up a thrilling murder mystery! Most people are not who they appear to be. I can't give away the really shadowy characters or the killer, but there is a killer—and this killer means business!"

—Gabi Kupitz

Key Lime Pie

"I had a great time following the ever-delightful Sadie as she ate and sleuthed her way through nerve-racking twists and turns and nail-biting suspense."

—Melanie Jacobsen, author of *The List* and *Not My Type*,
http://www.readandwritestuff.blogspot.com/

"Sadie Hoffmiller is the perfect heroine. She's funny, sassy, and always my first choice for crime solving. And where better to solve a mystery than the Florida Keys? *Key Lime Pie* **satisfied with every bite!**"

—Julie Wright, author of *Cross My Heart*, www.juliewright.com

"The title of *Key Lime Pie* will make you hungry, but the story will keep you too busy to bake. Even when oh-so-busy amateur sleuth Sadie Hoffmiller vows to stay out of police business, life comes up with a different plan. **A missing girl, a very interesting man with bright blue eyes, and plenty of delicious recipes all create a combination even Sadie can't resist.**"

—H.B. Moore, www.hbmoore.com

Devil's Food Cake

"Josi Kilpack whips up **another tasty mystery where startling twists and delightful humor mix** in a confection as delicious as Sadie Hoffmiller's devil's food cake."

—Stephanie Black, four-time winner of the Whitney Award for Mystery/Suspense

"There's no mistaking that Kilpack is one of the best in this field and not just in the LDS market. *Lemon Tart* was good, *English Trifle* was better, but with *Devil's Food Cake* she delivers **a polished novel that can hold its own anywhere.**"

—Jennie Hansen, *Meridian Magazine*

English Trifle

"*English Trifle* **is a delightful combo of mystery and gourmet cooking,** highly recommended."

—*Midwest Review Journal*, October 2009

"*English Trifle* **is an excellent read** and will be enjoyed by teens and adults of either gender. The characters are interesting, the plot is carefully crafted, and the setting has an authentic feel."

—Jennie Hansen, *Meridian Magazine*

Lemon Tart

"**The novel has a bit of everything. It's a mystery, a cookbook, a low-key romance and a dead-on depiction of life.** . . . That may sound like a hodgepodge. It's not. It works. Kilpack blends it all together and cooks it up until it has the taste of, well . . . of a tangy lemon tart."

—Jerry Johnston, *Deseret News*

"*Lemon Tart* **is an enjoyable mystery** with a well-hidden culprit and an unlikely heroine in Sadie Hoffmiller. Kilpack endows Sadie with logical hidden talents that come in handy at just the right moment."

—Shelley Glodowski, *Midwest Book Review*, June 2009

"Josi Kilpack's new book *Lemon Tart* takes everything I love about a culinary mystery—the food, the humor, the intrigue—and blends it all at high speed with a dash of spice in the form of our main character, Sadie. **A must-read for those who enjoy well-crafted mysteries.**"

—Tristi Pinkston, http://www.tristipinkston.blogspot.com

BAKED
ALASKA

OTHER BOOKS BY JOSI S. KILPACK

Her Good Name
Sheep's Clothing
Unsung Lullaby
Daisy

CULINARY MYSTERIES

Lemon Tart	*Blackberry Crumble*
English Trifle	*Pumpkin Roll*
Devil's Food Cake	*Banana Split*
Key Lime Pie	*Tres Leches Cupcakes*

Rocky Road (coming Fall 2013)

❦

Baked Alaska recipes

Kara's Bread Pudding and Caramel Sauce	10
Sausage Wontons	29
Crepes and Toppings	40
Salmon Caesar Salad	93
Glazed Salmon	100
Carrie's Crunchy Caramel Popcorn	156
Fruity Popcorn	157
Chef Ferguson's Stuffed Mushrooms	233
Lemon-Zucchini Fettuccine	278
Baked Alaska	284
Baked Alaska Cupcakes	285
Salmon and Red Potato Chowder	341

Download a free PDF of all the recipes in this book at
josiskilpack.com or shadowmountain.com

BAKED ALASKA

A CULINARY MYSTERY

JOSI S. KILPACK

SHADOW
MOUNTAIN

Visit us at ShadowMountain.com

Library of Congress Cataloging-in-Publication Data
Kilpack, Josi S., author.
 Baked Alaska / Josi S. Kilpack.
  pages cm
 Summary: Sadie Hoffmiller has gathered her family together to enjoy an Alaskan cruise and to help plan her daughter's wedding. But when her son's birth mother shows up on the ship, relationships become complicated. And once the dead bodies start appearing, Sadie realizes more than one person on the cruise is keeping secrets.
 ISBN 978-1-60907-328-2 (paperbound)
 1. Hoffmiller, Sadie (Fictitious character)—Fiction. 2. Cooks—Fiction.
3. Ocean travel—Fiction. I. Title.
 PS3561.I412B35 2013
 813'.54—dc23   2012047362

Printed in the United States of America
R. R. Donnelley, Crawfordsville, IN

10   9   8   7   6   5   4   3   2   1

To my writing group: Becki, Jody, Nancy, Ronda.
There are specific points in this story I owe completely to you guys.
You have been a foundation for me for so long and I so appreciate
your friendship, support, and continual encouragement. I love
you gals and am blessed to have you in my life!

CHAPTER 1

ᘡ

"Don't be a snob, Mom."

Sadie didn't look up from the gelatinous bread pudding she was poking with the serving spoon. "Bread pudding should not jiggle. If this is any indication of the food I can expect on this cruise, it's going to be a very long week."

"It's the first buffet," Breanna said as she spooned some berry cobbler onto her plate. "Don't judge the food so harshly from just one meal."

The cobbler looked okay, so Sadie took a small amount, then followed her daughter down the buffet line.

"You never get a second chance to make a first impression," Sadie said, narrowing her eyes at what was supposed to be cheese-cake but looked like stiff pudding. She settled for a cherry turnover that looked exactly like the ones Arby's sold for a dollar. "On that cruise I took with Gayle in January, the food was awful."

Sadie had always loved cruises, but just over a year ago, she had undergone some traumatic experiences associated with water, so the inexpensive, three-day Baja cruise with Gayle had been a test to see

1

if Sadie could handle being in a floating hotel. The cruise convinced her she was okay *on* the water, just not *in* it.

The food on that ship, however, had been very low quality. It was a cheap cruise, though, so perhaps that was to be expected. Now she was on another cruise—a longer, more expensive one—with a different cruise line, and the first foray into the menus had shaken her confidence. Good bread pudding should be dense, flavorful, and topped with a creamy caramel sauce—like her cousin Kara's recipe which Sadie had made for years and years. It wasn't difficult to make good bread pudding. If the ship's cooks couldn't do right by a basic dessert, what would their beef Wellington be like?

They finished the dessert segment of the buffet and made their way to the salad bar—dessert first whenever possible.

"If you don't mind my saying so, you seem a little uptight," Breanna said once they finished dishing up and were winding their way through the dining room in hopes of finding an empty table. "Is everything okay? Have you already found a dead body you're afraid to tell me about?"

Sadie scowled at her daughter's back. "I'll have you know I haven't seen a dead body for eight months, if you don't count Brother Harper from church, but he was eighty-seven and properly laid out in his coffin when I saw him at the viewing. It was a lovely service."

"Eight months—that's got to be some kind of record, right?"

"Oh, stop it," Sadie said, wishing she had a free hand so she could playfully slap her daughter's arm. "I think that phase of my life is over." She scanned table after table filled with people already eating. "Is there not even one empty table in this entire dining room?"

"There are some back there," Breanna said, nodding toward the back of the ship. "Just calm down."

They made their way past their fellow passengers and finally slid into their seats, officially staking their claim at a table for four near a window that looked out over the Seattle pier. The ship wouldn't sail for another two hours.

"Seriously, though," Breanna said once they were seated, "are you okay?"

Sadie took a breath and decided to spill it. "I'm worried about this trip."

Breanna unwrapped her silverware from her napkin, placed the cloth in her lap, then raised her brown eyes to meet Sadie's blue ones. Both of Sadie's children were adopted, and not for the first time Sadie thought that Breanna's birth mother must have been very beautiful.

"*You're* worried? This whole trip was your idea."

"I know, but I guess the worry didn't hit me until I realized Pete and Shawn would be on the transfer bus together. They were on that bus for half an hour, then in line for another hour. What if they decide they hate each other by the time they get here? Then we're stuck together for seven really lousy days."

"Shawn and Pete have spent time together before," Breanna said. "I'm the one who hardly knows your boyfriend."

"Oh, don't call him that," Sadie said, feeling her cheeks heat up. "It sounds so . . . young." Sadie had recently turned fifty-eight years old. Young was feeling further and further away as she tried to wrap her head around her impending AARP membership.

Breanna laughed and stabbed a bite of her salad with one hand while tucking her long, straight, brown hair behind her ear with the other. "I'd call him your fiancé, but he hasn't made it official yet, though I don't know what he's waiting for."

Sadie took a bite of her own salad to stall before she answered. The truth was that she and Pete had talked about marriage often during the last few months as Pete's retirement grew closer and the threat Sadie had been running from felt more and more distant—she'd been safely living back in Garrison, Colorado, since December and nothing had happened. But, even so, Sadie had always stopped the wedding discussions when they got to the point of timing and specifics.

Breanna had been engaged for more than a year now, and the happy couple had finally set the date for October nineteenth. Sadie was loath to take any attention away from her daughter's special celebration of a joined life.

Pete understood Sadie's reasons to delay their own vows, but two and a half years was a really long courtship. This cruise therefore, had multiple purposes: to celebrate Pete's retirement from the police department, to allow Sadie's children to get to know him better, and to allow Sadie to catch up with Breanna's wedding plans. Seeing as how Breanna lived in London and Sadie lived in Colorado, mother and daughter hadn't had a lot of time to talk things over.

"So?"

Sadie looked up, her fork halfway to her mouth. "What?"

"I asked if Pete was going to make an honest woman of you or not?"

"Breanna Lynn!" Sadie said, lowering her fork as her cheeks heated up again. "Are you implying that my relationship with Pete Cunningham is anything less than respectable?"

Breanna's grin widened, and she pointed her fork across the table. "Bazinga."

"Bazinga? What does that mean?"

Breanna laughed again and took another bite.

It must be European humor.

"Isn't this whole cruise about you making an announcement to Shawn and me?"

"No," Sadie said, shaking her head. Is that what they thought? "It's a family vacation . . . with Pete, and my chance to get caught up on your wedding plans."

"Oh," Breanna said with a shrug of one shoulder, showing how unconcerned she was about the information. "Shawn and I both like Pete, so I don't know why you're worried."

Sadie considered how best to proceed as she and Breanna took a few more bites of their meals but decided she may as well lay all her concerns on the table. "I'm also a little worried about Shawn."

Bre kept her eyes on her food, a sure indication that she knew something, and Sadie's stomach fell. As much as Sadie hated being left out, if Shawn were in *serious* trouble, he wouldn't only talk to Breanna about it, right? One thing was for certain, if Sadie hoped to get information from Breanna, she couldn't push too hard or her daughter would clam up. She wasn't one to be casual with other people's confidences. "Does he seem okay to you?" Sadie asked innocently.

"Well, you know, he's finishing up school this summer and . . . it's not the best time to get a job and, well . . . it's a big transition."

While Shawn had walked with his graduating class just last month, he still had two online classes he needed to finish up over the summer in order to complete his degree in criminal justice.

But it was obvious to Sadie that school and the inevitable transition that followed wasn't *it*. "Why wouldn't he talk to me about that?"

Breanna still wouldn't meet her mother's eyes. "Um, well, have you asked him what's wrong?"

"Of course I have. He's assured me everything is fine, but he only calls me back about half the time these days. I can just feel this . . . vagueness from him."

"Maybe don't worry about it, then," Breanna said, attempting a smile as she finally made eye contact. "When he's ready, he'll tell you."

"So he *is* having trouble that he doesn't want to talk to me about."

"Mom," Bre said, but the roar of a lion cut her off. Breanna rummaged in her bag and pulled out her phone. She'd majored in zoology and currently worked as a docent at the London Zoo, so of course her text message tone was a lion's roar. Because they were in port, there was still cell service, but once they headed out to sea, cell phones would only be useful to check the time and to take pictures.

"They're checked in," she said while typing a response.

"Shawn and Pete?" Sadie asked, sitting up straighter and instantly dropping her concerns in favor of an appropriate welcome for her two favorite men. "Where are they?"

"Shawn says they just had their 'Welcome Aboard' photo taken."

"Together?" Sadie said, a tender lump in her throat at the thought of Pete and Shawn superimposed in front of their boat, the *Celebration.*

Breanna smiled at her and sent the text message. "They're on their way up. Shawn said to save him some bacon."

"Even if it's undercooked?"

❦

When Pete found them, Sadie jumped up for a hello kiss and hug. It had only been a week since he'd dropped her off at the Denver airport so she could fly up to visit some friends in Portland before the cruise, but she'd missed him. Only when she pulled back from the embrace did she realize he was alone. "Where's Shawn?"

"He said he'd catch up. I think he saw someone he knew."

"Really?" Sadie asked with heavy skepticism in her voice as all her concerns came rushing back. What were the chances of him knowing someone other than Pete, Breanna, and herself on this cruise?

"He told me to go ahead and he'd be right behind me." They all looked behind Pete, but there was no 260-pound Polynesian man with an Afro bringing up the rear.

"You go get yourself some food—avoid the bread pudding, though—and I'll find my boy," Sadie said to Pete. She hadn't seen Shawn since Christmas—almost six months—which was far too long to go without one of his signature bear hugs. She knew she'd feel better once she saw him in person.

"Okay. He was one level down, in front of the elevators when I last saw him. Hurry back." He gave her a wink, and she felt all jiggly inside for a moment.

Sadie made her way out of the dining room and down the set of stairs just outside the entrance to the buffet. Unlike deck twelve, deck eleven was primarily a cabin deck, though a sign indicated that the security office was forward on the starboard side and the bridge was forward on the port side of the ship. Although there were several people waiting for an elevator when Sadie arrived, Shawn was not one of them. If she didn't find him soon, she'd call his phone, but she liked the idea of finding him on her own.

She headed to the port side and glanced down the long narrow hallway lined with turquoise doors that led to the passenger cabins. There was a younger couple coming out of a room, but no Shawn. She crossed in front of the elevators to the starboard side, glanced right, and then left, relieved when a familiar set of shoulders and six inches of picked-out curls caught her eye. She smiled to herself and headed toward Shawn's towering form when she realized he was talking to someone. And he didn't look happy about it.

Sadie slowed her steps and observed the scene with a little more interest. The woman Shawn was talking to was a light-skinned black woman with hundreds of long thin braids pulled back into a bulky ponytail. Some of the braids were dyed hot pink. She wore a black cotton sundress and was very engaged in whatever it was she was explaining to Shawn, who had his arms crossed over his chest and a scowl on his face.

The woman was gesturing with her hands, but the expression on her face was somewhat pleading, as though she was trying to convince Shawn of something. As Sadie got closer, she realized the woman was older than Shawn. She was thickly built and at least six feet tall. The two of them completely blocked the hallway.

Sadie stopped about twenty feet from them, not wanting to be rude and interrupt, but not inclined to back away either. Why was Shawn upset? Who was this woman?

The woman said something, then leaned forward slightly, awaiting his answer. Shawn shook his head and began to speak, then saw Sadie out of the corner of his eye and pinched his lips together. She smiled, but he didn't smile back and instead turned to the woman with some urgency. Sadie couldn't hear what he said, but the woman looked at Sadie too. She didn't smile either, and Sadie found herself taking a step backward. Were they angry with *her*? What for?

Shawn said something else, and the woman nodded, turned away from Sadie, and proceeded down the hall. Shawn looked after the woman for a moment, then turned back to Sadie. It took him ten feet before he managed to put a fake smile on his face.

"Who was that?" Sadie asked.

"Don't worry about it."

"But it seemed like the two of you—"

"Gosh, Mom," Shawn snapped, "can you please just not worry about it?"

Sadie lifted her eyebrows in surprise. Shawn never talked to her like that. At least not since he was twelve and she'd grounded him from his GameCube for sassing her.

His expression softened and he took a breath. "Sorry. I've got a lot on my mind right now. Where's the buffet?"

Sadie opened her mouth to ask what he had on his mind, but the way he was holding himself and shifting his weight from one foot to the other kept her quiet. She forced a smile of her own and tucked her wanting-to-know-everything instinct away while putting out her arms, her signal that she wanted a hug from her favorite boy. "It's great to see you."

Shawn wrapped his strong arms around her back, but he didn't squeeze her quite as tight or hold on for quite as long as she'd expected. "Good to see you too, Mom." He pulled back and headed toward the elevators. "Is the food on deck twelve, then? I'm starving."

"Yeah," Sadie said, following him down the hall. "One deck up."

Just before they left the hallway, Sadie looked over her shoulder. The woman Shawn had been talking to ducked out of sight around a corner.

A heavy feeling settled into Sadie's stomach as she and Shawn climbed the stairs leading to deck twelve. Over the last few years, Sadie had developed an extreme dislike for secrets. And now, it seemed, her son was keeping one from her.

Kara's Bread Pudding and Caramel Sauce

Caramel Sauce
1/3 cup white sugar
1/3 cup brown sugar
6 tablespoons butter
2/3 cup corn syrup (maple syrup works well, too)
3/4 cup heavy whipping cream

Bread Pudding
1½ cups sugar
4 eggs, beaten
1¼ cups heavy whipping cream
1½ cups milk
½ teaspoon cinnamon (optional)
1 teaspoon vanilla
½ cup butter, melted
1¼ pounds white bread, cubed
½ cup Caramel Sauce

Preheat oven to 350 degrees.

To make sauce, combine sugars, butter, and syrup in a pot. Cook over medium heat until ingredients liquefy and sugar is dissolved. (Caution, this sauce gets very hot, so be careful. Also, this recipe does not thicken like traditional caramel; you should have a thin sauce.)

Remove from heat and add the cream. Set aside.

To make pudding, combine the sugar, eggs, cream, milk, cinnamon (if desired), vanilla, and butter in a bowl or blender and mix together well. Put cubed bread in a very large mixing bowl. Pour milk mixture over the bread, folding ingredients together until bread has absorbed the liquid.

Pour the mixture in a greased 9x13-inch pan. Pour ½ cup of the caramel sauce over the top of the bread mixture. Bake for

30 minutes; rotate pan and bake another 30 minutes until crust is golden brown and the center doesn't jiggle when you shake the pan. (Depending on your oven, the bread density, and type of pan, it could take up to an additional 30 minutes to cook through the middle.)

Serve bread pudding warm and top with leftover caramel sauce. Serves 12.

Note: Any type of bread works for this recipe—hot dog buns, end pieces, etc. Just go by weight.

CHAPTER 2

S adie stood at the railing with Pete and her children at her side
as the engines roared to life and confetti burst out of the chim-
neys at the top of the ship. She watched the Space Needle disappear
behind them.

"And we're off," Breanna said, her long hair dancing in the
wind. Though Sadie had suggested the cruise, Breanna was the one
who requested Alaska as their destination. She'd never seen whales
in the wild. Seeing her daughter's excitement validated Sadie's decision to fulfill the request despite knowing she would miss the
warmer climates of the Caribbean and Mexican cruises she'd been
on before.

Liam, Breanna's fiancé, had been invited to attend, but since
taking over the affairs of his family's holdings in England, it was
difficult for him to leave for long periods of time. He'd sent Sadie
a very gracious thank-you card for the invite though. Sadie liked
Liam quite a lot, but his responsibilities to his heritage—his father
was an earl—had posed many challenges for the engaged couple.
Despite the difficulties, Liam and Breanna were both working hard
to make the compromises needed for a future together, and Sadie

was proud of her daughter for finding a place of independence amid the obligations.

After the pier faded into the horizon, the Hoffmillers and Pete returned for another round at the buffet. Or, rather, Shawn headed back for another round while the rest of them settled for something to nibble on. Breanna and Pete went with cookies while Sadie got another roll. The bread pudding might be subpar, but the rolls were excellent.

Shawn's lingering tension seemed to dissipate in direct correlation to how much food he ate, but the woman in the hall was never far from Sadie's mind. Each time she considered bringing it up again, however, she remembered Shawn's request to leave it alone and she recommitted to respect that . . . for now. Shawn had been through a lot the last couple of years, and she wanted this to be a true vacation for him, which meant not pushing him too much.

The mandatory evacuation drill went well—the crew didn't make the passengers put on the ugly orange life vests, which Sadie appreciated—and the first evening's entertainment was a preview of the different shows that would be playing in the ship's theater throughout the week. After the performance, Sadie and her family enjoyed a late dinner in the Tiara Room, one of the onboard restaurants, and Sadie was pleased to note that the food there was much better than at the buffet. Everyone got along well, and Sadie was relieved that Pete and her children seemed to be enjoying one another's company.

By ten o'clock, the sky was mostly dark—she wasn't sure it ever got fully dark this far north this time of year—and their bellies were full as they headed to their cabins. Breanna and Sadie were sharing a room on deck eight, while Shawn and Pete each had their own cabins; Shawn on deck seven and Pete on deck ten. Sadie had expected all three rooms would be close to one another, but she must not have checked a box for that request when she submitted the reservation. Oh well, going up and down the stairs would be good for her glutes.

Sadie had stuck to a pretty regular exercise routine since having stayed in New Mexico last fall. Pete's cousin, Caro, had been her inspiration, and Sadie had maintained a better weight than she'd had in several years. She'd given up on ever having the word "slender" be an adjective anyone would use to describe her figure, but she could live with "curvy." It beat "round" any day of the week.

Breanna hadn't quite recovered from her transatlantic flight yesterday, and though Sadie had encouraged her all evening to go to bed early, Breanna hadn't wanted to miss anything.

Once in the room, however, she wilted fast, which meant grilling her about Shawn wasn't the best idea. Breanna managed to brush her teeth, send Liam a quick good night e-mail from her laptop—at approximately $1.25 per minute, Sadie didn't imagine any of them would be spending much time online—and change into her kitten-print pajamas before falling into bed. Within a minute, she was out.

Sadie changed into her own PJs—plaid, not kittens—and was considering checking on Shawn when she heard a tapping at her door. She peered through the peephole and smiled to see that her late-night visitor was Pete. She opened the door quietly and eased out of the room, keeping her hand on the doorknob so it wouldn't lock behind her.

"I tried to text you," Pete said quietly, "but we must be out of cell range now that we're in open water. Did you get settled in okay?"

Sadie nodded. "Breanna's already asleep."

"Good. Then she won't know you snuck out. I want to see what the stars look like from the Pacific Ocean."

Sadie was sixteen all over again, although she'd never actually snuck out when she was sixteen. Still, she felt a little scandalous as she tiptoed back inside her room, put on her slippers, grabbed a jacket, and slid her room key into the pocket. Thank goodness she hadn't taken off her makeup yet; hopefully that made up for the fact that she was in her pajamas.

"Do you mind if I stop by Shawn's cabin to say good night on our way?" Sadie asked after she'd closed the door and tested the handle to make sure it was locked.

"Uh, sure," Pete said.

Sadie pretended not to notice that he wasn't thrilled with the idea. On the way to Shawn's room, Sadie explained that she was worried about him and wanted some reassurance that he was okay.

"Why are you so worried about him?"

"I'll tell you later," she said, dropping her voice since they'd reached Shawn's cabin: room 749. She didn't want him to overhear them talking about him. She tapped on his door and waited for him to answer. His stateroom was the same size as the one Breanna and Sadie were sharing, which meant he could get to the door in about five steps no matter where he might be inside. Sure enough, a few seconds later, he pulled open the door, completely filling the door-way. Sadie smiled and was relieved when he smiled back.

"I just wanted to say good night before Pete and I go look at the stars," Sadie said.

She put out her arms for a hug, and he complied, holding her tighter than he had that afternoon, which went a long way toward easing her worries.

"Good night, Mom," he said when he let her go. He glanced at Pete and raised one eyebrow. "Don't keep her out too late."

"Well, you know what they say—what happens on a cruise ship, stays on a cruise ship."

Shawn chuckled while Sadie shook her head and hoped her embarrassment didn't show. The phone in Shawn's cabin rang, and his expression instantly hardened as he glanced over his shoulder. "I better go," he said, stepping back and closing the door halfway. "I'll catch up with you for breakfast, okay?"

"Okay, what . . . time?" But he'd shut the cabin door before she finished. She blinked at the door for a few moments, until Pete took her hand and pulled her toward the stairs.

"Who would be calling him?" Sadie wondered. "It's almost eleven o'clock." But even as she asked it, she had a strong suspicion about the answer. There was only one other person on this boat whom he seemed to know besides his family—the woman with the braids.

"Stand down, Mama Bear, we'll see him in the morning."

Pete guided her down the hall, but Sadie kept looking over her shoulder at the closed door to Shawn's room.

They took the elevator up to deck twelve, then followed a short hallway to the automatic doors that led to the open portion of the deck that held the swimming pools, hot tubs, and outside grill—none of which she expected would get much use since the temperature wasn't expected to go past the low sixties all week. This late at night, it had to be in the forties. Though June was technically summer in Colorado, it seemed to still be early spring in the Pacific Northwest.

She was surprised to see a few of her fellow passengers braving the hot tubs, and she shivered at the thought of how cold they would be once they ran for their towels. She zipped her jacket up to her chin and pushed her hands into the fleece-lined pockets as she followed Pete up a set of stairs that led to the highest deck on the ship. Thirteen-forward, like its sister deck, thirteen-aft, were partial balconies, set up with a few tables and a dozen or so deck chairs. It was a perfect place to get away from the bustle of the ship, which was still going strong despite the late hour.

Sadie and Pete had the deck to themselves, probably because it was also the coldest part of the ship with nothing to protect them from the bracing breeze coming off the ocean. Sadie had hoped to see the northern lights on this trip, but in her research prior to the cruise, she had learned they probably wouldn't be far enough north to see them, especially this time of year. But she still hoped all the same.

Though clouds covered the sky, the moonlight that filtered through lit the ocean like an undulating mirror. Sadie felt a moment of misgiving, imagining the depths below the surface of the water, but then Pete put his arms around her from behind and pulled her close. Was there a better antidote to her anxiety than Peter Cunningham's embrace?

"So this is what retirement is like," Pete said after they spent a minute just enjoying the togetherness of it all. He rested his chin on her shoulder and stared across the ocean. "I think I could get used to it pretty quickly."

"It hasn't even been a full weekend," Sadie teased. Her face was already tingling from the cold.

"But there's no desk waiting for me on Monday, and no one will be calling me at three in the morning. Just knowing that makes this a very different weekend than any other weekend I've had before. I might even learn how to sleep in again."

"You're not going to be one of those retirees who ends up watching *Wheel of Fortune* reruns all day and showering once a week, are you?"

Pete laughed. "Somehow I don't think you'll let that happen."

Sadie smiled at the inclusion of her in his life and snuggled into his chest a little more. She breathed in the scent of his cologne—something musky—mingled with the ocean breeze.

"Besides, I'll still be doing some consulting, and there's talk of opening up a tri-county cold case squad; I'll put in for that. *And*, believe it or not, there are things I've wanted to do other than work."

"Like what?"

"Fishing and hiking and raising chickens—I've got a list."

Sadie laughed out loud and turned her head to look up at him. "Raise chickens?"

"I grew up with chickens. We had a flock when my kids were little, but they got tired of them, and I was busy and Pat never liked them. I think I'd like to start up again. They're a fun hobby."

"Chickens," Sadie repeated, shaking her head and looking out across the ocean again. "I'd have never guessed you were a wannabe chicken farmer." Fresh eggs were fabulous in baked goods, however, which offset Sadie's qualms about supporting such an endeavor. She wasn't keen on cleaning out the chicken coop though. They would definitely need to negotiate terms of the chicken-related duties down the road.

"I'll have you know I took the blue ribbon in the Santa Fe county fair for my Ameraucana bantam rooster when I was twelve. His name was Elvis."

Sadie laughed again. "Oh, Pete, you continue to surprise me."

"That's good. Because once you figure me out, I'll be boring."

"I can't imagine that."

He kissed the top of her head, and she turned in his arms so that they were facing one another. They went quiet, and Sadie closed her eyes and rested her head against his chest while she listened to the passengers below them and the sound of the ship cutting through the water. For a moment, Sadie pretended they were married and this was their honeymoon.

Sadie had never enjoyed waiting, but this kind of waiting was taxing her more than anything else had in her life. And it was all her fault. Pete would likely marry her next week if she said she was ready, and she *was* ready in almost every way other than wanting her daughter to get married first so as not to take anything away from that event. It was a hard decision to stick to though, and she questioned her determination on a daily basis. Breanna's wedding was still four months away. *Four!* Would it be so bad if Sadie were a married woman on her daughter's special day?

"So, why are you worried about Shawn? You've been looking at him funny all day."

"I have?" Sadie said with a frown, opening her eyes and staring out at the water once more. "I didn't mean to be so obvious."

"Did something happen?"

Sadie explained about seeing the woman in the hallway and Shawn's reaction to her questions.

"Huh," Pete said in reply. "That's strange."

Sadie looked up at him. "Did you see her when the two of you parted ways?"

Pete shook his head. "We'd come on with a big group and opted for the stairs since the elevators were packed. It was slow going. When we reached deck eleven, Shawn said he'd catch up. I didn't see where he went."

"How would he know someone on board? And why not explain

it to me if it's innocent? I think Breanna knows something, but she fell asleep before I could get it out of her."

"Sadie, Sadie, Sadie," Pete said, shaking his head. "Don't do this."

"Do what?" Sadie asked innocently. "I'm a concerned parent."

He gave her a questioning look, and she narrowed her eyes, albeit playfully—sort of. "If it were *your* son, *you'd* be concerned."

"Being concerned and getting into it are two different things, and I can guarantee that I wouldn't *get into it*. He's twenty-two years old. Let him be a grown-up."

Shawn was actually twenty-three—he'd just had a birthday—but correcting Pete wouldn't help her case, so she refrained. "I don't want to *get into it*. And I know he's an adult, I just . . . " Her voice trailed off at Pete's incredulous look. "I'm just worried about him. I told you how aloof he's been the last few months—not returning my calls and being vague when we do talk."

"That doesn't justify you poking your nose where it doesn't belong."

Sadie frowned, mostly because he was right, but partly because she really, really wanted to know what was going on. "Things have been different between us since Boston," she said. Boston had been hard for everyone—Shawn, Sadie, and Pete too. "It's been a year and a half, and I keep hoping our relationship will repair itself, but sometimes I worry that something broke in him back there."

"Regardless of whether that's true or not, all you can do is love him as your son and respect him as an adult. Let this trip be about togetherness. He's doing good things with his life, and if you can respect his boundaries, he'll be much more likely to open up to you."

Sadie took a breath and nodded. "You're right."

Pete smiled widely. "I'm glad you think so."

"I think I'm getting frostbite in my toes."

"Well, then perhaps we're going to have to think of ways to warm you up." And in fact he did, kissing her until the soles of her feet, along with most of the rest of her, were on fire. Whoever said menopause interfered with the feelings of a red-blooded woman had been terribly misinformed.

CHAPTER 3

🍓

Pete had said he'd meet Sadie and her children for breakfast at 8:30. He was an early riser and wanted to get some reading done before the rest of them got up. When Sadie and Breanna stopped by Shawn's cabin, he said he was going to sleep a little longer. How long did he need to sleep? Didn't he know the onboard activities had already started? Some people vacationed differently than Sadie did, so she tried not to be judgmental, but she still couldn't help but wonder if his late night phone call had something to do with his slow start to the morning.

It was all Sadie could do not to grill Breanna for more information about her brother on their way to the dining room, but Pete's advice kept cycling through her head. *Togetherness. Respect his boundaries.*

She could do this.

Deep breaths.

It was an at-sea day as the ship made its way to the first port in Juneau, Alaska. Julie, the cruise director—just like on *The Love Boat*—had planned a full day of activities to keep the cruisers occupied and entertained. Sadie had offered to discuss the wedding with

Breanna that morning, but Breanna said they would have plenty of time for that later if Sadie would rather enjoy the onboard activities. Sadie smiled; her daughter knew her too well.

After breakfast, the three of them went to a program about the history of Alaska with an overview of the ports they'd be stopping at. She then dragged Pete and Breanna to another class highlighting the different amenities on the ship, and by the time they finished with *that*, it was lunchtime.

Shawn wasn't in his room when Sadie called to ask him to meet them at the Chinese restaurant for lunch, and she wondered if he was avoiding her. It hurt her heart to even think that, so she ordered wontons in the hopes that the deep-fried yumminess would distract her. Sadie had a good recipe of her own at home, but she didn't make them very often. When she took the time and allowed the extra calories, however, she enjoyed every bite.

After lunch, Sadie pulled out the onboard daily newspaper— it was more like a brochure, really—and started mapping out their afternoon activities, but after sharing a look, both Pete and Breanna admitted they had other things they wanted to do.

Breanna wanted to check her e-mail, and Pete wanted to visit the on-ship casino. There was a blackjack tournament scheduled for later in the week, and he was thinking about signing up for one of the qualifying rounds. After hearing his plans, Breanna decided to go with him before she caught up on her e-mail. Sadie wasn't a gambler, though her father had taught her to play twenty-one when she was young—with M&M's instead of money—and while she didn't like the idea of Breanna being in a casino, she *did* like the idea of Breanna spending time with Pete.

Pete assured Sadie he'd see to it that Shawn joined them for dinner, and then they parted ways outside the restaurant.

Sadie missed their company as soon as they were gone, but reminded herself they deserved to do what they wanted to do just as much as she did.

She headed for the presentation about on-shore shopping, where she met some new friends. Mary Anne was celebrating her forty-fifth wedding anniversary with her husband, Glen, who preferred the casino to shopping—something Sadie could relate to a little too well at the moment. Jen was a young mother of three whose in-laws had treated the entire family to the cruise. She would likely have gone to a tractor pull if it meant she'd have some time alone. "Right now the grandparents think the kids are cute. I'm taking advantage of that for as long as it lasts. Chances are they'll burn out by day three," she confided to Sadie.

After the shopping presentation, the three new friends attended a cooking class on how to make sushi—which convinced Sadie never to try to make it at home—and then enjoyed the afternoon movie, *An Affair to Remember*. Cary Grant was such a handsome man. Too bad he'd been a drug user. You never could tell by just looking at someone, could you?

By the time Sadie made it to the Tiara Room on deck ten for dinner, Pete and Shawn were already there. She hugged them both before taking her seat. Sadie hated that they'd been on the ship for a full twenty-four hours and she'd barely seen her son, but he seemed to be in a good mood and she took that as a step in the right direction. Pete had already ordered the spinach salad for Sadie so she was able to dig right in. Sadly, the dressing was a tad too sweet.

Sadie asked about the blackjack tournament, but Pete said he hadn't won the qualifying round and therefore didn't have a spot in the final tournament that would take place on Friday. She and Shawn both commiserated with him over the loss, but he shrugged and said he'd had fun anyway. Sadie asked Shawn what he'd done all day, but the only answer she got was "stuff."

"Where's Bre?" Sadie asked after her third bite. The sweet dressing was starting to grow on her.

"She was all stressed out about something when we stopped in to get her," Shawn said before taking a massive bite of his antipasto.

Sadie's fork paused midway to her mouth, and she straightened in her chair as her mama-alarm went off. "Stressed out? About what?"

"I don't know. Something to do with the wedding."

Had Sadie just started coming to terms with Shawn's secret-keeping only to have things with Breanna get topsy-turvy? She tried not to worry too much through dinner, but as soon as they finished, she told Pete and Shawn she'd meet them in the theater for the Broadway review—*after* she checked on Breanna.

"Bre?" Sadie asked as she entered the cabin a few minutes later.

Breanna looked up from her laptop set on the small desk at the foot of her bed and tried to smile. She had an open bag of chocolate-covered pretzels next to her computer.

"What's wrong?" Sadie asked, frowning. Breanna had never been an emotional eater.

Breanna let out a heavy sigh and looked back at the screen in front of her. "I'm instant messaging with Liam. Hang on, I'm almost out of words anyway."

Sadie sat at the end of her bed. "How long have you been instant messaging with him?"

"About a hundred dollars-worth of minutes," Bre said, typing, pausing, and then typing again.

Oh, dear. Breanna wasn't an emotional eater *or* a spender. There was no cell coverage on the ship, including Internet services for smart phones, and the on-ship Internet was atrociously expensive, even at the computer center. From the beginning, Breanna had said she was mostly bringing her laptop for when they were in port; she'd hoped to find some Wi-Fi hot spots that wouldn't cost an arm and a leg. That she was paying top dollar to IM Liam meant that this was serious.

"Is everything okay between you two?"

"Everything's fine with *us*," Breanna said. "Hang on."

After another minute, Breanna typed one last message and then shut her computer, dropping her head on top of it dramatically. Sadie moved to the end of Breanna's bed and brushed her daughter's hair away from the back of her neck. "What's going on, sweetie?"

Breanna let out a heavy breath and sat up. She looked exhausted. "Liam's mother has ordered carriages for the wedding party."

Sadie raised her eyebrows. "Carriages?"

Breanna nodded. "She's also ordered $8,000 worth of flowers. *Eight thousand dollars!* I know Liam is her only child, an heir and all that, but his mom is turning our wedding into a circus." Tears came to her eyes, and she quickly blinked them away. "I hate it so much, Mom."

Sadie pulled her into a hug. "Oh, sweetie, I'm so sorry."

There was more. Liam's mother had reserved an ornate church for the ceremony and had e-mailed pictures of an eight-tiered cake, even though Breanna had already found a cake she liked at a quaint little shop not far from her London apartment. Seeing the cake had overwhelmed Breanna, so she sent an instant message to Liam about it, but he was having a hard time understanding why it was such a big deal. He'd promised to talk to his mom, but Breanna didn't feel like he really understood where she was coming from.

"He thinks it's about the cake and the venue and the stupid carriages, but it's about so much more than that," she said. "It's *my* wedding—don't I get to have some input?"

"Has she planned everything?" Sadie said, trying to keep her emotion in check. Breanna was Sadie's only daughter, and she had looked forward to helping with her wedding all of her life. This trip was supposed to be *their* opportunity to plan Breanna's special day. Sadie had known Liam's mother would have a part in it—like Breanna had said, Liam was an only child and the heir to an earldom—but Sadie had still expected that as the mother of the bride, she'd be on the front lines.

"Pretty much," Breanna said with a nod. "And while I've accepted that Liam comes with a lot of . . . trappings, this kind of thing throws me back into those old concerns about maybe not being ready for this. I moved to London to be closer to Liam and to get more comfortable with his lifestyle, but I've kept my independence. I've paid my own way, worked, and created a life for myself. It's made me think that when Liam and I get married, I'll still be able to have some power, you know, but here I am losing control of my own wedding day. What will my marriage be like if I can't have a say in the beginning of it?"

"Are you reconsidering?" Sadie asked with her heart in her throat.

Breanna looked at the floor and tucked her hands underneath her thighs. "Why can't I just have Liam?" she said quietly. "Why does it have to be so complicated?"

"I could talk to Liam's mother for you, if you want. Maybe if I said I wanted to be involved, it would help soften her."

"Maybe Liam and I should run off to Monaco and get married on a beach."

Sadie's heart stopped for a split second, and she gripped Breanna's hand. "So help me, Bre, if you get married without me there, I'm not sure I'll survive it."

And that's when Breanna started to cry. Sadie's comment was supposed to be a joke, or at least a teasing truth, but it opened the floodgates instead. Over the next twenty minutes, Sadie came to realize just how stressed out her daughter really was—not only because of Liam's mother and her expectations, but because of Sadie's expectations too, and the difficulty of having to merge lives taking place on two different continents. By the end, Sadie was practically begging Breanna to elope if it meant she'd be happy.

"I need to go to bed," Breanna finally said when the tears subsided. "I'm such a mess right now. Thanks for letting me vent."

"Of course," Sadie said. Even with her swollen eyes and red nose, Breanna was lovely. "Tomorrow we can put together a plan. I'll back you up any way you need me to."

"Okay. Thanks, Mom," she said with a nod. "Go to the show. I'll be fine, I promise. I'm going to take a shower to wash the day off and then go to bed. Maybe I'm still jet-lagged and that's making me overreact. I'm sure things will look better in the morning."

Only after Breanna was in the shower did Sadie let herself out of her room. She felt overwhelmed by the weight of her children's problems. Knowing what Breanna was facing made her wonder whether or not she wanted to know what Shawn was dealing with after all. She wondered when her respect for his boundaries would lead him to open up to her, and she worried that when the moment arrived she might not be as much help as she wanted to be.

Sausage Wontons

1 pound sage-flavored sausage (lean works best; hamburger can also
   be used)
1 egg, beaten
1 (4.5-ounce) can tiny shrimp
1 (4-ounce) can water chestnuts, finely chopped (or ½ of an
   8-ounce can)
1 celery rib, finely chopped
3 green onions, finely chopped
2 (12- to 16-ounce) packages wonton skins
Vegetable oil, for frying

In a medium-sized skillet, brown sausage, breaking clumps into small pieces as it cooks; drain fat. Add beaten egg, shrimp, water chestnuts, celery, and onions. In a frying pan over medium heat, heat 2 inches of vegetable oil.

Put rounded teaspoonfuls of sausage mixture in the center of each wonton skin. (To keep skins from drying out, keep them covered with a damp cloth while working with them.) Dip finger in water and moisten edges of wonton skin. Fold wonton skin as desired to seal in filling. When oil is hot enough that a corner of the wonton immediately floats to the top, add uncooked wontons and cook 1 minute, or until golden brown. Turn wontons over and cook an additional minute (reduce heat if necessary to prevent overcooking). Remove wontons from oil with a slotted spoon and drain on a paper towel-lined cookie sheet. Once fried, keep wontons warm in a 190-degree oven until ready to serve. Serve with Saundra's Sweet and Sour Sauce.

Makes approximately 48 wontons.

Note: Wontons can be fried ahead of time and reheated in a 450 degree oven for 5 minutes.

Note: Shawn likes 2 ounces of softened cream cheese added to the sausage mixture.

Sandra's Sweet and Sour Sauce

2 tablespoons cornstarch
½ cup honey
½ cup apple cider vinegar
1 clove garlic, minced
½ teaspoon fresh ginger, grated (or ¼ teaspoon dry ginger, ground)
5 tablespoons ketchup
6 tablespoons pineapple juice

Mix all ingredients in a medium-sized saucepan. Bring to a boil over medium-high heat, stirring constantly. Simmer 1 to 2 minutes until mixture thickens and becomes clear. Serve warm.

CHAPTER 4

🍓

Because of her discussion with Breanna, Sadie had missed the first half of the one-hour show. But she was no longer in the mood for show tunes anyway—a rare thing for her since she usually loved the upbeat tempos and easy-to-recall lyrics she'd known since she was young. Cruise ships were a mecca for such nostalgia, and since there was a show every night, she didn't worry about missing out on too much.

Pete and Shawn seemed to be getting along, which helped her feel less guilty about ditching them, though she wondered if either of them would have gone to the show if not for her being excited about it. She'd have to find a way to make it up to them later.

Instead of going to the show, she went to the coffee counter on deck seven and ordered a hot cocoa, then wandered over to the photo gallery, which was just a hallway displaying all the welcome pictures taken by the ship photographers that were available for purchase.

The welcome photos from yesterday were organized by time of arrival in half-hour intervals. She and Breanna had arrived at 1:45, and Sadie found their picture quickly. She frowned at how wide her hips looked and immediately determined never to wear those shorts again. She turned the picture around and returned it to its place on the rack, indicating she wasn't planning to purchase it. She found Pete and Shawn's picture in the 3:30 to 4:00 section and decided to buy that one. Seeing the two of them together made her a little misty-eyed.

She was on her way to the counter when she caught a flash of black and pink braids from the other end of the hallway. Sadie turned her head quickly and made eye contact with the woman for a split second before the woman turned and began walking away, casting an anxious look over her shoulder after just a few steps.

Sadie followed her without considering whether it was a good idea. She wouldn't need to get answers from Shawn if she could get them from this woman instead. But why was the woman in a hurry to get away? There were so many other people around that Sadie refrained from calling out to the woman, but she really wanted to.

"Ma'am!" someone said behind her. "Excuse me, ma'am!"

She looked over her shoulder as the cashier from the photo gallery walked toward her with his hand outstretched.

"You must pay for your photograph."

Sadie realized she still had Pete and Shawn's welcome photo in her hand. "Oh, I'm sorry," she said, handing it to him. She caught another flash of braids as the woman turned the corner into the foyer area in front of the elevators. "I'll come back and pay for it in a minute," she said over her shoulder as she began heading in the woman's direction.

The staff member said something Sadie didn't hear as she increased her pace, earning a curious look from a few of her fellow passengers who seemed shocked to see someone hurrying at all; this was a cruise after all.

Sadie turned the corner to see the woman one last time just as the elevator doors closed. She ran to push the button, hoping to reach the elevator quickly enough that the doors would open before the car left the deck, but she was too late.

"Biscuits," she muttered under her breath, then stepped back to watch the digital display above the elevator. It stopped on deck eleven, but did that mean the woman had gotten off? Or had someone else gotten on?

Another elevator opened in response to her button pushing, but she ignored it, waiting until the doors had closed before she pushed the button again. Two more elevators had come and gone before the original elevator finally returned after making a stop on deck nine. The woman with braids wasn't inside, rather there were two Caucasian women with perfect makeup and tailored clothes.

"Did you get on at deck eleven, by chance?" Sadie asked.

"I did," the younger of the two said.

"Did you see a black woman, with black and pink braids?"

"Don't you mean African-American?" the older woman said. Her age was difficult to determine, and Sadie guessed she had a plastic surgeon on retainer.

Sadie was embarrassed to have inadvertently used the wrong terminology. "Yes, sorry, African-American. She just went up on this elevator."

"And you're waiting for her?"

"Yes, kind of. Did you see her?"

"She got off when I got on," the younger woman said with a cute drawling accent. "On deck eleven, like I said."

"Thank you," Sadie said, then stepped back so the doors would close.

"Aren't you coming?" the older woman asked. Sadie thought she might be trying to raise her eyebrows—there was the faintest crease toward the top of her forehead—but the Botox made the expression awkward.

"No, I'm sorry. I'm going up. Thank you for your help, though."

As soon as the doors closed, Sadie hit the button again, this time getting into the first elevator going up and hitting the button for deck eleven. It was the same level where she'd seen Shawn talking to the woman yesterday afternoon. Did that mean something? Was this woman's cabin on deck eleven?

She spent fifteen minutes walking forward to aft in search of the mysterious woman, only to give up when a steward turning down beds on the starboard-aft side started looking at her funny on her third pass. She smiled at him and took the stairs down to deck seven, where she headed back to the photo gallery. She graciously thanked the clerk for holding on to the photo of Pete and Shawn and then explained she needed to buy another photo before he rang her up.

She found the black and pink braids easily enough; the woman had arrived in the same time period as Pete and Shawn. There was another woman in the photograph as well: younger, shorter, and darker-skinned, but with clearer skin, brighter eyes, and better teeth. The two women had their arms around each other's backs, their heads leaned in while they smiled for the camera. Mother and daughter, perhaps? Sadie stared at the image for several seconds, then pulled the photo from the rack. There was another copy behind it, which made her decision to buy this one a little easier. She wasn't taking away their chance to own a copy too.

She worried the clerk wouldn't let her buy someone else's photos, but he was happy to charge her ship-card $34.99 for the two photographs. She thanked him and slid the photos, complete with cheap cardboard frames, into the shoulder bag she wore slung across her chest.

She would need to think of a good reason why she'd bought the photo in case she ended up needing to explain herself, but she wasn't sure she *had* a good explanation. Maybe she just wanted proof that the woman was real. Maybe she'd show Shawn the photo to remind him that he couldn't pretend the woman in braids didn't exist. Maybe then he would confide in his mother. Pete, however, would likely not approve.

Sadie reached the theater in time to stand in the back for the last two minutes, but she couldn't focus on the grand finale of the show. Why had the woman run away? Had Shawn told her not to talk to Sadie? What was her connection to Shawn? How on earth was Sadie supposed to enjoy herself on this trip without knowing the answers to her questions? How long could she be expected to respect these boundaries of Shawn's that she simply did not understand?

CHAPTER 5

Shawn wanted to hit the buffet again after the show; Sadie would get her money's worth with his ticket for sure. She wasn't particularly hungry, but took a chance on some made-to-order crepes with a variety of yummy toppings and was pleasantly surprised by the quality. Perhaps the buffet wasn't a lost cause after all.

As they ate, she kept looking across the table at Shawn, wondering what he was hiding about the woman in braids. But Pete was watching *her* and she was pretty sure he could read her mind even though he didn't know about Sadie's most recent encounter with the mystery woman. Would he approve of Sadie's chase? What would he think of the photo she had in her bag hanging on the back of her chair?

Pete and Shawn talked about the show, while Sadie ate another crepe and turned her worry from Pete's opinions of her actions to Breanna's conflicts with the wedding. She couldn't believe Liam's mother would take things over so completely. Carriages? Eight thousand dollars in flowers? Did the woman not know Breanna at all? Had she no respect for Sadie's position as mother of the bride?

When those thoughts got too heavy, she ate yet another crepe and worried about Shawn again. Finally, when she felt ready to explode from both crepes and worry, the three of them made their way out of the dining room, and Shawn said he was going to check out one of the clubs.

Sadie stiffened. "You go to clubs?"

"Mom, I'm twenty-three."

"What does being twenty-three have to do with going to clubs? I was twenty-three once, and I never went to clubs. Breanna didn't go to clubs when she was twenty-three."

Yes, Shawn had been away at college for four years, but she always pictured him studying when she worried where he was or what he might be doing at any given time. Could he be one of those college kids who went to frat parties and locked their friends in the trunk of a car as a joke? Oh, she certainly hoped not. She'd been locked in the trunk of a car before and it had been horrid.

"Pete, maybe you can explain it to her," Shawn said as they stood outside the dining room.

Pete draped his arm over Sadie's shoulder and gave Shawn a nod. "I've got your back." They tapped their fists together. What on earth was that all about?

Sadie looked at Pete. "You're supporting this kind of behavior?"

Pete steered her toward the open deck, away from Shawn. "We talked about this," he reminded her as the doors whooshed open.

He guided her across the open deck toward the stairs that led to deck thirteen-forward. The ever-determined hot-tubbers were there again, basking in the steaming water and occasionally running across the deck to jump into the swimming pool. She'd worn better pants tonight and wasn't so chilled by the dropping temperatures, but she couldn't imagine wearing a swimsuit, let alone getting wet. On the port side of the hot tubs, someone seemed to be asleep on a deck chair, and Sadie shook her head. Weren't they cold? It had to be close to forty degrees out here.

"I can't believe he goes to clubs," Sadie said when they reached the top of the stairs. They had the deck to themselves again. She narrowed her eyes at Pete. "And I can't believe you're supporting him in that."

"You're going to let Shawn be a grown-up, remember?"

Letting your children be grown-ups stunk like liverwurst.

There was less cloud cover tonight, leaving patches of starlit sky they both admired, though Sadie struggled to shake off the day, which had been full of difficult things. Finally, Pete asked her what was wrong, and she downloaded everything she'd been aching to tell him. He commiserated with the parts about Breanna, and then asked to see the picture of the woman with braids. Sadie reluctantly took it out of her shoulder bag, not sure if he was in support or not.

After looking at it for several seconds in the muted light, Pete passed it back to Sadie.

"Well?" Sadie asked.

"Well, what?"

"What do you think?"

"I think you're well on your way to driving yourself crazy, and if Shawn finds that photograph, it's going to make things even harder between you two. Why did you buy it?"

"I guess I just wanted to get a good look at her. Every other time I've seen her, she's hurrying away from me." Sadie let out a breath and put the photo back into her bag. Last night Pete had been holding her, but tonight, she and Pete were sitting side by side on deck chairs and the night felt heavy and cold. "How do I let this go?"

"You just do," Pete said, reaching over to rub her shoulder. "You focus on something else."

"Like my daughter who's miserable about her wedding that I apparently don't get to help with?"

"At least she wants your help. She invited you into that situation; you're not invited into Shawn's."

Sadie couldn't help but glare at Pete a little bit. "Is it a man thing to shrug things off like this? Or a cop thing?"

Pete smiled without answering and moved onto her deck chair. Squeezing both of them into the relatively small space was tricky, but a little exciting too. They ended up face-to-face, arms wrapped around each other.

"You could focus on us," he whispered before kissing her gently on the lips. "We're grown-ups with a future ahead of us as well."

"You might have a point," Sadie said as her worries began to drain away.

They stayed there until a group of teenaged girls coming up the stairs sent Pete back to his own chair, and then it was just too cold to enjoy the night—nevermind the giggling girls hanging over the railing and swooning over the boys getting out of one of the hot tubs below.

With a look, they agreed to go and made their way down the stairs. Sadie was disappointed when the girls followed them down; she and Pete could have stayed up there if the girls hadn't interrupted them. Still, it *was* cold. Cold enough that Sadie did a double take when she noticed that the passenger they'd passed earlier was still curled up on the deck chair.

She elbowed Pete in the side before pointing toward the dark form. "That person was there when we went up," she said. "It's freezing."

Pete scowled and then nodded. "They probably overindulged at the bar. Stay here."

It was silly for Sadie not to go with him, but his cop instincts must have kicked in, and she wasn't a fan of dealing with drunks anyway. The hot-tubbing boys and giggling girls left through the automatic sliding doors, leaving silence in their wake save for the bubbling hot tubs.

"Drinking makes you even more susceptible to hypothermia, you know," Sadie added as Pete moved away. "Alcohol lowers your internal temperatures."

Pete smiled at her over his shoulder and wound through the deck chairs while Sadie shifted her weight from one foot to another. He leaned down, shaking the person's shoulder and talking softly enough that she couldn't hear what he said. She watched as he paused, then seemed to pull back the blanket covering the person's head.

The increasing cold Sadie felt wasn't from the weather. Something was wrong.

She quickly joined Pete, and he looked up at her with an anxious expression on his face. "I can't find a pulse."

"What?" Sadie stepped around him so she could get a better view, then gasped as she saw the black and pink braids spilling over the side of the chair.

Crepes and Toppings

4 eggs
1 cup milk
1 cup water
½ teaspoon vanilla extract (optional)
2 cups all-purpose flour
½ teaspoon salt
¼ cup melted butter

Put eggs, milk, water, and vanilla extract (if desired) into a blender. Blend until smooth. Add flour and salt. Blend until smooth, using a knife or rubber spatula to get all the flour off the sides of the blender. When blended, add butter and mix until combined.

To cook, heat a crepe pan or medium-sized frying pan on medium heat. Brush pan with butter or spray with nonstick cooking spray. Pour approximately ¼ cup of batter into pan (bigger pans will require larger amounts of batter) and tilt the pan until the batter covers the bottom of the pan in a thin layer.

Cook until top is dry. Flip crepe over with a rubber spatula or fork. Cook for an additional few seconds. (If you like darker crepes, increase heat.) Remove to a plate and add toppings as desired.

Serves 6.

Note: You can roll the crepe once it is filled, or fold it in half and then in half again, which is the traditional method.

Cream Cheese Filling
1 (8-ounce) package cream cheese, softened
1 cup sour cream
1 cup powdered sugar

Beat cream cheese until smooth. Add sour cream and powdered sugar; beat until smooth. For a less-sweet version, reduce the powdered sugar by ½ cup.

Vanilla Sauce
2 cups whipping cream
1 cup sugar
2 tablespoons all-purpose flour
½ cup butter
1 teaspoon vanilla extract

Whisk cream, sugar, and flour in a saucepan. Add butter. Cook over medium heat until butter is melted and mixture begins to boil, stirring constantly. Cook an additional 3 minutes or until mixture is slightly thickened. Remove from heat, and stir in vanilla. Serve warm.

Additional Toppings

Lemon juice and powdered sugar
Jam
Pie filling
Fresh fruit
Whipping cream
Nutella
Cream cheese
Sour cream and brown sugar
Maple syrup
Bacon
Chicken gravy
Diced ham
Cheese

CHAPTER 6

🍓

"Maybe my fingers are just cold," Pete said, withdrawing his hand and raising his fingers to his mouth so he could blow on them.

"That's the . . ." Sadie was having a hard time forming words as she stared at the woman in the chair. The entire ship seemed to spin beneath her feet. "Pete, that's the woman Shawn was talking to yesterday." She placed her hand on the outside of her bag. "She's the woman I chased tonight. I bought her photo."

"I know," Pete said, sounding frustrated, as though he'd been trying to talk himself out of believing it. He placed two fingers on the woman's neck, then shook his head and rolled the woman onto her back.

Sadie heard a gasping breath come from the woman due to the change of position.

"She's breathing!" Sadie said. But the woman didn't move, didn't open her eyes.

"And I found a pulse. It's weak though, and . . . " He lightly slapped the woman's cheeks, but she didn't respond and her head lolled to the side. He shook her shoulder. "Ma'am? Ma'am, can you hear me?" She still didn't respond.

"What's wrong with her?" Sadie asked, relieved that the woman wasn't dead.

After a few more seconds, Pete dropped his hand to his side and looked up at Sadie. "Go get security," he said. "She needs medical attention. Can you smell the alcohol?"

Sadie was still staring at the braids; the woman's face was turned away from her.

"Sadie."

She looked up at Pete and blinked, not knowing what to say or what to think.

Pete stared at her a moment, then guided her to another chair. "You sit. I'll get security. Don't go anywhere."

Sadie nodded as Pete took off toward the doors. Sadie hadn't gotten a good look at the woman's face. Maybe it *wasn't* the woman Shawn had been talking to. Could there be two women with the same hair on this boat?

Sadie stood up and walked closer to the deck chair. The woman's head had fallen to the side and her hair—there was so much of it—covered part of her face. She reached out to move the woman's hair out of the way.

She hesitated when her hand was a few inches away, but she couldn't stop herself and carefully brushed the braids back from the woman's face, touching the woman's cheek in the process. It was cold. Her eyes were closed and her mouth was slightly open. Her face looked soft in the dim light. She was definitely the woman Shawn had been talking to. Sadie had seen her just a couple of hours ago. Had it been two hours? Two and a half? Who was this woman?

Sadie pulled her hand away, and her eyes traveled to a wine bottle placed near the leg of the deck chair. She bent down to read the label because her investigative mind couldn't *not* do it. Pinot noir. There was a pale green ribbon tied around the neck and what looked like a gift tag attached to it, though it was facing the bottle. Sadie put her hand in the pocket of her jacket like a glove and leaned forward awkwardly so she could turn the label around.

To Ben & Tanice—
May you continue to find every happiness together.

"Tanice?" Sadie said as she dropped the label and looked at the woman again. Like Janice but with a T? In her photo, this woman had been with a younger woman, not "Ben."

The sound of the whooshing door and footsteps on the deck broke the spell, and Sadie jumped to her feet moments before two security officers, someone who looked like a doctor, and Pete arrived.

Pete and Sadie backed up while the men assessed the woman in the chair. One of the security guards picked up the wine bottle, and Sadie considered telling him not to tamper with evidence. He wasn't even wearing gloves. Were these men trained for this kind of thing? Wait, why was she acting as though a crime had been committed?

The security guard shook the bottle. From the sloshing of the remaining wine inside, it sounded nearly full.

"Too much alcohol," he said in thickly accented English.

The medical staff member told the other security guard to alert the onboard physician and order a stretcher.

"I need to talk to Shawn," Sadie whispered to Pete a minute later when it seemed the men had forgotten all about them.

"Not yet," Pete whispered back.

Another medical worker joined the group, and a few minutes later two more security guards arrived with a gurney.

Eventually, another man joined the others and, after talking with everyone already there, introduced himself to Pete and Sadie as the head of security. Officer Jareg was from the Philippines like many of the other staff members on the ship, but he carried himself with a more official air. He asked both Sadie and Pete to explain how they'd found the woman. He took notes on their answers in a small notebook just like the ones Sadie had seen numerous detectives and police officers use.

"Do you know her?" he asked after they finished recounting what had happened.

"Um, no," Sadie said. "Though I've seen her on the ship." She wanted to talk to Shawn before she told this man too much.

Officer Jareg asked for their cabin numbers and told them he'd contact them if he had any questions; he also invited them to come to him if they remembered anything else. "Unfortunately this happens from time to time," he explained. "Too much vacation." And yet, when he looked back at the woman in the chair, he looked decidedly worried. As though there was something about this situation that bothered him more than he was letting on. Or perhaps Sadie was simply paranoid.

He turned back and smiled reassuringly. "If you should need me, the security office is located on deck eleven, starboard forward." He put his notebook away. "We would very much appreciate for you to keep this quiet. A problem like this can be very upsetting to the other passengers. You understand?"

Sadie and Pete both agreed. "Is she going to be alright?" Sadie asked.

"I'm sure she will be fine. The doctor will see to her."

They were told they could return to their rooms, and together they moved toward the closest set of doors leading into the ship. A security guard had put up plastic signs around the area that said "Maintenance in Progress."

The guard let Sadie and Pete through the doors, and they walked to the stairs, their moods sufficiently troubled.

"Do you think she'll be alright?" Sadie asked Pete. "I got the impression Officer Jareg was more worried than he let on."

"She was completely unresponsive," Pete said. "Even a drunk will usually move or attempt to speak or something. But she was breathing and had a pulse and those are both good signs."

Sadie nodded. "We need to talk to Shawn." This wasn't how she wanted to learn about his connection to this woman—Tanice—but it seemed as though the time had arrived.

When they reached Shawn's cabin, Sadie knocked, waited, then knocked again.

Shawn didn't answer.

CHAPTER 7

He might still be at the club," Pete said when Sadie knocked for the third time.

"We need to find him." She hadn't paid much attention to the different nightclubs on the ship since they held no interest for her, but now she scanned her memory banks. She thought there was one on deck ten. Was another one on deck twelve? She tried to remain calm, but her anticipation of explaining this to Shawn was rising.

"*I* will find him," Pete said, pulling Sadie toward the stairs. "Why don't you go to your cabin?"

"There's no way I'm going to my cabin right now," Sadie said. "I need to find out what Shawn's relationship is to that woman. I need to see his face when we tell him what's happened."

"This is not an opportunity for you to satisfy your curiosity."

"Pete," Sadie said, exasperated, "I'm worried about my son, and now this woman he knows is ill or drunk or something. Who is she, Pete? Why wouldn't she talk to me earlier? What if Shawn told her to avoid me?" She could hear her own voice rising as she spoke and stopped to take a deep breath.

"This isn't the time to interrogate him," Pete said. "This will likely be upsetting for him to hear—especially if you're there watching his reaction. Just let me bring him up to speed on my own, okay?"

Sadie shook her head. "He's *my* son, and *I'll* find him." She tried to sound confident, but it came across more panicked than she'd have liked.

"Sadie," Pete said, lowering his chin and holding her gaze with his eyes. "There is obviously some history between him and this woman that he didn't want to tell you. You being there when he learns that she's sick—really sick—isn't a good idea. Let me take care of this, please."

She didn't want him to take care of this, but she could also picture exactly what she would do when she found Shawn. She'd either cry or get angry, and neither would be effective. Pete was right, this news would probably be upsetting for Shawn. She didn't want to make it worse, so she finally gave in. "Will you bring him to my room after you talk to him? Just so I know he's okay?"

"He's fine, Sadie, just because she—"

"Pete, with all I've seen in the last few years, I want to see for myself that he's okay. I need that, okay? And I won't push for any information from him. I won't freak out."

He paused a moment before nodding. "Okay."

Breanna was still asleep when Sadie entered the cabin, which meant Sadie couldn't turn on the lights or the TV. She settled for propping open the bathroom door which gave her just enough light to see and then spent half an hour pacing the same six-foot area of carpet until she heard a tap on the door. She hurried to the door and pulled it open.

Shawn stood in the doorway, and Sadie took a step into the hallway and threw her arms around his neck, all her determination to be calm drowned out by her concern for him. Shawn let her hang on for a few seconds, but stepped back as soon as she loosened her grip. Pete stood to the side, but Sadie only had eyes for Shawn. "Are you okay? Where were you? Who is she?"

Shawn glanced at Pete, giving Sadie a chance to read the fearful expression on Shawn's face. "What's wrong?" she asked, looking between the two of them. Pete had his detective face on, which meant she couldn't read any of his thoughts. He rarely used it with her these days, and she hated seeing it in place again. It shut her out, and more than anything right now, she didn't want to be shut out. "What's going on?"

"I told Shawn he needed to come tell you he was alright, but that the rest could wait until morning," Pete said, giving her a pointed look. She remembered her promise that she wouldn't grill Shawn if Pete would bring him to her cabin. So much easier said than done.

"The rest? What's the rest?"

"I've got to go talk to security," Shawn said, looking to Pete for help, which raised Sadie's blood pressure even more. Were they ganging up on her? Had Pete told Shawn to wait to tell her whatever she should know right now? Or had Shawn asked Pete to support him in keeping Sadie in the dark?

"Why?" Sadie asked.

"He just needs to talk to them," Pete said. "To see if he can help. He also needs to find out if she's okay. We'll have more information in the morning."

"You can tell me who she is before you go. Why won't you tell me?" She looked at her son, who was obviously upset. Why wouldn't he want his mother to comfort him?

"Mom . . ."

"Can I come with you?" she asked, trying to think of any way to be a part of this.

"I think it's best if Shawn and I go to security alone for now. Meet us in the library tomorrow morning at eight, okay?"

"I don't understand why you won't talk to me," Sadie said, hearing her desperation.

Pete took her hands, gave them a squeeze, and told her in a gentle voice that everything would be fine.

They really weren't going to tell her anything.

She finally nodded, as much out of embarrassment to be losing it as in agreement. But her backing down seemed to be all Shawn needed to excuse himself from the situation. He started down the hall without another word.

Pete glanced at Shawn, and then back to Sadie. "Please trust me on this. We'll see you at eight. Take one of your sleeping pills; make yourself get some rest. Tomorrow might be a long day."

"Pete Cunningham," Sadie said, her voice shaking as tears filled her eyes. She took as deep a breath as she could before she continued. "Not telling me what's going on is only making me panic more. Don't—"

Pete glanced down the hall again, but Shawn was almost out of sight. "Please trust me, Sadie. Please sleep." He squeezed her hand quickly, then hurried down the hall, catching up with Shawn just as he rounded the corner toward the elevators.

CHAPTER 8

Sadie stood in the teeny-tiny bathroom of her cabin and held the small pill in the palm of her hand. She hadn't taken one of her prescribed sleeping pills for a few months—not since the nightmares had subsided, at least the really bad ones that left her confused, sweating, and shaky in the middle of the night. When she'd packed her medications for the trip—bringing this one, just in case—she never imagined she'd need it because Shawn was talking to the ship's security officers about a woman he didn't want to tell Sadie about, and that he and Pete were in cahoots to keep her out of it.

She stared at the pill, considering her options. Instead of following Pete's suggestion, she could leave the cabin and go to security herself. If she were obnoxious enough, they would likely take her to Shawn and Pete. They might even tell her something themselves—on purpose or on accident, depending on how she worked it. She could do obnoxious, even if it wasn't her favorite part to play, and it might be worth it. But both Pete and Shawn had asked her to stay away. Would she betray their trust and perhaps complicate whatever it was they were doing?

Another option was to snoop around on her own and see what

she could learn about this Tanice woman . . . at midnight . . . on a ship with three thousand passengers, not counting at least a thousand staff members. That didn't seem like it would be a very effective use of her time.

She could wake up Breanna and force some answers regarding what *she* might know, but that was assuming what Breanna knew was connected to the woman. And Breanna had already been so stressed out tonight.

Why was Pete so supportive of the idea of waiting until tomorrow to tell her what he knew? That was perhaps the scariest part—whatever it was must be *so* bad that Pete needed time to figure out his approach.

Without thinking about it any longer, Sadie popped the pill into her mouth and chased it with a glass of water from the bathroom sink. She went through her nightly routine while obsessing over what Shawn and Pete were doing, wondering if Tanice was coming out of her stupor and, if so, what she and Shawn might talk about.

Not long after climbing into bed, her thoughts began jumping in and out of reality, a sign that the pill was kicking in. Hadn't Jennifer Hudson once been a cruise ship performer? Was Jennifer Hudson on this ship? Was Steven Tyler a merman?

The final thought she had before she fell asleep, however, was remarkably lucid. What was Ben from the wine bottle gift tag doing right now? And why hadn't he been in the welcome photo?

CHAPTER 9

S adie's brain woke up several minutes before her body recovered
from the chemically induced sleep. It was why she'd stopped taking the pills unless she absolutely had to—waking up felt like swimming through oatmeal. Or Jell-O. Or the ship's bread pudding.

Finally she was able to open one eye, then the other. She stared
at the darkness since she couldn't yet move her head. There wasn't a
window in the room, so there was no indication of daylight or time.
She heard the movement of passengers in the hallway on the other
side of the door, though it wasn't loud.

She was eventually able to sit up, and a minute later, she stood,
and once her brain accepted that she was officially awake and in
motion, she moved toward the bathroom where she turned on the
light, blinking as her eyes adjusted to the brightness. She undressed
and then stepped into the shower. The water ran over her head for
a solid five minutes before her brain finally remembered what had
happened the night before. She straightened up so fast that she hit
her head on the side of the tiny shower. She quickly washed her hair,
then shut off the water, stepped out of the shower, and dried off as
quickly as she possibly could. She hadn't gone to bed until nearly

midnight; it had to be close to eight o'clock by now. Shawn and Pete
might already be waiting for her in the library.

Having not thought to bring her clothes into the bathroom with
her, she wrapped herself up in a towel and opened the door slowly.
She didn't want to wake Breanna, so as soon as there was enough
light in the cabin for her to see the drawers of the tiny dresser opposite the bathroom door, she moved as quickly and quietly as possible, gathering her underthings and a pair of jeans from the drawers before moving toward the closet for a shirt. A quick glance at
Breanna's bed caused her to do a double take, however.

Breanna's bed was empty, her pajamas wadded up near the pil-
low. Sadie hit the main lights, illuminating the room. Where was
Breanna? What time was it? She hurried for her cell phone on the
nightstand. It didn't have reception, but it still had the time.

"Ten fourteen!" she said aloud, then dropped the towel and proceeded to get dressed a whole lot faster. Once dressed, she returned
to the bathroom and scrunched some gel into her hair. She'd spent
a year transitioning from brown to salt-and-pepper gray with textur-
izing tones of blonde and brown throughout. It didn't make her look
as old as she'd once feared it would, and it worked well with her
coloring. She usually blow-dried her hair with a large round brush
to soften her natural curl into a stacked A-line bob—a more elegant
style than she'd had the last few years—but there was no time for
elegance today. She had to settle for curls she knew would dry as stiff
as a Brillo pad.

Her skin had tightened as it dried, so she rubbed moisturizer
into her cheeks and forehead while using her feet to kick her shoes
out of the closet. There wasn't time for her full makeup regime; she
was eager to get to the library and learn the answers she'd been

wanting since first getting onto this ship. By the time she ran out of the cabin, slinging her bag over her head and shoulder, it was 10:28.

The library was on deck twelve, and she had to pass the hot tubs and the chair Tanice had been in on her way. There were people soaking in the tubs, eating at the tables that flanked the windows, and lounging in the chairs.

The library was the second door on the right once she passed through the interior doors at the forward end of the open deck. She pulled the glass door open and then stopped at the threshold, scanning the dozen or so people inside the room. Her shoulders slumped as she realized that Pete, Shawn, and Breanna were not here. She knew she was two and a half hours late, but couldn't they have waited? Or left a note or something?

Had she taken the time to actually look for a note in her room?

What she wouldn't give for cell phone reception that could put her in touch with anyone in her family in mere seconds. She blew out a breath, loudly, which earned her disapproving looks from a few of the library patrons. She didn't know where to start looking, and after standing there for several seconds, she headed back to her cabin—the only option she could think of. She let out another exasperated breath when she found a note sitting on top of Breanna's computer.

Mom,

Didn't want to wake you. We went to the security office but will come back here if we don't see you there.

Love you,

Bre

She knew where they were, that was good, but knowing they were at security was uncomfortable. Shawn and Pete had headed there last night and still went *back* this morning? What did that mean? Tanice should be sober by now, right?

Sadie hurried up the aft stairs to deck eleven while half a dozen scenarios of what Shawn was hiding—and Pete and Breanna were in on it, too!—ran through her mind. She should never have taken that pill last night.

When she reached deck eleven, she saw the sign for security beside the starboard hall and headed toward the front of the ship, mindful that deck eleven was where she'd first seen Shawn and Tanice on Sunday—the same deck she'd walked around and around last night.

Her steps slowed, and she walked more carefully, as though there might be a clue on the carpet somewhere that would explain everything that had happened in these hallways. Of course, finding that kind of clue rarely happened outside of Agatha Christie novels, but it was always a possibility.

She passed a room steward who nodded at her before entering a cabin, propping the door open. It was several yards before Sadie passed the doorway leading to the forward elevators. She passed by the place where the hallway jogged right—where Tanice had disappeared on Sunday. It felt surreal to be covering the same ground after so much had happened. A door opened farther down the hall, and a woman stepped out, causing Sadie to slow down even more.

"I know, alright? I'll be back in an hour," the woman said into the open doorway.

She pulled the door shut and turned in Sadie's direction. They both recognized each other at the same time—the woman had been in the elevator last night—and Sadie smiled politely.

"Hi, there," the young woman said with her cute Texan drawl.

"Hi, again," Sadie said.

"Did you find your friend last night?"

"Um, eventually, yes."

"Oh, good," the woman said, showing her bright white teeth. She was a beautiful girl with large green eyes and chestnut hair that fell in big loopy curls down her back. "I'm glad to hear it."

Sadie stepped aside so the woman could pass her. "Have a lovely day," the girl said as they continued in opposite directions.

"You too," Sadie said back, then hurried farther down the hall, her thoughts centered on her son and the events of last night.

There was a curtain at the end of the hall, and she slowed down again, then pulled it to the side when she saw the sign confirming that she had reached the security office. It fell back into place behind her, separating a twenty-foot section of hall from where the cabins had been. The carpet and wall paneling matched the rest of the deck, but the two doors—one marked "Security" and the other marked "Staff Only"—were stark white against the more colorful décor.

The security office was a small room, utilitarian, about eight feet by twelve feet, with white walls and the same flat carpet as the rest of the ship. A desk was set in one corner and four plastic chairs were lined up against the opposite wall just past the doorway. A hallway led to the left.

A young woman with her dark hair pulled into a bun so perfect it looked plastic was seated behind the desk. She was dressed in a maroon-colored uniform shirt and black slacks; all the staff members wore something similar, though the colors of their shirts seemed to be different depending on their position. Her name tag said her name was Hazel, from Turkey. She said hello with a Middle Eastern accent.

"Hi," Sadie said as she approached the desk and looked down the hallway lined with four solid white doors. Which room was Shawn in? What about Breanna and Pete? Or had they already left and she'd have to track them down all over again? "I'm looking for my son, Shawn Hoffmiller. Is he still here?"

"Ah, yes. You must be his mother. He said you might come." She picked up the receiver of the phone on her desk. "I'll let the investigator know you're here. Your daughter and husband are here as well."

"Thank you," Sadie said, barely acknowledging the tenderness she felt at having Pete referred to as her husband.

"Please have a seat."

Sadie sat in the chair she was waved toward and tried to focus on remaining calm. Knowing her loved ones were safe and accounted for should have helped her relax, but relaxation was hard to come by. It felt as though her anxiety had been put into a soda bottle that was being shaken, and shaken, and shaken, and at any minute the lid would come off and she'd explode. She focused on her de-escalation exercises: ignoring the shaken-bottle imagery, and concentrating on breathing, counting, and thinking happy thoughts.

A few minutes into the wait she hoped wouldn't be a long one, the door to the waiting area opened and Sadie looked up at a young woman who, upon second glance, she identified as the other half of the photograph still in Sadie's purse. The young woman wasn't smiling like she'd been in the photo.

"I have my mother's documentation," the woman said when she approached the desk, her voice sounding tired and flat. Her smooth black hair was pulled into a ponytail, and she was dressed in gray yoga pants and a plain white T-shirt that didn't completely camouflage her curves, though the clothing didn't emphasize them either.

"Very good," Hazel said. "Have a seat. Officer Jareg is with someone just now. I will let him know you're here."

Hazel picked up the phone again as the young woman turned toward the row of seats where Sadie was sitting. The woman chose the last of the four chairs, leaving an empty chair between her and Sadie. Her eyes were puffy, her face free of makeup, and the dullness of her eyes reflected the same thing her voice had already communicated—she was exhausted. Her bright pink acrylic nails seemed out of place in the solemn room.

Shawn knew Tanice. Did he know this girl, too? Did she have the answers Sadie was desperate to know?

When the young woman sniffled, Sadie couldn't get her package of tissues out of her bag fast enough. She lifted the strap over her head to make it easier to dig through and to make sure she didn't inadvertently show the photo hiding there. She wished she'd thought to leave it in her room.

"Thank you," the woman said, taking the proffered tissue a few seconds later and dabbing at her eyes.

"You're welcome," Sadie said. She wondered how to start a conversation, but then realized that she didn't know what had happened after she'd left deck twelve last night. Shawn was talking to security, and this girl was obviously upset. Had Tanice's condition become worse? Could she have . . . died?

Heat grew in Sadie's chest at the thought, and she wondered how much longer she'd have to wait to talk to her son.

"Ms. Lewish," the receptionist said.

"Yes?" the woman answered.

"Officer Jareg said you can leave the papers with me if you'd like. He hates to take more of your time."

"I'm fine to wait," Ms. Lewish said, smoothing the papers on her lap. "I have some questions for him too."

"Okay," the receptionist said. "I'll let him know you're waiting."

The sound of a door opening and voices talking from the hallway caused both Sadie and Ms. Lewish to come to their feet, then look at one another. Sadie looked away first while she fumbled with her bag, holding it tight against her stomach.

The sound of people approaching the waiting area drew their attention, and Sadie let out a breath when Officer Jareg and Shawn appeared from around the corner.

"Shawn," she said, unable to keep his name in her mouth a second longer. She took a step toward him before realizing he was looking past her at Ms. Lewish.

Ms. Lewish also said his name, but so softly Sadie almost didn't hear it. She was unable to read the expression on the woman's face. Surprise, maybe?

Shawn's expression was definitely one of surprise—*unpleasant surprise*—then he looked at Sadie and an equally certain look of fear replaced his expression.

"Do you two know one another?" Sadie asked.

"Pete and Bre should be right behind me," Shawn said quickly, looking over his shoulder.

Ms. Lewish was still staring at him, though he was clearly ignoring her.

"You're Shawn Hoffmiller?"

Sadie and Shawn both looked in Ms. Lewish's direction. She was scrutinizing Shawn, looking him up and down but not out of admiration, which set Sadie's back up a little bit. Ms. Lewish narrowed her eyes slightly, her expression tight.

"Let's wait out in the hall," Shawn said. He took Sadie's arm and pulled her toward the door.

"Wh-whoa," Sadie said, stumbling behind him and trying to keep from dropping her bag. "Hang on."

Shawn didn't hang on. He opened the door with one hand and was in the process of pulling Sadie through it with the other when Pete and Breanna entered the tiny room, made even smaller by the seven adults now crowding it.

"Shawn," Sadie said in reprimand, trying to catch her bag that was sliding toward the floor, but without success. The bag hit the floor and Sadie's tissues, nail clippers, gum, wet wipes, useless cell phone, a roll of Ziploc bags, and both pictures spilled across the security office. The picture of Pete and Shawn landed face up, but Sadie's breath caught in her throat as she watched the other picture slide across the slick commercial carpet—face down, at least. It bounced off Pete's foot before shooting to the right.

She twisted her arm out of Shawn's grip and shot him an annoyed look as she stepped over everything else in hopes of getting to the picture before anyone else did. Hazel bent down and picked up the photograph before Sadie had the chance, automatically turning it over as she stood.

The room was silent as everyone stared at the faces smiling back from the photograph—Tanice and Ms. Lewish, both unaware of what the next thirty-six hours held for either one of them.

CHAPTER 10

❦

W hat are you doing with that?" Ms. Lewish asked at the same time Shawn said, "Mom!"

"Uh, I . . . "

She looked from the picture to Pete, whose expression seemed to be asking why she still had the picture in her purse.

After a few more awkward seconds, Officer Jareg took the photograph from the receptionist's hand and took a step toward Sadie; there wasn't room for much more than that one step, the room was packed. "This is yours?"

"Um, well . . . I *did* buy it. Yesterday, though, before all . . . of . . . this."

He handed it back to her, a question in his eyes. She swallowed as she took the photo, shifting her weight from one foot to the other as she glanced at Ms. Lewish, who was a few inches taller than Sadie's five foot six. Sadie made a split-second decision and extended the photo toward Ms. Lewish.

"Why do you have this?" Ms. Lewish asked, taking the photo from Sadie's hands.

"I . . . uh . . ." What could she say? Because *I'm obsessing about how your mother might be connected to my son*?

"Mom, let's go," Shawn said. He took Sadie's arm again and tried to pull her toward the door, but she twisted out of his grip immediately. His insistence to talk to her *right now* made her nervous, and she used the excuse of cleaning up the contents of her purse to stall for time. That bottle of anxiety started getting shaken up again.

Breanna stepped around Pete and bent down to help Sadie finish cleaning things up. When Sadie looked over at her, Bre gave her a sympathetic smile, which only compounded Sadie's fears.

"Ms. Lewish wanted to speak to you, Officer Jareg," Hazel said in a timid voice.

Sadie glanced up at Ms. Lewish, who held the photograph on the top of the stack of documents she'd brought with her. Was this the first time she and Shawn had met?

Officer Jareg turned slightly and extended his hand toward the hallway. "Ms. Lewish, if you'll come with me."

Sadie returned the last item to her purse—a small first-aid kit packed into an Altoids container—and stood while putting the strap of her bag over her head so that it rested on her shoulder again. Secure. If she'd been wearing it correctly when Shawn tried to yank her from the room, the picture would never have ended up on the floor.

Sadie felt like she owed Ms. Lewish more of an explanation, but what could she say? Pete took her arm, turned her toward the door, and walked her out of the office. Shawn led the way and Breanna brought up the rear. Sadie felt surrounded.

They all seemed to let out a collective breath once they left the office. Well, everyone but Sadie, whose tension was still rising. The narrow confines of the hallway required Pete to let go of Sadie's arm so that the four of them could walk single file in the direction of the elevators.

"Where should we go?" Shawn asked over his shoulder after they pushed through the curtain that separated the security office from the passenger cabins.

"How about the card room?" Pete suggested. "It was empty this morning."

"There was a bridge tournament at ten," Breanna said from the back of the line. "I saw the posting for it when we were at the library earlier."

"How about the Good Times Café? It doesn't open until noon, but they only use those velvet cords to close it off," Shawn said.

"Good idea," Pete said. "I'm sure—"

Sadie stopped in the middle of the hallway, forcing Pete and Breanna to stop as well. It took Shawn a few steps to realize they weren't behind him anymore. Sadie waited until he turned around. "How about you tell me what's going on. Right now. Why are you acting so strange? Is Tanice okay?"

"Who?" Shawn asked, looking confused.

"The woman from the deck last night, the one I still know nothing about. She's doing better, right?"

Shawn exchanged a look with Pete or Breanna—or maybe both of them—over her head, and it made Sadie's frustrations rise even faster.

"They said not to talk about it," Pete reminded her. "If we could find somewhere private—"

Sadie shot a glare over her shoulder before looking at Shawn again. "Well, you all get a gold star for doing what they told you to do."

"Maybe we should just go to one of our cabins," Pete said, putting a hand on her shoulder.

She shook off his hand as her concerns and frustration began morphing into anger. She was not a child, nor was she some delicate collectible that needed special treatment. Sadie opened her mouth to once again demand an answer when a fifth voice joined the melee.

"Why did you have my mother's picture?"

They all turned around to see Ms. Lewish coming down the hallway, the picture in her hand, though she no longer had the documents.

Ms. Lewish reached Breanna and pushed her aside before Bre had a chance to hold her ground. They were similar in height, but Ms. Lewish was built larger and was sturdier than Breanna's more willowy form. Pete wouldn't be so easy to get past, and Ms. Lewish stopped a few feet away from him. Her eyes cut past Pete to land on Sadie, who returned her stare. As they faced off, Sadie was surprised to feel an odd bond with the younger woman; she wanted answers, just like Sadie did.

"What were you doing with this?" Ms. Lewish asked again, holding out the photo.

Pete turned sideways, looking back and forth between the women on either side of him.

Sadie couldn't think of any reason not to be honest. "She was talking to my son on the first day of the cruise, but he wouldn't tell me who she was. I don't really know why I bought it. Just wanted answers, I guess, and thinking it might have some."

Sadie didn't expect her words to affect the woman so strongly, but the confrontational look on Ms. Lewish's face disappeared. The photograph dropped to her side as she looked past Sadie to Shawn.

"This is your . . . *adoptive* mother?"

A flash of heat landed in the middle of Sadie's chest. *Adoptive mother?*

Shawn's hand was suddenly at Sadie's back, pulling at her shirt as he moved down the hall, taking her away from Ms. Lewish. "Mom," he said from behind her, but didn't finish his thought as Sadie fought and pulled against his attempts to remove her from this confrontation.

"She doesn't know?" Ms. Lewish continued, still looking at Shawn.

"No, I don't know," Sadie said quickly, finding her voice and trying to dig her heels into the cheap carpet. She threw an elbow behind her and hit Shawn, but it didn't seem to faze him. "I don't have any idea what's happening here."

"Sadie," Pete said.

"Mom," Breanna said at the same time that Ms. Lewish also spoke.

"I'm Shawn's birth sister," she said. She lifted the photo and pointed at Tanice. Sadie's entire body froze in dreadful anticipation. "This is our birth mother."

CHAPTER 11

❦

As a reminder, disembarkation is taking place on deck seven, midship and aft, with a wheelchair-accessible exit on deck four, aft. Please join us back on the ship tonight at eight and ten for the tribute to the Temptations in the Starlight Theater on decks nine and ten, forward. All passengers must be back on the ship by nine thirty tonight. Have a lovely afternoon in Juneau, Alaska."

Sadie let the cruise director's words go in one ear and out the other while she leaned against the railing of deck thirteen forward and stared at the expansive forest that made up the backdrop of Alaska's capitol city. It was obvious that the city planners had tried to preserve the land as much as possible. In the class about the different ports, Sadie had learned that Juneau was only accessible by boat or plane—there were no roads that crossed through the mountains. Though it taxed Sadie's levels of poetry, she could relate to the feeling of stuckness that some of the Juneauites must feel from time to time. If the weather was bad, or the water too rough, they had no choice but to stay put, right? Kind of like she had no choice but to stay and deal with everything she'd learned, everything Shawn had been keeping from her.

Shawn's birth mother was named Lorraina Juxteson—not Tanice—and had discovered his profile on an adoption reunification website eight months ago. He'd only posted his profile a couple of months earlier but hadn't determined how to tell Sadie about his search before they found each other, so he chose simply to not tell her anything at all. He'd pursued the relationship with his birth mother without Sadie's knowledge. In fact, the reason he'd only stayed in Colorado for a few days at Christmastime wasn't because of work, it was because he'd spent the rest of the break in Knoxville, Tennessee, with his *real* mother. That's not what he'd called her, of course, but it's how the term "birth mother" sounded to Sadie's ears. He'd met some of Lorraina's family; they had a single picture of him, taken at the hospital before Lorraina had signed the paperwork putting him up for adoption.

A stiff breeze came at Sadie from behind, barely moving her gelled-stiff curls, and she shivered. She looked around for a deck chair she could settle into, as though being more comfortable would help her work things out in her head. She'd always known her children might one day want to seek out their birth parents. Both adoptions had been closed, with minimal information about the birth parents made available to Sadie and her late husband, Neil. Today, birth parents often received pictures or even had visits with their biological children, but twenty-something years ago, things had been different. Even so, Sadie would have told them everything she knew and helped them in their search, even if it were painful. It was far more painful to be left out; being excluded from this important discovery made her feel so oddly insignificant.

And after all these years, this woman—Lorraina—could waltz in and share Sadie's motherhood? Just like that?

Sadie had thought that the woman's obvious drunkenness of the night before would have worn off by morning, but the opposite had taken place. Lorraina had gone into arrhythmia not long after being taken to the infirmary and had stopped breathing at one point, requiring a breathing tube. As her condition worsened, the medical staff onboard the ship reached the limit of care they could give her and the decision had been made to transport her to a hospital in Juneau. A helicopter had picked her up early in the morning while Sadie had been fast asleep. Lorraina was now in the Intensive Care unit in Juneau. Shawn said that Lorraina was a recovered alcoholic with a bad liver. Her condition was serious.

Sadie's feelings were twisted and complicated and hard to make sense of in her own head, let alone put into words. That's why she'd excused herself after Shawn's rushed explanation. She needed some time alone to line up her thoughts.

Now that she'd had that time, she could admit she was angry, but felt guilty for it. Sadie was hurt that Shawn hadn't told her, but felt guilty about that too. She knew his pain was greater than hers, and yet she still hurt so much that she didn't know how to talk to him about what he was feeling. She was also sad, and that just made her feel silly because, regardless of how she felt, the birth mother Shawn had only recently met was fighting for her life. It said a lot about Lorraina's condition that she had been life-flighted off the ship just a few hours before they docked.

Sadie closed her eyes and leaned back in the chair while zipping her jacket up a little higher. It wasn't all that cold—mid-50s—but her lack of movement made her more sensitive to the chill.

Shawn, Breanna, and Pete were probably worried; she'd been gone for nearly an hour. There was cell service now that they were in port, but Sadie had ignored the text messages that had chimed on her phone, certain they were from the three people she really didn't want to talk to right now. Surely there was a thought or realization on the fringe of her consciousness that would help even out her jumbled emotions. Surely if she took enough time to meditate and think things through, she'd find salvation somewhere.

"Mrs. Hoffmiller?"

Sadie looked at the top of the stairs where Shawn's birth sister stood, looking at her with trepidation.

"May I speak with you?"

Sadie didn't want to talk to *anyone*, and yet the fact that this woman had told her the truth before Sadie's own family had counted for something. Not only had Shawn hidden the truth from her, but Breanna had known for a few months. When Pete had learned about it last night, he had agreed with Shawn that telling Sadie in the morning was a better choice. It galled her to have been the one left out when she felt as though she deserved to know more than any of the rest of them, other than Shawn. But Ms. Lewish had nothing to do with all that, and it was nice not to be angry at *someone*.

Sadie smiled, patting the chair next to her. "Call me Sadie."

Ms. Lewish looked down the stairs and waved at someone before making her way to the chair Sadie had indicated. "I'm Maggie," she said.

"I assume they're down there?" Sadie asked, nodding toward the stairs where Ms. Lewish—Maggie—had waved.

Maggie nodded, and once again Sadie felt left out, though this time it was her fault.

"How did you guys know I was here?"

"I passed your family when they were heading this way looking for you. I offered to go first when they started debating who would be the best choice to send up. If you have any demands, you're in a perfect position to get them."

She spoke so formally, Sadie noted, smiling politely at the attempted humor. "I'm not sure my demands are the kind that anyone can meet." What she wanted was a do-over. She wanted Shawn to have told her the truth from the beginning. She wanted to have given him her blessing—which she totally would have done—and then process through this transition as it unfolded, rather than trying to untangle the ugly mass of feeling she had now. She wanted to feel included, not discounted simply as the woman who had raised Lorraina's child until that child decided he wanted his birth mother back. Hot tears rose with that thought, and she quickly blinked them away. These were thoughts she could never say aloud.

Maggie sat down in the deck chair next to Sadie, her hands in her lap. She had changed into jeans and a hooded sweatshirt, but her hair was still in a ponytail. She was a pretty girl—wholesome looking, which Sadie liked—though Sadie struggled to see the resemblance between Maggie and Shawn other than skin, eye, and hair color. Maggie was darker-skinned than Shawn, with a thinner nose and more pronounced cheekbones that gave her a leaner look than Shawn had.

Knowing what she knew now, Sadie recognized the commonalities between Shawn and Lorraina: a similar roundness of their faces, and the same shape of their big, brown eyes. Maggie must have taken after her father; Shawn's Polynesian heritage probably came from his father as well. Maggie and Shawn clearly didn't share a paternal line, though Sadie hadn't asked. She hadn't asked anything at all following Shawn's rushed explanation. Perhaps she should have.

"I'm sorry to bother you," Maggie said, shifting awkwardly and making Sadie wonder why she'd come at all, "but I wanted to apologize for what I did this morning. I was out of line."

"You were exactly what I needed. I don't like secrets."

Maggie looked at her hands in her lap. She sat on the edge of the chair, as though not wanting to get too comfortable or stay too long. "I also wanted to thank you for the picture. I hadn't even thought about getting it from the gallery, what with everything happening. I don't have many pictures of Lorraina, and I'm glad to have this one before I leave the ship. I'm grateful for the tender mercy of the gift. Thank you."

Sadie felt humbled by this girl's gratitude. She had no reason to seek out Sadie, and far less reason to apologize for anything. "I'm sorry about the way it happened, and about everything else, of course. I can imagine this has been very difficult for you." Maggie had come aboard with her mother and was leaving without her.

Maggie blinked quickly and looked across the deck to the city below them. "It's all pretty intense."

"You're getting off the ship in Juneau?" Sadie asked, changing the subject just a little bit. "For good?"

"I'm going to go to the hospital, first. I'll decide what to do from there, I guess. Thank goodness my dad talked me into getting travel insurance for both of us. This would have cost a fortune otherwise."

"Your dad?" Sadie asked. Her curiosity about Maggie's life was growing.

"He's in Northern California—just south of Sacramento, where I live."

Lorraina lived in Tennessee, not California. Maggie seemed to read Sadie's thoughts. "I didn't grow up with Lorraina either," she said. Sadie had suspected as much; Maggie was so comfortable with adoption terminology—birth sister; adoptive mother.

"You were adopted too?" Sadie asked, then held up a hand. "I'm sorry, it's really none of my business."

Maggie waved away Sadie's feigned politeness. "Lorraina found me a couple months ago through an adoption reunification website."

Lorraina, Sadie repeated in her mind. She hadn't broached the name confusion of Tanice versus Lorraina in her own mind yet, let alone bring it up with someone else. The wine bottle obviously wasn't Lorraina's. Where did Lorraina get it? Why was she drinking at all if she had a bad liver?

"You found each other so recently," Sadie commented.

Maggie nodded; her smiled faded as she continued. "It's been a gift from God to have her in my life again. No matter what happens next, I will always have that."

Sadie tried to keep her own smile in place, but she had to look away under the guise of scanning the shoreline of Douglas Island, which was connected via a bridge to Juneau. Did Shawn feel that the reunion with his birth mother was a gift? Sadie hated how her jealousy festered in light of this consideration.

"I'm sorry," Maggie said, apparently reading Sadie's thoughts again. "I know this is difficult for you too. My dad had a hard time when I told him I was looking for my birth mom."

Sadie took a breath and turned her attention back to her companion. "How did your mother react?"

Maggie looked at her pink fingernails and smoothed her hands over her thighs. "Mom passed away when I was fourteen."

"Oh, I'm sorry," Sadie said. That chipped away at Sadie's hurt more than anything else had so far.

Maggie took a deep breath. "She was first diagnosed with cancer when I was three and fought a very good fight through a couple remissions and some surgeries until God finally called her home."

"I'm so sorry."

"Yeah, so am I," she said, shrugging slightly. "But I can see I'm a stronger person for it, and I have faith that one day I'll see all this as part of God's road for me as well. There is always something to learn, right?"

"You have beautiful faith, Maggie." Had Sadie given Shawn the kind of foundation that would make him open to seeing things from that type of perspective? She hoped so, but then Sadie thought she'd given him the kind of foundation that would let him know, without any doubt, that Sadie would support him in his search for his birth parents. She'd been wrong about that. How many other failures had she made along her path of motherhood? Was it because he'd grown up without a father? Was Sadie too smothering? Did she encourage too much independence?

They sat in silence for several seconds, then Maggie stood. She didn't have a purse or anything and seemed unsure what to do with her hands. Finally she clasped them in front of her. "Well, it was nice to meet you, even this way. And I am sorry for bursting into a private conversation like I did earlier; my parents raised me with better manners than that."

"No apology needed. And I appreciate you coming to say goodbye. Thank you."

"You're welcome." She glanced toward the stairs and then back at Sadie. The wind shifted and blew her long ponytail over her shoulder. She had black hair, but with lighter highlights that softened the color. "You're not what I expected, but it looks like both Shawn and I got lucky with our adopted families."

Not what she expected? Why would Maggie have any expectations of Sadie?

Suddenly Sadie wasn't as eager to let her leave. Had someone given her a poor impression of Sadie? "Had you ever met Shawn before this morning?"

Maggie tucked her hands in her pockets. "I didn't even know he was on the ship until yesterday, and I didn't know he was with his family until this morning—though in hindsight I should have figured out your connection to him. I wasn't thinking clearly."

Sadie straightened slightly, her curiosity piqued. "You didn't know he was on the ship?"

Maggie shook her head. "Lorraina said she was going to surprise me with it. I'd wondered why she'd insisted on us taking *this* cruise."

Sadie thought back to the conversation she'd interrupted between Shawn and Lorraina that first day. Shawn had seemed angry, and Sadie hadn't thought to ask why. "Did Shawn know you guys would be here?"

Maggie shrugged. "When I realized Lorraina hadn't told me what to expect, I suspected she hadn't let Shawn in on it either, but I'm really not sure."

"I see," Sadie said, then lapsed into silence, lost in her thoughts.

"Anyway, I better get going," Maggie said again.

Sadie stood and walked with Maggie to the stairs, not remembering until she was a few feet away that Shawn, Breanna, and Pete would be at the bottom waiting for her. She stopped, not sure she wanted to face them, even though she knew she had to. They had a shore excursion planned to pan for gold at 2:30, and though it was the last thing she wanted to do, maybe being with a group of other tourists pretending like they were real prospectors was just what they needed. Or maybe Shawn wanted to go to the hospital with Maggie. Either way, this conversation had reminded her that she didn't want to hold on to her hurt to the detriment of her most valued relationships.

Maggie realized Sadie had stopped walking and turned to face her again. "Well, I hope you enjoy the rest of your cruise. Sample some of the chocolate buffet on Thursday for me."

Sadie smiled. "I'm not sure how much of this trip will be salvaged, but I appreciate you coming and talking to me. It's easier to understand other people's stories sometimes, and you've helped me better know how to make sense of Shawn's perspective."

Maggie's smile fell a little at the mention of Shawn's name. "It's none of my business," she said, lowering her voice, "but I don't think Shawn has been as . . . fulfilled by his relationship with Lorraina as I was, so maybe this isn't as difficult for him."

As an adoptive parent, Sadie had read about birth-family relationships. She knew natural sibling relationships were almost as anticipated as reuniting with birth parents—but Maggie didn't seem excited about connecting with Shawn, and Shawn hadn't seemed excited to meet his sister either. Why was that?

"You know," Sadie said, taking a half step closer, a reckless idea grabbing hold of her. The wind had picked up, and she pushed her hair out of her face. "You and Shawn haven't really gotten to know one another, and yet you share something important."

"He's made himself pretty clear about not wanting a relationship with me," Maggie said. The bitterness in her voice was impossible to mistake for anything else.

"Really?"

Maggie nodded. "It's okay. He's already got a sister, right?"

Sadie was surprised. Shawn had obviously been interested in his birth parents, why not his birth sister too? "I'm sorry," she finally managed.

Maggie looked away, but Sadie saw the glimmer of tears in her eyes and wished she felt like she could comfort this poor girl.

"If there's anything I can do to help," Sadie said, "anything at all,

I'd be happy to do it. It's too bad that we all can't help each other heal a little bit more."

"Like I said, Shawn doesn't want me around."

Sadie had no idea what Shawn's thoughts were on this topic so she didn't push the issue. She talked Maggie into trading cell phone numbers with her and offered, again, to help any way she could. Maggie thanked her, and Sadie wished her luck before they descended the stairs together, three eager faces watching them as they came down. Before reaching the end of the steps, Sadie took a deep breath and prayed for peace, and forgiveness, and healing. For all of them.

CHAPTER 12

🍓

The small talk at the base of the stairs was awkward, and Sadie watched Maggie avoid even looking at Shawn until the conversation had begun to ebb. "Are you coming to the hospital?" Maggie asked suddenly, looking at Shawn for the first time.

"No," he said without looking at her.

Maggie didn't seem surprised and turned away from him in order to say good-bye to Sadie one last time.

It took conscious effort for Sadie not to search Shawn's expression for a reason behind the tension between the two of them. She instead focused on Maggie and smiled. "I'd love to know what your plans are, once you have them figured out. And if for some reason you choose to stay on the cruise, we would love to get to know you better." The words just kind of came out, and yet they felt right to Sadie.

Maggie blinked in surprise, but there was a glimmer of interest that validated Sadie's spontaneous suggestion. She wasn't sure that Pete or her children were as convinced that this could be a good thing, but none of them argued the idea.

As they exited the ship a while later, Pete and Shawn fell in step with one another and pulled ahead. Sadie wondered what they were talking about but didn't try to catch up. She still had so many thoughts in need of processing, accepting, and understanding.

"Mom," Breanna said, once Pete and Shawn were out of eaves-dropping range. "I'm so sorry about the way everything happened this morning. Are you okay?"

"I'm getting better," Sadie said, answering Breanna's apologetic look with a forgiving smile. "I certainly didn't see it coming. When did he tell you about her?"

Breanna tucked her hair behind her ear, and Sadie noted that Breanna wasn't pulling her hair back as often as she used to. For years she had worn her hair in a ponytail or French braid. Wearing it down made her look older, more grown-up. "March," she said. "Not long after Liam officially proposed. For what it's worth, I told Shawn to tell you."

"Why didn't he?" Sadie asked. They both watched the pavement at their feet while they talked, as though eye contact would make this conversation more difficult.

"He was really worried about hurting you, Mom, and with everything that's happened—Boston, your anxiety, my being so far away—he didn't want to add to it. And I think he was still trying to decide if he'd done the right thing. We've talked about this stuff be-fore, ya know—our birth parents." She lifted her hands and fluttered her fingers. Sadie wasn't sure what she was trying to insinuate, but Breanna followed with an explanation. "When you grow up knowing that you weren't made by the people you belong to, you can't help but wonder who those other people are, where they are, why they didn't raise you themselves, and if they would look like you or act like you or like the same things you like."

Sadie wanted to cover her ears. What she wouldn't give for her and Neil to have been the only parents in her children's lives. She remembered the years of infertility and hoping and longing that had been her life before she and Neil had made the decision to adopt. Biological children would never have fantasized about their *other* parents . . . but then again, if she'd had biological children, they wouldn't have been Breanna and Shawn. This situation and the feelings it had triggered were complex, but her love of her children and deep assurance they belonged to her was simple, real, and certain.

"You understand why *I* couldn't tell you what was going on with Shawn, right?" Breanna asked after they'd walked in silence a little longer. They fell into line behind a dozen or so other passengers waiting for the bus to arrive that would take them from the pier to Juneau, just a mile or so away. Pete and Shawn were several people ahead of them, and Pete said something that brought a smile to Shawn's face, softening Sadie even more. She'd wanted to see how Pete and her children got along on this trip and, difficulties aside, she could not have hoped for better connections to be developing between them.

"I do understand why you didn't tell me," Sadie said, choosing her words carefully so as not to take out any of her hurt on Breanna just because she could probably get away with it. "And I'm glad you were a good sister to him. When did you know she was on the ship?"

"This morning," Breanna said, looking toward the driveway leading to the pier. The bus wasn't yet in view. "You were still asleep, and I didn't know what the breakfast plans were so I went to Shawn's room. I'd have slapped him upside the head for not telling all of us as soon as he knew Lorraina was here if not for the fact that he's pretty tormented by all of this. He really does feel terrible for the way everything happened, and I don't think he slept a wink last night. I'm not sure what he'll do if she . . . doesn't make it."

They both looked toward Juneau automatically. Somewhere in that city was a hospital, and in that hospital was Shawn's birth mother, fighting for her life. What *would* Shawn do if she died? And what had Maggie meant when she said she didn't think Shawn was as fulfilled by his relationship with Lorraina?

"Are you okay?" Breanna asked softly.

Sadie smiled as genuinely as she could at her daughter just as the bus turned the corner into the pier. "I will be," she said. "I just need to process through this—we all do. But we're a family, and we'll get through it."

They got on the large bus to Juncau and then transferred to a small shore excursion shuttle that took them toward the river where they would pan for gold. It wasn't until they were on the shuttle and listening to the history of Juneau that Sadie wondered if they shouldn't have skipped this activity entirely. Talking with Maggie and Breanna had helped her feel better prepared to talk to Shawn— really *talk*. But that was impossible to do on a bus with twenty-five other people while a cute college girl dressed up like Jessie from the Toy Story movies entertained them with trivia over a loudspeaker. Maybe Sadie should have encouraged Shawn to go to the hospital. What if the reason he wasn't going was because he thought Sadie would be hurt if he did? Maybe he'd be right.

Pete and Sadie were sitting next to each other, and he took her hand and gave it a squeeze. She took it as an apology and squeezed back in hopes he would know he was forgiven, though she still wanted answers when the time came. It was nice to feel as though she'd worked through her initial anger. She wasn't mad anymore, but there was still a lot to come to terms with.

At the shallow river, their guide showed them how to pan for gold—the tiny bits of gold dust were already seeded in their pans, but it was fun to try not to lose them back into the river. After the instruction, the tourists spread out across the shoreline, staking their "claim," and tapping their pans while swishing the water in hopes that the flecks of gold, which were heavier than everything else, would fall to the bottom of the pan.

Sadie was on her third pan—she'd already put fourteen flecks of gold in her tiny plastic container—when she heard someone come up behind her. She looked over her shoulder and felt her stomach flip. Shawn's smile looked repentant, and Sadie braced herself for what might be a difficult discussion—difficult but necessary. She liked that he'd come to her, though. She liked that a lot.

Shawn crouched beside her and dipped his pan, already full of dirt and rocks, into the water. "I'm really sorry, Mom," he said a few seconds into their shared pursuit of treasure. "If I'd had any idea things would turn out the way they did, I'd have told you a long time ago."

"Why *didn't* you tell me a long time ago?" Sadie asked, proud of herself for keeping her voice calm and non-accusatory. "I've been aware of this possibility all of your life; I would have understood."

"Yeah," Shawn said, agreeing without explaining. "It's just . . . I guess . . . I knew it would hurt your feelings."

"I'm not so fragile and delicate," Sadie said, looking up at him and reviewing in her mind the murderers she'd faced off with and the peril she'd found herself in many times over the last few years. "It makes me feel like you don't trust me."

Shawn said nothing, and Sadie wondered what she'd done to lose his trust. "I don't know how to explain it, Mom, but I just didn't want to talk about it. Not with anyone. If I'd told you, you'd have asked questions, and it was all really intense, and I couldn't handle more than what I was already dealing with. I guess that doesn't make sense, but it's how I felt."

"You told Bre."

He was quiet for another few seconds, and Sadie waited him out. Finally, he dipped his pan again, continued swirling, and nodded. "Yeah, I guess I did."

"I'm not critical of that. It makes sense," Sadie said, offering an olive branch. "She has a birth mom out there, too, so it's reasonable for you to go to her."

Shawn sighed and sat back on his heels. "I thought she'd be supportive."

Sadie looked at him, reading the heaviness of his words and re-membering Breanna's tone when she'd told Sadie about Shawn con-fiding in her. "She wasn't?"

Shawn shook his head. "She doesn't feel like she needs to know her birth parents—at least not right now—and she was mad that I lied to you about Christmas."

Sadie mentally gave Breanna ten bonus points for having such integrity.

"I'd planned to talk to you about everything on this trip."

"But then Lorraina was here." Sadie was down to some dirt and a few small pebbles in her pan and could see tiny flecks of gold as she swirled the water. She tried to plan where to take the conversation, feeling glad to be having it at all. "Maggie said she didn't think you knew they were going to be on the ship. Is that true?"

Shawn picked the larger stones out of his pan and threw them back into the river. He shook his head.

"No, it's not true, or no, you didn't know she would be on the ship?"

A slight smile touched his lips. "I didn't know she'd be on the ship. I'd told her we were going when you first booked it, but I had no idea she'd follow me here. When I saw her after we boarded, I couldn't believe it, and it threw me for a loop. I'm sorry, Mom. I should have told you right then, or months ago, or last night. I thought I was doing the right thing, but then the way it came out couldn't have been worse. I just kept thinking that a better moment would come around, ya know?"

Sadie put her pan to the side and placed a hand on his arm. She remembered Pete saying that Shawn didn't owe her every detail of his life. She *had* to accept the fact that her boy could make his own choices and that she wasn't entitled to know about each one of them. Lorraina was part of his story that had taken a difficult turn. Sadie didn't want to make that any harder for him than it already was. It certainly helped that he was repentant, however, and wanted things to be okay between them. He looked at her hand on his arm, then into her face, and she could see the hunger for her reassurance in his eyes.

"I love you, and there's nothing you could do that will change that," she said quietly. "I hope that Lorraina will be okay and that you can continue building your relationship with her."

Shawn looked away, but not before Sadie saw a flicker of guilt in his eyes. Maggie had said that Shawn's relationship with Lorraina might have had some problems. But how could she ask about that right now? It would feel so self-serving.

"Thanks, Mom," Shawn said. He rinsed his whole pan in the river and stood up. Sadie winced at the potential treasure he'd just washed away—two or three dollars' worth of gold!

Raised voices a few feet away caused both of them to look upriver.

"I don't need you to do it for me," a redheaded woman said,

standing with her hands on her hips as she looked down at a bald man crouched at the edge of the water with his back to her.

"I'm not doing it *for* you," the man said, obviously frustrated. "I'm just showing you how to do it right."

"Oh," she said, crossing her arms over her chest, "because you're an expert at panning for gold, now?"

"No, because I paid attention when they showed us how to do it. You have to hold the pan like this."

Sadie was about to look away, embarrassed for them both, when the woman lifted one foot and kicked the man in the tush, upsetting his center of gravity and sending him face-first into the shallow water. He dropped his pan and spread his arms in an attempt to catch himself, but ended up spread-eagled in the muddy water.

An awkward hush fell over the rest of the gold-panners as the woman marched toward the shuttle parked several yards away behind some trees. One of the tour guides went after her while the man got out of the river, spitting water. He turned toward the woman's retreating form as he wiped mud from his face. "For heaven's sake, Tanice!" he said, storming in her direction.

Sadie watched Pete and another guide hurry in the man's direction, intercepting him before he covered too much ground. Sadie stayed put, repeating the woman's name in her mind. "Tanice," she said aloud. "Like Janice but with a T."

"What?"

Sadie looked up at a confused Shawn.

She stood, still holding her pan in both hands, looking at the place where the woman had disappeared into the trees. "The wine bottle Lorraina had last night had a gift tag on it for Ben and Tanice."

"A gift tag? What gift tag?"

CHAPTER 13

🍓

"Didn't Officer Jareg tell you about the gift tag? That's why I thought Lorraina's name was Tanice."

"He told me about the wine but he didn't say anything about a gift tag. Lorraina had someone else's wine?"

"I guess so," Sadie said.

"And that woman"—he nodded toward the trees—"is named Tanice? The same name from the gift tag?"

"Same name, yes. But I have no idea if it's the same Tanice, though it can't be a very common name. I've never heard of it before." The pure coincidence that the Tanice and Ben from the gift tag might be on the same shore excursion as Sadie's family seemed far-fetched, but she could feel her investigative mind clicking into place all the same. She wondered if Shawn was experiencing the same thing.

"I wonder how Lorraina got their wine," Shawn said.

"Or when," Sadie added. "I saw her just a couple of hours before Pete and I found her on deck. Even then she hadn't drunk much of the wine after she got it."

"But it was enough," Shawn said quietly, sadly.

Sadie looked at the man still standing on the shore, talking with Pete and the guide. Was that Ben? The guide left, and Pete led the man over to a fallen tree where they both sat down. Sadie could tell, even from a distance, that Pete was working his magic; he was a master at calming people down in intense situations. Heaven knew he'd calmed Sadie down more than once.

"Ten more minutes," Jackpot Jessie, one of the guides, called out to the tourists. Some were still bent over the river, others were standing around the rickety tables placed here and there, picking the gold out of their pans with tiny eyedroppers. "When you're finished, please return the pans to the equipment box. I hope prospecting helped you work up an appetite 'cause we'll be taking you to the salmon bake just as soon as we finish up."

Sadie looked at the gold and dirt still in her pan, then at Shawn who was watching an eagle circling in the sky above them. He seemed deep in thought.

Sadie finished swirling her pan, ending up with four more flecks of gold. She was one of the last to get her gold into her little container, but Shawn and Breanna waited for her. Pete had walked back to the shuttles with the man Tanice had pushed into the river, but then sat next to Sadie when they got on the bus. Tanice was sitting in the very back row of seats fiddling with her iPhone, making the most of having cell service. Her companion sat at the front, behind the driver, Nugget Nick, with a garbage sack spread over the seat to protect it from his muddy pants.

Sadie let Pete get comfortable before asking him, in a whisper, what he'd talked to the man about. Pete kept his voice low as he explained that apparently the couple's marriage had been rocky for a few years and this trip was supposed to help repair their relationship.

"I don't think it's working," Pete said when he finished.

Sadie nodded in agreement. "Um, did you happen to catch the man's name?" she asked, not sure if she'd told Pete about the wine bottle gift tag either.

"Kirby," Pete said. "Kirby Tucker."

Sadie slumped slightly.

"Why?" Pete asked.

Sadie opened her mouth to answer just as Nugget Nick got back on the loudspeaker and began touting more facts about Juneau. It was home to the second-oldest surviving totem in all of Alaska, which he would take them past in a few minutes.

Before Sadie knew it, they'd arrived, along with several other shuttles from other excursions, at an outdoor restaurant where a full-fledged salmon bake was on. It had started raining, but each table was covered by a large umbrella and outfitted with heaters at the top. The buffet was set up under a covered pavilion. The four of them filled up their plates with salad and side dishes—the salmon was still cooking—and made their way through the crowds, eventually finding an empty table.

The rain pattered on the canvas over their heads, and Sadie felt herself slowly unwinding thanks to the soothing atmosphere, good food, and even better company. She knew what Shawn had been hiding, and they had had a good discussion about it. The mood was feeling better, and Pete began telling them about an actual gold panning trip he'd taken several years ago. He was a great storyteller and the more he talked, the more relaxed everyone became.

After a few minutes, Sadie's phone dinged with a text message, and she reluctantly put down her fork—the Salmon Caesar Salad was delicious—in order to get her phone out of her bag. With Pete, Bre, and Shawn all here, Sadie wondered who was texting.

Pete continued his story, and Sadie unlocked her phone so she

89

could see the message. She was surprised to see that the text was from Maggie.

Do you have a minute?

"It's Maggie," Sadie said to her companions as she stood up from the table. She caught a flash of Shawn's unhappy expression before moving away. "I'll be right back," she said.

The overhanging roof of the gift shop provided some protection from the rain away from the tables and tourists; Sadie hurried to an empty section while calling Maggie's number.

"Hi," she said when Maggie answered. There was no heater under the eaves, and she wrapped her free arm around her stomach to try to retain some body heat.

"Hi," Maggie said back. She sounded nervous.

"Is everything okay?"

"Um, I don't know," she said, then let out a breath. "They're taking Lorraina to Anchorage in about an hour."

"Oh, dear! Did something happen?"

"No, she's about the same. She's actually breathing a little better and her vital signs have been stable, but the doctors think another hospital can do more for her than Juneau can."

"I see. Are you going to Anchorage with her?"

Maggie paused. "That's what I wanted to talk about. I talked to my dad and told him how you suggested I stay on the cruise. He thought it was a good idea."

"He did?" Sadie said, blinking in surprise.

"Yeah, I mean, I had such little time to get to know Lorraina, and he felt that since I'd come all this way, and paid for the cruise and everything, that maybe I should stay and see if Shawn and I can come to understand each other a little better or something. Maybe I can learn more about Lorraina, too. I can't really do anything for her in Anchorage, and I don't have the money to fly there without a good reason, but . . . I don't know. I'm just trying to figure out what to do, and since you offered . . ."

"I agree with your dad. Staying on the ship would give you and Shawn a chance to get comfortable with each other. And I think Shawn has questions, too. Together you might be able to help each other find the answers and prepare for what to do next depending on what happens with Lorraina."

"You're sure you don't mind? I realize this was a family vacation and everything. I don't want to intrude."

Maggie intruding was not going to ruin this vacation—much bigger things had already taken the trip off the rails. But that didn't mean that good couldn't come of this. "We'd love to have you. Truly."

Maggie was quiet for a minute. "Do you think Shawn will be okay with it? I'm not trying to force him to accept me or anything, but I want to learn more about Lorraina, and he knows her better than I do."

"I think Shawn will be okay." She'd seen his interest spark when she told him about the gift tag, and she knew he had questions he hadn't yet posed for answers. Sadie was a big believer that information was power, and she felt it was in Shawn's best interest to connect with Maggie, even if he might need time to adjust to the idea.

They made plans to meet when they all returned to the ship. Maggie didn't want to leave the hospital while Lorraina was still there, and she needed to talk to the captain about staying longer since the staff had anticipated her leaving the cruise all together.

Sadie agreed to text Maggie when they were back at the pier, which she assumed would be in an hour or so.

They said their good-byes, and Sadie returned to the table. "Shawn, can I talk to you for a minute?" It wasn't that what she had to say was secret, but the moment just seemed to belong to him.

He looked hesitant, but then put down his silverware and stood from the table. She led him back to the gift shop. He folded his arms across his chest and raised his eyebrows expectantly.

"Lorraina's being transferred to Anchorage," Sadie said, watching as his eyes shifted to the ground at the mention of Lorraina's name. They'd discussed her twice now—once in the hallway outside the security office and once at the river—but it felt as though he'd broken the topic up into bite-sized pieces and could give them up only when he was ready to let them go. She waited for him to say something or ask a question, but he continued to stare at the ground. "Are you okay?"

"When does she go?" Shawn asked. His expression and tone were blank, which was unusual for him; he was usually so easy to read.

"In about an hour."

Shawn let out a breath and looked toward the parking lot at the front of the pavilions. They weren't the only shore excursion that had ended up at the salmon bake and numerous shuttles were waiting to take the cruisers back to the various ships. "Do you think there are any taxis out there?"

"Why?"

"I think I should go to the hospital before they transport her. Talk to her doctors and stuff."

"I don't know that—" She stopped herself and thought things through for a few seconds. Did she really want to talk him out of seeing Lorraina? There was no way to know what would come next for her, or for him. For them.

"Do you want me to come with you?" she said instead.

He immediately shook his head, then gave her a sympathetic look. "There's stuff I know I need to explain—stuff I *want* to explain—but if she's leaving so soon, I think I need to see her first. Can we talk later, though?"

Being told to wait *again* was so much like last night that she wanted to insist he tell her now, but he was genuinely asking for her patience this time. She nodded, and he gave her a quick hug. As he turned back to the table, Sadie remembered the other thing she needed to tell him and grabbed his arm. "Also, Maggie isn't going to Anchorage. She's staying on the ship instead. I really think you two should connect, at least try to."

Shawn let out another heavy breath and stared at the ground. She felt him tense beneath her hand, and for a moment, she thought he was about to explain his feelings toward Maggie. The moment passed.

"I better get to the hospital," Shawn said.

Salmon Caesar Salad

Dressing
1 coddled egg
⅓ cup olive oil
⅓ cup lemon juice (fresh is always best)
3 gloves of garlic, pressed
2 tablespoons Worcestershire sauce
2 tablespoons Parmesan cheese, grated
1½ teaspoons anchovy paste (more to taste, but the flavor is strong)

½ teaspoon Dijon mustard (or ¼ teaspoon mustard powder)
½ teaspoon freshly ground black pepper

To coddle the egg, boil enough water in a small saucepan that the egg can be covered. Add egg (still in the shell) to boiling water, and boil for 4 minutes. Remove with a slotted spoon and run under cold water until cool enough to hold. Crack shell with a hard tap of a butter knife and pull both halves of the egg apart, careful not to spill the yolk and still-liquid portions of egg white. Using a spoon, scoop egg out of shell; be careful not to get any bits of shell in it. Put both halves of coddled egg in food processor or blender.

Add additional dressing ingredients to food processor or blender and blend until well combined. Put in fridge until ready to serve. Mix before serving.

Note: You can use a raw egg in place of a coddled egg, but don't store dressing for more than an hour before serving.

Note: Anchovy fillets can be used in place of paste; 1 fillet equals ½ teaspoon anchovy paste.

Salad
1 large head of romaine lettuce, washed and chopped
8 ounces cooked and cooled salmon, shredded (can use canned salmon or chicken in a pinch)
Croutons
Grated Parmesan cheese, to taste

Toss lettuce, salmon, and croutons together in large bowl. Drizzle refrigerated dressing over the top and toss together until lettuce is well coated. Top with grated Parmesan cheese.

Note: Great option for using up leftover salmon.

CHAPTER 14

Pete went with Shawn to get a taxi. Sadie and Breanna took a few bites in silence before Sadie suddenly put down her fork and said, "Oh, I haven't even followed up on the wedding stuff. I'm so sorry—are you feeling better today? Have you had a chance to talk to Liam?"

Breanna smiled. "Don't feel bad. My wedding woes are micro-scopic compared to what's going on with Shawn right now."

"No, they aren't," Sadie said, shaking her head. "So where are things at? Did sleeping on it make you feel any better?"

Breanna shrugged and scooped up a bite of baked beans.

"Have you talked to Liam?"

"I texted him earlier, gave him a summary of what was going on—it sounded like such a soap opera. I'm not sure I want to get all dramatic about a stupid wedding in light of everything else."

"Breanna," Sadie said with her head cocked to the side, "this is your wedding day. *Yours.* All this stuff with Shawn is going to work out. Don't sell out on what should be the most important day of your life simply because this other stuff looks bigger right now."

Breanna looked hesitant, but that was all Sadie needed to know;

Breanna was being gracious, but was open to some advice. For the next ten minutes, she worked hard to convince Breanna of what she'd said yesterday—that if Breanna could stand her ground now, she'd increase the potential of having the future she wanted.

"And Liam should be backing you up on this," Sadie added as Pete walked back up to the table. "I know he's a great guy, but it's not just him anymore. It's good for you to talk to him about this and insist on his support. You're not out of line to remind him that the two of you are getting married, which means he needs to be his own man. Well, more like *your* man, but his own man too. You know what I mean."

"Really?" Breanna said after Pete had slid into his seat and agreed with Sadie's advice. "I feel like I'm being a brat. I mean, Liam's mom has worked really hard on the wedding plans. I feel bad saying I don't like it."

"It's the first battle of many," Sadie said. "I'm not telling you what you should do or how you should do it, but I think if you stand down and just let Liam's mom take over, you'll regret it one day. Right now is when it's going to be easiest for you to be heard—before she takes things any further."

Breanna's expression was lighter than it had been. "Maybe I should call him before we leave port."

"Excellent idea," Sadie said just as their hosts rang the bell indicating there was more salmon ready. Sadie had been on the phone with Maggie when the last round had been served. Sadie and Pete got in line while Breanna retreated to the quiet spot beneath the dripping eves to call Liam.

Sadie and Pete enjoyed several minutes of one-on-one conversation, and she appreciated his concern as well as his encouragement at how she was handling things. He apologized for not telling her who Lorraina was when he and Shawn had come to the cabin last night, but Sadie now understood why Shawn hadn't been ready to talk about it right then.

Breanna returned with good news: Liam had listened to her explanation and agreed to talk to his mother as soon as possible. He assured Breanna that he was on her side and that everything would work out. "Thanks for giving me the push I needed, Mom," Breanna said. "I feel so much better. I think everything's going to be okay."

After dinner, they headed to the shuttle that would take them back to the pier, and Sadie was able to reflect on the fact that though the day had gotten off to a horrible start, the afternoon and evening had redeemed it somewhat. Of course things were far from over, considering Lorraina's future was uncertain, and Shawn had things he hadn't yet told Sadie about. But she felt as though she'd connected with both of her children today, and as of eleven o'clock that morning, she could not have foreseen that happening.

When they slid into their seats on the shuttle—Sadie and Bre sitting together while Pete gallantly sat alone—Sadie was surprised to see Tanice and Kirby sitting toward the back of the bus. Tanice was looking out the window, and Kirby was on his phone, but they were together.

Breanna turned to follow Sadie's gaze when Tanice caught Sadie staring. Sadie quickly looked away.

"Do you know her?" Breanna asked.

Sadie quickly—and quietly—told Breanna about the gift tag on the bottle and what she had witnessed at the river.

"And you think *she* owned the wine bottle?" Breanna said, nodding her head toward the back of the bus.

"Her husband's name isn't Ben," Sadie said. "But Tanice is such a unique name. Have you ever heard it before?"

"I think there was a Tanice in one of my classes a few years ago," Breanna said. "But it's certainly unique."

"We had a woman named Tanice who worked the dispatch for a while back in New Mexico." Pete leaned forward in his seat to join the conversation. "And there are three thousand people on the ship. Two Tanices is possible."

"And there are probably seventy-five Bens on board," Breanna added.

"How would Lorraina get someone else's wine in the first place?" Sadie asked.

"I've seen a few bottles left on dinner tables," Pete said. "Maybe she snagged it after Tanice and Ben—whoever they are—left it on their table after dinner last night."

"But so little of the wine was gone," Sadie reminded him. "Why would anyone leave a nearly full bottle of wine on a table? And if they had just had one glass, for example, how much could Lorraina have had and still left the wine bottle that full? Not much, I don't think."

"Maybe she'd had drinks at the bar before she got the wine," Breanna suggested.

They continued discussing theories and possibilities, which only served to frustrate Sadie with how little they knew. After a few minutes, she shelved both her curiosity and her frustrations and turned the attention back to Breanna. "Tell me about the cake you picked out."

Breanna's face lit up like a lightbulb. "It's so pretty, Mom. Simple and elegant."

"Just like you," Sadie interjected with a smile.

As Breanna described the cake in detail, Pete sat back in his seat and pulled out his phone.

After five minutes, the shuttle pulled into the parking lot on the pier. As everyone filed out, several people put a few dollars in Jackpot Jessie's hat. Sadie was feeling generous and gave her a ten-dollar tip, which earned her a "Yee-haw!"

Once off the shuttle, Sadie noticed that Kirby, Tanice's husband, was standing to the side of the gangplank, talking on his phone, while Tanice was standing in line to reboard the ship. There were a few people behind her, but Sadie had an idea and quickly explained to Pete and Breanna that she'd catch up with them later. With so many people on the ship, she might never see this woman again, and she wanted to rule out the possibility, no matter how slight, of the wine bottle belonging to her. If the wine *did* belong to her, maybe it would help them figure out how and when Lorraina had gotten it.

There wasn't much form to the line, and Sadie was able to make her way up until she was right behind Tanice. Tanice was an average-looking woman with thick bottle-red hair and a profusion of freckles on every bit of exposed skin, which wasn't much because the temperature was still in the fifties. Her face was tight, and she stared at the ship's entrance at the top of the gangway as though it were impossibly far away. There were almost thirty people ahead of them in line, which was moving slowly.

"Hi," Sadie said, leaning forward.

Tanice looked over her shoulder. "Hi," she said back, sounding confused. She immediately faced forward again.

Sadie smiled. Confusion was good; it often meant people would say more than if they were fully aware of what was going on. "I was on the same excursion as you and just wondered if everything was okay," Sadie said.

Tanice once again looked over her shoulder, this time with a frown.

This felt more awkward than Sadie had expected it would, but hadn't Pete said similar things to Kirby? Kirby had opened up just fine. Surely Tanice was just as eager for a new friend with a listening ear.

Tanice narrowed her pale blue eyes, then looked forward again. Hmm. This wasn't going nearly as smoothly as Sadie had hoped it would.

Sadie leaned forward so that she could keep her voice down. "I saw the, uh, argument. Are you okay?"

"I'm fine," Tanice said. She took a step forward even though the line hadn't moved.

"Are you sure?" Sadie pushed.

Tanice's head whipped back around and she spoke loud enough for everyone within several feet to hear her. "I'm sure, okay? Mind your own business. What's wrong with you?"

Glazed Salmon

1½ teaspoons lemon pepper
1 pound salmon
2 tablespoons soy sauce
4 teaspoons sugar (brown or white)
4 teaspoons olive oil

To bake, sprinkle lemon pepper over fish. Place in a greased 8x8 pan and cover with foil. Bake at 350 degrees for 30 to 40 minutes or until fish flakes.

Mix together the remaining ingredients in a small bowl for a basting sauce. When the fish has finished baking, turn oven to broil and baste or brush the fish several times with the sauce until nicely browned.

To grill, sprinkle lemon pepper over fish. In small saucepan, heat the soy sauce, sugar, and olive oil, and add 1 teaspoon cornstarch. Heat over medium heat to a boil, stirring constantly until sugar crystals are dissolved.

Heat grill to medium. Place salmon on grill and baste with glaze. Cook 3 to 4 minutes, turn, and baste again. Continue basting and turning until fish is cooked through.

CHAPTER 15

🍓

Sadie fell back a step, her cheeks heating up as several people in line looked at her in the wake of the reprimand. *Sheesh, I must be losing my touch.* "Sorry," she muttered, then fell back to join Breanna and Pete, who thankfully said nothing about her failure, though there was no doubt they'd heard the exchange.

Tanice looked back at her, but Sadie quickly busied herself with her phone, sending Shawn a text message to ask how things were going. She was embarrassed by Tanice's reaction and frustrated that she hadn't even asked about the wine.

Shawn texted back that Lorraina had been taken to the helipad and he was finishing up a few things at the hospital. Sadie asked if Maggie was there, and Shawn said no. Sadie texted Maggie, telling her they were nearly back on the ship, and Maggie texted back saying she'd been held up and would let her know when she got on the ship. Sadie put her phone in her bag and updated Breanna and Pete about the plan.

"So are we going to the show tonight?" Breanna said, looking between them both. "Or is it totally inappropriate for me to ask?"

Sadie shared a look with Pete and then lifted her shoulders. She didn't know the answer. Shawn had promised her information, and she was eager to talk in more detail with Maggie, but neither of them were here right now.

"Isn't it the Temptations tribute tonight?" Pete asked. "It looked like it would be a good show."

Sadie did like the Temptations, and there wasn't anything else to do until Shawn and Maggie joined them, so she agreed. It would be fun, and they could save Shawn and Maggie a seat in case either of them were interested.

After they were checked onto the ship, Pete headed to his cabin while Sadie and Bre went to theirs to change their clothes.

They met at the theater twenty minutes later and found five seats together. Because of Shawn's size, they had to be strategic to make sure he wouldn't block anyone's view, which put them against the back wall on the first level. Sadie texted both Shawn and Maggie with the location of their seats while her fellow passengers filled up the seats around them.

There was a plethora of "Juneau, Alaska" T-shirts and jackets among the crowd. One woman had a purse with the word "Juneau" written out in rhinestones on the front. Sadie wondered if such treasures would seem quite so cute once the owners were back home in Ohio or Alabama or wherever they were from. Then again, the entire point of the souvenirs was to be a conversation starter: "Oh, did you go to Juneau?"

Cruise-director Julie came on stage at exactly eight o'clock and pumped up the crowd with talk of the next day's visit to Skagway. She wore a semiformal gown and obviously had a big personality that helped her do her job with confidence. After finishing the Skagway talk, Julie reminded them that the ship would be leaving port in less than two hours and then introduced the cover group for the Temptations.

While the real Temptations were African-American, this version was a mixed group: three black men, one white man, and one Hispanic or Greek who wore his hair in a faux-hawk—something the original Temptations never did. The five men wore bright blue tuxedos with sequined bow ties reminiscent of the original group, and they sounded amazing. If not for checking her phone every five minutes in hopes of an update from Maggie or Shawn, Sadie would have thoroughly enjoyed the show.

Thirty minutes in, Shawn tapped Sadie on the shoulder, and they all moved over so that Shawn could have the aisle seat. Sadie wanted to ask him how it had gone at the hospital, but it was poor etiquette to talk in a theater.

Within just a few minutes of Shawn's arrival, she received a text from Maggie.

Can we meet at the Lamplighter Lounge after the show?

Sadie replied that the Lamplighter would be great and returned her phone to her purse. She heard the vibration of another incoming text message a minute later and reached for her phone before realizing it was Pete's phone, not hers. Pete pulled his phone from the pocket of his sport coat, read it, and replied. Who was he texting? He responded to additional texts several times, increasing Sadie's curiosity. A minute later, her phone signaled a text message too. It was from Pete.

Pete: **Tox screens are showing something unusual in Lorraina's system.**

Sadie: Who told you?

Pete: I made an arrangement with one of the medics on the ship. Keep it on the down low.

Sadie: Look at you, Mr. Police Detective. Are they thinking overdose?

Pete: Medications would show up on the initial tests. They're wondering if there was something else in the wine. It would explain her extreme reaction. Also, you're the only one who saw the gift tag. Security wants to talk to you about it.

Sadie read the message twice, then replied just as the group started in on "Papa Was a Rollin' Stone."

Sadie: Tonight?

Pete: Tomorrow morning.

Shawn-to-Sadie: Are you guys seriously texting each other?

Sadie-to-Shawn: It would be rude to talk out loud in the theater.

Pete-to-Sadie: How cute is it that we're texting like teenagers while sitting right next to each other?

Sadie-to-Pete: Adorable ☺

Shawn-to-Sadie: Where's Maggie?

Sadie-to-Shawn: She'll meet us in the Lamplighter after the show.

Pete-to-Sadie: I think you're cute.

Sadie-to-Pete: I think you're cute, too. Wanna go out?

Shawn-to-Sadie: I should probably tell you something before we meet up with her.

Sadie's smile fell, and she sat up a little straighter.

Sadie-to-Shawn: What?

Pete-to-Sadie: You mean go steady?

Sadie's palms were starting to sweat in anticipation. What did
Shawn need to tell her?

The singers broke into "My Girl," and several members of the
audience started singing along. Sadie glanced to her left and could
see the glow of Shawn's cell phone in the darkened theater as he
typed on his phone.

Pete-to-Sadie: If I still had my high school letterman's jacket,
I'd let you wear it. ☺

Shawn-to-Sadie: I don't think Maggie's really my sister.

CHAPTER 16

♦

Somewhere between Sadie's gasp, Pete's confused look, and the singers finishing the song to a standing ovation, Shawn sent one more text:

I'll explain when we finish here.

The lights came on, and the entire theater got to their feet. The buffets were still open, and no one looked as though they wanted to delay their fifth meal of the day for even a few extra seconds.

Sadie turned toward Shawn, eager for the explanation, but immediately realized it was too loud for her to hear anything. She pointed toward the crowds now filling the aisles that led to the doors, and Shawn nodded. Sadie blinked beneath the bright lights of the hallway once she got through the doors, glad that Pete was right behind her; his hand had stayed at the small of her back the whole time. She looked over her shoulder, trying to keep track of Shawn and Breanna, who seemed to be getting farther and farther behind them. She grabbed Pete's hand and pulled him out of the crowd. They stood against the wall to allow the hordes of their fellow passengers to pass by before Shawn and Breanna caught up. Sadie grabbed the sleeve of Shawn's jacket and twisted it tightly in her grip to pull him from the crowd. No way was she letting go of him before he explained himself.

"Lamplighter," Sadie said loudly when they were all together. Shawn, Bre, and Pete nodded, and the four of them managed to stay relatively close until the hallway opened up into the foyer in front of the elevators. Pete was in the lead and took the stairs. The rest of them followed—all three flights—to deck twelve-forward where the Lamplighter Lounge was located. Sadie hoped she could catch her breath and that Shawn could explain himself before Maggie's arrival.

The crowds thinned out the farther up they went, but they weren't the only people heading for the Lamplighter, which was touted as a drink-and-dessert bar. When Sadie saw the old-fashioned lantern hanging next to the sign over the door, she attempted to pull Shawn aside when a familiar voice said her name.

"Sadie?"

Sadie looked around to see Maggie standing a few feet away. She was dressed in a lovely yellow dress with matching peep-toed heels, and a flower in her hair, which she'd pulled up into a side bun. She held a small purse in both hands, and it looked as though she'd applied fresh makeup to her puffy eyes.

"Maggie," Sadie said as she took a few steps toward Shawn's sister . . . uh, or *not sister*. Her being here meant whatever Shawn was going to explain would have to wait. "Are you okay?"

"I'm fine," Maggie said with a forced smile. Her tone was less than reassuring, and the fragility that surrounded her triggered all of Sadie's motherly instincts.

"Are you sure?" Sadie said, taking another step forward. Of course she'd had a terrible day, what with spending it at the hospital and then having Lorraina taken away. Did she know about the toxicology reports? Did Shawn?

"I'm sure," Maggie said, but her smile seemed even weaker than it had been a moment earlier.

Sadie considered her options, then turned to the rest of the group, who hung back as though awaiting instructions Sadie had no qualms about giving. "Why don't you guys go in and get a table before they're all taken? We'll be right there."

Breanna nodded, and Pete led the way while a hesitant Shawn followed. Sadie turned back to Maggie and eased around her so that they were face-to-face, shoulders against the wall. It was almost like a private conversation except for the three-dozen people around them at any given moment.

"What happened?" She braced herself to hear that Lorraina's condition had worsened since Sadie had last talked to Maggie.

Maggie shook her head in a vain attempt to pretend everything was okay, but her trembling chin betrayed her.

Sadie looked around for somewhere they could go to talk and saw a small glass door with the word "Chapel" above it. A chapel had been built next to the entrance to a bar? Well, engineers couldn't be expected to consider all facets of a layout.

She put her arm around Maggie's shoulders and steered her toward the chapel, which turned out to be a tiny room with plush benches around three walls and a podium in front. Royal blue floor-to-ceiling draperies were set as a backdrop behind it. A very nice artificial flower arrangement was currently set on the pulpit, but it would be easy enough to move if someone wanted to speak to a group, though no more than a dozen people could comfortably fit in the room.

They sat side by side on one of the benches, and Sadie rubbed Maggie's back while she cried quietly. After nearly a minute, Maggie straightened up and wiped at her eyes. She looked at her fingers to see if her mascara was running—which it was. Sadie hadn't brought her shoulder bag with her, but she found a box of tissues on a shelf behind the podium. Maggie took two tissues from the box and dabbed carefully at her eyes. Sadie didn't have the heart to tell her that her makeup was beyond saving.

"Thank you," Maggie said. "I should have just flown home. I'm sorry."

"You're fine," Sadie assured her. "Really. We're . . ." She was going to say they were family, but according to Shawn, they weren't. Oh, she wished she knew what he'd meant by that. "We're here for you," she amended. "Did something happen to Lorraina? Did she get to Anchorage okay?"

"Yes," Maggie said. "I mean, I wasn't there when she left. I had to go to the police station because . . . " Her chin quivered, and she took a deep breath. "When the Juneau doctors got ahold of her family, they . . . they didn't know anything about me. They said that . . . that Lorraina doesn't have a daughter. In fact, they didn't believe it was really Lorraina they were calling about at all. They didn't even know she'd gone on a cruise. The hospital had to send them a picture before they would believe it, and then they freaked out and demanded I not be treated like family because clearly I was some kind of fraud." She dissolved into sobs and put her hands over her face.

Sadie steered Maggie into her shoulder and rubbed her back. *This poor girl,* she thought to herself. She glanced toward the door and prayed no one would interrupt them. It was frosted glass, but she could see the forms of people walking past, and the steady thump of the music from the lounge was like a muted heartbeat in the walls.

Maggie pulled away after a minute but kept her face averted until she'd wiped at her eyes again and straightened up. She'd gotten most of the smeared mascara but not all of it. "I'm so sorry," Maggie said sincerely. "I thought I could handle coming here tonight, but I fell apart as soon as I got back to our room. I think I should have just gone home." She moved as though to stand, but Sadie put a hand on her arm and kept her from rising.

"I'm so sorry you had to face all that on your own," Sadie said. "Did they say anything about Shawn? Did they know about him?"

Maggie nodded, and Sadie looked down to hide her reaction. It was embarrassing to admit, even to herself, but she'd been hoping that maybe Lorraina *wasn't* Shawn's birth mother and that's what he meant when he said Maggie wasn't his sister. That Sadie should want such a conclusion made her feel like a terrible person.

"It doesn't make sense," Maggie said. She had a mascara streak running down the left side of her face, but Sadie didn't point it out. "Lorraina knew things about me that no one else could know." She said it as though it were a question Sadie could answer for her. "But why would she hide *me* if she didn't hide Shawn's adoption?" She paused and shook her head. "And . . . I can't even ask her."

Sadie pulled her into another hug while offering whispered bits of comfort as Maggie fell apart again. Lorraina's family knew about Shawn, but not Maggie. So when Shawn said Maggie wasn't his sister, what *exactly* did that mean?

"We argued the last time I saw her," Maggie said softly as she tried again to get ahold of herself.

"What did you argue about?"

Maggie took a deep breath. "Things had been strange ever since we got on the ship. She'd disappear for periods of time, and she was always looking around when we were going somewhere—you know, like she was looking for someone. Yesterday afternoon I asked her what was going on. She tried to come up with all these excuses, but she finally admitted that Shawn was on the ship, but he didn't want to see *me*."

"You?" Sadie had interrupted one of the conversations Shawn had with Lorraina, and then Shawn had received a phone call in his cabin Sunday night, which Sadie already realized had likely been from Lorraina. But Sadie didn't know what they had talked about. And why would Lorraina not tell Shawn or Maggie about the other one coming on the cruise? She didn't know enough about Shawn's interactions with Lorraina to guess. She would remedy that as soon as she could, but for right now, Maggie was divulging information, and Sadie was in a position to try to help her feel better, while picking up important details. "You're sure it's you he didn't want to see?"

Maggie nodded. "I already knew Shawn didn't want to meet me. Lorraina showed me those horrible e-mails he'd sent."

What horrible e-mails?

Maggie continued before Sadie could ask for an explanation. "So when I found out she was trying to trick us into meeting, I was really mad. I told her I wished I hadn't even come, and she totally freaked out and said she wished *she* hadn't come either, that Shawn was ruining everything."

"Everything? What's everything?"

"Us meeting," Maggie said. "That's why she did all of this— because she really wanted Shawn and me to meet and get along, like a real brother and sister. She said all she ever wanted was for us to be a family."

It took a whole lot of self-restraint for Sadie not to blurt out that *she* was Shawn's family, not Maggie or Lorraina.

"But Shawn was so mad when he found her on the ship and he didn't want you to know about either one of us, which had Lorraina all stressed out and nervous."

Sadie couldn't help but feel a little responsible for the fact that Shawn was unhappy to see Lorraina on the ship, and by default, Maggie, too. Having Sadie and his birth mother on the same ship had put him in a difficult position, but he'd made things far more complicated than they'd needed to be by not coming clean about everything in the beginning.

"Anyway," Maggie continued, "I talked about leaving the cruise when we got to Juneau, and Lorraina told me to go ahead." Tears filled Maggie's eyes again, and she looked at the tissue she was holding in her lap. "Then she left the cabin. I had a mini-breakdown but tried to get centered for when she got back." She paused, then took a ragged breath. "The next time I saw her, she was in the ship's infirmary. I think . . . I think she was so upset about our argument that she went on that drinking binge. And now she's in a coma."

Maggie stared at her hands, her tears falling down her face. She looked completely exhausted.

"What time did this argument happen?" Sadie asked after a few seconds.

"It was around seven," Maggie answered. "We'd just gotten back from dinner."

So *before* Sadie had seen Lorraina at the photo gallery. "And did you stay in the cabin the rest of the night?"

Maggie nodded.

"And Lorraina never came back—even for a little while?"

Maggie shook her head.

Sadie thought for a moment. "What deck is your room on?"

"Eleven," Maggie said.

Sadie had assumed as much, since that's where she'd seen Shawn and Lorraina talking the first day. Lorraina had also gotten off on the eleventh floor at around 8:40 after Sadie had chased her from the photo gallery. Why would Lorraina get off on her floor but not go to her room? "You never left your room after seven o'clock?"

Maggie shook her head again. The tissue in her hands was now a damp, fuzzy ball of disintegrating paper. "I watched a couple of movies, then finally fell asleep around midnight."

The inconsistency bothered Sadie. She couldn't think of any other reason Lorraina would have gone to deck eleven except to return to her room. But according to Maggie, Lorraina never came back. Sympathy aside, Sadie didn't know Maggie very well, and if Shawn was right, and if he and she weren't siblings, that meant that Lorraina had lied about something. Something *big*.

"What time did you find out about what happened to Lorraina?"

"The medical staff woke me up with a phone call around two o'clock and confirmed my name and everything, then sent someone to talk to me."

Sadie handed Maggie a new tissue, then helped her clean up the last of the smudges. She thought through everything she'd learned and tried to come up with a hypothesis. Without any background information on Lorraina or her family, though, it felt far more like conjecture.

"You should go back to your family," Maggie said. "I really shouldn't have come tonight."

"Yes, you should have," Sadie said. "Come have some dessert with us. Let's talk about this with everyone there and see what we can make of it."

Maggie shook her head. "Shawn already didn't want to meet me. He certainly won't want to spend time with me now. Maybe the captain can help set up a flight for me from Skagway tomorrow."

"Maggie," she said, feeling a little desperate to have her stay, "I haven't had much time to talk to Shawn, but I do know he has questions about Lorraina he wants answered, too."

Maggie didn't respond, but Sadie was encouraged by the fact that she seemed to have moved through the worst of her emotion.

"I think maybe you could help him find the answers he's looking for. And maybe he could help you find some answers, too. This isn't just a hopeful suggestion; Pete's a retired police detective, and Shawn and I have run our own private investigating company. Obviously, there are some things going on that none of us understand, but if we could figure them out, I think we would all feel better. You are an essential part of that process. We could really use your help."

Maggie looked up, intrigued but cautious.

"We like having answers to questions," Sadie added. "And we've found that knowing the truth, even when it's painful, is usually better than wondering about it. Maybe by the time Lorraina gets well, you will have a better idea of what's going on."

Maggie nodded, as though not quite sure she wanted to commit but at least open to the idea.

"Would you be interested in helping us?"

Maggie looked into her lap again.

Sadie allowed the silence to build for several seconds before she spoke again. "There are no wrong decisions here. If you want to go home tomorrow, I will completely understand. But if you want answers, and if you want to be a part of this process, we would welcome you. I promise to help you find whatever peace we can."

She waited with bated breath for an answer, and when Maggie lifted her head, Sadie knew by the spark of curiosity in the girl's eyes that she was interested. Sadie knew that look all too well.

CHAPTER 17

🍓

Sadie could feel the tension between Maggie and Shawn as soon as they sat down.

When the waiter came around asking if the newcomers wanted anything to eat or drink, Sadie shook her head. Breanna, Pete, and Shawn had nearly finished their drinks, and it looked like they had shared a large piece of cheesecake.

"I really should get some sleep," Maggie said after attempts at small talk fell flat. She didn't mention Lorraina, and everyone else seemed to follow her lead. "Today's been one of the longest days of my life. Can we talk more tomorrow?"

"Of course," Sadie said, standing and giving Maggie a hug.

"I have some of Lorraina's things," Maggie said. "I can bring them with me tomorrow morning if you want, and we can look through them to see if we learn anything. I'm just worn out tonight."

"I could walk you to your room and get whatever you have," Breanna offered, putting her napkin on the table. "That way we could get a head start." She looked to Pete and Sadie for support, and they both agreed that was a good idea, if Maggie didn't mind, which she didn't.

"Wonderful," Sadie said, grateful for Breanna's offer. "Should we meet for a late breakfast in the Tiara Room? Say, nine thirty?" That would give Sadie's group a chance to meet up and talk about the situation before Maggie arrived.

They all agreed to the place and time, and after Breanna and Maggie left the lounge, Sadie returned to her seat and zeroed her focus in on Shawn. She had liked the idea of Maggie joining them, but now that she was gone, Sadie was relieved to have the chance to talk to Shawn.

The engines began to rumble, and Julie came over the intercom to inform them that they were leaving Juneau. She reminded the passengers to check out the daily onboard paper that was delivered to their rooms every evening and wished them all a good night.

After Julie finished her announcements, Shawn, Sadie, and Pete moved closer to each other around the table, and Sadie updated them on the discussion she'd had with Maggie in the chapel. Shawn took a drink from his water glass. He looked nervous, and Sadie and Pete shared a glance acknowledging that they'd both noticed it.

"So, fill in the blanks for us," Pete said once Shawn had returned his glass to the table. "What don't we know?"

"There's a lot *I* don't know," Shawn said, staring at his glass. He hadn't used a coaster, and the glass had left a water ring on the Formica tabletop. He lifted the glass and set it back down an inch to the right, then did it again, making an interlocking chain pattern. Sadie had to sit on her hands to keep from taking the glass away from him. She wanted his focus, but needed his cooperation.

"Tell us what you *do* know," Pete amended.

"I know that a woman named Lorraina Juxteson had a baby boy on April twelfth at the Nebraska Medical Center in Omaha. That boy seems to be me, and the lady they took to Anchorage today seems to be Lorraina."

"You requested your original birth certificate?" Sadie asked. Upon adoption, a new birth certificate was created. Sadie had the paperwork explaining the process that could be used to get a copy of the original, ready for the day when her children might want or need it. They'd never asked. The irony of this did not escape her.

"Seems to be?" Pete repeated. "You're not sure?"

"I'm not sure of anything," he said, sounding as worn-out as Maggie had.

"Why don't you start from the beginning?" Pete suggested. "How did you find her?"

Sadie sensed that Pete already knew some of this, but she appreciated that he could bring her up to speed with the recap.

Shawn nodded and took a breath. "I put up a basic profile on a few reunification websites last August, listing my date of birth, gender, ethnicity, and hospital—stuff from the certificate you had for me, Mom." He glanced at her quickly, then continued. "Two months later, Lorraina replied with additional information like my birth weight and her full name, which matched the original birth certificate I was able to get via an official request from the county of record. We e-mailed for a while, and I was able to get enough information to do a background check that seemed to verify that she was who she said she was."

"So you do believe that the woman you met on this ship is your birth mother?" Pete asked. Sadie's heart clenched just a little.

Shawn hesitated but then nodded.

"But you have some concerns as well," Pete added.

Shawn nodded again. "She had some arrests for things like bank fraud and check kiting. Not serious, and nothing recent, but enough for me to be on guard. Still, things were going well; she was really funny and . . ." He glanced at Sadie, and she sensed his hesitation to say whatever it was he was about to say. She was glad he'd paused. This wasn't easy to listen to.

"Anyway, in February, Lorraina asked if she could borrow a few hundred dollars; she was short on rent. I'd read about *a lot* of birth family reunions online, and one of the red flags is when either party asks for money from the other one. But it was just $300, and she swore she'd pay me back, so I loaned it to her." He paused to take another sip of his drink. "She asked for another loan a month later, and I said no. I didn't have it anyway, and I reminded her about the money I'd loaned her in February. She got mad about it, saying how she'd thought we'd be a family, and how she'd help me out if I needed it—stuff like that. It made me really uncomfortable, and I started pulling back."

Sadie nodded. His response seemed perfectly reasonable.

"When she realized what was happening, she apologized about the money and for losing her cool. Then she told me she'd been sick for a really long time and that sometimes it made her moody and stuff. I still wanted some space, and while she respected that at first, after a week she was calling me four times a day and sending me all these e-mails asking me to call her. A few weeks later, she left a voice mail asking me to come to a doctor's appointment with her—in Tennessee—and said she would explain everything.

"I'd stopped calling her back by then—the conversations were just too frustrating—so I e-mailed her and told her I couldn't miss school for her doctor's appointment and to please back off. I said I would contact her when I was ready to talk. She got all ticked again, saying how I didn't care about her. She started leaving these long messages on my voice mail. It was so weird."

Sadie agreed with him completely; it was very strange behavior.

"I mean, I *was* worried about her, but . . . I don't know, I just needed some space to think about things, ya know? Even a week without her bombarding me would have helped, but she wouldn't stop. By April, I was ignoring her completely, and then a couple of weeks after the whole doctor thing, she e-mails me to tell me I have a sister, even though she'd told me back in October that I didn't have any brothers or sisters."

"You think she lied about Maggie?" Sadie asked.

Shawn shrugged. "It felt like she was just pulling one thing after another to hook me in or something. I felt manipulated by the whole thing, and so I told her, again, that I needed some time to figure things out and I needed her to back off and stop contacting me for a while. In the next e-mail, she drops this bombshell about needing a liver transplant."

Sadie startled. She hadn't seen that coming.

"A liver transplant?" Pete repeated, leaning in and glancing at Sadie—apparently he didn't know this part either. "From you?"

Had Shawn really said a liver transplant or had both Sadie and Pete heard it wrong? Maybe he'd said *river houseplant?*

"She said I needed to be tested as a possible donor, that she hadn't told me sooner because she thought I would think that's why she found me and stuff—it was all so crazy."

"You can't just give someone your liver," Sadie said.

"You can give them part of it," Pete said. "It's called a living donor liver transplant. Is that what she called it, Shawn?"

Shawn nodded. "Yeah, I read up on it, and it's a legit procedure. They take part of the donor's liver, which grows back eventually, and put that piece into the recipient. It eventually grows into a whole liver for the recipient too. They're getting more and more common, but she has a really rare blood type and none of her family was a good match."

Shawn's blood type was AB negative. Very rare. Did Lorraina have the same type?

Shawn rubbed his hand over his forehead, looking tired. "But after everything had happened, I couldn't help doubting her. I mean, as soon as I start pulling away, she tells me she's sick, and when *that* doesn't work, I suddenly have a birth sister, and when I *still* want my space, she needs me to give her part of my liver?" He shook his head. "I thought she was messing with me," he said, his voice soft. He looked at Sadie. "I didn't know what to think, Mom. I wanted to talk to you about all of it on this cruise and then decide what to do when I got back . . . and then Lorraina was here and sent me into this panic and then she went on a drinking binge last night."

"No one is blaming you for anything," Sadie said, reaching out and giving his arm a squeeze.

"I want to make sure I understand what you are telling us," Pete cut in. "If you were tested and found to be a match, she wanted you to donate part of your liver to her?"

Sadie felt like she was in *The Twilight Zone*. The whole transplant thing was ridiculous, like those stories of people waking up in their hotel bathtub without a kidney.

"She never came right out and said that, but why else have me tested?"

"When did she first tell you about the transplant, again?" He'd told them, but Sadie wanted to be sure.

"About three weeks ago."

"And you didn't get the test done because you didn't believe her?" Pete asked.

"From what I'd read about liver transplants, they were rarely something that happened quickly—not like a heart transplant or something like that. She said she'd been in liver failure for a couple of years, and I figured I had at least a few weeks to get things worked out with you and stuff." He groaned slightly and shook his head. "I wish I could find the words to help you guys understand that what I felt was just so . . . so out there, ya know? So weird, and not what I was expecting when I put up those profiles. It was like I hadn't even caught up with wanting to find her before I found her, and I hadn't gotten used to having her before she started bombarding me with these expectations I couldn't understand." He took a breath and scrubbed a hand across his forehead. "I just didn't know what to think or what to believe or what to do."

"Of course," Sadie said, smiling at him and rubbing his arm again. "You did the best you could do under the circumstances."

"So where does Maggie fit in?" Pete asked without allowing the tenderness to draw out too long. He was all business. Sadie appreciated his ability to keep Shawn talking.

"I never even met her before this morning," Shawn said. "And I can't help but wonder if she is part of this game Lorraina seems to be playing with me. That's why I didn't want to meet her in the first place. I mean, Lorraina's family says she doesn't have a daughter, did you know that?"

Sadie did, but wanted to hear Shawn's information so she just nodded rather than get off track.

Shawn shook his head. "I met some of Lorraina's family when I went back at Christmas. They had a picture of me and everything, plus pictures of Lorraina for a few years after I was born and before Lorraina got all messed up with alcohol. I don't know how Maggie could have been born during that time without them knowing about it; Maggie's only two years younger than me. Lorraina would have only been eighteen years old back then, and she still lived with her sister. I don't see how it's possible."

"I think *Maggie* thinks she's Lorraina's daughter," Sadie said. "Or at least she thought she was. You said Lorraina had told you back in October that you didn't have any natural siblings. How did she explain the fact that, come April, you did?"

"She said she wanted to wait until she and I knew each other better. She said she hadn't wanted to get my hopes up, so she didn't tell me until after she found Maggie."

"So," Pete said, "it looks like we have three possibilities. One, Maggie *is* your sister and Lorraina was telling the truth and somehow hid Maggie's existence from her family. Two, she *isn't* your sister but was tricked by Lorraina into thinking she is. Or three, she isn't your sister, knows it, and was going along with Lorraina's story for some reason. Does that sound like it covers the possibilities in regard to Maggie?"

Shawn and Sadie both pondered for a few seconds, then nodded.

"Do you have any kind of verification about Lorraina's liver disease?" Pete asked.

"The doctor at the hospital tonight confirmed it. There was a big name for what she has and I can't remember what it was, but it's real and it's really serious. They said there's more testing they'll need to do in Anchorage, but there's a chance she'll need a new liver in order to recover from this—assuming she's strong enough for the operation." Shawn hesitated, then said, "They took some blood from me at the hospital to see if I'm a match."

Both Sadie and Pete lifted their eyebrows. Shawn pulled up the sleeve of his sweatshirt, revealing a purple bandage wrapped around his elbow, holding a cotton ball in place. He looked at Sadie as he pulled the sleeve down again. "I don't know what will come of it.

Maybe I'm not a match, but knowing that she really is sick . . . well, it changes things I guess. Some things, anyway."

"So, she *was* telling the truth about the liver disease," Pete said. "Does that make you think she could be telling the truth about Maggie, too? Maybe there is an explanation for why no one knows about Maggie."

"I honestly don't see how," Shawn said, looking at Pete. "I've got my notes at home, but after I learned about Maggie I found a couple of things that prove my point—like Lorraina being in jail when she would have been six months pregnant. And her second arrest was within like a week of Maggie's birth date. It just doesn't seem possible. I told Lorraina that when I discovered it. She just kept saying that I had a sister, and asking why I wasn't happy about that, and why we couldn't be a family. It was all just so weird."

Pete sighed. "Maybe we can go back and verify that information while we're in port tomorrow. In the meantime, while Maggie's reaction to the possibility of Lorraina not being her birth mother seems sincere, we'd be well-advised to not be too trusting until we have more answers. We don't know her, and we need to be careful and double-check the facts as quickly as we can."

Shawn nodded his understanding and Sadie reluctantly accepted that Pete was right. She'd had a similar thought earlier, about not knowing Maggie well enough to know whether or not she was trustworthy, but it felt different now that there was the possibility that Maggie might have been tricked all along. Then she remembered the information Maggie had given her about Lorraina not coming back to the room last night and how it hadn't made sense. Perhaps Pete's caution was more warranted than even he thought.

She took a few moments to fill Shawn and Pete in on those details from her conversation with Maggie, then finished, "And since

Maggie was alone in her stateroom, supposedly waiting for Lorraina's return, no one can corroborate her story."

Pete and Shawn's expressions matched Sadie's thoughts perfectly. What had been going on with Lorraina? She could only hope that their search for information in Skagway tomorrow would give them the answers they all needed.

"Are we all in agreement not to share our concerns with Maggie at this point?" Pete asked. Sadie and Shawn both nodded. "I think it's in everyone's best interest—Maggie's included—to see what we can learn one way or another before we make a big deal out of this to her."

Shawn and Sadie nodded again.

"Good, then as I see it, we now have a double investigation going: Is Lorraina Maggie's birth mother? And what happened yesterday in the time between her argument with Maggie, Sadie seeing her at the photo gallery, and us finding her on deck—basically, how did she get the wine, why did she drink it, and why is she now in a coma?" He looked between them as they agreed to the goals he had outlined. He was really good at this.

"I'm glad we're on the same page. The other thing we need to consider is that the abnormal tox screen is going to change things."

"What abnormal tox screen?" Shawn asked.

"They didn't tell you at the hospital?" Sadie asked.

Pete relayed what he'd learned from his contact on the ship. "It's not a medication she was taking or something common that is tested for automatically. The doctors are running additional tests now to determine what it is, but something is showing up that absolutely should not be there."

Shawn stared at the tabletop but said nothing, so Pete continued. "Up until now this has been treated as a binge on Lorraina's part, but now that there's something unusual, the police might open an investigation and your conflicts with Lorraina will be something they are going to scrutinize. Ship security has already requested that Sadie come in to tell them about the gift tag on the bottle of wine—no one else saw it, including me—and that makes me think more than ever that they are going to investigate this. Because of that, we need to know if there is anything"—Pete leaned forward slightly while jabbing his finger onto the top of the table—"*anything* at all that might strengthen an investigator's reason for thinking you could have had anything to do with what's happened to Lorraina."

"That's ridiculous," Sadie said, incensed by the suggestion. She looked to Shawn for confirmation of his protest, but Shawn didn't look shocked; he looked decidedly worried. "Shawn? Isn't it ridiculous?"

CHAPTER 18

W ell, yeah. I wouldn't have done anything to hurt her." He still had that look on his face that could stop a mother's heart, though. That look that clearly said there was still something else Sadie didn't know.

Sadie glanced at Pete and could tell he saw the same thing she did in Shawn's face.

Pete held Shawn's eyes as he continued. "Is there anything that someone who doesn't know you might not understand? Anything that would make you look suspicious?"

As soon as Pete asked the question, Sadie remembered something Maggie had said. "Did you send Lorraina some e-mails? Mean ones?"

Shawn's eyebrows went up. "You know about those?"

Sadie's stomach sank. He *did* send horrible e-mails? "Maggie told me. She said Lorraina forwarded them to her."

"What e-mails?" Pete cut in.

Shawn hesitated, and Sadie braced herself as he started talking. "Like I told you guys, Lorraina wouldn't back off, and over those weeks I was trying to get her to just leave me alone, I sent some e-mails asking her to give me some space. She never listened to any-thing I said. I was pretty rude in that last e-mail."

Sadie was sympathetic of his position; her poor boy had been through so much. Pete was impossible to read since his detective-face was masking his feelings.

"When was the last e-mail sent?" Pete asked.

"Um, about a week and a half ago. After that, I blocked her e-mail address. I figured that e-mail worked, because she didn't text or call me, and she didn't just get a new e-mail address and start harassing me again. I had planned to contact her after the cruise, I swear. After I'd talked to Mom and everything."

Pete nodded. "Okay. Would you mind sending the e-mails to me?"

Shawn shifted slightly in his chair. "Uh, is that really necessary? I mean, they're personal."

Sadie looked at the tabletop and tried to pretend she wasn't con-cerned about why he wouldn't want them to know what was in those exchanges.

"It would be really helpful if *I* could read them and therefore know what to expect, should it come up later." Was it Sadie's imagi-nation that Pete emphasized that *he* would read them, not Sadie?

"Okay," Shawn said in surrender. "I'll have to use the ship com-puters to access my e-mail, though; I didn't bring my laptop."

"Breanna brought hers," Sadie offered. Breanna was probably back in their cabin by now. Shawn could have those e-mails sent to Pete within just a few minutes, or Shawn could log in and Pete could read them right there in the cabin . . . while Sadie peeked over his shoulder.

"I'll just use a ship computer," Shawn said before pushing away from the table and letting out a breath. He wasn't happy about this. "Are we done here, then?"

"Yeah," Pete said, getting to his feet. "We're done."

Pete didn't invite Sadie to look at the stars tonight—or, more realistically, the clouds—but that wasn't really why they'd gone to deck thirteen on the other nights. Instead, they parted ways with a good-night kiss at the elevators on deck twelve. Pete took the stairs to his room on deck ten while Sadie opted to take the elevator.

Breanna wasn't in their cabin when Sadie arrived, which she hoped meant that she was having a good discussion with Maggie— maybe even getting important information in the process. What would Breanna think of the things Sadie had learned from Shawn tonight?

Sadie got ready for bed and laid out the clothes she wanted to wear to Skagway tomorrow. They had signed up for a whale watching tour, though Sadie couldn't say she was looking forward to it any longer. The gold panning today had been a nice distraction, and an important opportunity for her and Shawn to talk, but they hadn't had an investigation to work on when they decided to keep that appointment. Now there was work to do, and yet whale watching had been one of the main reasons Breanna chose *this* cruise. Sadie took a deep breath, released it, and tried not to scream in frustration. Yesterday had been such a hard day. Today had been hellacious.

Breanna came in around 10:40, saving Sadie from having to reorganize the closet by color in a vain attempt to distract herself from her growing anxieties induced by waiting and wondering what was taking Breanna so long.

Maggie had given most of Lorraina's personal papers to Officer Jareg that morning, but there were some miscellaneous items that Breanna had brought back for Sadie to look at—including Lorraina's purse.

Sadie started looking through everything while Breanna filled her in on what a sweet girl Maggie was and how sad this whole situation was. Sadie nodded in agreement while separating the items from the purse into two piles—"of interest" and "everything else."

"Did Shawn say anything about some e-mails he sent to Lorraina?" Breanna asked after changing into her kitten pajamas and pulling her hair up into a high ponytail on the top of her head.

"Yes," Sadie said, pondering over a receipt from an airport gift shop. It was for two magazines, but Breanna hadn't brought any magazines back with her—Sadie hoped they wouldn't be important. She put the receipt in the "of interest" pile, just in case. So far everything was in the "of interest" pile, including a tube of ChapStick Sadie thought might have DNA evidence. "He said he'd asked Lorraina for some space."

"Is that how he explained it?" Breanna said, sitting down on her bed and tucking her long legs underneath her. "Space?"

Sadie looked up, a parking stub from the Memphis airport in one hand. "He said he told her to back off while he tried to work things out. Why? Did Maggie say something different?" Maggie had used the word "horrible" to describe the e-mails. Had she simply misinterpreted them because her feelings were hurt?

"Shawn told Lorraina to never contact him again and that if she did, he'd call the police—or worse."

"Or worse?" Sadie repeated, lifting her eyebrows and sitting up straighter. "That's what Maggie said?"

"No, that's what *Shawn* said. It really hurt Maggie's feelings that Shawn didn't want to meet her, and Lorraina forwarded the e-mails to prove that she wasn't making it up."

Sadie leaned forward. "You *read* the e-mails? They were threatening?"

Breanna nodded and made a concerned face. "Mom, they were . . . scary."

"What *exactly* did they say?"

"At first, Shawn told her to leave him alone for a while, but then he got meaner and angrier. In the last one, he called her a liar and a . . . a really bad name you once washed my mouth out with soap for saying. He told her that she was trashy and that he was embarrassed to have her be a part of his life or a part of him and that he had no interest in meeting Maggie, who was probably just like her. He said he never wanted anything to do with her and, word for word, that if she didn't leave him alone he'd call the police *or worse*."

Heat filled Sadie with every word. "Breanna, he would never say those things. You know he wouldn't, right?"

"I wouldn't have thought so," Breanna said, putting her hands up as though in surrender. "But I read them, Mom. They were sent from his e-mail address and, well, he's been really struggling since all that stuff happened in Boston. I just wonder if maybe he hit his limit, ya know, and kind of exploded. I don't think he meant it, though," she quickly added. "I know Shawn would never hurt anyone."

Sadie stared at the covers of her bed. Was that why Shawn was hesitant to send the e-mails to Pete? Because he knew what they really said and didn't want it verified?

She shook her head, refusing to believe Shawn would say those things, or lie about it to her and Pete. Shawn was as honest and trustworthy as anyone Sadie had ever known . . . except that he'd hidden the fact that he'd found his birth mother and lied about going back to Michigan after Christmas. She'd told Pete that she was worried something had broken in Shawn when they'd been in Boston. What if she was right? What if he wasn't the same man he'd been before all of that happened?

She closed her eyes and pressed her hand to her forehead. She couldn't think this way. Shawn was her son; she knew his heart and had no doubt that he was a good man. Could Lorraina, or even Maggie, have changed the e-mails? Maybe Lorraina wanted to make Shawn seem worse than she'd already made him out to be. Sadie couldn't think of what Maggie's motivation would be but that didn't mean she didn't have one.

"Did Maggie say anything about *me?*" Sadie asked. "She made a comment earlier that I wasn't what she expected."

Breanna paused, and Sadie gave her an "I can handle it" look. "Lorraina told Maggie that you were super-controlling and that's why Shawn hadn't talked to you about them reconnecting—because you'd freak out about it. One of the e-mails said something to that effect as well."

Sadie was offended, but tried to keep her cool.

"But she doesn't believe that anymore," Breanna assured her. "In fact, I think it's part of what's making this harder for Maggie. She was told things about you and Shawn that, now that she's met you, aren't adding up. Couple that with the fact that Lorraina's family didn't know anything about her, and I can see why she's questioning everything. I feel *so* bad for her."

"Did Shawn share his concerns about Lorraina with you? That she was making him uncomfortable or that she'd asked him for money?"

Breanna shook her head, and when she spoke, her voice was quiet. "No, he never said anything about that, but after the first conversation he and I had about her, he didn't seem to want to talk to me about it anymore. When I asked about her, he'd change the subject."

Sadie relayed what Shawn had told her about Lorraina's requests for money, the convenient timing of Maggie's arrival on the scene, and the liver transplant. By the time she finished, Breanna looked completely stunned.

"Maggie didn't say anything about her birth mom being that sick," she said. "She knew Lorraina had a bad liver, but not that she needed a transplant. Do you think Maggie didn't know?"

"I have no idea. I can't figure her out. If Maggie's role in this was to draw Shawn in—whether Maggie knew it or not—then why would Lorraina send the angry e-mails to Maggie and prejudice her against him? And why do all that, then try to arrange for them to meet on a cruise ship of all places? And why lie to Shawn about having natural siblings when he asked in October? There's so much that doesn't make sense."

Breanna telling Sadie about the e-mails had sapped Sadie's energy, and her motivation to go through Lorraina's belongings was gone. She put everything back in Lorraina's purse and set it on the floor next to her bed. "We're going to see what we can find out when we're in port tomorrow, and we don't want to talk to Maggie about this stuff until we know more, okay? Breakfast might be a little awkward, but we just need to take things one step at a time. Pete will probably lead the discussion; he's good at knowing what to keep to ourselves and what to share with her in order to learn what we need to know."

"Sure, of course," Breanna said with a nod. "But I don't think she was in on whatever it was Lorraina was doing. I think she truly believes—or believed—that she is Lorraina's daughter. I got the impression that finding her birth mom really filled in some holes in her life, ya know? Did she tell you that her dad remarried and has two little kids—bio-kids—now? I think it's just one more thing that's been really hard for her since her adoptive mother died."

Adoptive mother. The term rankled Sadie so badly, but she

refused to say so out loud. She went to the drawers by the closet and got out her pajamas. When the bathroom door was open, it closed off the hallway between the bathroom and the cabin door, making it a perfect dressing room.

"Did Maggie say anything about how she reunited with Lorraina? It's only been a couple of months, right?" Sadie asked.

"Yeah, she said it was right before Easter, which Maggie found very comforting. She's pretty religious."

Sadie had noted that as well. She got undressed, leaving her clothes in a pile on the floor. "How did they find each other?"

"Maggie started looking for her birth mom as soon as she turned eighteen."

"How old is Maggie now?"

"I'm not sure—twenty-one or twenty-two, I think. And Lorraina found *her*. Maggie had tried to do the search herself a couple of years ago, but her adoption records were sealed—not just regular sealed—something that required an attorney and a civil case. She couldn't afford to hire an attorney so she hooked up with a bunch of adoption-reunion websites instead. I guess they have all kinds of forums and things. It sounds like Maggie really liked being a part of that community. When Lorraina found her on one of those sites, Maggie said that she felt like it was an answer to her prayers."

Sadie pulled her pajama top over her head and contemplated the sheer horribleness of Lorraina pretending to be Maggie's mother, if that's what had happened. "I'm looking forward to filling in the blanks." She pulled on the bottoms and scooped up her discarded clothes before shutting the bathroom door and taking a minute to put everything away. There was no room for disorganization in this small space.

"I think we all are," Breanna agreed.

Sadie got her notebook and pen from her bag and sat on the bed. She started writing down everything that had happened last night; she knew from experience how quickly details could be forgotten. Breanna finished getting ready for bed, then turned her back toward the light on Sadie's side of the room.

Twenty minutes later, Sadie had written down as many details as she could about her encounters with Lorraina, her conversations with Maggie, Shawn's version of the story, and Breanna's experiences from tonight. She developed a preliminary timeline dating back to October of the prior year when Shawn first got in touch with Lorraina and ending with Lorraina being transported to Anchorage. Had Shawn gone through the same website as Maggie had to find Lorraina?

Sadie wrote down that question, then filled the rest of the page with additional questions she hoped they could find answers for tomorrow. When she finished, she felt completely overwhelmed. There were so many details to discover.

It was after midnight; day four of the cruise had begun and the heaviness she'd felt when she first saw Shawn talking to Lorraina had only gotten worse. She let out a sigh, put down the pen and paper, and rubbed her eyes.

She wasn't sure she'd be able to sleep without a sleeping pill, but remembering how mixed up this morning had been when she'd overslept helped her commit to a lousy night's sleep if it meant not sleeping through tomorrow morning. She went through her nightly routine of removing her makeup, brushing her teeth, and slathering herself with creams that promised younger-looking skin in less than a week. Never mind that she'd been using them for years and was still aging, albeit gracefully. Just before she got under the covers and turned out the light, she said a prayer for her son. And Maggie too.

CHAPTER 19

♦

Sadie slept for a few hours, but started checking the time on her phone around five o'clock, waiting for a more reasonable time to wake up. She *was* on vacation, after all. Or at least, she was supposed to be. She tried to fall asleep again but finally, a little after six thirty, she got up and took her clothes into the tiny bathroom. She got dressed by the light of her phone, careful not to bang her elbows on the walls and wake Breanna up.

She used her lipstick to write a note on the mirror telling Breanna she was going to walk around the track that circled deck five and would meet her at the Tiara Room at nine for the pre-breakfast discussion, as planned. She grabbed her jacket and her ship-card and let herself into the hallway.

Worried about getting crossed wires within the group, she borrowed some paper from the customer service desk and wrote notes to both Pete and Shawn about where she was, then slid them under their doors. She hoped that would make it easier for everyone to meet up. She liked everyone being on the same page. She should have brought her walkie-talkies from home.

It was cold on the track, colder than she'd expected it to be, and she zipped her jacket up all the way and walked faster in order to stay warm. It took two and a half laps before she wasn't shivering anymore, and from that point on, it was a nice stretch of the legs. The ship was moving south toward Skagway, and the shoreline was still a thick forest as far as the eye could see in every direction. The water was an angry gray, but gentle as it lapped against the sides of the ship and carried them forward.

She reviewed everything she'd learned last night, over and over again, until she felt as though she knew every detail backward and forward and round and round. She needed a good solid conversation with both Shawn and Maggie, and there was the pending discussion with the security office about the wine. Why wouldn't they know about the gift tag? It was right there!

She was on her tenth lap around the track—just starting her third mile—when she came up alongside Mary Anne, one of the women she'd met that first day along with the young mom, Jen. Sadie slowed her stride and fell into step with her new friend. After saying hello and some general small talk, Sadie asked about Mary Anne's husband. She said he was resting up before the next qualifying round of the blackjack tournament at eleven o'clock. He'd played in the first qualifying round Monday, but hadn't made the top score.

"Pete played in one of those rounds, too. He didn't make it, though."

"Glen's very good. He's won these things more times than I want to admit," Mary Anne said, leaning closer to Sadie as though sharing a secret. "He once earned enough to pay for all our on-ship expenses."

"Nice," Sadie said with a smile, grateful to be able to push away the difficulties she'd been pondering all morning.

"So, what are your plans for Skagway?" Mary Anne asked.

"We have a whale watching trip planned," Sadie said, even though she wasn't sure her group would go.

"I guess they'll remove the body from the ship once we pull into port," Mary Anne said.

"What?" Sadie asked, unable to hide her surprise. She automatically thought Mary Anne was talking about Lorraina, but "body" denoted someone had died, and Lorraina was in Anchorage, alive at the last update.

Mary Anne shrugged. "I think it would make more sense to keep it here until we return to Seattle, don't you think? I bet it's expensive to ship a body back from Alaska. And there's no doubt they've got extra freezer space now that we're halfway through the food they loaded from Seattle."

Sadie was thoroughly confused and a little disgusted by the idea of storing a body in freezers meant for food. Been there, done that, couldn't eat salad for a month. "What body?" Sadie asked, hoping for some clarification.

Mary Anne turned toward her with an animated expression. "Didn't you hear?"

"Hear what?"

"A gentleman died last night, at the buffet. They do try to keep these things quiet, I suppose. In fact, they tried to tell us that he was going to be okay, but he was dead before he hit the floor."

Lorraina was in a coma with an abnormal tox screen—could the wine she drank have been poisoned?—and the next night someone dies? What kind of cruise was this? "What happened, exactly?"

"Heart attack," Mary Anne said with a sharp nod.

"What time did this happen?"

"Oh, eleven thirty or so. Glen and I had gone to the late show at ten. You know, you always get a better show the second time around;

all the performers are warmed up by then. Besides, we have our dinner reservation in the Chandelier dining room at seven thirty every night. They have the best food on the ship. After the show, we went to the buffet and were just finishing up when a woman screamed. All these crewmen came running and closed off that part of the room."

Sadie had been in the Lamplighter Lounge until ten thirty, but the lounge was on the opposite side of the ship from the buffet. Still, she expected that there would have been some kind of alarm, or at the very least gossip, if someone died so publicly. Then again, Mary Anne was the first person, other than Pete and her family, that Sadie had talked to since last night.

"That's terrible," Sadie said. She kept to herself her experience of when her husband, Neil, had collapsed. Even after all these years, she wasn't prepared to face that memory right now.

"It is, but I wouldn't be surprised if they lose one or two every trip. I mean, you know what they say about Alaskan cruises, right?"

Sadie shook her head.

"They're for the newlywed and the nearly dead." She laughed at her joke. All Sadie could manage was a weak smile.

CHAPTER 20

♥

Sadie knocked on Pete's door until he answered, his hair sticking up in a hundred directions and his eyes puffy as he squinted into the bright light of the hallway.

"Sadie," he said, scrubbing a hand over his face. "What's the matter?"

"I was just talking to Mary Anne," Sadie said.

"Who's Mary Anne?"

"One of the women I went to all those classes with on Monday. The older one. Remember?"

"Oh, right," he said, but Sadie suspected he didn't really remember. He'd seemed only partially attentive when she told him about Mary Anne and Jen.

"She said a man had a heart attack at the buffet last night."

Pete blinked and looked thoughtful, as though trying to determine why this was important enough for her to have woken him up so early. "That's terrible," he said, but still sounded confused.

In the wake of his reaction, Sadie wondered if she was being paranoid. There were a lot of elderly people on the boat; Sadie had seen some in wheelchairs and others with portable oxygen tanks.

Maybe it *was* to be expected that not everyone would make it back to port. But she'd gone to the trouble of waking him up, she might as well explore her reason behind that. "I was thinking—what if the wine Lorraina drank was poisoned? It might explain the strange tox report, right? And if so, then that would mean someone was poisoned *and* someone else died two days later. Doesn't that seem weird to you?"

"First of all, we don't know that Lorraina was poisoned, though I suppose it's possible," Pete said. "Second, did this man who had a heart attack have a history of heart disease? Was he over the age of seventy? Had he just eaten a double bacon cheeseburger with extra mayo?"

"You think I'm being dumb," Sadie said. It wasn't a question.

Pete smiled and reached out to grab her hand and pull her toward him.

She stopped at the threshold; they'd made a rule a long time ago about going into one another's sleeping space. It was a good rule.

"I think I could really use a cup of coffee," he said, giving her a quick kiss. She was careful not to inhale in case he had morning breath. She wanted nothing to shatter her belief that someone as wonderful as Pete could never have halitosis.

"I'm sorry I woke you," she said, feeling sheepish and a little bit too warm being so close to the man she loved when he wore nothing but a white T-shirt and a pair of athletic shorts.

"Why don't I take a quick shower, and we'll talk this over before everyone else gets up. Then we can make a plan for the day," Pete said.

"You say the sweetest things," Sadie cooed. He knew how much she liked plans, and the offer helped dilute her embarrassment of possibly making too big a deal about this.

He winked and gave her hand another squeeze before promising he'd be ready in fifteen minutes. Sadie didn't know how that was possible, but she agreed to meet him at the Coffee Counter by the reception desk.

She'd read the entire four-page onboard paper from Monday by the time Pete joined her. The ship was in sight of the Skagway pier; they would be docked in an hour.

His hair was still wet, but his expression looked more awake. They ordered their morning beverages of choice, and Pete asked what she knew about the man who died the night before.

Sadie had already told him everything she knew, but she didn't mind repeating herself and stretched out the information to make it feel more substantial. In the end, she had to admit that the connection was still rather weak, but Pete was too polite to say so.

"So, did Shawn send you those e-mails?" she asked, changing the subject.

Pete glanced at her with an uneasy expression that made her tense, then shook his head. "I didn't check my e-mail this morning, but I waited 'til almost midnight last night. I bet I spent $30 in Internet fees waiting for him to send them over."

"You didn't call his room to ask him where they were?"

Pete paused, that uneasy expression still in place. "Actually, I did. He didn't answer."

"What?"

"Don't freak out," Pete said, putting up one hand. "And let me talk to him about it, okay? I think I'm a safer choice right now."

Sadie clenched her jaw and took a breath even though she knew he was right. "Breanna read the e-mails," she said. "Or at least the versions of them Lorraina sent to Maggie. What if Lorraina changed them? It's easy enough to do, and it could explain why they sounded as mean as Breanna said the e-mails were."

"What did they say?" Pete asked, frowning.

Sadie summarized what she knew, and Pete looked more worried than ever. As much as she appreciated that he didn't use his detective-face around her as much these days, seeing his true fears reflected in his expression made her nervous.

"Why don't we go find Maggie and see if she'll let us read them too?" Pete said. He picked up his coffee cup and quickly emptied it; he was suddenly in a hurry.

Sadie didn't love the idea of bombarding Maggie with such an uncomfortable request so early in the morning, but she couldn't deny her own anxiety about seeing the e-mails for herself. "Okay," she said, not bothering to finish her tea.

They stood just as the cruise director made an announcement that they were approaching Skagway and would be docked in half an hour.

"What's Maggie's room number?" Pete asked.

Sadie made a face. "I don't know."

"Okay, so we need to ask Breanna then," Pete said. "Should we call the cabin to save time? She's up by now, right?"

The large clock on the wall behind the reception desk read 8:40—Breanna should be up. "Yes," Sadie said, looking around. "Where's the closest courtesy phone?"

Pete pointed toward a phone on the wall just to the right of the customer service desk, and they wound their way through the other tables and passengers to get to it.

Sadie accidentally kicked a woman's purse and stopped to apologize just as Pete put a hand on Sadie's arm. She lifted her head and looked at whatever *he* was looking at. Two police officers were walking toward the reception desk. Regular ship security wore white shirts; these men were dressed in blue, like regular street cops. Pete stepped ahead of her, and she stayed close as he began moving toward the officers instead of the phone. She sensed he was trying not to be obvious.

The two officers approached the desk, turning enough that Sadie could read SKAGWAY POLICE DEPARTMENT above the name tags on their shirts. How did the Skagway police get on board when the ship was still half an hour from docking?

The desk clerk made a phone call, and a minute later, a security guard met them. Sadie stepped forward and pretended to read the day's itinerary posted on the customer service desk about ten feet away from them. Pete had moved to the other side of the officers and pulled out his cell phone as though checking a text message. If the officers were worried about being overheard, they would likely have moved away, but that didn't seem to be a concern.

"Thank you for coming," the security officer said. Sadie didn't recognize him from the other interactions she'd had with security so far. The three men exchanged handshakes.

"Where is he?" one of the officers said.

He? Were they talking about the unfortunate heart attack victim?

"We've had his steward keeping an eye on his room. He hasn't left yet."

Not the dead guy then.

"It's good you had us come. We wouldn't want him to get off the ship without us."

The security guard agreed, and Sadie tried to catch Pete's eye. They really needed to see those e-mails as soon as possible, preferably before they had to confront Shawn about not having sent them.

And yet Pete was still intently listening, though seemingly focused on his phone.

"Certainly," the security officer said. "I'll escort you. It's room 749."

Sadie gasped. Pete's gaze snapped to hers in an instant. Room 749—*Shawn's room?*

CHAPTER 21

S adie headed for the closest stairway. She didn't know how long it
took her to push past other passengers and run down the stairs
to deck seven, but she was out of breath by the time she banged on
Shawn's door. She scanned both ends of the hallway but the officers
didn't appear.

She heard Shawn's doorknob turn, and as soon as he pulled the
door open an inch, she pushed her way through, forcing Shawn to
walk backward until his legs hit the double bed in the middle of the
room and he was forced to sit. Sadie shut the door behind her.

"What was in those e-mails?"

"Wh-what?" Shawn said, standing up. He didn't have a shirt on,
so Sadie grabbed one out of the closet and threw it at him.

"Those e-mails. What did you say? Did you threaten Lorraina?
Did you tell her you'd call the police on her or worse?"

"Mom," Shawn said, looking completely shocked and just offended enough that Sadie felt some relief. He pulled the T-shirt over
his head, his puffy hair springing back after being pushed though the
neck hole. "What are you talking about?"

Her brain was moving too fast for her to keep up with his

questions. If she didn't know two police officers were on their way to his room right now, she'd have backed off. "Why didn't you send those e-mails to Pete last night?"

"The onboard Internet wasn't working."

"Shawn, don't you dare lie to me."

His eyes narrowed. "I'm not lying," he said, sounding angry. "I went to the computer center and the Internet was down."

"So, then, what did you do? Did you go to your room?"

"No, I went back to the Lamplighter. Are you going to chew me out for that, too? They had that magician guy doing the grown-up magic show."

Sadie wasn't sure she wanted to know what happened at a grown-up magic show. "You went alone?"

"Yes, alone. I waited for the Internet to get fixed, but when I went back to the computer center, it was closed. I figured I'd use Bre's laptop this morning. What's your deal?"

"My deal is that two police officers from Skagway are on the ship and coming to *your* room. Maggie showed Breanna the e-mails Lorraina forwarded to her, and in *those* e-mails you threatened her if she didn't leave you alone. I think the police are going to arrest you!"

"What?" Shawn said, his eyebrows going up and his eyes going wide. He shook his head. "I didn't threaten her—I swear I didn't—and the computers were down, Mom. Let's get Bre's laptop right now and—"

A knock at the door silenced him, and Sadie spun around to face the door, the only thing separating them from the police officers. She turned back to Shawn. "Okay," she said, making a calming motion with her hands as she took a step toward him. "We need to handle this the right way, okay?"

Another knock. Sadie closed her eyes. What was the right way to handle this?

"Mr. Hoffmiller?" a voice called from the hallway. "Please open the door."

Sadie opened her eyes, feeling the tears rising as she looked up at the scared expression on Shawn's face. She put a hand on his arm. "It's going to be okay," she said. "Just do what they say. We'll follow you to the police station and get this figured out."

"Mr. Hoffmiller," the voice said again. "This is Officer Wells from the Skagway Police Department. If you don't come out of your room, your steward has been given permission to let us in."

"I'm coming," Shawn said. He pulled Sadie into a bear hug that lifted her off the floor, held her tight for a second, then turned and put her down in front of the bed, placing him between her and the door. He grabbed his wallet off the counter beneath the TV and put it in his pocket.

"Shawn," Sadie said in a shaky voice, though she had nothing to add.

He looked over his shoulder at her for one grim moment before opening the door and looking down at the officers. They moved back half a step, likely because they realized that if he wanted to, he could make this situation very difficult. He was bigger than both of them combined.

Sadie told herself to be calm, but watching Shawn step into the hall was too much for her, and a moment later, she ran after the officers. "Don't say anything without an attorney," she shouted in a panic. Shawn turned to look at her in surprise. "And don't—"

"Sadie," Pete said, taking her arm and pulling her away from the officers. Where had Pete come from? Where were the officers taking Shawn?

CHAPTER 22

L et go," Sadie said, trying to twist out of Pete's grip, but he knew her tricks and had anticipated them, so his hold remained strong. He backed her up against the wall between two cabin doors and took her face in both of his hands, forcing her to look up at him. She tried to see where Shawn was going, but Pete held her head in place.

"Sadie," he said, quietly, calmly, and with tender understanding that made tears spring up in her eyes. "It's going to be okay."

She tried to shake her head, but then he said her name again, and when the first tear started running down her cheek, he wiped it away with his thumb. "Get Breanna," Pete said, his voice calm and even. "Meet us at the police station. They've agreed to let me go with him."

"Why you and not me?"

"I'm cooperating," he said with a slight smile. "And not telling Shawn to act like a criminal. Get Breanna. Meet us at the police station. I'm sure someone in town can point it out to you."

She swallowed and nodded. Pete leaned in, kissed her once, then turned and started walking down the hallway after Shawn.

Sadie stayed right where she was, pressed against the wall, and taking deep breaths until she had counted to one hundred. She was afraid that if she moved, she'd chase Shawn down and go bonkers all over again. When she was certain she had control over herself, she hurried to her cabin. Breanna was still asleep, but Sadie flipped on the lights and told her to get up. She tried to give her a coherent version of what had happened, but the story was disconnected and rushed. Sadie had to stop and breathe again before she managed to relay all the information.

It was nearly forty minutes before the doors of the ship were opened to allow passengers to disembark. Breanna and Sadie were the very first ones down the gangplank. Pete had texted Sadie the address for the police station, and though she'd replied with a request for an update, he hadn't responded.

The port was right next to the town of Skagway, and a helpful dockworker pointed them toward the police station, which was just a few blocks from the pier. Even though the wait to get off the boat had been excruciating, it had helped Sadie feel more centered. Now was the time for a plan. She'd already rehearsed how she'd demand—as kindly as possible—that a computer forensics crew determine if the e-mails had been compromised after Shawn originally sent them. They could do that, right? It seemed like the right place to start.

At the police station, they checked in with the officer sitting behind a glass panel and were told to take a seat in the waiting room. Ten minutes later, Sadie's center was fading when Breanna received a text message from Liam.

"I need to talk to him," Breanna said, making an apologetic face. "Is that okay?"

"Of course," Sadie said. "I'll come get you once they're ready for us." A few minutes after Breanna stepped outside, Pete came through the door at the other end of the room. Sadie was on her feet in an instant and felt her calm focus abandon her.

"What's happening? Is Shawn all right? Can I see him?"

"He's talking to the police," Pete said as he approached her. He took her hands and guided her back into her chair. "Things are going as well as can be expected."

"Are they arresting him? Do we need to get an attorney? Is the FBI involved? Do they know what was showing up in Lorraina's tox screen yet?"

"Sadie," Pete said, "take a breath." He watched her until she obeyed, then gave her a smile that would have been patronizing if it had come from anyone else. "It's going to be okay. Shawn has done nothing wrong."

"They didn't bring him in for questioning because they think he's innocent."

"They brought him in for questioning because they have in their possession several threatening e-mails addressed to a woman who is in a coma under suspicious circumstances. I also understand that it's the cruise line that's making a big deal about this. They asked a bunch of questions about if he's been on other cruises and which ones. That makes me think they're fishing for something, but I don't know what. I'm hoping they'll reveal more information as the day goes on. But the police are doing their job, and Shawn is cooperating, which is exactly what he should do. You freaking out makes it look as though he has something to hide."

"I'm his mother. I think freaking out because my son was escorted off a cruise ship and taken to the police station is completely acceptable."

"Acceptable, yes. Helpful, no."

"Um, Mom?"

Sadie turned to see Breanna standing not far away, holding up her cell phone. "Maggie's wondering if we're still meeting for breakfast. I guess she's been waiting at the Tiara Room."

Maggie. Sadie wasn't sure she could focus on her right now. However, she connected some possible dots in Sadie's mind as well. "Did she send the e-mails to the police?" she asked, then looked at Pete. "Could Maggie be the reason all of this happened? Is she trying to get Shawn in trouble?" She'd no sooner said it than she saw it all laid out in front of her. "Maybe Shawn's concern that Maggie was a part of Lorraina's whole scheme was spot-on. Maybe *Maggie* was out to make Shawn into the bad guy, which meant she might have something to hide!"

"Slow down," Pete said, lowering his voice, which reminded Sadie to lower hers as well. He let go of Sadie's hands and stood, taking two steps toward Breanna, who was still standing a few feet inside the waiting area. "Ask Maggie if she wouldn't mind coming to town for breakfast instead." He looked around the waiting area thoughtfully. "I heard the officers talking about a café on Broadway—Sweet Tooth, I think? Have her meet me there."

"Why you and not us?" Sadie asked.

"'Cause you're a basket case," Breanna said while texting on her phone. "You need to chill."

"Chill?" Sadie repeated, throwing her arms up in exasperation. This was ridiculous. Her son was in jail! "Chill? And *where* am I supposed to *chill*? Here? In this waiting room while the police interrogate my little boy and—"

"Okay," Pete said, taking Sadie by the shoulders and turning her around so she faced the doors. "Breanna, will you get her out of here? Take her on a walk, or back to the ship, or something. I'll meet

Maggie at Sweet Tooth, and we'll move forward from there. I'll update you guys when I have something to tell you."

"Got it," Breanna said, hooking her arm through Sadie's and pushing her through the door. Pete followed as though worried Sadie might try to run back inside. Which she might have done if she thought she'd make it or if she had any idea what she'd do once she got back in.

Sadie tried to argue, but before she knew it, they were on the streets of Skagway. Breanna received a text, presumably from Maggie, and showed it to Pete, who nodded and pulled out his phone before typing a text of his own. Sadie had all these arguments she wanted to make but it was as though the words were tripping over one another on their way to her mouth. She could feel her heart racing similar to a panic attack except that she wasn't anxious, she was just mad and scared. But Pete was distrustful of her because of her emotions, which meant she had to find a way not to show them right now if she wanted to be of any help to her son.

"'Kay, Mom. Let's go back to the ship."

"That's silly," Sadie said, trying to keep her voice reasonable. Pete had slipped back into the police station, so Sadie turned her focus on Breanna. If she could convince Breanna that she was up to this, Breanna could talk to Pete. "I don't need to go back to the ship. I can go to breakfast with Pete and Maggie."

"Have you noticed that, like, every store here sells popcorn?"

"What?" Sadie asked, thrown off her train of thought. She looked around and realized they were back on Skagway's main street, which was called Broadway. It looked like something from an old Western movie set, except with brighter paint jobs. There were boardwalks instead of sidewalks and hand-painted signs hanging above the covered doorways of the different facades.

"Seriously," Breanna said, pointing across the street to a window display featuring at least six different types of popcorn. "That one has caramel and raspberry, and is that lime, do you think? It's green—they wouldn't make mint popcorn, would they?"

"You're trying to distract me," Sadie pointed out, and yet she couldn't help but wonder if it was indeed mint-flavored popcorn. She looked farther down the street and saw at least three more shops with popcorn displays in the window.

"We should buy some," Breanna said, pulling Sadie across the street. "I wonder if the caramel corn is as good as Aunt Carrie's."

Sadie had a strange relationship with her sister-in-law these days, and they had never been particularly close, despite living next door to one another for more than twenty years. Even on days when Sadie was annoyed with her brother's wife, she couldn't deny the fact that Carrie made the most amazing caramel popcorn. Dry rather than chewy, it never got stuck in your teeth or made your fingers sticky. And it had just the right blend of butter and brown sugar.

"Well, I guess we could buy a bag."

"Two," Breanna said. "One caramel—to compare with Aunt Carrie's—and then the green kind."

They entered the store a few minutes later, and the teenage boy behind the counter scrambled to help the pretty lady wanting two bags of popcorn at ten in the morning. Even with only a few minutes to get ready that morning, Breanna's natural beauty shone through. Everyone saw it, except maybe her.

Sadie inhaled the scent of caramelizing sugars, and now that she was removed enough from the situation at the police station, she could admit that she had perhaps overreacted. Well, maybe not overreacted—her son *was* at the police station—but he hadn't been arrested and he wasn't guilty and Sadie *did* believe in the judicial process, most of the time. She knew Pete would take good care of him and that he'd get whatever information from Maggie he could, whereas Sadie might be too intense right now to be effective.

Breanna handed Sadie the bag of caramel corn and set about opening the bag of green popcorn she was holding. They exited the shop and headed back to the pier.

"Lime," Breanna said as she held out the open bag of green popcorn to Sadie. "I win."

"I didn't know we were competing," Sadie said, shifting her bag of caramel corn in order to take a handful of green kernels. It was good. Sadie had a recipe for fruity popcorn in her Little Black Recipe Book—it used Jell-O.

"We weren't competing, but I thought lime first, then mint as a second possibility, so I won by choosing correctly the first time."

Sadie eyed her daughter while Breanna took another handful of popcorn. "Why are you so calm about what's happening with Shawn?"

Breanna looked at her with a serious expression. "Because my mom has told me all my life that *I* am in charge of *me*. Shawn knows that too, and I think he's handling this rather well—talking to the police and all that. You need to have faith in him and calm the heck down enough to be helpful 'cause *you're* in charge of *you* too. And right now you're making yourself look bad."

Sadie felt herself flush under the reprimand, but she also took the words to heart. She was in charge of her own reactions, just as Shawn was responsible for his. She knew he was innocent, so why was she so scared?

"Do you think he said those horrible things in the e-mails? You read them; did they sound like him?"

Breanna took another handful of the lime popcorn while

thinking over her answer. Finally, she met Sadie's eyes. "I don't know, Mom. I don't want to think he did, it's not like him, but sometimes we find ourselves feeling things and doing things that are out of character."

Sadie didn't like that answer and looked down the street of colorful shops that were slowly filling up with tourists. A second cruise ship was maneuvering into the port, and a third could be seen a half a mile or so away, likely waiting its turn to dock.

"But Shawn's in charge of Shawn," Breanna continued. "And *if* he wrote those e-mails, it's okay for him to be accountable for it. You should want him to be."

Carrie's Crunchy Caramel Popcorn

8 cups popped popcorn
1 cup brown sugar
½ cup butter
¼ cup light corn syrup
¼ teaspoon salt
¼ teaspoon baking soda
¼ teaspoon vanilla

Put popped popcorn in large bowl (the bigger the better) and set aside.

Combine sugar, butter, corn syrup, and salt in medium-sized saucepan. Cook on medium heat, stirring constantly, until mixture comes to a boil. Decrease temperature to medium-low, and simmer for 5 minutes, stirring constantly. (If mixture begins to scorch, remove from heat and lower temperature before returning to the stove top.)

Remove from heat, and add baking soda and vanilla. Mix well.

Pour sauce over popcorn. Use a spatula coated with a nonstick spray to stir the popcorn, being careful not to crush the kernels.

Spread coated popcorn on a cookie sheet and bake at 250 degrees for 1 hour, stirring every 15 minutes.

If made in the oven, it may overflow the pan as it bakes; line your oven, just in case.

Note: You can also make this recipe in a large electric roaster oven. Put popped popcorn in roaster oven with heat turned off. Add sauce and turn on heat to 200 degrees. Stir popcorn every couple of minutes for about 20 minutes or until caramel has coated and hardened onto kernels. Turn off heat before you stop stirring.

Note: This recipe doubles well!

Fruity Popcorn

8 cups popped popcorn
1 cup sugar
½ cup butter
¼ cup light corn syrup
¼ teaspoon salt
1 (3-ounce) package Jell-O, any flavor

Put popped popcorn in large bowl (the bigger the better) and set aside.

Combine sugar, butter, corn syrup, and salt in medium-sized saucepan. Cook on medium heat, stirring constantly until mixture comes to a boil. Decrease temperature to medium-low, simmer for 2 to 3 minutes, stirring constantly. (If mixture begins to scorch, remove from heat and lower temperature before returning to the stove top.)

Add Jell-O, mix well, and simmer 1 minute or until gelatin is dissolved. (Mixture will be thick.) Remove from heat and pour over popcorn. Stir to coat the kernels, being careful not to crush kernels. Work quickly as syrup will harden as it cools. Let popcorn sit in bowl for 10 minutes or until cooled. Break into large chunks. Store leftovers in large, zip-top plastic bag.

CHAPTER 23

S adie felt her mind clearing in response to Breanna's wisdom. Shawn was responsible for himself. If he wrote those e-mails—so help him—he had to make that right. If he didn't write them, then he needed to clarify that with the police so they could move on.

She thought back to Maggie's original opinion of Sadie: *super-controlling, would freak if she knew the truth.* Sadie was not that woman. She would prove it by not freaking out and by letting Shawn handle this. He was innocent; Sadie needed to show her faith in him by not being defensive. She wondered why the officers had asked him about other cruises. This was the first one he'd been on since his high school graduation when the three of them had cruised the western Caribbean.

"There's Maggie," Breanna said, pointing ahead of them. Maggie was wearing a bright purple top, white jeans, and cute purple leopard-print heels. She was texting on her phone while she walked and hadn't seen them yet.

Sadie grabbed Breanna's arm and pulled her into a gift shop, not wanting to get in the way of Pete and Maggie's meeting now that she'd accepted that Pete was right about her backing off a little.

Breanna went along with the unexpected detour, and Sadie had purchased two Christmas ornaments, a magnet, and a bright pink jacket with "Alaska" embroidered on the front before they went back out to Broadway. Maggie was nowhere in sight by then, but Sadie spotted the sign for the restaurant where Pete said he'd meet her. She wasn't going to be a super-controlling-freak-out-mom, but she did wish she could be a fly on the wall and listen to their conversation.

"Can we go to the ship now?" Breanna said. "I'm actually getting hungry, which I wasn't sure was possible since I feel like all we've done is eat since we left Seattle."

Really? Sadie felt like all she'd done was worry since leaving Seattle. "Breakfast does sound good," she said.

But Sadie still wanted to help her boy. So, what could she do without taking things too far?

Shawn had said he hadn't sent the e-mails last night because the Internet was down and the computer center was closed when he returned. Sadie could possibly verify that information. She was also supposed to meet with security to tell them what she knew about the gift tag. Maybe she could even learn more about the man who'd died last night. Mary Anne hadn't seemed to think it was strange for someone to die on the cruise; maybe it wasn't. Maybe she could find enough information to either alleviate her worries about a connection between his death and Lorraina's poisoning, or to support those concerns. Either way she'd feel better, more confident, because she'd be making an informed decision rather than jumping to an emotionally driven conclusion.

Knowing there was something she could do gave her a sense of purpose and immediately Sadie felt better.

She had direction.

Breanna's phone chimed. She handed Sadie the bag of lime

popcorn and dug her phone out of her back pocket; Breanna hated purses. She frowned at her phone and stopped walking. Sadie stopped too, holding a bag of popcorn in each arm.

"What? Is it Pete? Did Maggie admit to something?"

"It's not Pete," Breanna said without glancing up from her phone. "It's Liam. We talked earlier, and he said he was going to talk to his mom about the cake."

"Did it not go well?"

"I am so sick of this *stupid* wedding," Breanna said with uncharacteristic bitterness. She started typing a response. "Apparently, his mom broke into tears." She paused, sighed, and then turned to Sadie. "What do I do?" She shook her head without waiting for an answer. "I'm sorry. It's stupid to be worried about a cake with everything else going on." She waved a hand toward the police station.

"It's not stupid," Sadie said. She worked hard to focus on this aspect of Breanna's life for the moment, pushing aside Shawn. "Do you want me to call her?"

Super-controlling-freak-out-mom.

"Thanks, but I need to do this on my own," Breanna said, going back to her phone with a more determined look. She started typing. "And I need Liam to understand it and back me up—like we talked about last night. I assumed that's what he was doing, but she cries, and now he's wondering if we're making too big a deal about this. By *we* he means *me*, though."

Sadie shifted her weight back and forth over the next few minutes as Breanna continued texting. Based on Breanna's sighs and groans each time a text came in, the conversation wasn't going well, but she didn't pause long enough to fill Sadie in. Finally, she pushed a number and put the phone to her ear. "Sorry. This might be a minute. Can we just meet back at the ship?"

"Sure," Sadie said. "I still need to talk to security anyway."

Breanna nodded and turned to walk to a wrought-iron bench a few storefronts away. "Liam," Sadie heard her say just before she went out of range. After that, all Sadie could see was Breanna's expression, which was intense as she tried to explain something.

Sadie headed back to the ship, though other passengers were still coming ashore in droves. Most people headed for the train station; Skagway was famous for its White Pass and Yukon Route Railway.

For Sadie, going up the gangplank with a bag of popcorn in each arm and a bag of souvenirs in each hand while a hundred passengers were coming down was like swimming upstream, but she was pondering on which task to tackle first once she got on the ship and so she wasn't too anxious about making good time. The first thing she needed to do once she got back to her cabin was make a list of everything she needed to do!

She was struggling to shift the popcorn she was holding so she could get her ship-card from her purse when she heard a familiar voice.

"Do you need a hand?"

Sadie looked up and smiled at the cute mom she'd attended classes with on Monday. "Hi, Jen," she said. She nearly dropped one of the bags of popcorn, but Jen quickly stepped up and took it from her. "Thanks," Sadie said, feeling silly. If she'd known she was going to make any purchases, she'd have brought her reusable nylon shopping bag that folded up to the size of a deck of cards.

Sadie showed her card to the security officers who scanned it, verified she matched the picture that came up on the computer, and handed it back. Sadie reached for the popcorn once she'd put away her ship-card.

"Are you going to your room? I can carry it for you."

"I can get it. Aren't you on your way into town?"

Jen nodded, but didn't hand over the popcorn. "I have a few minutes to help you to your room."

"You're a sweet girl," Sadie said. "Thank you." They headed toward the stairs, and Sadie asked about Jen's day in Juneau yesterday—her family had gone up the tram, which the kids had loved—and Jen asked Sadie if she'd seen Mary Anne recently.

"I did this morning," Sadie said. "Did you hear about the guy who had a heart attack at the buffet last night?"

Jen looked surprised. "Yes, that's what I wanted to talk to her about. I heard he was from our dining room."

Our dining room? "What do you mean?"

"We have the same dining room time as Mary Anne. Frank's parents stay with the boys so we can have that one time a day together. Frank went to the gym this morning with another guy from our table who told him Ben was from our dining room. I wondered if Mary Anne knew him. She said he had a heart attack?"

Sadie's brain had stopped at "Ben." "Wait, the guy who died was named Ben?"

Jen's eyes went wide, and she stopped walking. "He died?"

Mary Anne had said he died, hadn't she? "I guess I don't know that part for sure," she said. "Mary Anne thought he did. But you're sure his name was Ben?"

"That's what the guy Frank talked to thought his name was. We were trying to figure out who it was, and I wanted to ask Mary Anne about it. Not that it's important or anything. I guess we're just curious is all. If it's who we think it was, he's a young guy—close to Frank's age. I feel so bad for his wife."

Jen bit her lip, and Sadie felt sure the young mother was wishing there was something she could do to help—Jen struck Sadie as that kind of woman.

"That's just horrible," she said, but her mind was racing. The gift tag on the wine bottle had been for a "Ben" and now a young man name Ben had had a heart attack? Sadie couldn't ignore the wine bottle connection any longer—not that she'd ever dismissed the idea entirely.

They reached Sadie's room before she could figure out how to pick the conversation back up. "Thanks for your help," Sadie said after opening her room, depositing her things on the floor, and taking the caramel corn from Jen. "I appreciate it. If I see Mary Anne around, would you like me to tell her you want to talk to her?"

"That would be great," Jen said. "I'm in room 991, though we'll be on the train most of the afternoon. There's no rush; in fact I could probably just wait until I see her in the dining room tonight—unless she's eating in town."

"Well, I'll let her know if I see her."

"Thanks," Jen said. "If it didn't look like you'd already done your shopping, I'd invite you to come to town with me. Frank took the boys to the game room so I could have an hour or so to myself—I didn't get any shopping done yesterday."

"That would be fun," Sadie said, thinking *on any other day but this one.* "And if you do find Mary Anne and figure out if this Ben-guy is the one from the buffet last night, I'd love an update."

"I'll let you know what I find out." She looked at Sadie's door, then typed Sadie's room number into her phone.

They said their good-byes, and as soon as Sadie was alone, she grabbed her notebook and wrote down everything from her conversations with both Jen and Mary Anne. Jen thought the heart attack victim was named Ben; he had the same dinnertime in the same dining room as Mary Anne. Sadie thought hard on what Mary Anne had said, then added "7:30 Chandelier dining room." That's what Mary Anne had said was her standard dinner reservation, and why she'd gone to the late show last night, which put her in the buffet at the time Ben died. She hadn't mentioned recognizing the guy as being from her dining room, though. Maybe she hadn't seen him up close.

And maybe the dining room had a list of the people scheduled for each seating.

So maybe Sadie could figure out who Ben was—and whether or not he was married to a woman named Tanice!

CHAPTER 24

●

Plans on finding out more about Ben began instantly download-
ing into Sadie's brain, but she put a stop to it as soon as she
remembered that she was supposed to meet with security about the
gift tag. It was the perfect opportunity to talk to them about what
she'd discovered today. A possible poisoning and a sudden heart attack had felt like too much of a coincidence *before* learning the man
who died—assuming he had died—was named Ben.

She took the stairs to deck eleven and followed the signs to the
security office. She passed the place in the hall where she'd first seen
Lorraina and Shawn talking, and shivered slightly. How different
would things have been if she'd confronted the two of them right
then?

The hall jogged to the right and she followed the bend, finally
reaching the curtain that separated the cabins from the security office door.

"Hello," Hazel said a few seconds later, smiling. "Can I help
you?"

"I'm supposed to come by and talk to security," Sadie said.

She glanced at the clock; it was almost eleven o'clock. "I'm Sadie Hoffmiller."

"Okay," Hazel said in her lilting accent. "Officer Jareg isn't available right now. Would you like to set up an appointment for later?"

"Um, sure," Sadie said, disappointed not to be able to talk to him right now, when all her thoughts and concerns were at the forefront of her mind. Was he not available because he was in Skagway, working with the local police to question Shawn?

They set an appointment for four that afternoon—five hours from now—and Sadie headed back to her cabin. Once there, she spent several minutes updating her notes and rewriting a couple of earlier pages of notes that didn't seem as clear as she'd like them to be. She wrote out a to-do list and tapped her pen on the three bullet points she'd written down:

- Verify that the computers were down last night
- Learn more about "Ben"
- Meet with security

She couldn't meet with security until later, but the other two items on her list were doable right now. Having not taken the time to put on her makeup this morning, she decided to take a few minutes to make herself presentable. The steward had made up the beds but hadn't washed the mirror—probably because he thought the note was important. She attempted to clean off the lipstick but made a mess of it in the process and finally gave up.

The computer lab was located on deck five, in a little office behind one of the lounges that offered live entertainment every night. Sadie was halfway through the cruise, and though she'd seen the shows in the theater, she hadn't visited any of the other entertainment venues on the ship—such a waste.

There was a sign next to the door that said the computer center's hours were 8:00 a.m. to midnight. Shawn was right about them closing, though she wondered why he hadn't noted the closing time when he checked in the first time.

She had to scan her ship-card to get into the room, where a staff member sat behind a desk.

"Are you here to use the computers?" he asked with barely a hint of an accent, though his name tag said his name was Henry and he was from the Philippines—a lot of the staff was from the Philippines, Sadie had noticed. The next most common country of origin was Indonesia.

"Um, no, not really," Sadie said as she approached. No one else was in the computer center, which she was glad of. It was always better to interview someone in private. "I'm wondering if you can tell me if the Internet was working last night. Were you here by chance?"

"I wasn't here last night," he said, shaking his head slightly and furrowing his brows.

Sadie could tell he was wondering why she needed such specific information. Surprisingly, she could be perfectly honest about her reason. "My son was supposed to use the computers last night to get some information for me, and he claims they weren't working. I just need to know if that's true or not."

Henry smiled and sat back down at his desk, turning so he could work on the computer set up on one side. "I don't like to ruin the trips of teenagers," he said with a sly grin in Sadie's direction that told her she'd found a friend in Henry. "But I hope to put your mind at rest. What is his name? I have a record of who entered the center, which computer they used, and how long they were logged on."

"Shawn Hoffmiller," Sadie said. Even though she knew it was impossible, she worried for a moment that Henry would recognize the name as the man being questioned by police.

"Room number?" he asked, showing no reaction to Shawn's name.

"Seven forty-nine."

He typed for a minute, and then leaned closer to the screen. He glanced up at her with a blank expression that made her stomach clench, then he smiled, showing bright white teeth—the front two had a small gap between them. Henry turned the computer screen toward her and used a pen to point at a line. "He entered the room at a quarter to eleven but never logged into the computers."

"Oh, good," Sadie said, but she still had questions. "Can you tell for sure that the Internet was down? Could he have come in, but then not tried to go online?"

"You are a very suspicious woman," Henry said with a smile Sadie was sure was intended as a joke. But she *was* suspicious, and fearful for her son. Henry typed on the computer for a few more seconds, then sat back. "Ah, you will be glad to know that last night's attendant noted that the Internet was down from nine o'clock until midnight. The system must have reset itself during the night, however, since everything was working fine when I opened this morning."

Sadie felt like she'd lost ten pounds of dead weight off her shoulders with the news. "Oh, good," she said. "Thank you so much."

"You're welcome," he said, closing out the screen and settling back into his chair. The page that came up on the monitor looked like a textbook. He caught Sadie looking at it and gave her a sheepish grin as he turned the screen away from her view.

"Are you going to school?" Sadie asked.

His cheeks turned pink. "The Internet is working now if your son would like to come in."

"I'm not going to get you in trouble," Sadie said, assuming that studying on the job was likely against the rules. "I've been an advocate of education all of my life. I was a teacher for many years."

He just smiled at her, and she understood that he didn't want to discuss it at all.

"Good luck to you," she said. "And thank you so much for your help. I appreciate it very much."

"You're welcome. Have a nice day."

Sadie let herself out of the computer center, relieved to know that Shawn had told her the truth. She pulled her phone out of her bag and frowned when she saw there were no text messages. Why hadn't Pete sent her an update? She'd left Skagway over an hour ago.

It's not about me, it's not about me, it's not about me, she chanted as she typed out a text, telling him that she'd verified Shawn's story about the Internet last night. She hit SEND, hoping for a quick answer, but after a full minute of waiting, she put her phone back in her bag and tried not to think too hard about why no one seemed to want to tell her what was going on. Was Breanna still hashing things out with Liam? Was Pete still talking to Maggie?

She shook off her anxiety and frustration about the lack of communication and moved to the next item on her list. Until her appointment with Officer Jareg later that afternoon, all that was left for her to do was find out more about Ben. It was actually rather perfect. If she could find more about him, and maybe even uncover some connections between him and the suspicious wine bottle, she could take that information to security when she met with Officer Jareg, making his job easier and speeding up the process with Shawn so that he could leave sooner rather than later.

Sadie knew exactly where to start her search for more information about Ben—the Chandelier dining room. From there she hoped to learn his wife's name, maybe even his room number. It was tempting to let her thoughts spiral forward from there to what she would do with that information, but she tried to keep her focus.

She texted Breanna to see where she was.

> *Breanna:* Almost back on the ship.
>
> *Sadie:* I need to do a little investigating. Want to help me?
>
> *Breanna:* Can I eat first?

Sadie frowned; she wanted to execute her plan *right now.* And yet, food was important too.

> *Sadie:* Sure. Let's meet at the buffet.

When they met up for their late breakfast/early lunch, Sadie asked Breanna how her conversation had gone with Liam.

"I think he's frustrated," Breanna said before taking a bite of her sandwich. "He's trying hard to stand up to his mom, but I think his heart isn't really in it. He just doesn't care about all the fluffy stuff—that's what he calls it."

"That's frustrating," Sadie commiserated.

"It doesn't help that this is coming at a really busy time for him. They're selling off a piece of property, and he's been overseeing the deal. The sale is supposed to close tomorrow, but he's really stressed out about it. This is the first time he's done anything like this on his own. He wants to make his dad proud and all that. If I didn't think his mom would hire the Spice Girls to sing the wedding march, I'd back off." She took another bite, then looked up at Sadie. "So, what was the investigating you wanted help with?"

Sadie didn't realize that Breanna didn't know anything about the heart attack last night until she started talking as though Breanna knew the whole thing. When her daughter responded with shock, Sadie had to back up to that morning and start the story with her morning walk with Mary Anne.

As Sadie filled in the details, she glanced around the buffet, wondering where in this space Ben had been last night. She realized that even though she had no official confirmation that the heart attack victim was named Ben, she assumed he was.

Breanna listened dutifully while she ate. "Wow," she said when Sadie finished. "So, you're going to talk to Officer Jareg about all of this, right?"

"Eventually, yes," Sadie said. "But my appointment with him isn't until four o'clock and the more info I can give him at that time, the better. I mean, what if Ben's wife or girlfriend is named Tanice? What if I can confirm that the wine bottle belonged to them? If there was something dangerous in the wine that sent Lorraina into her coma, then Shawn's off the hook and he can come back on the boat, right?"

"You really think you can figure all of that out?"

"I'm not sure, but I've found that oftentimes it's like pulling a loose thread—it goes further than you expect. The alternative is to sit and do nothing until my appointment. That sounds impossible."

"That does sound impossible," Breanna agreed. "Sitting still has never been your strong suit."

It was a relief to have Breanna agree so readily that Sadie had good reason to seek this information. "I thought we could start with the Chandelier dining room. I bet they have lists and charts of who sits at which table."

Breanna sat up straighter, intrigued. "So we go to the dining room and ask to see the lists, right?"

"It *might* be that easy," Sadie said with a hesitant smile. "But it might not. Sometimes people don't offer up information quite so easily, in which case we might need to be . . . creative. If you're uncomfortable with it, you don't have to come with me."

"No, I'm good," Breanna said. She took the napkin from her lap and put it on her plate, then smiled nervously. "Just tell me what to do."

CHAPTER 25

❦

The Chandelier dining room was designed for those people who'd chosen, at the time of booking, reserved seating for their evening meals— people like Glen and Mary Anne who liked a more traditional cruising experience or like Jen and Frank who wanted an excuse to sit down together at a set time every day.

Because Sadie's group had chosen the flexible eating option, she'd never been to the Chandelier, but it was easy to find thanks to the color-coded maps of the ship posted in numerous locations. The outside of the restaurant was painted with an elaborate mural depicting a 1920s-type ballroom, with men in zoot suits and women with feathered headbands kicking up their heels around a dance floor. The large doors leading to the dining room itself were closed; only dinner was served in the Chandelier, and it was barely noon.

Sadie tried the doorknob. "It's locked."

"Really?" Breanna said from behind her where she'd been casting nervous glances left and right since their arrival. "Maybe we could ask someone in one of the other restaurants. I bet they could put us in contact with whoever is in charge."

Josi S. Kilpack

Sadie had to keep herself from frowning. Breanna was already anxious even though all they'd done was check the lock?

"Except that whoever is in charge might not give us the lists, which puts us in an awkward position if we try to get them after being told not to."

It took a few moments for Breanna to figure out what Sadie meant, but then she smiled wryly. "Ask for forgiveness instead of permission?"

"Sort of," Sadie said. She took a step back to get a better look at the double doors—big, heavy, commercial-grade fire doors that were up to code for a ship of this size. But the lock was standard, and Sadie could see the latch in the space between the doors. She reached in her pocket for her ship-card and slid it in between the two doors, below the latch. Breaking into a locked door with a credit card was cliché, but that was because it worked so well—on the right kind of lock.

"The ultimate goal is not to have to ask for either one. If no one knows we took the list, then there's no need to even ask for forgiveness."

"That sounds so blasphemous," Breanna said.

"It's not," Sadie said quickly. "God believes in justice, and we're working toward that. He gets it. You stand in the hall and let me know if you hear anyone coming."

Breanna looked at the door. "You're really going to break in there?"

Sadie looked at Breanna's doubtful expression and tried to hide the slight annoyance growing in her mind. She was used to working alone, which meant no one questioned her—at least not until they realized what she'd done. "Would you rather go back to the cabin? It's okay if you do."

"No, it's fine. I mean, we're not going to steal anything, right?"

"Just information, and it's for a good cause." Sadie was beginning to feel like the little devil on someone's shoulder, while Breanna was taking the more angelic route.

"I can't believe I'm doing this," Breanna said, looking both ways as she moved back a few feet toward the hallway.

"Just signal me if someone's coming." Sadie slid the credit card upward, twisted it as much as she could to put tension on the latch, and then pushed up ever so slightly. It made progress one millimeter at a time, but it was progress all the same.

"How should I signal you?" Breanna asked from where she'd posted herself about ten feet away. "Liam and I always use bird calls, but there aren't a lot of birds inside a cruise ship."

"Why don't you cough?" Sadie said, keeping her focus on the latch, which was still moving. She increased the pressure, but it was still slow going.

Seconds later, Breanna coughed, and Sadie straightened and stepped back from the door. A moment later she heard voices, and gestured Breanna to come toward her. She looked up at the mural as though admiring it.

"Isn't it lovely?" Sadie said to Breanna just as two staff members walked past carrying what looked like table linens and speaking in a language Sadie had never heard before.

"Um, yeah, truly . . . lovely," Breanna said with her arms folded tightly across her stomach. She looked more ill than anything else.

Sadie glanced over her shoulder and acted surprised to see the staff members. She said hello, which they returned before going back to their indecipherable words. After they turned the corner, Sadie waited a few seconds to be sure they were gone, then shooed Breanna back to her post. She hurried back to the door.

"That was close," Breanna said anxiously, looking both ways again.

It wasn't really, but it was kind of cute how worried Breanna was. Compared to other places Sadie had broken into, a dining room wasn't a big deal at all. Sadie got back to work, slowly using the tension from the card to slide back the latch, bit by bit by bit. After nearly a full minute, Breanna coughed again. Sadie was so close to having the latch completely pulled back that she increased the tension on the card and moved faster. Sweat beaded on her forehead.

Breanna coughed again, loud hacking coughs.

"Come on," Sadie whispered under her breath when she heard footsteps. She'd managed to pull the latch back almost all the way and if she stopped now, she'd have to start all over again. She just needed a mere fraction of a centimeter in order to . . . finally!

The latch pulled back and Sadie quickly slipped the card into the empty space. She looked up at a frightened Breanna at the same moment she twisted the handle and opened the door enough to dart through. There wasn't time to do anything else, but she cringed at having left Breanna outside the door. They should have planned this part out a little better. She pulled the door closed, straining to hear what might be taking place on the other side.

"Oh, hi," she heard Breanna say in a high-pitched voice that hopefully didn't sound as nervous to whoever had approached as it did to Sadie. She heard the murmur of another voice, then Breanna said, "I'm just waiting for my mom. We're meeting here in a few minutes."

There were more murmurs and then silence. She counted to three before opening the door an inch, but Breanna gestured at her to close it again. "Hurry!" she whispered, then looked both ways and took a deep breath. She gave Sadie a shaky thumbs-up. "I'm good."

Sadie closed the door and faced the room for the first time, half expecting to see a bunch of workers staring at her, but she was alone.

An ornate staircase led down a few steps to the actual dining room. The same mural from outside the room was repeated on the inside walls, complete with intricate crown molding along the upper edge, velvet valances on the windows, and more than a dozen huge chandeliers hanging from the ceiling. It was lovely, but Sadie hoped Mary Anne was wrong about it having the best food on the ship since that would mean Sadie would never get to try it. Flexible dining had seemed like such a good idea at the time.

She heard the sound of dishes clinking together somewhere to her left and quickly moved into action. There was a podium at the bottom of the stairs with a door panel on the front. It made sense that there would be a seating chart, and it made even more sense that the seating chart would be stored near the entrance.

The door panel was unlocked, which was a relief. Sadie smiled as she opened the panel and pulled out a three-ring binder with "Seating" on the front. Perfect!

She sat on the bottom step and opened the book to find several pages of instructions in plastic sleeves. She flipped through them until she reached a page showing a diagram with several circles. A quick glance at the dining room showed that all the tables were round and sat eight people. Sadie went back to the book and located a time stamp on each page. There were four dinner shifts: 5:30, 6:30, 7:30, and 8:30. She went to the page for 7:30 and scanned the seating arrangement, disappointed not to have names listed on the tables, just room numbers.

"Biscuits," she muttered. The sound of voices coming from the same direction as the clanging dishes didn't allow her the luxury of thinking through her options. She snapped open the three-ring binder and removed the page. They were on day four of a seven-day cruise and surely everyone knew where their seats were by now, right? She rolled up the seating assignment, slid it into her bag where it promptly unrolled itself, hurried up the stairs, opened the door carefully, and stepped back into the hallway. She took a deep breath and let it out slowly.

"That was absolutely terrifying," Breanna said as she and Sadie quickstepped away from the restaurant. "It reminded me of that sick-to-my-stomach feeling I'd get when I'd play hide-and-seek as a kid. I hated that game."

Sadie had used the exact same description to describe her own feelings during earlier investigations. "You were a great lookout," Sadie assured her. "Thank you for your help."

"Sure," Breanna said, but she still sounded nervous. "So, did you find out if there was a Ben and Tanice at the 7:30 seating?"

Sadie patted her bag. "No names, just room numbers."

Breanna glanced at the bag hanging across Sadie's chest and came to a stop. "You took the list?"

Sadie stopped too, looking around to make sure no one would overhear their exchange. The ship was pretty much empty since most of the passengers were in Skagway. "Just the one page."

"You took it, though?"

"I had to. There were people in the kitchen, and I worried they would come out before I could copy down the chart by hand. I had hoped for names too, believe me."

Breanna pursed her lips in disapproval, but Sadie took her arm and kept walking. "We'll talk about it in the cabin, okay?"

As soon as they entered the cabin, Sadie sat on her bed and removed the seating chart from her purse, giving herself a little pat on the back for having been successful in her quest. One look at

Breanna, who had remained standing, however, caused her to drop the smile. "It's just a list, Breanna."

"Someone else's list. I didn't think you were going to do anything illegal."

Sadie put the paper down and looked up at Breanna. "It's a list, and not even a list of names. Everyone knows where they sit by now, and I think the end justifies the means."

"Is this the kind of thing you and Shawn do?" Breanna said. "Take stuff and—"

"Spy on people and gather information and catch bad guys?" Sadie finished up with a nod. "What did you think we did as investigators?"

"It doesn't feel right."

Sadie took a breath and tried not to be dismissive of Breanna's feelings. "I'm sorry, I didn't mean to make you uncomfortable. And I didn't do this, or anything else I've done in the past, flippantly. But a man is dead, and Lorraina is in the hospital, and this"—she lifted the list—"might help us figure out how both of those things happened, and more importantly, if they are connected."

Breanna still looked concerned but sat down on the bed next to Sadie without further comment.

Sadie slid the seating chart out of the sheet protector so she could fold the paper and used her pen to circle all the repeating room numbers.

"You're circling everyone who shares a room together?"

"Yes," Sadie said. "Unfortunately, most of the seats are taken by shared room numbers. Still, narrowing the list is important."

"Maybe if we leave a bigger tip for our steward, it will satisfy karma for us having stolen the list."

"That's a good idea," Sadie said. "Especially if it will make you feel better."

"It will," Breanna said nodding, but then she smiled slightly. "It is kind of exciting, isn't it? I mean, now that it's over and stuff."

Sadie smiled back. She didn't want to encourage rebellious behavior in her daughter who had never been one to break the rules, but there *was* a thrill of discovery that permeated these kinds of things.

"So, now what?" Breanna said, after pointing out the final set of room numbers Sadie had missed. "How do you find out which room number belongs to this Ben guy?"

"Well, Jen and Mary Anne both eat at the same time, and Jen thought she knew who it was. Maybe she could look at the list and help us narrow it down, at least to the table he sat at. She said she was taking the train with her kids this afternoon, though I don't know what time. She seemed to think Mary Anne would be able to verify the guy too, though, so I'm wondering if Mary Anne could be just as helpful. She might be easier to find; I think all she planned to do in town was shop."

"What do we do if we figure out what room Ben was in? Knock on the door and see if the widow answers?"

Sadie grimaced. "I haven't thought that far out. Let's just find Jen or Mary Anne and see what they can tell us. Keep in mind that the plan is to be able to give as much information as possible to the investigators I'll be talking to at four. We'll go as far as we can, but if we reach a stopping point, no worries. It's still beneficial."

"That makes sense. So how do we find Jen or Mary Anne?" Breanna asked. "There are three thousand people on this cruise, and most of them are in Skagway along with the passengers from the two other ships that docked today."

If Jen hadn't left on the train yet, she'd likely be getting lunch with her family or visiting the train station, which had a gift shop and a museum. Mary Anne could be anywhere. The bigger problem was that Breanna didn't know either one of the women, so she couldn't really look for them.

Or could she?

There had been hundreds of photos taken since the first time Sadie had made her purchases from the photo gallery, and it took some time to find one of each of the women. Because of how badly it had turned out the last time Sadie purchased someone else's photo, she thought hard about buying these before taking them to the counter and charging them to her ship-card. If asked, she could always tell the ladies she'd purchased them as gifts.

Breanna opted to search on the ship, keeping the photos with her for verification purposes. She put them in Sadie's bag and carried it over her shoulder so it wouldn't be obvious that she was consulting the photographs as she wandered the ship. Sadie would look through Skagway—bagless.

"You're sure you're okay with this?" Sadie said as they approached the gangway and she pulled her ship-card out of her pocket.

"I've totally got this," Breanna said, though she still looked nervous. "But we better leave an extra big tip for the steward."

CHAPTER 26

🍓

Sadie checked the train station first in hopes of finding Jen and her cute family before they headed to the Yukon, but they weren't at the depot or the gift shop or the museum. She then turned her attention to the more touristy shops, thinking that was where she'd likely find Mary Anne. After the third store, Sadie sent a text to Pete, requesting an update about his visit with Maggie, but he didn't respond, which made her even more intent on finding Jen or Mary Anne. Any time her thoughts dwelled on Shawn for too long, her chest would get tight and her motherly instincts would tempt her to go back to the police station and make a scene.

Bre sent periodic updates each time she finished searching an entire floor. She'd found the kids club and talked to a worker who recognized Jen's kids, but said they'd gone ashore with their parents for the day. Breanna also thought she recognized Mary Anne's husband in the casino, which had Sadie shaking her head for not thinking of looking there first.

Sadie: Did you ask him where Mary Anne was?

Breanna: No. He looked grumpy. I think he was losing.

Sadie considered going back to the casino herself to talk to Glen, but she wasn't a big fan of grumpy people either. If she didn't end up finding Jen or Mary Anne, she could stop by the casino on her way to the security office that afternoon. She had a feeling Glen would still be there.

> *Sadie:* Let's keep looking. We've got two hours until my appointment.

Two shops later, her diligence was rewarded when she spotted Mary Anne in the far corner of a little shop. She sent a quick text to Breanna before putting the phone in her pocket and hurrying forward.

"Mary Anne," Sadie said as she came up behind her.

Mary Anne turned around and smiled. "Sadie! How wonderful to see you."

Sadie was immediately pulled into the woman's squishy hug, which she gladly returned. "You too."

Mary Anne immediately held up the bag on her shoulder. "Look at this beauty," she said triumphantly. It was navy blue pleather with "Alaska" embroidered in silver thread and a map of Alaska outlined with tiny diamonds. It was big enough to fit a small child or a medium-sized dog, though the stitching didn't look as though it would hold up to that kind of load. "I chose navy because I think that makes the design look like a constellation. Don't you agree?"

"I get it," Sadie said. "The diamonds are like stars."

"And look at this," she said, unzipping it. "It has not two but *three* separate compartments, along with a hidden one inside, see?" She slid her hand into a side pocket that didn't look all that hidden.

"Wow," Sadie said, trying to sound interested.

"And there's this little pocket right here. I think it's for a cell phone, but it's perfect for my ship-to-shore card." She pulled up the flap and withdrew her ship-card just enough for Sadie to see. "It's like it was made for it, don't you think? Such clever merchandising. I don't have to pull out my wallet every time I need to use my card anymore."

"Genius," Sadie said, admiring Mary Anne's knack for finding joy in the simple things and yet also eager to get her help.

Mary Anne admired the purse again before letting it drop to her side. "My friend Millie is going to be so jealous. She's one of those purse-hounds, you know; I bet she has no less than thirty purses in her closet. She doesn't have anything like this, though, no sirree. And it's blue, so it matches everything."

"It's lovely," Sadie said; it was the kind of lie you couldn't not say. "Um, do you have a minute?"

"I have lots of minutes," Mary Anne said, grinning widely. "I'm on vacation!"

Sadie smiled, sincerely that time; Mary Anne's joy was infectious. "I was wondering if you could help me figure out the seating arrangement in your dining room."

"Whatever for?" Mary Anne asked, pulling her eyebrows together.

Sadie explained her conversation with Jen and then removed the seating chart from her pocket, showing it to Mary Anne. "Do you know who she's talking about? A younger guy named Ben. Jen seemed to think he was married."

"If you don't mind my asking, why is this of any interest to you? You don't even eat in our dining room."

Sadie didn't want to get into everything that had happened with Shawn or Maggie or Lorraina. "I'm worried about Ben's

BAKED ALASKA

wife—assuming it *was* Ben who died at the buffet. I wanted to see if she's okay."

She'd hoped that would buy her some sympathy with the older woman, but Mary Anne looked unimpressed. "You don't even know her."

"I might, actually. I'm wondering if we were on a shore excursion with them yesterday," Sadie admitted. "Beyond that, I was widowed when I was younger and left to raise two small children. I thought maybe I could give her some advice."

Mary Anne was not thawed by Sadie's second attempt at an explanation either. Sadie tried to think of another reason she'd want to find Tanice, other than the truth, when Mary Anne made it easy on her.

"I bet that boyfriend of yours is an attorney, isn't he?" She nodded, ready to believe it without Sadie's confirmation. "And he wants to represent the widow in a lawsuit, right?" She pushed her glasses up on her nose. "I don't blame you for a second. It's highway robbery what they charge on this ship. Back in the day, everything was included, you know, now you have to pay extra for certain restaurants, some of the onboard ship tours, *and* the shuttle transportation. It's ridiculous if you ask me. If you can get some money out of the cruise line, I'm all for it."

Sadie didn't know what to say to that.

Mary Anne adjusted her glasses again and then cocked her head to the side. "You'll need to turn the paper, otherwise I'm not properly oriented."

Sadie turned the paper, and Mary Anne leaned closer, scrunching her nose slightly.

"Do you know who it is Jen's talking about?"

"I think so, yes," Mary Anne said. "I saw him last night so if

185

we're thinking of the same person, I should be able to figure this out."

"I'd sure appreciate it," Sadie said. "You'd be my hero for the day."

Mary Anne looked at her over the top of her glasses. "I do love playing the hero role." She smiled, then looked back at the chart. "Well, that's our table," she said, pointing to one of the tables on the left side of the dining room. "And that means that Ben's table would be right . . ." She paused and looked up at Sadie. "Where did you get this?"

"Oh, uh, from the dining room," Sadie said, shrugging in hopes of keeping it casual.

"They just hand out maps of where people are seated? That's got to be a breach of privacy."

"Oh, no, it wasn't like that."

Mary Anne put one hand on her ample hip. "They employ all those foreigners and they don't always understand the laws around here. We live in the U. S. of A. and we're entitled to our privacy. Who knows what could happen if this ended up in the wrong hands? They'll never learn if we don't teach them the right and proper way to do things, and if they lose their jobs for it, so be it. These jobs are a privilege, and they are lucky to have them. I'm going to talk to my steward—"

"I stole it," Sadie said, hoping to forestall a scene. "I snuck into the dining room and stole the seating chart."

Mary Anne looked shocked and blinked at her from behind her glasses.

Sadie felt herself squirming. First Breanna and now Mary Anne was standing in judgment of her choices. Was she out of line here? She didn't have time to consider that as Mary Anne finally spoke.

"So your boyfriend is the ambulance-chasing type, huh?"

Sadie shrugged, relieved when Mary Anne looked back at the chart. After a few seconds, she tapped a finger on one of the central tables. "There it is. Ben's party was seated right here."

Sadie made note of his table. "His party?"

"There were eight of them, all from Texas, I think. Friends, or associates or something. He was a handsome man."

"Jen said he was young, in his thirties." She looked back at the seating chart and the table Mary Anne had pointed out. Four of the seats shared the same room number while the other four spots were made up of two sets of two. One set was on the tenth floor, but Sadie's eyes zeroed in on the numbers 1184. Lorraina's room was on deck eleven and that was the floor where she'd gotten off the elevator when Sadie had been trying to catch up with her.

What if she'd gotten off the elevator, heading toward her room, but somehow come across the bottle of wine en route? Considering the disastrous turn of events on the cruise thus far, perhaps she couldn't resist taking the wine bottle to deck twelve, where she planned to drown her sorrows. Had she considered the damage it might do to her already failing liver? Did she care? Sadie felt her neck flush at the questions and the potential answers.

"Do you know which of these seats would have been his?" Sadie asked.

"Well, from my seat, I could see the man in profile," Mary Anne said, drawing Sadie's attention back to her. "He had a nose kind of like Tom Cruise—flat on the tip, you know—though he was several inches taller. Did you know Tom Cruise is only five foot seven? And he wasn't nearly as sexy as Tom is. Anyway"—her finger hovered over the table—"I guess this is him here." She pointed to the numbers 1184 on the seating chart. Sadie felt the rush of discovery course through her.

"Do you remember much about Ben's wife? Was she a redhead?"

Mary Anne lowered her chin in thought. "I don't really recall," she said with a shrug. "So did I give you the help you needed?"

Sadie smiled at Mary Anne's eager face and gave the woman another hug. "You were exactly what I needed. Thank you."

"Anytime, dear," she said, waving away the compliment. "Make sure your boy toy hits 'em where it hurts and helps that lady out. If you can't have love, you should at least end up with money, that's what I always say."

Sadie's smile was a bit more forced at that, but she thanked Mary Anne again and turned to leave.

"Are you heading back to the ship now?" Mary Anne asked.

"Actually, I was planning to meet my daughter."

"Oh, wonderful. For lunch? I'm absolutely starving, and I'm sure your daughter is lovely."

Ten minutes later, Sadie and Mary Anne were sitting across from one another at a little table outside a store that sold Sarah Palin merchandise. Sadie had texted back and forth with Breanna, who was happy to give up the search in favor of a nap in the cabin. Her interest in dining with Sadie's new friend was minimal, so Sadie didn't force it.

Pete still hadn't responded to Sadie's texts, but his silence reinforced Sadie's desire to stay in Skagway a little longer. Breanna could rest, and Sadie would be close by whenever Pete finally let her know what was going on. She had the information she needed about Ben, but since she wasn't sure what to do with that information other than tell security about it when she met with them later, taking a break didn't seem like a bad idea.

It wasn't until Sadie ordered some sweet potato fries that she noticed the clock in the window. It was after two o'clock, and she realized the whale watching trip had left half an hour ago. Why hadn't Breanna mentioned it? Had she forgotten too? Sadie couldn't imagine that either of them would have wanted to go without Shawn or Pete, but missing the trip made her sad. Here they were, in Alaska, and not able to do the adventure Breanna had most looked forward to.

"Did you vote for Sarah Palin?" Mary Anne asked as she picked up her hamburger. Though in her seventies, Mary Anne obviously still had all her own teeth and took a massive bite out of the burger.

Sadie gingerly sidestepped the question and waved toward the store dedicated to the former vice-president hopeful. "Can you believe they have a whole store for her?"

"They *should* have a whole mall for her!" Mary Anne said, and quickly launched into explaining why the Republican party would be ushering in the Second Coming sooner than anyone could say "Here's what I think about gun control."

Sadie was relieved when the familiar Nokia ringtone started playing from the recesses of Mary Anne's new pleather monstrosity. The phone stopped ringing before Mary Anne managed to find it, though a moment later, she held up the phone, victorious.

Honestly, if Mary Anne still owned that purse a year from now—once the blinding thrill of the purchase had faded enough for her to see it for what it really was—Sadie would eat canned peas. And Sadie *never* ate canned peas.

Mary Anne scrunched up her nose as she looked at the screen on her phone. "Glen," she said simply, before pushing some buttons and putting the phone to her ear.

"Hi, sweetie. . . . Just having lunch with Sadie. . . . Yes, that's the one. . . . You didn't tell me to wait for you for lunch. . . . No, I'm not full. I can eat again. . . . All the way back on the ship? . . . Oh, well, you don't want to miss that. . . . Okay, I'll be there in a few minutes. . . . I'll meet you at the buffet then. Kiss, kiss." She hung up the phone and took another huge bite of her burger. "Did I mention my husband is crazy?"

"Really?" Sadie asked, casually glancing at the clock again. Why hadn't Pete texted her back yet? Why wasn't he giving her an update?

Mary Anne nodded. "See, we owned a pet store in Kansas City—built it from the ground up, and managed it for almost thirty years."

"Oh, wow. That's impressive." Sadie ate another fry.

"It was impressive, until a big-box store moved in and took our business—and our tagline: 'A pet store with so much more.' Well, we contacted an attorney, and ended up with a nice chunk of change when the store decided to settle with us. They even bought the slogan from us, so I guess it worked out pretty well, but we were forced to close our store."

A text message lit up Sadie's phone, and she reached for it, but Mary Anne went quiet.

"You're going to text while we eat?"

"Um, no," Sadie said, pulling her hand back. Hadn't Mary Anne just talked to her husband?

Mary Anne smiled. "I knew you had better manners than that. Anyway, Glen's never really been the same since then. He has these . . . moods, you know? We went to couple's therapy for a while, and the therapist talked about taking back your power and not letting anyone hold you down. I love that empowerment stuff, don't you?"

"I'm glad you found something to help you cope," Sadie said, sincere but impatient as she kept looking at the phone. Had Pete finally texted her? Or maybe Shawn? She'd been waiting for hours to get an update, and Mary Anne was only halfway through her burger.

Mary Anne told Sadie about the medication Glen's doctor had told him to take, but that Glen hadn't liked the side effects. She said that last bit with a wink, and Sadie smiled in hopes that would be enough of a response to keep Mary Anne from explaining what those side effects were.

"He's doing better, now," Mary Anne said. "But I have to be real careful with him, you know. Make sure he's taken care of and feeling okay."

"I'm sorry," Sadie said. "That sounds difficult."

Mary Anne stared at her hamburger, her expression falling for a moment before she forced a smile and looked back at Sadie. "For better or for worse, right? And besides, it's not all bad. He loves to go on cruises, and he does really well in the casinos—part of that 'embracing your power' the therapist taught us. Did I tell you he once won enough to pay for all our onboard expenses?"

A second text message chimed on Sadie's phone. She stared at it while Mary Anne began telling Sadie about her children and grandchildren—seventeen total—and as much as Sadie sensed Mary Anne needed a friend, was she really going to ignore her own son in order to listen politely while Mary Anne talk about hers?

She was just about to explain to Mary Anne that she had to go when her phone rang, giving Sadie the perfect excuse all on its own. "I'm sorry, Mary Anne, but I really do have to take this."

She didn't look at Mary Anne's expression or listen to her response as she grabbed the phone and glanced at the caller ID. It was Shawn! "Hi," Sadie said as she stood and walked a few steps away from the table. Sadie felt bad for leaving Mary Anne, but it was *Shawn.*

"Hi, Mom," Shawn said. He sounded worn out and dejected. He'd never been good at hiding his feelings.

"What's wrong?" Sadie asked, all her mom-worries triggered at once.

"The police want Maggie and me to stay in Skagway."

CHAPTER 27

🍓

Sadie put her free hand to her chest and felt her heart rate speeding up. "Oh, my gosh. Why? Did something happen to Lorraina? Are you under arrest?"

"No," he said quickly from the other end of the phone. "Lorraina's fine—well . . . I mean . . . anyway, I don't *have* to stay, but there's some federal guy coming in the morning, and they asked me to stay. Pete thinks it's a good idea."

"Pete said that?" Sadie said, feeling oddly hurt. "Why didn't he call to talk to me first?"

"He sent you a couple texts, but you didn't answer so he suggested I try calling. He's talking to Bre right now to see if she can stay in town with me but asked me to keep calling you until you answered."

"*Both* of you would stay in Skagway? I don't understand. What exactly is going on?"

"Pete explained it better than I can," Shawn said, the strain in his voice clear. "Here . . . hang on."

Sadie heard the phone shuffling, some muted voices, and then Pete's voice came on the line. "Sadie—"

She didn't give him a chance to finish. "Why does Shawn have to stay? Does this have something to do with those e-mails? Or—"

"The police have the tests back on the wine bottle. They found cyanide."

"Cyanide?" Sadie said, all her breath leaving her in one rush. "Is Lorraina—?" She couldn't finish the question.

"They aren't telling us much right now, but she's still in a coma. If her condition were to worsen, or if she were to . . . " Pete trailed off.

Sadie closed her eyes. She didn't want to think what it might mean to her family—to Shawn—if Lorraina never woke up from the coma.

Pete continued. "The cruise ship staff dumped out the contents of the bottle, so they only have trace amounts on the inside of the bottle. There's still a lot of work that needs to be done to prove that Lorraina ingested the cyanide from the wine, and that the cyanide is what sent her into the coma, but it looks like the poison is what showed up on those initial toxicology reports. Skagway is talking with Juneau, and then coordinating with both federal agents and the labs in Anchorage. It's getting complicated, but I'm hopeful that the federal agent can clear things up."

"And Shawn?"

"He's been cooperating, and if he continues to cooperate, he puts himself in a much stronger position. I know it's not what you want to hear, but it's not that unusual considering the circumstances, and I'm not sure having Shawn leave is worth the risk." He was quiet for a moment, and the background voices got quieter, making Sadie think he'd moved away from whomever he was with. "Honestly, Sadie, I worry that if he refuses to stay, he *will* be arrested in order to keep him here. We don't want that."

Sadie raised a hand to her forehead. Of course she didn't want that, but she didn't want Shawn to stay in Skagway either.

"I'm sorry, Sadie," Pete said.

As was usually the case, his sympathy unraveled her. "You really think it's best for him to stay?"

"*Them* to stay," Pete clarified. "Maggie too."

Shawn had said that but Sadie hadn't paid it much attention. "Why Maggie?"

"Same reason as Shawn—she was close to Lorraina and had motive to poison the wine. She might have had the opportunity too—we just don't know. I had a good talk with her over breakfast. When we finished, she went to the police station on her own. She's been in questioning ever since."

Sadie tried to stay calm. She leaned against a brick wall and took a breath. "Can I talk to Shawn again?"

"Of course," Pete said, and she heard the muted rustle of the phone being passed from hand to hand.

"Mom?" Shawn's voice was subdued.

Sadie felt tears in her eyes, which she tried to ignore. She had to be strong for her son. "Are you okay?"

"I don't know, Mom. I'm just . . . this is all so much, you know?"

"Yeah," Sadie said. "Can I come down and see you?"

"I don't know if that's a good idea," Shawn said. "I mean, I just feel like I'm on the edge and seeing you might undo me completely."

It was perhaps the only thing he could have said that would keep her from insisting on a face-to-face meeting, even as she worried that he said it because he didn't really want her to come and didn't know how else to tell her. She felt so disconnected from him right now. Her heart ached to have him so close, and yet still be so distant in the ways that mattered to her the most.

"I understand," Sadie said, even though she didn't. "Do you need a change of clothes from the ship?"

"That would be great. A couple days' worth since I won't be able to rejoin the cruise until at least Ketchikan, if everything goes well."

Ketchikan. That was two more days. Shawn and Breanna would miss even more of the cruise, and yet from the minute Shawn saw Lorraina, the trip had no longer been what Sadie had hoped it would be.

And now with Lorraina still sick, and Shawn still being questioned, it wasn't hard to imagine that at some point the police might feel he was a suspect and arrest him. Could she really leave him here with that possibility hanging over his head?

"Here's Pete," Shawn said, a moment before Pete's voice came over the line.

"Are you still there, Sadie?"

"Yes," she said. "Why can't I stay in Skagway with Shawn? It would make me feel a lot better."

"You could," Pete said, but from his tone it was obvious that wasn't his first choice. "But there's still no sign of the gift tag, and while I know the security team is now much more invested in this situation, I have found at least a dozen extreme miscarriages in basic procedure, and I'm wondering if they could use a helping hand on the ship. We still need a lot of answers, and I don't think either of us can do much good if we stay here. Also, my contact on the ship said that something has come down from the cruise line headquarters about problems on other cruises—I don't know what it is, but the police have questioned both Maggie and Shawn about other cruises they've taken. This is Maggie's first cruise ever, and Shawn says he hasn't been on a cruise for five years."

"He hasn't," Sadie said.

"Right, so why are they asking? They've asked the same question three or four different ways and have gotten all these passenger manifests from other cruises. They even asked if he's ever gone by other names—it's really strange. If we're on the ship, I think I can learn more about that. Here in Skagway, I worry that we'll just be underfoot. They were open to my involvement in the beginning, but they're starting to shut me out; I've been relegated to the waiting room."

"Sadie."

Sadie startled and turned around to see Mary Anne standing a few feet away, smiling broadly, her eyes blinking behind her bifocals. "I'm ready to head back to the ship. Are you coming?"

"Just a minute, Pete," Sadie said before taking the phone away from her ear. "Actually, I'm going to meet up with Pete here in town."

"Your boyfriend, the attorney?" Mary Anne asked.

Sadie hesitated but nodded.

"Ah, yes," Mary Anne said, as though in on a secret. "You probably need to discuss his new client, right?"

Sadie just smiled. "Hopefully I'll see you later, though."

"I'm going to the karaoke show tonight at nine—want to join me? Glen can't sing a note."

"Well, I'll need to see what my family has planned," Sadie said, still smiling. Her cheeks were starting to hurt. She leaned in to give Mary Anne a hug; the woman smelled like lavender soap and hamburger grease. "Thanks for lunch," Sadie said even though she'd paid for her own fries.

"My pleasure. See you soon, dear." Mary Anne hiked the strap of her new purse higher up on her arm and headed toward Broadway.

Sadie put the phone back to her ear. "I'm back," she said,

relieved to have severed the connection with Mary Anne without hurting her feelings in the process.

"You have a boyfriend who's an attorney?" Pete asked.

"It's a long story," Sadie said. A story she wasn't even sure she understood. "I'll tell you about it later. Anyway, Shawn said you were talking to Breanna about her staying in Skagway?" She quickly returned to the table and cleaned up her lunch mess with one hand by dumping it into an old barrel that served as a garbage can.

"Yes, and she said it might be for the best if she could stay where she has cell coverage—I guess things are kind of rough with the wedding? She said she'd just gotten an e-mail from Liam's mom. I don't think it was good news."

"She did?" Sadie asked. Breanna hadn't said anything, but then again Sadie still hadn't read the texts that had come in while she'd been having lunch with Mary Anne.

"Shawn and Maggie don't have to stay at the police department, and Breanna said she'd get some hotel rooms for everyone. That way, the three of them can really dig into Lorraina's history. That will be a lot easier to do here than on the ship."

Sadie hated this. Both of her children staying in Skagway without her? And yet, was there really a better option? She liked that Shawn wouldn't be alone and that they could use the time to learn more about Lorraina. And she liked that Pete felt she could be helpful in doing what could be done on the ship . . . unless he was just trying to keep her from making a scene in Skagway. "You really think this is best?"

"I do," Pete said, and his sympathy brought tears to her eyes. He was all business, but he *did* understand.

"Breanna will miss Glacier Bay tomorrow. We already missed the whale watching today."

Pete didn't answer. They both knew it wasn't a deal breaker, just one more disappointment in an extremely disappointing situation.

"And what about Maggie? How is she doing?"

"Well, I was hoping you would be able to sit down with her and explain about Breanna staying and them using the time to research Lorraina."

Sadie felt so grateful to be included and immediately headed for the police station. "Really?"

"When she and I were talking earlier, she was really worried that you were mad at her."

Sadie was quiet as she walked. She wasn't *mad* at Maggie, but she felt cautious. "Did she send those e-mails to the police?"

"No," Pete said. "But she did give the security department a bunch of Lorraina's papers. She had them when she came into the security office yesterday—remember?"

"Right."

"Lorraina had the printed e-mails in that folder. When security asked for Lorraina's documents, Maggie handed them all over."

It was a reasonable explanation, but Sadie still felt as though being too supportive of Maggie somehow took her support away from Shawn.

"I think Maggie really respects you, Sadie. It's upsetting for her to think that you're angry with her. If you could talk to her and help her feel better about all of this, I think it would mean a lot to her."

Would she join them in Ketchikan, too? Sadie wondered. Did Sadie want her to? "I'm almost at the police department. Can I talk to Maggie right now?"

"Let me see what I can do. Hang out in the waiting area until I come for you, okay?"

CHAPTER 28

Maggie was obviously nervous when she met Sadie in the waiting room ten minutes later. She had her hands between her knees, palms together, and kept glancing at the desk clerk as though making sure the woman wasn't eavesdropping. As soon as Maggie opened her mouth, the words just tumbled out. Sadie sensed that she'd been holding in a lot of emotion, as every word seemed encapsulated by her feelings.

"They're talking to Lorraina's family," she whispered, each word agonizing. "And they already contacted my dad for the adoption information. It's a sealed record, so the courts can't open it without a warrant from a judge, but they grilled my dad about it anyway. Then they took blood samples and sent them to a lab here in Skagway that can run blood-type tests to see if that tells them anything—there are certain types that don't match up and Lorraina had a rare blood type, I guess. They said they'd tell me the results when they know." She'd cried off any makeup she'd put on that morning, but she still wiped at her eyes carefully, as though she didn't realize she had nothing left to protect. She lowered her voice even more; Sadie leaned in to hear her. "I think they think I did something do her."

"But you've told them everything, right? About the argument and all that?"

Maggie nodded and tucked her hair behind her ear. Her hair was sleek and straight, while Shawn's was a mass of tight curls. Did that mean anything? She could have had it relaxed professionally. Sadie wondered when the blood-type test would be back, and then wondered what any of them would do about the results, regardless of which direction the results took them. What if Shawn and Maggie *were* related to each other? What if they *weren't*?

"I think telling them all that made it worse," Maggie said. "I mean, if she's not my birth mom and she's lied to me all these weeks, it gives me motive or something."

"But if you're not guilty, then you don't have to be scared," Sadie assured her. "They're going to look into everything, and it's not like you have some kind of connection to cyanide that could give you opportunity, right?"

Maggie's expression fell even more, and Sadie's heart skipped a beat. "You *don't* have a connection to cyanide, do you?"

"I work for a paper manufacturing company, and we use cyanide in the production process of most of our products. I work in receivables, where all the different raw materials come in."

"Oh," Sadie said. "So, you had access to cyanide, and Lorraina might have been lying to you about being your mother."

"It sounds so bad," Maggie said, looking terrified. "Plus I paid for our trip. She said she was going to pay me back with her next paycheck, and I really wanted to spend time with her so I put it on my credit card. But now the police are saying she doesn't have any money, that she hadn't worked in weeks. I completely lost it." She wiped at her eyes again. "It was just one more thing, ya know? One more hurt in all of this, but I think they saw it as proof that I'm some kind of loony; one more reason I could be mad enough to want to punish my birth . . . Lorraina. Did you know she has a criminal history for stuff like bad checks and things? I mean, everyone makes mistakes, and I know she didn't have an easy time of it, but she never told me she'd been *arrested* for anything."

Sadie didn't comment because she didn't trust herself to be objective and instead shifted the conversation ever so slightly. "Can you tell me about how she found you?"

"It was through a website that reunites birth families. She found me through a profile I had put up."

"That's how she and Shawn found each other too."

"Yeah, after Shawn had his profile up for just a few months." The bitterness in her tone put Sadie on edge, and she straightened slightly as Maggie continued, "I put my profile up as soon as I turned eighteen and participated on forums and answered people's questions for almost three years. Do you have any idea how many people I saw get reunited with their natural families? When Lorraina found me, it was like . . ." She looked upward, as though trying to find the right analogy hanging from the ceiling. After a few moments, she looked at Sadie again. "It was like Christmas and Easter and my birthday all rolled up into one moment—one event."

Sadie hated this topic. She hated thinking that Shawn and Breanna had voids she could not fill. "What kind of things did you talk about on the forums?"

It was Maggie's turn to pull back. "I know what you're getting at. The police already suggested that Lorraina used the information from my posts to make herself seem like my mother."

"Could it be what happened?"

Maggie slumped in her seat, unable to keep up her confidence. "I don't *want* to think that," she said, softly. "Even after all of this,

I still want her to have been telling me the truth. Why would she pretend? Why go to that forum and read through all my past posts to learn about me and my history? But that's what the police think she did. Do you know she told me she was allergic to bees, just like me? And she didn't like asparagus—neither do I. But Shawn said she cooked asparagus for him at Christmastime. I don't know about the bees yet."

"Did you post about those things on the forum?" Sadie asked.

Maggie nodded slowly, and her chin quivered, prompting her to take a deep breath and sit up a little straighter. "What kind of person would lie about those things?" She shook her head. "I *have* to believe she wasn't lying—that she *is* my birth mother. I honestly can't comprehend believing anything else. It's felt so . . . good to have her. So . . . important and healing and right."

Sadie wished she could believe Lorraina hadn't lied about all of this. And yet, if Lorraina wasn't Maggie's birth mother, that meant that Maggie's real birth mother was still out there. Maybe. Would Maggie search for her again? "Did Lorraina ever explain why your adoption record was sealed?"

Maggie looked into her lap, smoothing her pants over her legs. "I never asked her. I was born in Ohio, and I petitioned the probate court to open my records almost two and a half years ago. It took forever for me to get an answer, but what I got back was that an affidavit had been filed that wouldn't allow me to open them. They wouldn't tell me who filed the affidavit, but it's usually a birth parent. I talked to a lawyer, but she wanted a large retainer and thought I should hire a private investigator to help get information. I didn't have the money, and Ohio was so far away. So I just kept hoping that I'd find my birth mom another way, which is why I went to all those websites. I never imagined in a million years that someone would take advantage of the information on the site. I still can't believe it. Lorraina and I talked on the phone a dozen times. We exchanged e-mails. I knew her. *I did.*"

"And this cruise was the first time you'd met in person?" Sadie thought Maggie had said something about that when they had talked before, but she couldn't be sure.

Maggie nodded. "We met up in Seattle before getting on the ship. This was our big face-to-face after weeks of getting to know one another. I can look back on it now and remember that she talked a lot about Shawn and how she hoped that one day we would have a relationship. She said that he probably didn't mean what he'd said in those e-mails and she wished she hadn't sent them to me. Knowing that she knew he was on the ship makes me realize she was prepping me to meet him. I guess she thought we would make up and get along and everything, but at the time I just thought she was sad he'd cut her off, maybe obsessing a little bit. This whole thing was supposed to be . . . life-changing."

It had been life-changing, but in such a different way than anyone expected. Sadie processed through all the information and wondered if she should remind Maggie that Sadie and Shawn had once had a private investigating business and that Ohio was a border state to Michigan, where Shawn lived. Once Shawn was back home, it wouldn't be difficult for him to sniff out the information about who had filed the affidavit, possibly leading her to her birth parents. It didn't feel like the right time to say it out loud, though. "I'm so sorry," Sadie said instead.

"But I know there's purpose in this," Maggie said, straightening her back and trying to look confident. "I know God's trying to show me something, and I'm trying to keep an open heart about it. I just wish I understood better than I do."

Sadie nodded her agreement with the sentiment. She'd seen that very thing play out in her life so many times that she couldn't discount it. But just because God was leading you through a journey with a meaningful end didn't mean the brambles along that course didn't draw blood sometimes. "Did Lorraina ever tell you that she was sick?"

Maggie looked at her hands again. "I knew she was a recovered alcoholic, and she told me she had a bad liver, but I didn't know how bad it was until Juneau." She glanced at Sadie fast enough for her to see the smallest amount of censure in her eyes. "I didn't know anything about her needing a transplant or Shawn not being willing to be tested to see if he could save her life."

Oh, dear. Sadie could feel her mama bear instincts shifting around in her chest. She was not in a good place to hear even the mildest of condemnations against Shawn. She took a deep breath before she spoke and tried to take a diplomatic approach. "He was having a difficult time trusting what Lorraina told him, and he just needed more time to figure things out—time she wasn't giving him."

Maggie's eyes narrowed slightly, and it was enough to put Sadie even more on edge. "I know he's your son, but it was cruel of him to deny her the peace of mind to at least have been tested. If he wasn't a match, then fine, but to not even try? I just . . . I just can't understand that."

Sadie felt her sympathy closing off even more as her hackles rose in defense of her son. "He was feeling very manipulated by the situation. She'd borrowed money she hadn't paid back and told him things that weren't lining up."

Maggie gave a halfhearted shrug. "She borrowed a couple hundred dollars and was having a hard time keeping up with her hours at the dry cleaners because she was so sick. A person's life is on the line, and he can't even get a blood test for her?"

"It's not that simple," Sadie defended. "And he hadn't said no. He was just taking a little time to try to understand the situation better. It all felt very rushed for him, very strange."

"I would have been tested in an instant if she'd asked me."

Sadie's mama bear claws were out in full force, and though she knew the next words she said should be more carefully considered, having Shawn villainized in any way was more than she could stand. "I don't know much about the testing behind this transplant thing, but the fact that she never even asked you to be tested makes me wonder if it was because you weren't biologically linked to one another and Lorraina knew it." That hit Maggie hard enough that she flinched. Sadie wasn't done. "After all that's happened, can't you see that the chances are that she was manipulating *everyone*? If she knew she was sick when she first found Shawn, it puts a whole new spin on why she reconnected with him at all. And then, six months *after* she'd told Shawn that she'd never had any other children, she tells him that he has a birth sister and wouldn't he love to meet her? When he says he doesn't want to, she plans for this cruise that *you* pay for in order to put it all right in front of him. She was probably hoping to make him uncomfortable enough that he'd get tested just to get her out of his hair." It wasn't until Sadie stopped talking that she saw the growing expression of horror on Maggie's face.

"What are you saying?" she asked, her voice squeaky with rising emotion. "That I was some kind of . . . bait for Shawn?"

Oh gosh, Sadie thought, realizing what she'd said and what it would feel like to hear it laid out like that. "I'm sorry, I didn't mean it to sound that way. I'm just trying to explain why Shawn acted the way he did. She was harassing him."

"She was sick," Maggie said, tears spilling out of her eyes. "He was her last hope, and he turned his back on her." She got to her feet and Sadie did as well.

"Maggie, I—"

"Margret Lewish?"

They both turned to look at an officer who had approached them.

"Yes?" Maggie said.

"Officer Daltron would like you to come back."

Maggie avoided Sadie's eyes and seemed glad to have a reason to leave. "I'm sorry I bothered you to come in."

"You didn't bother me," Sadie said, feeling terrible and yet still defensive. The officer walked to the door at the far end of the waiting room, and Sadie took the opportunity to loop back to their initial conversation and hopefully end this conversation on a higher note than the one they'd sunk to. She spoke softly, though, so only Maggie could hear her. "I don't think you hurt her, Maggie. Even if she wasn't who she said she was, I don't think you'd do anything to hurt her."

Maggie made eye contact with Sadie, but her expression didn't soften. When she spoke, her words were barely a whisper. "Maybe you don't, but if I have a stronger motive than Shawn does, it changes things for him, doesn't it? If I *did* poison her, then he's off the hook."

Sadie had to really think about that. Did she believe, even just a little bit, that maybe Maggie *did* have something to do with Lorraina's coma? If it turned out that Lorraina had targeted Maggie on that website and faked everything as a ploy to get Shawn's cooperation through his interest in having a birth sibling, and if Maggie found out, wasn't that a pretty good motive for attempted murder?

And Maggie worked with cyanide! How many people had access to something so deadly in the course of their nine-to-five job? And yet to look at her, and to have felt the pain in Maggie's voice as she talked about what she was learning about Lorraina, set all those suspicions on their ear. "I don't think you tricked her into drinking cyanide-laced wine, Maggie. But I just . . . I just don't know how to deal with this. I don't know how to help you."

"Right, because Shawn needs you. I get it."

"Ms. Lewish?" the officer said.

Maggie turned and walked out of the room, not even acknowledging Sadie's weak "Good-bye." She felt horrible but didn't know how to make it right. She pulled out her phone to check the time and saw it was nearly three o'clock; she had her appointment with Officer Jareg in an hour. Breanna was probably packing for the stay in Skagway.

Sadie looked at the door Maggie had disappeared through one last time before she left the police station. Unraveling who Lorraina was had turned out to be an emotional minefield for everyone involved, and Sadie didn't like that she'd thrown more pain into Maggie's path.

Sadie hurried toward the ship, her mind filled with thoughts of Maggie. What was Sadie supposed to do to help her? She hated that Maggie's guilt could work in favor of proving Shawn's innocence and wished there was something else, or someone else, on the radar to take the attention away from both of them. The only possible connection was the wine bottle.

Thinking about that fueled her fires all over again. She needed to find out more about Ben and Tanice. Had the poisoned wine been meant for one of them? And how had it gotten into Lorraina's hands? If they could prove that someone else had tampered with the wine, that could get both Shawn and Maggie off the hook, right? Could Shawn get back on the ship tonight if the police could get enough information to clear him before the ship left port?

Her phone chimed with a text shortly after she reached Broadway, and she stepped out of the flow of pedestrians to read the message. It was from Maggie, and Sadie held her breath as she opened it.

Blood test came back. Lorraina isn't my mother.

Sadie groaned, knowing that despite the crisp explanation, this had to have hit Maggie like a boulder to the head. She texted back.

I'm so sorry.

She hoped Maggie would reply right away, but when nothing came in, she sent one more text.

I really am sorry. I know this must be hard for you.

No response.

Sadie's heart was heavy. Lorraina had preyed upon Maggie's vulnerability and inflicted more pain than Sadie could possibly imagine. And Sadie had pushed Maggie away to the point where she could offer no solace to the poor girl who needed support now more than ever.

A text came in from Pete telling her the same information, and Sadie thanked him without telling him she already knew. He promised her more information as it became available. Sadie thanked him again and headed for the ship.

Could she send a note to Maggie explaining her position? It

would allow Maggie the chance to read it on her own and ponder Sadie's words without the pressure of having to respond. She was deep in thought as she reached the gangplank and glanced up in time to see a familiar face.

"Tanice!" she said automatically, causing the other woman, who was coming down the gangplank, to flinch. She didn't respond, but gave Sadie a dirty look as she passed by, reminding Sadie of their less-than-enjoyable conversation following the gold panning expedition yesterday.

And yet Sadie was turning around before she could consider any other alternative but to talk to this woman.

So help her.

CHAPTER 29

🍓

"Tanice," she called out, pushing down all her feelings of embarrassment by reminding herself that Shawn and Maggie were being questioned by the police and this woman might know why. She noted that Tanice only had her purse with her; like every other passenger infiltrating the city, she was probably going shopping. Would she do that if her husband were dead? Except, Sadie remembered, Tanice's husband's name was Kirby. Maybe Ben was Tanice's boyfriend and the reason for her marital problems. Maybe Kirby was trying to poison him!

"Tanice," she called out again, picking up her pace.

Tanice looked over her shoulder but kept going, taking longer steps, which spurred Sadie to speed up even more.

"I just need to talk to you for a second," Sadie said when she was just a few feet away from the woman. Tanice showed no signs of stopping, so Sadie reached out and grabbed Tanice's arm in an aggressive gesture that caused Tanice to stop, turn, and pull her arm back.

Sadie let go—she didn't have to, she chose to—and came to a stop in front of her.

Tanice obviously didn't know what to do as her eyes darted from side to side as though looking for someone to save her. They were in broad daylight, in the middle of the pier. Tanice was perfectly safe, but her fear worked in Sadie's favor.

"I'm sorry," Sadie said, trying to catch her breath, "but it's important."

Tanice regarded her with suspicion, but finally said, "What?"

What indeed. Sadie could think of several questions she *couldn't* ask, but a few that she could.

"Is your husband's middle name Benjamin?"

"What?" Tanice said, sounding incredulous and backing up a step.

Oh, please don't run away, Sadie thought to herself. She did not want to tackle this woman in front of all these people, but she would if she had to. "Is your husband's middle name Benjamin?"

"It's none of your busine—"

"Just tell me!" Sadie interrupted. "The sooner you do the sooner we can both walk away from this. Is his name Ben?"

"His name is Kirby."

"Is his middle name Ben?"

"No, it's Jonathan. Why are—"

"Is Ben his nickname?"

"Are you drunk?"

Sadie took a deep breath. "Okay, look, I found a wine bottle with a gift tag that was written to Ben and Tanice—was it yours?"

"I have no idea what you're talking about. I don't—"

"Would anyone send a bottle of wine to you and someone named Ben?"

"Other than a cousin of mine, I don't know anyone named Ben.

Besides, my husband and I don't drink, so no one would be sending us a bottle of wine in the first place," Tanice said, her voice clipped.

"And you don't know anyone who would send a bottle of wine to you and someone named Ben?"

"I think I already said no to that question. What is wrong with you?"

Sadie let out a breath. She could officially rule out *this* Tanice. What a relief. "I'm looking for someone named Tanice; it's an unusual name."

Tanice nodded warily, and her expression wasn't showing any good faith in Sadie.

"Do you know of any other people named Tanice on this ship?"

Tanice shook her head. "But I didn't come here to meet people. I've met other Tanices in my life, though some of them spell it T-A-N-I-S. Was the name on this gift tag spelled that way?"

"No, do you spell yours like Janice with a T instead of a J?"

"Yes," Tanice said.

"That's how it was spelled on the gift tag."

They lapsed into silence, and Sadie hurried to put an end to the conversation, glad she'd made a fool out of herself to get the information, though it would have been nice to get the information *without* having to make a fool of herself. "If you by chance run into anyone with that name, could you let me know? I'm in room 829."

"Um, yeah," Tanice said. "Why do you need to find her?"

"Just . . . because." She wasn't about to reveal more information than she had to.

Tanice's expression was turning curious, a very dangerous thing Sadie needed to nip in the bud.

"So, how are things with you and Kirby?"

That did the trick, turning off Tanice's curiosity to make room for her to be offended by Sadie's nosiness. Tanice reminded Sadie that it was none of her business and quickly headed into town once more.

When Sadie got back to her room, she found Breanna zipping up her suitcase. It drained Sadie for the moment and she sat on her bed. "Pete said you got an e-mail from Liam's mom."

Breanna let out a breath and nodded. "She thinks Liam and I are being ungrateful for her help, and then she listed everything she's done for this wedding." She paused, her shoulders slumping as she stared at her suitcase for a few beats, then she lifted the suitcase off the bed and placed it on the ground. "She sent it to Liam too, and he's finally mad. It's no longer about just trying to make me happy; he can see she crossed a line with the accusations she made. The bad news is that what was already ugly, just got a whole lot uglier." She sat on her bed across from Sadie. "When I told him I was stay- ing in Skagway, he set up a conference call for all of us—he's in London and his mom's at the estate."

They were quiet for several seconds until Sadie finally spoke. "I'm so sorry, Bre."

Breanna smiled wanly at her. "Thanks for supporting me," she said quietly. "I know none of this is easy for you either—it's not what you dreamed for me—and I appreciate that you're letting me do this my way."

That brought tears to Sadie's eyes, but she tried to blink them away. "I want you to be happy, Bre, and Liam makes you happy."

"Shouldn't that be what Liam's mom wants for us, too?"

"She does want that," Sadie said, thinking back to something Pete had said once. "Everyone has motives for what they do. Maybe if you can find out what her motivation is, you can find a middle ground."

Breanna nodded and put her hands between her knees before glancing up at Sadie. "Are you mad I'm staying in Skagway?"

"Disappointed, but I'm glad Shawn won't be alone. And I'm relieved that you get to work things out with Liam and his mother."

"I need to get this wedding settled or I might lose my mind."

"If eloping in Monaco is the best idea, I won't say a word against it, I promise."

Breanna smiled. "Thanks, Mom."

Sadie would have liked some reassurance that they *wouldn't* elope, but Breanna wasn't offering any.

"We can use my computer to look up information about Lorraina—Pete said Shawn knows where to look. And Maggie will be there, too, so hopefully between the three of us, we can make some progress with that side of things. I've already found a hotel with free Internet."

It took a few phone calls in order for Sadie to get access to Shawn's room. She didn't pack everything from his room, though. She couldn't face the idea of his presence not being on the ship at all; it seemed to say he wasn't coming back. Shawn *was* coming back—she had to believe that.

Sadie tried not to get emotional as she put the strap of Shawn's bag over Breanna's shoulder. The ship would sail at seven that night. If Sadie had time after her meeting with Officer Jareg, she promised Breanna she'd come to town and see them both before the ship left port. Maybe she'd have another chance to talk to Maggie too, and try to repair the things she'd broken.

After watching Breanna walk down the gangplank, Sadie returned to her cabin—alone—and clenched her fists to her sides. "This is not fair," she said out loud, then pulled her notebook out of her purse and got to work. The best remedy for feelings of insufficiency was to do something. She ripped out a sheet of paper and began writing a note to the *right* Tanice, not the redheaded Tanice who had pushed her husband into a river, but the woman who sat a few tables away from Mary Anne in the dining room.

As far as etiquette went, it was completely out of line to pester a woman who had just lost her husband, Sadie knew that, and yet she was feeling desperate. Mama bear was not taking this sitting down. If they could get to the bottom of this and clear Shawn's name, she could have her family around her again. Not doing what she *could* do to help was out of the question.

Rather than try to explain why she was contacting Tanice at such a difficult time, she decided to simply focus on what she needed to know. If that didn't work, she'd be more direct with her next attempt, but she didn't have a whole lot of room for "next times" in her schedule right now. She needed her son back.

Dear Tanice,

I wonder if you know anything about a bottle of wine with a gift tag that said "To Ben & Tanice—May you continue to find every happiness together." I'm in cabin 829. It will be very helpful to many people if you would contact me with what you know.

Sincerely,
Sadie Hoffmiller

CHAPTER 30

🍓

At the last minute, Sadie included her cell number on the note since they would be in port for a little longer. She folded up the paper and headed to deck eleven, moving slow enough to read the room numbers on the cabin doors. She wondered which of these cabins was Maggie and Lorraina's? How close was it to Ben and Tanice's cabin?

A young man came down the hall, and Sadie moved to the side so he could pass her.

She looked at the next cabin and continued counting: 1176, 1178, 1180, 1182. She stopped in front of 1184—Ben and Tanice's assigned cabin per the seating chart and Mary Anne's verification.

Sadie looked at the note in her hand, wishing she could have a face-to-face with Tanice, but knowing that in the wake of the tragic loss of her husband, it was better to let her come to Sadie when she felt up to it. Hopefully that would happen before the cruise came to an end. Then again, Tanice might have left the ship entirely by now. Still, Sadie needed to do what she could do, so she squatted down and slid the folded paper underneath the door, then stood again, staring at the place where her request had disappeared.

She had a meeting with Officer Jareg in a few minutes. When she finished there, maybe she'd get a little more aggressive about finding Tanice. It was insanity-inducing to question every possible option every single time she did anything. It was often far more efficient to follow her gut, and her gut was telling her she was on the right track.

Sadie headed toward the security office and hoped that maybe she would learn as much from them as they learned from her. Police rarely shared information, but as Pete had pointed out, the security officers didn't operate the same way actual police officers did.

"I have an appointment with Officer Jareg at four," Sadie said to Hazel, who was still behind the desk. Did the girl ever get a break?

"Yes, I am sorry, but he won't be back in time. Can you come back at five?"

Disappointment washed over Sadie. "Yes, that's fine," she said, trying not to sound too put out. It wasn't Hazel's fault that things were complicated. She wrote Sadie into the calendar; Sadie noticed that her four o'clock appointment was already crossed out.

She left the office and headed toward the elevators while texting Pete that she was on her way back to Skagway—was there anything she could do to help while she was in town? She finished the text and slid her phone into her purse just as she reached the doorway leading to the elevators.

"Thank you so much for your help," a woman said, the emotion in her voice causing Sadie's steps to slow. There weren't many reasons to be so upset while on a cruise.

"Are you sure you don't need help packing your things?" another woman's voice asked while Sadie scrambled to make a possible equation for this situation. She was exiting the hallway containing the door to the cabin of a woman who'd just lost her husband. Could it be . . . ?

"No, I'm fine. Thank you for going to the coroner's office with me. I'm so sorry it took as long as it did. I just . . ." She paused to sniffle a very dainty sniffle.

Sadie inched closer to the doorway, not wanting to interrupt and yet trying to come up with the best approach. It sounded like this woman—Tanice, if Sadie were correct—was dismissing her friend, meaning she'd be alone. Meaning that Sadie could talk to her. Holy cow!

"I just need a little time alone, you understand, right?"

Sadie was leaning against the wall dividing her from the elevators and heard the rustle of movement and change of tone which led her to believe the two women hugged one another. They said goodbye, and Sadie listened for the elevator door to shut before backing up a few steps so that it wouldn't look like she'd been listening. She started walking toward the elevators again, waiting for the woman to turn the corner but stopped when she reached the doorway, again, and heard the woman speaking. "Bunch of busy-bodied boon flies, every last one of ya."

It was the same voice she'd just heard, but a completely different tone, and yet there was something familiar about it. Had Sadie met this woman already? Why wasn't she coming around the corner?

Sadie paused, waiting for the woman to come toward her, but when there was no movement, she couldn't hold back her curiosity any longer. She turned the corner and saw the woman finger combing her hair in the mirrored door of the elevator. Sadie almost missed a step as she recognized the woman as the one she'd met on the elevator a few days earlier when Sadie had been chasing after Lorraina.

This was the girl who had told her that Lorraina had gotten off on the eleventh floor. Sadie had run into her a second time yesterday—right down the hall! She hadn't been paying attention to which room this woman had been exiting when they had passed one another yesterday, but thinking back on it now, it could have been the same door Sadie had just slid the note under. Sadie was processing this information when the woman turned and smiled at her—a fully lit, kind as they come, smile.

"Oh, hey there," she said with the little drawl Sadie remembered. She was dressed in a charcoal velour sweat suit, and though her hair was done, her makeup was not. "How ya doin'?"

"I'm fine," Sadie said, slower than she meant to. If she looked closely enough, the woman's eyes looked red around the edges, but just a little. Sadie tried to remember exactly what she'd heard before she turned the corner into the elevator area. The woman had been mournful when her friend was there, then snide once her friend left, and now she was bubbly?

"Glad to hear it," the woman said, moving toward the hallway Sadie had just vacated.

Sadie realized she'd come to an awkward stop, so she hurried forward and pushed the button for the elevator. "It sure is a nice day," she said, wanting to keep talking but not sure how to do so.

The woman didn't stop walking, but she did look over her shoulder and smile. "I hope you get to enjoy it, then." She put her hand on the frame of the doorway, gave Sadie a flash of an even bigger smile, and then disappeared.

Sadie counted one, two, three, four, five hippopotamuses, then moved toward the hallway and peeked around the corner just as the elevator doors opened behind her.

The woman was walking down the hall with a swing of her hips, her long brown hair moving slightly as she did so. She turned the corner in the hallway, and Sadie counted two more hippopotamuses before hurrying down that section of hallway and peering around that corner too.

Sadie held her breath as the woman stopped at room 1184 and removed her card key from her back pocket. Sadie pulled back so that she only had one eye visible, should the woman—who seemed to be the recently widowed Tanice—look her way, but the woman disappeared inside the cabin without a backward glance. The door clicked shut, and Sadie leaned against the wall, taking a deep breath. That woman was not acting *at all* like a woman in mourning. The only reason Sadie could think of as to why was if her husband's death wasn't tragic. At least not to her.

Sadie was scrolling through her mind in search of who to call about this first—Pete, probably—when the ringing of her phone startled her. She pulled it out of her purse and looked at the numbers on the screen. She didn't know the number, and it had an unfamiliar area code. *Tanice?*

"Oh, boy," Sadie whispered as sweat instantly bloomed on her forehead and her heart took off running. She wasn't able to get a handle on herself before the call went to voice mail, which was probably for the best. She took the stairs down to her cabin where she let herself inside and then called her voice mailbox.

The voice she now believed belonged to the widow Tanice was just a little bit frantic. "I just found a note in my room, and I don't know what you're talking about. Please leave me alone." Sadie listened to it twice more, then disconnected from her voice mail and sat on the edge of her bed, considering her options. She could call Pete. She could save all this and take it to Officer Jareg. Or . . . she could call the woman back. Her insides flip-flopped at the idea, and yet she had only to think about Shawn at the police department, and Breanna disembarking the ship, to find the motivation she needed to drive her forward. Her thumb hovered over the CALL button for a few seconds before she took a breath and called Tanice back.

CHAPTER 31

Worried that Tanice would recognize her voice, Sadie pitched the tone of her voice so she sounded a little like Minnie Mouse. "Hello. This is Sadie. You just left me a message?" As soon as she spoke, she knew she'd made a mistake. It would be hard to keep up the high-pitched voice for the entire phone call.

"I believe I was very clear that you weren't to bother me." This time the woman's tone wasn't mournful or snide or bubbly, but instead swung back and forth between anger and fear.

"Yes," Sadie said in that squeaky, high-pitched voice. She wished she'd gone with a Boston accent. It was her favorite one to impersonate—wheh did you pahk the cah?—but it was too late now. "I just wanted to make sure you didn't lose a wine bottle."

"No," she said, her words sharp. "I don't just go 'round losin' bottles of wine. Why are you askin' me about it?"

"You're sure you aren't missing one?" Sadie's throat was starting to hurt from the forced pitch.

"Look," Tanice said, lowering her voice. "I don't know what you're talking about, but you better leave me alone." The line went dead, and Sadie pulled her phone away from her ear, staring at it and wishing she had recorded the conversation.

This was not the reaction of a woman who was sad to see her husband gone, yet a sense of relief filled Sadie as well. If Tanice had something to do with the poisoned wine, that would get Shawn and Maggie off the hook. Once they were cleared of suspicion, Sadie could work on rebuilding her relationship with Shawn and making things better with Maggie. She was so eager for those two things to happen that she hurried out of her room and up the stairs. She would wait in the security office, going over her notes, and then, as soon as Officer Jareg was ready, she'd be right there.

She took a deep breath as she entered the hallway that led to security.

As she approached Tanice's door, she tensed and took longer strides for fear that Tanice would open the door and confront her.

She doesn't know it was you who left the note, Sadie told herself, but she was still relieved when she'd passed the closed door. The farther she got from Tanice's room, the better she felt. It wasn't until she was in the security office, however, that she felt she could really breathe normally again.

Her new appointment was at five o'clock, and she was forty minutes early. After reviewing her notes in her notebook, she texted Pete, but he didn't reply. Again! She texted Breanna, too, who responded to tell Sadie that Pete and Shawn were still at the police station while she was at the hotel getting ready for the conference call with Liam and his parents. Sadie wanted to be a part of that discussion, but both she and Breanna knew that was impossible. Sadie wished her luck and asked her to let her know how things went, and that if she saw Pete, to have him call her. Breanna said she would.

It was disappointing how quickly Sadie ran out of things to do; her notes were better honed than she'd thought.

The only magazine in the room was a guide to cruising that Sadie suspected was printed by the cruise line itself. Other than what looked like a really wonderful recipe for stuffed mushrooms by Chef Ferguson which she copied into her notebook, Sadie had a hard time finding anything else of interest. She checked her phone again, then put it on silent for the pending interview.

It used to be that she could deal with her impatience better than this, but since her recent bouts of anxiety, it was much harder for her to control her racing thoughts. By the time Hazel motioned her back to Officer Jareg's office a few minutes before five, she felt as though she'd drunk three cups of coffee.

When she entered the room, Officer Jareg was finishing a phone call and writing a few words on a notebook on his desk. She sat down and waited until he hung up the phone and turned his attention to her.

"Thank you for coming in, Mrs. Hoffmiller, and for being patient with the change in appointment. I'm afraid it has been a very busy day for me. I'm glad, however, that we have a chance to talk."

"So am I," Sadie said, but once she'd said those words, the floodgates opened and she began jabbering away about everything, barely able to get the words out as fast as her mind was working. Several times, Officer Jareg stopped her and asked her to back up and start again. Each time that happened, her tension increased. Finally, he put up both hands.

"You must slow down, Mrs. Hoffmiller," he said, frustrated. "This is not making sense. What do you mean you sent a note to his wife? Whose wife?"

"Ben's wife," Sadie said, knowing she'd explained that. Was the fact that English wasn't this man's first language getting in the way of this discussion?

"Ben who?"

"I don't know his last name," Sadie said. "But it's the man who died last night of a heart attack at the buffet."

Officer Jareg clamped his mouth shut in surprise, paused a few moments, and then asked her how she knew about that.

She told him about what Mary Anne had said happened and then about Jen talking about it as well. "It's hard to keep these kinds of secrets," Sadie said.

Officer Jareg's expression became increasingly concerned while she spoke, which she couldn't understand. Ben had collapsed in the buffet, right? Any number of people must know about it.

"Perhaps it would be best if you could write down what you have learned," he said, pulling open a desk drawer and removing a spiral-bound notebook—the kind you could buy for twenty cents at back-to-school sales. No official forms?

He handed her a Seven Seas Cruise pen along with the notebook. "I have some phone calls I need to make, but I'll use another office. I'll be right back." After taking a step away from the desk, however, he paused, then returned and tore off the piece of paper he'd been writing on when Sadie entered. Sadie didn't see what it said, and he smiled slightly as he folded it in half and tucked it into the front shirt pocket of his uniform.

He then left her alone with the notebook.

Though frustrated with the lack of procedure, she gathered her thoughts and wrote about the gift tag it seemed only she had seen, and then about her conversation with Mary Anne and how it led to the note Sadie had left under Tanice's door. She included every detail she could think of, even the ones she didn't want to admit, like breaking into the dining room. She worried she would get in trouble for that, but what was the worst thing the cruise line could do to her? And if it helped get Shawn out of trouble with the police, then it would be worth every embarrassing detail. She didn't say anything about Breanna helping her, however.

Officer Jareg peeked in on her twice, but she wasn't done either time so he shut the door. She wasn't about to be chintzy with her report; this was about her son's future. When she finished—four pages in all—she reread it, corrected a misspelled word here and there, inserted the proper punctuation, and then put the pen on top of the notebook and pushed it toward Officer Jareg's side of the desk.

She had every intention of waiting patiently for him to return, but then she looked at the notepad on his desk. Officer Jareg had taken the top sheet before leaving the room; she couldn't help but wonder what it said.

From where she sat, she could see indentations in the top sheet of paper, left over impressions from whatever had been written on the paper above it. For the first minute, she looked away and distracted herself with other things in the office. However, the room was very sparse. For the second minute, she stared at the paper and listed all the reasons not to mess with it. After *those* two minutes, though, her curiosity got the better of her.

It likely has nothing to do with my interests anyway, she told herself as her eyes rested on a mug on the far side of the desk. It was filled with pens, markers, and, more important, pencils.

She stood rather casually, ready to abandon her plan at the first hint of Officer Jareg's return. She picked through the pencils until she found one with the sharpest point—still glancing at the door every couple of seconds—then quickly snatched the pad of paper. She was now too far in to be able to explain what she was doing if he returned, so, as fast as she could, she lightly rubbed the lead of the pencil over the surface of the paper, starting at the top. The indentations remained white while the surface of the paper turned light gray.

Sadie frowned as it became apparent that the words appearing on the paper weren't in English. They weren't in any alphabet she recognized. Perhaps it was in Filipino since that was Officer Jareg's nationality.

"Biscuits." He may as well have left the note in the office, it wasn't as though she could have read it.

She nearly gave up but decided there was no reason to stop now, and continued lightly coloring the paper. More words showed up white against the gray. None of them could be read, except near the end where some English words were written in list form.

SEABOARD
RYDELL
BAKER
JENSKOWSKI

Sadie said the words out loud. Were they brands of something? Last names? For all she knew they were ports of call—though she'd never heard of Jenskowski, Alaska. Then again, she'd never heard of Skagway either, until she looked up the ship's itinerary.

Remembering she could be caught at any moment, she tore the paper from the pad, folded it in half, and put it in her back pocket, a little disappointed in herself for having been left alone in the security director's office and finding nothing of any significance.

Her eyes wandered to the filing cabinet behind the desk and the pile of papers on top of that cabinet, which led her to thinking about the drawers on the other side of the desk. The sheer possibility of available information created an intense temptation, but coloring on a pad of paper was much easier to justify than going through files. And less illegal. She'd already incriminated herself by telling about breaking into the Chandelier dining room and stealing the seating chart. She couldn't afford to make things worse.

To keep her mind occupied, she pulled the notebook back in front of herself and turned to a fresh page where she sketched out the wine bottle and the gift tag, adding all the details she could remember. When she finished, she cocked her head to the side, rather impressed with her drawing since she'd never thought of herself as much of an artist. She attempted the scrolling letters on the wine bottle but knew she wasn't getting it right. There had been a cluster of grapes in the center of the label, though; Sadie was certain of that because she found it rather cliché.

When Officer Jareg opened the door a few minutes later, she startled slightly, so carried away in her artwork that she'd forgotten about him coming back in. She was instantly aware of the folded paper in her pocket, however, and sat up straighter as though that would somehow keep her from looking suspicious.

"Finished?" Officer Jareg asked as he came around to his side of the desk. He looked at the bottle of wine she'd drawn.

"It's just a rough sketch," Sadie said, her tone caught between pride and embarrassment.

"I'm most interested in the gift tag," Officer Jareg said. "You seem to be the only person who saw it. You say it was written to a Ben and Tanice?"

Sadie nodded. "And a man named Ben with a wife named Tanice died last night." She looked at him expectantly, waiting for him to show the impact of that summation on his face, but he kept a poker face. Did security personnel take a class on that expression like she assumed detectives did?

"What more can you tell me about the tag?"

"Well, it was tied to the bottle with a green ribbon."

"Was it handwritten or printed?"

"Uh, printed, I think. Not many people can write that pretty. The gift tag was brown, like paper-bag brown, with a black border."

"How did you see it so well? It was dark on the deck when the men arrived, and the wine bottle was under the chair, if I'm not mistaken."

"It wasn't very far under the chair," Sadie said, squirming slightly. "I bent down to read the tag. I'm good at remembering details." She almost added that she had past experience as an investigator, but she kind of liked that Officer Jareg didn't know her history. In the past, it had worked against her to have been involved in so many investigations, and she didn't want to add that concern to this situation.

"Did you touch it?"

"I . . . yes, I touched it, but just to see what it said. I didn't know Lorraina's name at that time, but I'd seen her on the ship, as I think my son told you. I thought her name was Tanice after I read the tag."

"So you did touch the gift tag," Officer Jareg repeated.

"Yes, but I had my hand in the pocket of my jacket so I wouldn't mess up any fingerprints."

"Perhaps you loosened the tag and it fell off," Officer Jareg said.

Sadie considered that, but shook her head. "I was very careful, and I don't remember it being loose at all." She wondered if he was trying to come up with a reason so as to spare the accusation of the missing gift tag being put upon his officers. "What is the onboard procedure for chain of evidence? Depending on who had access to the bottle, any number of people could have removed it, accidentally or on purpose."

"Why would they remove it on purpose?" Officer Jareg said, looking back at Sadie's sketch.

She couldn't help herself from adding more to her theory. "Look, the widow of this man isn't brokenhearted by his death. How many couples made up of a Ben and a Tanice are on this ship? I'm sure you've spoken with her, right? She talked about having gone to the coroner's office, and I'm sure she had to arrange for her husband to be shipped home, and through it all she had to have played the role of weeping widow, right? She isn't a weeping widow, I assure you. I think you have enough circumstantial evidence to hold her for questioning. You're holding my son based solely on your suspicions that he might have had something to do with Lorraina's coma. But a man is dead, and my son didn't have anything to do with *that*. Surely Tanice deserves some of your attention in the matter of her husband's death."

He was silent for a few seconds, then met her eyes and gave her a polite smile. So be it, but she had no doubt that as soon as she left this office, he would be on the phone to the federal authorities. Sadie could only hope he would get the go-ahead to detain Tanice before she left the ship.

"She's probably packing as we speak—unless she's left the ship already," Sadie said. "And her cabin is right down the hall."

"This is a police matter," Officer Jareg said, getting to his feet. "I will let you know if we need anything additional from you."

Sadie suppressed a sigh; bureaucracy was such a slow animal sometimes. But she understood the ship wouldn't want to make a big deal about something that might upset the passengers. Maybe they preferred the idea of locating Tanice at the airport in

Skagway—there was only one—rather than making a scene here. Either way, Sadie had done everything she could do—perhaps a little too much, if Officer Jareg's expression was any indication.

Sadie thanked him and left the office, a little frustrated, but content in the fact that she'd done her best. It was a few minutes before six o'clock. She might still have time to hurry to town and see her children before the ship left port.

Sadie didn't think to be worried about passing Tanice's room again until she realized the door was open. She came to a stop several feet away, but to get to the elevators, she would have to pass in front of the open door. The hinges on the cabin doors had springs to ensure they always shut behind the guests. For it to be open meant something was propping it open; the stewards used little wedges as they were going back and forth between the rooms and their carts. Sadie retrieved her phone from her purse. Pete had texted her, but, more importantly, Tanice had called her twice. She turned the ringer back on before returning the phone to her purse and looking at the open door again.

Every second she delayed was less time she'd have to say goodbye to her children, so she raised her chin and told herself she was being silly. Tanice didn't know it was her who had slid the note under the door or answered her phone call. She would call her back in a few minutes.

She had taken a single step forward when Tanice startled her by coming out into the hall. "Hey there."

"Oh," Sadie said quickly as she fell back a step, then cleared her throat. "Hi." She started walking again, but Tanice quickly moved in front of her, forcing Sadie back another step.

"You sure do spend a lot of time up here on deck eleven," Tanice said.

"Well, my . . . um, this is the only access to the security office." She attempted to angle past Tanice on the other side of the hallway, but Tanice blocked her once more.

"What are y'all doin' at the security office?"

"I had an appointment. Now, if you'll excuse me." Sadie's heart rate began to pick up, and she forced herself to take a full breath. She was feeling increasingly threatened.

"Really?" Tanice drawled. She reached into the pocket of her sweat pants, pulled out her phone, and pushed a button. For a moment, Sadie was confused—was she calling security because she felt Sadie spent too much time on deck eleven?

An instant later, Sadie's phone started ringing in her bag.

Chef Ferguson's Stuffed Mushrooms

8 ounces bacon
16 ounces white button mushrooms (can use a larger mushroom, if desired)
½ cup finely minced sweet onion
1 clove garlic, minced
1 (4-ounce) package cream cheese, softened
¼ cup grated Parmesan cheese
Pepper, to taste

Preheat oven to 350 degrees.
Using scissors or a sharp knife, cut raw bacon into small pieces. In a large sauté pan, cook bacon over medium heat until crispy. While bacon is cooking, remove mushroom stems from caps and chop stems into small pieces; set caps aside to use later.

When bacon is done, remove from pan and drain all but 2 tablespoons of bacon grease from the pan. Set bacon aside.

In the remaining bacon grease, sauté onion over medium heat until soft, about 5 minutes, scraping up any brown bits on bottom of pan. Add garlic and cook 30 seconds before adding the chopped mushroom stems. Reduce heat to low. Add cream cheese and Parmesan cheese. Stir until cheeses are melted and ingredients are combined.

Add reserved chopped bacon and season to taste with pepper. Remove mixture from heat and generously stuff each mushroom cap with mixture. Bake for 20 minutes or until mushrooms are soft and filling is hot.

Note: To keep mushroom caps from drying out during the baking process, put caps in a zip-top plastic bag. Add a tablespoon of olive oil and shake bag until caps are lightly coated, being careful not to crush the caps. You can also spray or brush them with olive oil.

Note: Mixture can be made, cooled, and stored (covered) in the fridge for up to two days.

CHAPTER 32

🍓

How 'bout that?" Tanice said while Sadie's ringtone filled the air. "You sounded different on the phone." She pushed a button on her phone and the ringing in Sadie's bag stopped.

The only escape Sadie could think of was to run back to security, but when she looked up at Tanice, it wasn't to see a cocky expression or even an angry one. Instead, she looked almost contrite.

"Would you come inside so we can talk for a minute?" Tanice stepped to the threshold of her room and waved her arm inside. It was a nicer cabin than Sadie's group had booked, and though she admired the size, there was no way on this green earth she was going to go inside with this woman.

"I would rather not," Sadie said as diplomatically as possible.

"Well, I don't much like the idea of talkin' here in the hall."

"Perhaps we could go to the card room or the chapel or something."

Tanice shook her head and ran her fingers through her long thick hair, trailing it over one shoulder. "I'm supposed to get off this ship within the next hour." She lowered her voice. "But I'd like to take that wine with me, and I'm willin' to compensate you for your help with that."

"So you do have a bottle of wine that went missing."

"I tried to bring it on the ship," Tanice explained. "But they took it away and said they would return it when I left. If you saw it, though, then obviously someone else got a hold of it, right? Was it you?"

Sadie remembered hearing something about not bringing alcoholic beverages on the ship. It made sense that if Tanice's wine bottle was found when the bags were scanned, it would be held somewhere. But how would Lorraina have gotten it if it were in a hold somewhere? It made far more sense for Lorraina to have gotten it in close proximity to her room, which was nearby Ben and Tanice's room, than for Lorraina to have somehow gotten it from wherever confiscated items were stored.

"Why did you say you didn't know anything about it?" Sadie asked.

Tanice let out a pretty sigh. "Maybe it's hard for you to understand, but a whole lot has been going on the last little bit. I wasn't thinkin' straight when I first read your note, but now that I've had time to think about it, I really don't have time to have a big discussion. I'm willing to pay a reward for it."

"I don't have it," Sadie said, and watched Tanice's jaw tighten. "A friend of mine found it, and she—"

"Found it?" Tanice interrupted, betraying the tension she was trying to conceal. "Where's your friend? I'll give *her* a reward." She stopped herself, repaired her expression, and then smiled before she continued. "And a little somethin' for you as well, since you helped me track it down."

Did Tanice not realize that *Sadie* knew Ben had died?

"Actually, I was just talking to the security office about it and—"

Tanice jolted and that reaction, combined with what Sadie had overheard by the elevators earlier, convinced Sadie that her hunch was right: Tanice knew there was something wrong with the wine.

A door opened farther down the hall, and Tanice quickly looked over her shoulder.

"Please," Tanice said, sounding more desperate than she had before. "Come on in. I'll keep the door open if it will make y'all feel better."

Sadie debated, but finally nodded. Tanice entered first, which Sadie appreciated since that kept her closer to the open door. She stopped just a few feet inside, not wanting to get any farther than necessary while still ensuring them some privacy.

Once inside, Tancie turned to Sadie, her jaw tightening again. "What did you tell security?"

They stared each other down for several seconds, but Sadie was a master at staring contests, and Tanice finally blinked and looked away. She took a deep breath. "Okay, look, I'm real sorry to say this but your friend *stole* that wine. I don't know how she got in my room, but I paid good money to get the bottle out of the hold. I put it on ice for after dinner and the show, but when my husband and I got back to the room, it was gone. If your friend had kept her hands to herself, she wouldn't have gotten sick."

"How did you know she got sick?"

Tanice blinked, her face turning pale. "You said—" she stammered.

Sadie shook her head. "No, I didn't."

When Tanice didn't reply, Sadie pressed her advantage. "Do you know what I think? I think the wine you smuggled onboard was poisoned. And I think you intended it for your husband."

Anger flared in Tanice's eyes. "I've had a real miserable few months, lady, and it was only fair that he have one miserable week in return."

Sadie considered that. Nothing Tanice had said suggested that she'd expected the wine to kill her husband, but her husband didn't have liver disease. "And yet he died, even without the wine. Interesting."

Tanice's eyes went wide with the realization that Sadie knew about Ben's death. Sadie suspected that Tanice was also mentally reviewing the interactions she'd had with Sadie this afternoon—how very non-widow-ish she'd been acting.

Tanice opened her mouth to speak but obviously hadn't expected this direction and wasn't prepared.

Sadie waited her out, letting the moment grow more and more uncomfortable.

Finally, Tanice put up her hands. "Okay, I'm sure you're judgin' me pretty harsh right now, but people grieve in different ways. I didn't *kill* my husband. You have to believe that I wouldn't do that. We have children; I'm not a murderer." By the time she finished, the arrogant defensiveness had seeped back into her words.

"So the heart attack last night was, what? A happy accident that conveniently happened after your attempt to give your husband poisoned wine didn't work out? That might just make your husband the unluckiest man in the entire world."

"Until this moment I thought him droppin' dead like that was an answer to prayer, tell you the truth," Tanice said, her tone sounding desperate. "Heaven knows I've been prayin' for months for help on how to get that man out of my life. I saw it as a faith healin' . . . of sorts—more for me than him, I guess, but either way, I was free, and I'm not one to look a gift horse in the mouth."

"So, you prayed for your husband to die and yet expect me to believe that you only intended to make him sick on this cruise?"

"I didn't pray for him to die—I prayed for a way out of my misery," Tanice said, taking a step closer to Sadie and lowering her voice. "He's been foolin' around with a woman five years *older* than me. I've spent the last several weeks gettin' my affairs in order and preparin' for the day when I tell him that *he* ain't leavin' *me*. No, I was going to leave *first*.

"This cruise was the last part of the plan. He was gonna get sick, and I was gonna take care of him when he was upchuckin' into the toilet. We've got some friends on this trip with us, and I wanted everyone to see me bein' the best wife any man could hope for—in sickness and in health and all that." Her face was starting to turn red, and Sadie prepared herself to run if escape became essential. "Two weeks from now, I planned to tell him I was leavin' 'cause he was a no-good cheatin' never mind. Our friends would have seen me bein' so attentive on this ship, *before* they learned that he was a complete scoundrel. It's how I was going to preserve my honor when everythin' he's been doin' became the talk of the town."

"And then the wine disappeared," Sadie filled in.

Tears filled Tanice's eyes as she nodded, though Sadie didn't trust those tears for a minute. She'd already witnessed Tanice's mood going from hot to cold at the drop of a hat.

"Everything was going so well," she said, her voice shaky. "I was being the doting wife, and he was smiling like the jerk-faced-dog he is, and then the wine disappeared. I had no choice but to play the part of his arm candy instead of his nurse. I wasn't sure I could pull it off all week long. When he keeled over after the show last night, I took it as a sign from the heavens that they couldn't stand to watch it anymore either. I'm a God-fearing woman and to my mind what happened to Ben was something right out of the Old Testament—a lightning bolt if I ever did see one."

Sadie was processing the information as quickly as she could. "What if the wine *had* killed him? Seems quite a risk to simply hope it would just make him sick and not something worse."

"Ben wasn't a big drinker, just one glass of wine after dinner, that's all. One glass would make him sick, and a glass the next night would make him a touch sicker, and so on. I knew what I was doing." She looked at Sadie as though begging for her understanding.

Sadie felt *some* sympathy for this woman, but not enough to have her change what she knew to be right and wrong.

"You can see why I need that wine back—whatever's left. I'll cover all your friend's expenses for the trip, and yours too if that will help keep you quiet about this. I need to get back to Texas and have a proper funeral for my wanderlust husband, and I need that wine bottle in hand when I get off this boat."

"The wine isn't here," Sadie said.

"What do you mean?" Tanice said, taking a step closer to Sadie, which caused Sadie's muscles to tense. "Where is it?"

"The police in Juneau have it," Sadie said, watching Tanice's eyes go wide while the pallor of her skin went paler. "My friend drank it and went into a coma Sunday night. She's currently in critical care at the hospital in Anchorage. No one knows if she'll recover."

Tanice's mouth fell open as she stared at Sadie, disbelief and shock embedded into her features.

"You're foolin' with me," she said, but her voice was laced with fear.

"I'm not. So you can see why it's hard for me to believe that even though you wanted your husband dead, you didn't intend to kill him with that wine."

"I told you—I wanted him *sick*," Tanice said, her words clipped. "I wanted him humiliated. *That* was my payoff. As it is, I've had to accept the fact that everyone thinks he's going into the ground as an honorable man, instead of the dog he was."

She seemed sincere, but a woman who planned to nurse her husband through an illness she inflicted on him specifically to make herself look doting could surely feign sincerity.

Sadie glanced toward the door, already thinking of the next step of her plan now that she knew what she needed to know. Hopefully, Officer Jareg was still in his office. "I think it would be best if we went and talked to Officer—ooph—"

Sadie's head cracked against the wall and then the floor before she realized what had happened. The instant she figured out she was on the ground, she reached out and grabbed for Tanice, who was in the process of leaping over Sadie's body. She managed to snag the hem of Tanice's pants, sending her into a dive as she fell through the doorway.

Tanice rolled onto her back and kicked at Sadie's head, not holding back an ounce of her strength in the process. Sadie saw stars and was forced to let go of Tanice's pant leg. She rolled onto her stomach and grabbed again. This time she got nothing but air and lunged forward in time to see Tanice get to her feet and bolt down the hall toward the elevators.

"Security!" Sadie screamed at the top of her lungs as she tried to stand, blinking quickly in the hope it would help her head stop spinning. She heard a door open and looked to her right, where a woman with a pink turban wrapped around her head peeked out. "Call security!" Sadie screamed. The woman slammed the door.

Sadie made it to the far wall in the hallway and got to her feet, turning toward the elevators but knowing there was no way she could catch Tanice. The floor was pitching and rolling like they were in open sea instead of in port.

She headed for the security office instead, using the walls to keep her upright as she made her way down the hall. She was a few feet from the curtain when Hazel stepped out.

"Get Officer Jareg right now," Sadie said, her head throbbing. "Tanice is going to try to get off the ship!"

CHAPTER 33

🍓

D o you need more ice?" Pete asked, sitting across from Sadie in the ship's infirmary located on deck four. Sadie didn't remember how she got there.

She *did* remember Officer Jareg finding her in the hallway and asking her what happened. Seriously, she was attacked a few yards from his office; they really needed to get their security finer tuned than this.

She remembered telling him that Tanice was on the run, and then she slumped against the wall, nauseous and hurting. Someone called Pete from her cell phone—three times in a row before he finally answered, they said later—and about the time she realized she was in the infirmary, Pete had arrived, full of concern and questions. The nurse told her she might have a mild concussion, and she was supposed to stay still, sitting up in a very uncomfortable chair, for at least an hour so that the medical staff could keep an eye on her.

"It's fine," Sadie said to Pete. Her head had gone numb several minutes ago. The nurse had held the ice pack in place by wrapping what looked like plastic wrap around Sadie's head several times. It was quite likely a sight to behold, and Sadie was glad not to have to look at it herself. A part of her, though, noted the fact that she wasn't embarrassed to have Pete see her in such a state. That had to be a good sign about how their relationship was developing. "Did they find her?"

"I don't know," Pete said. "The ship's still on lockdown—no one on; no one off."

Sadie remembered him saying something about how the only reason he was able to get on the ship was because security officers had escorted him. The staff told the other passengers that it was a routine inspection of the ship and opened the dining rooms early.

"Are we stuck in port until they track her down?"

Pete lifted both shoulders. "I have no idea. I've been here for a good forty-five minutes, right?"

Sadie nodded even though she wasn't sure. Her head felt foggy, but she wasn't sure if it was because of having been kicked in the head or from the medication they'd given her to take the edge off the pain. "Have you talked to Shawn and Breanna?"

Pete shook his head. "Shawn was there when I got the call, though." He pulled his phone out of his pocket and hit a button. "When I got on the ship, I texted them both, telling them to hold tight, knowing they would want to try to come see you personally."

She didn't want them coming—they both had important things to do right now; it was bad enough for Pete to see her like this. "Will you call them and give them an update? Downplay it a little if you think you can get away with it. They have enough to worry about."

Pete nodded, then stepped out into the hall to make the phone calls.

The ship's engines started to hum, indicating that the ship was about to depart, and Sadie swallowed a lump in her throat as she thought about Breanna and Shawn still in Skagway, watching her and Pete sail away. And Maggie—where was she? Was she okay? Did the fact that they were leaving port mean that Officer Jareg had found Tanice? She'd wanted to ask someone about the possibility of Shawn and Maggie rejoining the cruise, now that they could point at Tanice for the wine—but she knew it was too late. Breanna had booked the hotel rooms, and a federal officer was on his way to Skagway. Revealing Tanice's motives hadn't happened soon enough to make a difference.

Sadie wasn't in a small exam room, rather she sat on a chair in the middle of what looked like the working part of the medical center. There was a stack of files on the far counter and an entire filing cabinet a few feet past that. Knowing information was so close made her wonder what she could learn in this room, and yet there was really nothing on this ship she wanted to know more about. The questions she had about Lorraina, Maggie, and the e-mails Shawn had sent wouldn't be answered here.

She closed her eyes and leaned back, and although she didn't like the fuzzy feeling in her head, it was nice not to feel so bombarded with trying to figure things out. A minor head injury was nothing compared to the satisfaction of knowing the answers had been found. Tanice had poisoned the wine, so of course she found another way to get rid of her husband when her first plan didn't work. Two cases solved—just like that. Tomorrow, the federal officer would get to Skagway, conduct his investigation, which would include the details of Tanice's plan, and know that Shawn and Maggie were cleared. Sadie would see them again on Friday. She took a deep breath and let it out, relieved to know that things were coming together.

She heard a door open and smiled in anticipation of Pete rejoining her, but opened her eyes to see Officer Jareg instead.

He attempted a smile as he walked toward her while she sat up straighter.

"How are you feeling?"

"Fine," Sadie said. It wasn't necessarily true, but she expected that she felt as well as she could under the circumstances and figured he had more important things to worry about right now. "Did you find her?"

He shook his head. "She may have gotten off the ship. We've alerted the airport and charter pilots."

"But she still might be on board," Sadie summed up.

"If she is, she'll be found. People cannot hide on this ship for very long. We will be making up posters and talking to the staff so they know to watch for her. We are unable to stay in port any longer; there are tight schedules, not just for us but other ships as well." Apparently nothing was more important than keeping the cruise going unhindered. "I don't believe you are in any danger, if you are worried about that. She has nothing to gain from hurting you now."

Strange how that didn't make her feel much better. She liked Officer Jareg and his staff, but she didn't feel that they had Sadie's best interests in mind. At the same time, she didn't know what Tanice would gain from coming after her either. If she were still on the ship, her only goal would be to get off of it, right?

"I spoke with Mrs. Jefferies's steward, and he admitted to getting her wine out of storage and later coordinating with another staff member to remove the tag from the wine bottle to hide his breach of policy."

"Will he lose his job?"

Officer Jareg paused, and Sadie suspected he was considering what he could, and should, say. "When you are at sea for months at a time, trust is essential. We know that things happen, unfortunate things, and we have to deal with them strongly to keep other staff from feeling there are any allowances. You understand."

Sadie nodded. She did understand, but she also knew how important these jobs were to the staff. If the steward had had any idea the impact that wine bottle would make, he'd have thrown it off the ship.

"I wanted to ask you some additional questions," Officer Jareg said as he pulled a stool on castors out from under a desk and sat down a few feet away from her.

"Okay."

"Has your son been on any other cruises to your knowledge?"

She bristled automatically but remembered Pete's concern regarding this line of questioning. "No, but I would know if he had been on other cruises. He's a college kid, and I talk to him all the time."

"But you did not know he was in Tennessee with Ms. Juxteson," Officer Jareg pointed out.

Sadie bristled even more and took a breath. "He's not a frequent cruiser. Why does any of this matter?"

"What about Ms. Lewish—do you know if she's attended other cruises?"

"I have no idea," Sadie said, trying to puzzle this out but knowing her brain wasn't in top form. "But I believe she told the police in Skagway that this was her first cruise. Why is this important?"

The door opened and Pete came in, shutting the door softly behind him before approaching them. Officer Jareg stood and they shook hands while he updated Pete on what he'd just told Sadie, though he left out the new line of questioning and didn't answer her question about why he'd asked about other cruises.

"I'll be sure I'm with her whenever she goes anywhere just in case this woman is still on the ship and has some kind of vendetta," Pete said. "Is Sadie medically stable enough to sleep without supervision tonight? We're staying in separate rooms."

"I'll be fine," Sadie said, not liking the idea of a babysitter. To prove her point, she stood and thought she did a really good job of hiding how much the room spun once she got to her feet.

"Let me have the nurse give her another assessment."

Sadie sat back down while Officer Jareg called the nurse in from another room. The attendant removed the ice pack and looked at Sadie's eyes, checked the swelling on her head, and had her complete a few exercises like following her finger and walking in a straight line.

"She'll be fine," the woman said, smiling at Sadie. "You must have a very hard head."

Sadie glared at the smile on Pete's face, but he didn't remove it as he took her hand. "Do you need anything else from us?" he asked Officer Jareg.

"I will contact you if I do. I hope you get some rest and feel better in the morning."

The remainder of the evening was a somber one, and though Sadie wasn't hungry, she sat across from Pete in the Tiara Room and picked at her food while they took turns updating one another on the details of what they'd done that day. There weren't many surprises, though Pete asked to see the paper Sadie had taken from Officer Jareg's office. He read it over, then handed it back without comment.

"I think Tanice's admission will go a long way toward clearing Shawn and Maggie," Pete said. "Of course it would be more effective if the ship's security team had Tanice in custody to verify everything."

"I'm sorry I let her get away," Sadie said.

"You didn't 'let her get away,' and I wasn't being critical, I just meant that it's always more effective when someone gives an official statement. Still, when I left the police department, the mood had changed, and they were treating both Shawn and Maggie more like information resources rather than persons of interest. I think things are going in the right direction. The police should be getting more test results from Anchorage in the morning as well. Did you know there are several different types of cyanide? Maggie works with one specific type, and if they can prove the cyanide in the wine isn't the same as the kind she works with, we'll all breathe easier."

"So what do we do tomorrow?" Sadie asked. She was relieved things were going well, but feeling a bit sorry for herself all the same. "We had planned to do all this investigative work, but we've already solved the mystery of the wine."

"True, but there might be more information coming out about that—we won't know until we get there." Their waiter came by and Pete ordered dessert; Sadie didn't bother.

"I asked my contact about all the questions regarding whether Shawn or Maggie had been on other cruises, and he said they're wanting to make sure the things that have happened on this ship aren't related to things that have happened on some other ships— but he doesn't know exactly what those things might be and admitted it might be nothing. I guess they have an entire department devoted to mitigating liabilities and that seems to be the group heading things up. Maybe it's nothing."

Nothing but the reason Pete wanted them to stay on the ship. Sadie kept her teeth clenched until the temptation to say that out loud went away. Everything seemed to be compiling in her head, depressing her more and more by the minute.

The plastic wrap had flattened her hair; she could feel it in the lack of movement whenever she turned her head, but attempting to revive her hairdo made her wince due to the tender spots on her skull. The people at the table next to them had had too many drinks and were talking and laughing really loudly, which was making her head hurt worse. She was ready for bed.

"Sadie," Pete said, reaching his hand across the table and putting it over hers. "They're okay."

She stared at his hand as tears sprang to her eyes. She tried to pretend it was the pain medication, but that wasn't really true. She'd gotten on this ship with both of her children, she'd learned hard truths, and now she'd left them behind. They might be cleared tomorrow, but how would Sadie even know that?

"They're okay," Pete repeated.

"I know that," she said, wiping at her eyes with her free hand. "But I'm not sure I am. I've failed them in so many ways on this trip."

"That's not true."

"It is," Sadie said, finally meeting his eyes. "Shawn didn't tell me about Lorraina, and I've been no help to Breanna with the wedding. You've been the rock—you're the one they've listened to. You're the one who's been there when Shawn needed someone. You're the one who's kept *me* level and sane. You've slid so perfectly into exactly what I wanted you to be, and in the process, I feel like I've crumbled." She looked at the plate of uneaten food in front of her. Saying so much of her heart out loud made her feel vulnerable.

"Crumbled?" Pete said. "You found the woman who brought poisoned wine onto the ship and discovered what put Lorraina in a coma. Your kids know, without a doubt, that you are here to back them up. No one is faulting you for being emotionally caught up in this, Sadie, and you've been remarkable in forgiving Shawn, embracing Maggie, and supporting both Breanna and me. You've failed no one."

She was embarrassed at his words because it felt as though she'd solicited the compliments, which wasn't what she'd meant to do. It had to be the pain medication; an unmedicated Sadie wasn't so self-indulgent.

"Sadie."

She looked up at him again.

"We love you."

"I know that," she said, wishing she'd kept her thoughts to herself. "And I'm sorry. I think it's the meds making me all funny in the head. I should probably turn in. I didn't sleep well last night and all this is catching up to me."

"Want to go look at the stars?"

She almost shook her head, but then she looked at him and felt his love and acceptance wash over her. Though she didn't know why she'd said all she'd said, she didn't doubt the sincerity of his assurances. "Are you sure you aren't tired of me yet? And I don't just mean this cruise—all I've done since we met is complicate your life." There went those meds again!

"And given me purpose," Pete said. He stood from the table, her hand still in his, and came around to her side, leaning down to kiss her on the lips in front of all these people. "You breathe energy into my world," he whispered, so close she could feel his breath move over her face. She felt the words down to her toes. He pulled her to her feet and smiled at her. "Come look at the stars with me. There is nothing better we can do right now than be together."

CHAPTER 34

🍓

Sadie slept fine, probably because of the pain medication she'd been given, but woke up with all the stress of the day before running through her head, which still ached terribly. Despite the tender reassurances Pete had reminded her of last night, there were still some dark thoughts that wouldn't leave her alone.

How had things gone in Skagway for Shawn and Maggie? Had they learned anything about Lorraina that could answer any of the many questions building up about her? Had Breanna been able to reach a compromise with Liam and his mother on the wedding? Were her children having a good, healthy breakfast?

She took a shower, wincing at the tender spots on her head—one in the back, and one just a few inches from her left temple—then did her hair and makeup. This morning, her gray-and-white hair made her feel old, and she wondered why she'd ever stopped coloring it. But then her hips felt bigger than ever as she pulled on her jeans, and her tummy felt pudgier, too. Maybe it was just one of those ugly days where she looked like she felt, and the best part of the day would be falling asleep at the end of it. She missed her children and worried about them—two things she couldn't turn off.

Her interest in Glacier Bay National Park, where the ship was headed today, was almost nonexistent. Though learning about Tanice's tampering with the wine bottle was good, knowing Tanice was still possibly hiding on the boat somewhere was less than comforting.

She met Pete for breakfast—not at the buffet—and then they went up on deck to see the forests that stretched out for miles and miles on either side of the bay. A ranger from the Glacier Bay National Park had gotten on board at some point and began speaking over the intercom about the unique features of the area. He pointed out the animals that he spotted on shore or in the water—a brown bear that Sadie and Pete took turns looking at through Pete's binoculars, lots of puffins with their colorful beaks, and even a pod of humpback whales that surfaced enough to spray water before going underwater again.

As they continued forward, Sadie saw more and more chunks of ice in the water. The ranger explained that the glacier at the far end of the bay was always "birthing" icebergs and ice shards, but assured the passengers that modern technology gave them the ability to see the larger pieces far enough away that the ship could avoid them. And none of the icebergs were anything like what the *Titanic* encountered. That was good to know.

It was all very interesting and beautiful, but Sadie couldn't help but picture Breanna sitting in a hotel in Skagway instead of being a part of this portion of the trip. Sadie didn't share her thoughts out loud, though. She didn't want to bring Pete down with her, especially after all the sweet things he'd said to her last night.

They had lunch in the Good Times Café and then went up to deck thirteen in time to see the glacier that gave the park its name. They got within a quarter mile of the huge mass of ice and snow and rock. Parts of it were blue, which the ranger explained was due to such intense compression that all the other colors reflected back, leaving the blue behind. What sounded like a crack of thunder was followed by an avalanche of ice—more bergs and shards birthed into the ocean. After half an hour of seeming to stand still, the ship proceeded to turn and head back out of the bay.

More animal sightings kept passengers on deck far longer than some of them should have been; too many people obviously hadn't prepared for the cold temperatures. Sadie and Pete, however, were outfitted with gloves and boots and warm jackets. Sadie had even brought a knit hat, though she knew once she put it on she'd have to commit not to take it off until she could fix her hair immediately upon its removal.

"So," Pete said when they'd gotten their fill of the sights of nature and wildlife. "What now? How are you feeling?"

"I'm feeling fine," Sadie said, trying to ignore the dull throbbing in her head. She'd managed to forget about Tanice being on the ship somewhere, and the sheer forgetting of it made her a little more nervous when she recalled the information. "I think I'd like to take a nap, though. Would that be okay? It feels strange to want to do something so . . . relaxing, but it does sound nice."

"Of course it's okay," Pete said with a chuckle, giving her a quick sideways glance. "I'll walk you to your room. Maybe I'll go to the casino."

Mention of the casino made Sadie realize she hadn't seen Mary Anne or Jen today. As opposed to the first day, Sadie no longer had an interest in doing any of the onboard activities but hoped the two women were having a good time, wherever they were.

At the door to Sadie's room, Pete gave her a kiss and Sadie promised to meet him in time for dinner. She felt a little bad about not spending every minute she could with Pete, and yet she appreciated the comfort of it as well. The fact that they didn't need to spend every minute in each other's company felt like a positive step in their relationship.

Sadie shut her door, removed her outerwear, and noticed the message light blinking on the cabin phone. It couldn't be a message from Pete; she'd been with him all day. She crossed the room and sat on the edge of the bed to pick up the handset and push the button. It was Officer Jareg asking her to come to the security office when she was able.

Sadie scrambled to find her shoes in a flash. What had Officer Jareg learned? Would her children be meeting her in Ketchikan tomorrow?

She didn't want to wear the Ugg boots she'd worn on deck—they made her feet sweat—so she went to the closet, pulling open the door and then screaming when someone stared back at her.

"Don't freak out!" Tanice said.

Sadie backpedaled into the bathroom door with a hand on her chest.

Tanice stood up from where she'd been crouched in the closet and put out her hands, palms out. She was wearing an oversized sweatshirt and jeans and had her hair pulled back in a ponytail. "Please, please, please don't freak out. I just need to talk to you."

"What are you doing in my room? How did you get in here? How did you know this was my room?"

"I got in the same way your friend probably got that bottle of wine from my room—the steward propped the door open while he was working on the room. When he went to the cart for linens, I slipped in here," Tanice explained. "And you gave me your cabin number on that note, remember?"

Sadie glanced at the cabin door, weighing her options, but the open closet door was in the way of her retreat, and she didn't dare look away from Tanice for long.

Tanice continued. "Look, I'm sorry about yesterday, okay? Really sorry. I just kind of lost it, but now I've had some time to think things through, and I think you might be the only person who can help me figure out what to do next."

Sadie considered this and, specifically, the help Tanice could be in fully clearing Shawn and Maggie if she told her side of things to security. "Go sit on that bed," she said, pointing to Breanna's bed.

Tanice nodded; Sadie pulled close to the bathroom door to make room for Tanice to pass by her in the tiny hallway. Tanice sat on the edge of Breanna's bed with her hands in her lap, as humble as a Sunday School student.

Sadie shut the closet doors, took a breath, and then stood close to the cabin door, determined to keep a steady eye on Tanice this time. She had already found this woman to be tricksy, and she had the headache to prove it.

"Did your friend *really* go into a coma from drinkin' that wine?"

Sadie nodded and Tanice's face paled. "Really? A coma? 'Cause it wasn't supposed to be *that* strong. I hated my husband, but I didn't want to kill him." She raised both hands to her face. "I can't believe this is happening. It should just have made someone sick." She looked at Sadie again. "Was she really old? Or really young?" Her face went even paler. "Oh, please tell me she wasn't a child. Oh my gosh, I'm going to throw up." She put a hand over her mouth and rocked back and forth slightly.

Sadie simply continued to watch her.

Finally Tanice stopped moving and dropped her hand from her mouth. "Was it a child? Did I put a child into a coma? 'Cause I double-checked the amount I put in that bottle, and it should only have killed someone who had health problems or someone who weighed less than seventy pounds."

Sadie went back and forth on what to say, or whether to say anything at all, but the torture on Tanice's face was impossible to ignore. "She had a bad liver," Sadie finally said, crossing her arms over her chest. She liked that she was standing and Tanice was sitting.

Tanice let out a heavy breath and put her hand to her chest as tears came to her eyes. "Oh, thank heavens," she said, her voice shaking. She then looked at Sadie, abashed. "I don't mean that like it sounded. I'm not glad this happened—I'm horrified by the whole thing—but my friend Joan said that if it can be proven that I didn't intend death, I might get a better deal from the DA." She closed her eyes and dropped her chin while putting her hands on her head and bracing her elbows on her knees. "I can't believe this is happening. Mama told me I shouldn't do it, but I was so determined to make Ben pay for what he'd done that I did it anyway. And now someone's in a coma."

"What kind of cyanide did you put into the wine?" Sadie asked, determined to build this case any way she could.

"Cassava root. My brother works with a company that has a hub in Peru. He got me some of the raw root. It's typically processed into—"

"Tapioca," Sadie cut in. "The processing destroys the cyanide." Tanice's brother brought her the cassava root, and her mother warned her against doing this but didn't make her stop? What kind of family was this?

Tanice looked surprised but nodded. "I put such a small amount in the wine that one glass of wine for two nights would be enough to make a grown man like Ben miserable for a few days, but not affect him so much that he'd even think to go to the doctor. He said doctors were for pansies anyway." She lifted her hands to her head again. "What will happen to my kids?"

"How many children do you have?" Sadie asked. *And you wanted to make their father deathly ill?*

"Two boys," Tanice said, her chin quivering. "I called them from port yesterday to tell them what had happened to Ben, and they fell apart. I told them I'd be home as soon as I could. I had a charter ready that was takin' me home last night. I'd be there by now if I'd made that flight, but then I couldn't get off the ship. My friend Joan let me stay in her room, but she's terrified they're going to find me and she'll be in trouble too. I don't have anywhere to hide. What am I going to do?"

"There's only one thing you can do, Tanice," Sadie said, keeping her arms crossed and watching the other woman closely. It was this part of their conversation yesterday that had spurred Tanice to run, but Sadie was ready this time. She could roundhouse this woman in point-two seconds if it came to that. "You have to go to security and tell them what you've done. Right now, they think you killed your husband *and* poisoned Lorraina. Running off like you did didn't help your case at all."

CHAPTER 35

🍓

They'll never believe me. People don't believe in lightning bolts from the Old Testament anymore, and if I admit to putting the cassava in the wine, they'll suspect I killed Ben—just like you do. And what if your friend doesn't get better?"

"There's no other way out of this," Sadie said, shaking her head and allowing a sympathetic expression. "I'm sure they're doing a full autopsy on Ben now, so they'll find the cause of death. If they can't tie it to you—if it was something other than the cassava—you can't be charged with his death. But honesty is your only hope."

"What if I end up in prison?"

Sadie thought Tanice would, and should, face charges. Her choices couldn't be undone. She also wasn't convinced that Tanice *hadn't* killed her husband, despite the assurances she'd tried to offer. "If you go in voluntarily and explain what you did, why you did it, and why you ran, I can promise things will be better for you than if they find you. And they *will* find you. They've put up posters throughout the staff quarters on the ship. You can't hide here."

"You're probably right," Tanice said, her shoulders slumping.

"Joan let me stay in her room last night, but it was a fright trying to hide from her husband in that tiny space. I can't do that again."

"I have a meeting with Officer Jareg right now," Sadie said. "Why don't you come with me?"

Tanice looked up at her, absolutely terrified. "Right now?"

"Why wait? This won't be easy, you know that, but the sooner you do the right thing and get a lawyer, the sooner you'll see your boys again."

Tanice started crying, and Sadie's instinct to comfort her was hard to ignore, but she did ignore it. This was a woman who'd tried to poison her husband and had given Sadie a concussion. Sadie needed all the distance she could get.

"Come with me," Sadie said after several seconds had passed. "I'll explain to Officer Jareg what's happened."

Tanice was terrified of being discovered before she turned herself in and she wanted to make sure she got the full benefit of taking the initiative, so she wore Sadie's knit cap and sunglasses as they made their way up to deck eleven. Sadie feared Tanice would run at any moment, but they reached the security office without incident. Sadie opened the door and waved Tanice in first.

Entering a moment later, Sadie could see right away that Hazel recognized her companion despite the glasses and hat. She was already on her feet, while Tanice looked around nervously.

"Hazel," Sadie said, drawing the young woman's attention to her. "Will you please get Officer Jareg?"

Hazel nodded and hurried around her desk and down the hall, either forgetting she had a phone or not wanting to be overheard by using it. Seconds later, quick heavy footsteps caused Tanice to tense up. Sadie put a hand on her arm and whispered that it was going to be okay.

As soon as Officer Jareg appeared, Sadie explained that Tanice wanted to turn herself in.

"Of course," Officer Jareg said, doing an excellent job of hiding his surprise. He put a hand out toward Tanice. "Come with me, please."

Tanice nodded and headed down the hallway. Officer Jareg stayed close behind her but looked over his shoulder at Sadie, who was following a few steps behind. "You wait in my office, alright?"

Officer Jareg led Tanice into the room at the end of the hall marked "Staff Only," and Sadie was able to share a quick look of encouragement with Tanice just before the door closed.

Once she was gone, Sadie leaned against the wall, closed her eyes, and let out a deep breath.

"Are you alright?"

Sadie looked up at Hazel. "I'm fine, just . . . a little overwhelmed. I'll be in Officer Jareg's office."

She expected to be kept waiting a long time while Officer Jareg questioned Tanice, but he returned in just a few minutes.

"Are you alright?" he asked when he sat down. Though Sadie had some complaints about the security team on the ship, she couldn't fault their kindness. She appreciated the sincerity of his sympathy.

"I'm fine," Sadie said. "And I'm relieved she decided to turn herself in. It helps my children, right?"

"I believe it will," he said.

"I can come back after you've questioned her—"

He shook his head. "No, she is comfortable and secure. I will talk with her later. I have important things to discuss with you first."

"Okay," Sadie said, but she still felt that Tanice ought to take priority.

A smile stretched across Officer Jareg's face. "I am pleased to tell you that your son has been cleared by the police and will join the ship in Ketchikan tomorrow. I believe he—along with your daughter and Ms. Lewish—will fly to Ketchikan first thing tomorrow morning."

"Really?" Sadie said, putting a hand to her chest and leaning forward. "They're cleared?"

Officer Jareg nodded. "There may be more questions, of course, depending on what happens with Ms. Juxteson, but they no longer need to stay in Skagway or be under the watch of the local or federal police. They have been very cooperative."

"Of course they were," Sadie said. As though her son would be anything but cooperative.

"The cruise line would like to cover the cost of their flight to Ketchikan."

"That's very generous. Thank you."

"And Captain Bormere has extended you a five-minute call from our satellite phone if you would like to talk with them."

Sadie's heart jumped. "Oh, that is wonderful!"

"However," he said, bringing his hands forward and putting a form on the table between them. Sadie braced herself. "We would like for you to sign this nondisclosure form which simply says that you will not discuss any of what has happened with other passengers or with the media or any other person. We work hard to ensure the safety of our guests, and in this industry, reputation is everything. Therefore, we would like your agreement not to use this information in any way that could be damaging to us."

Sadie looked at the form he pushed across the table and scanned the first paragraph enough to know that the language was quite technical and filled with words and terms she didn't understand. It was the type of document a lawyer should review before she signed it. And yet, the carrot he was dangling in front of her was a great big, juicy one. She looked up and met his eyes. "I get a *ten*-minute phone call with my children and my entire group gets a free shuttle to the airport when we disembark in Seattle on Sunday." The price they charged for shuttle service was exorbitant.

"Okay," he said.

"And I get half a dozen chocolate-covered strawberries delivered to my room at turndown service tonight."

He held her eyes, but his expression was amused. "You are a tough woman."

Sadie shrugged. "Take it or leave it."

"I'll deliver the strawberries myself."

Sadie was giddy as she signed the form and pushed it back to him. He took it, scanned her signature, and nodded. "I will get the satellite phone prepared."

CHAPTER 36

Sadie tried to call Shawn's cell phone first, but it went straight to voice mail. Had she remembered to pack his charger when she packed his things for the stay in Skagway? She called Breanna next and held her breath until she answered.

Sadie explained that she had ten minutes.

"I'll get Shawn," Breanna said.

A moment later, Shawn was on the line. "Mom?"

"Hey, buddy," Sadie said, feeling all warm and fuzzy to hear her name on his lips. "I can't wait to see you tomorrow."

"Me either," he said, and Sadie's warm fuzzies went through the roof.

"Did you guys learn anything about Lorraina?"

"I got in touch with Lorraina's older sister last night. Her name is Dot. I met her when I went out in December."

She was Shawn's aunt. Sadie was trying to find words for a response when Shawn continued. "Dot's the one who encouraged Lorraina to put me up for adoption so that both of us could have a better life. Only one of us did, though—she gave me details today that Lorraina never did."

"What did she say?"

Shawn went on to explain the difficult life Lorraina had after being a sixteen-year-old mother without her child. She had bouts of drug use, difficult relationships, and had struggled to remain employed. Sometimes Dot—who was more like a mother to Lorraina since their own had died when they were young—went years without knowing where Lorraina was. Each time Lorraina resurfaced though, Dot would help her. She believed Lorraina battled both depression and issues left over from a difficult childhood.

"But finally, about five years ago, Lorraina realized that she was making every wrong decision if what she wanted was to be happy. She went back to Tennessee and worked toward her recovery from the alcohol and drugs. And she started talking about finding me."

"So she *did* want to find you," Sadie said. She had mixed feelings about that and felt horrible that she was unable to be fully happy for Shawn.

"She did, but Dot said she was so afraid of rejection that she didn't dare risk it . . . until she got sick."

Sadie's heart dropped. Her illness *was* the motivation, then? "Because of the transplant?"

"I think that's part of it," Shawn said. "But Dot said it was also because Lorraina knew she might have limited time. In fact, it wasn't until February, when she took a bad turn, that she talked to Dot about being tested. Dot's the one who organized the testing for everyone else—except me. Lorraina told Dot that she didn't want to talk to me about it because she was worried I'd think that's why she found me."

"Oh," Sadie said, feeling her guilt rising. Had she really wanted to believe the worst about this woman?

"She got really sick, spent a weekend in the hospital, and was taken off her antidepressants because her liver could no longer handle them. Dot said after that, Lorraina started pulling away, becoming secretive—like she had before. Dot worried she was drinking again, but if that were the case, Lorraina would have been really sick. Meanwhile, none of Lorraina's other relatives who were tested were a match."

"When did all this happen?"

"Late March," Shawn said. "Before Lorraina found Maggie."

Sadie pondered that for a moment. "Lorraina didn't think helping her would be enough motivation for you, did she?"

"And she was right," Shawn said softly.

"No, it wasn't until after Maggie showed up so conveniently that you really began to question Lorraina."

"But she was still right," Shawn said.

"She also tricked Maggie into thinking she was her birth mother," Sadie reminded him. "I don't want you to blame yourself for any of this, Shawn. She obviously wasn't well, mentally or physically."

"I know that," Shawn said. "But at the root of all of this is the fact that Lorraina didn't find me originally because the potential rejection was more than she could take. I don't agree with the way she went about several things, but I think the fear of finding me and losing me again kind of took over, especially once she was off her meds."

"But that isn't your fault," Sadie said again.

"I know, Mom," Shawn said, sounding frustrated. They both paused and he took a breath. "I'm not blaming myself, okay? I'm just processing it. There's a lot to work through."

"Yes, there is." Sadie had to bite her tongue to keep from telling him how wonderful and nearly perfect he was, that everything would be okay, and that he'd done everything exactly right. Breanna's words from the other day came back to her: *You are in charge of yourself*. Shawn had made choices he was now responsible for. Sadie couldn't change any of that, and she wouldn't know how to change it even if she could.

"They ran those compatibility tests they drew blood for yesterday, and for the round of testing they did, I'm a match."

"For Lorraina's transplant?" Sadie slumped back in the chair. They were going to cut her baby open?

"I'd have to go to Anchorage for further testing, and they can't do anything unless she improves a little more, but the doctors want to know if I'm willing to do the further testing. They want to know—if everything lines up—if I'll donate."

Sadie was quiet as she absorbed that information.

"What should I do, Mom?" Shawn asked. "Talking to Dot answered a lot of questions and helped me not to see Lorraina in such a bad light, but . . ."

Sadie's throat thickened, and she blinked back tears. Shawn was asking her opinion—he was asking her as his mother. He trusted the advice she would give him, which meant she had to dig deep for the wisdom he deserved. "You go to Anchorage," she said softly, hoping her voice wouldn't catch. "You do whatever you can to do the right thing. And if it ends up that you can donate, and that she's well enough . . ."

Shawn was quiet so long that she wondered if her answer had surprised him. "You really think so?"

"You could save her life, and she gave you yours. But I suspect you already knew all of this. You don't need my permission to do the right thing."

Shawn let out a heavy breath. "Yeah, I guess I wasn't asking for your permission, Mom, but I wanted your support."

"And you have it. Fully."

They were both quiet again until Shawn spoke. "Well, Bre has some news for you, too, and I guess I need to make a phone call. Love you, Mom. Thanks."

"Love you, too, and you're welcome."

Breanna got on the line a few seconds later. "Crazy, huh?" she said.

Sadie tried to chuckle at the understatement but the sound came out as more of a grunt. "Completely crazy, but good. Shawn's handling it okay?"

"I'm actually really impressed with how he's dealt with all of this. You told him to go to Anchorage, right? I wasn't listening in."

"Of course."

"I knew you would, but I could also see that he couldn't make the decision until he talked to you. It's a good thing you're so awesome."

"Oh, well, thanks for that," Sadie said, a little flushed at the compliment she wasn't sure she deserved. "How's Maggie doing with all of this?"

"Ironically, now that they know they aren't related, Shawn's been a lot nicer to her. After talking to Dot, Maggie kind of lost it again—this has been so hard for her—but Shawn helped her pull herself back together. They went for a long walk last night and talked about who knows what, but when they came back, Maggie gave me a big hug and assured me she was going to be okay—that she could see God in this and she'd be stronger for it."

"I'm so glad," Sadie said. "And she's coming to Ketchikan with you guys, right?"

"She wasn't sure if she wanted to, but I talked her into it. Even though we aren't family, I think we're good for her right now. She seems most nervous about seeing you again, though. Did you guys have a fight or something?"

"Kind of," Sadie said, feeling sorry again for what she'd said yesterday. "But I'm glad she's coming to Ketchikan. It will give me a chance to make things right."

"Good," Bre said. "I'll tell her you said that."

"I'd appreciate that. And you can remind her about how awesome I am in the process—that might help my efforts."

Breanna laughed.

"How are things with the wedding?" Sadie asked. It had been more than ten minutes, but Officer Jareg hadn't come back, and she wasn't going to hang up a second before she had to. With how much the cruise charged for Internet, she felt sure they could afford this phone call.

Breanna was quiet for a minute. "I gave in."

Sadie straightened. "What?"

"We had the conference call last night—well, it was morning for them—and Liam did a great job of standing up for what we wanted. He even threatened the whole elope-to-Monaco scenario."

"But you gave in?"

"Remember how you told me to figure out her motivation? Well, I asked her about that and she talked about when she married Liam's dad. There were a lot of ugly feelings because she was an American and the earl's family was so traditional back then. She's always hated that her wedding was treated as an almost underground event—against family, against everyone's wishes. When they remarried, the earl was still really sick and, again, it was a small, quiet event. She was really sincere in explaining that she wanted something different for us, and as I listened to her, I realized that even if everything was exactly the way I wanted it to be, it wouldn't mean as much to me as the production of it would mean to her."

Sadie was stunned but didn't want to waste any of her precious satellite minutes with surprised silences. "You're really okay with that?"

"I am," Breanna said. "Liam's worried that I was just worn down by everything, but I assured him I wasn't. I should have talked to her in the beginning; that's a lesson I definitely learned through all of this."

Breanna did sound like she was at peace, but Sadie worried that she was being a martyr. "It's still your wedding, Breanna. And it's not a bad thing to want it your way. I don't want you to regret this."

"I want Liam," Breanna said simply. "And he wants me, and that's all that matters to us. Really, Mom, it's okay—you don't need to worry about me. Liam's mom agreed to let me wear the dress I picked out, and I made her promise to let you help with the rest of the plans."

Sadie made a face. Trying to help a woman with obviously strong opinions and an unlimited budget sounded miserable. Sadie's homemade coffee-filter garlands would look a bit out of place in a Church of England cathedral. But it was Breanna's wedding, which meant Sadie would do everything she could to be a part of it.

"I'm glad," Sadie said just as Officer Jareg came back into the room. "It looks like I'm out of time, but I'm so glad I got to talk to you both. And I'll see all three of you tomorrow, okay?"

"Yep. Don't enjoy having Pete to yourself too much."

"Oh, stop it," Sadie said, blushing slightly. "Love you guys."

"Love you, too."

She hung up the phone and tried to swallow the lump in her

throat. She couldn't wait to have her family back around her where they belonged.

"I have just one more question for you," Officer Jareg said after moving the phone out of the way.

"Okay," Sadie said.

"I read through your notes. This woman, Mary Anne—she is the one who told you that Mr. Jefferies died at the buffet?"

"I assume Mr. Jefferies is Ben?"

Officer Jareg nodded.

"Yes, Mary Anne said she and her husband were at the buffet when Ben collapsed, but she's not the one who told me his name— that was Jen. I don't know her last name."

"Which one said that he *died*?"

Sadie thought back over the conversations she'd had with both women. "Um, I'm not sure, really. I think they both said that he'd died. No, wait—Mary Anne said he'd died; Jen hadn't known for sure."

"Of a heart attack? How did either of them know that?"

"I don't know, but that is what happened, right?"

"Yes," Officer Jareg said. "But Mr. Jefferies didn't pass away in the buffet. He was taken to the infirmary and treated. He died several minutes after that. The passengers were told nothing about his condition, and in order to preserve the sensitivity of the situation, we have answered questions only with the fact that he got off the ship in Skagway. I am concerned that passengers are learning of this death. That will be a very difficult thing for everyone, you understand."

"I haven't told anyone," Sadie said, thinking back to the nondisclosure form. Should she have read it more closely? Was she being backed into some kind of corner?

"No, no, I am not worried about that. You and your party have been very discreet. I am concerned, however, that these women have been telling people this. I would like to talk with them. Do you know their cabin numbers?"

"Jen is in room 991," Sadie said. "I know Mary Anne's husband spends a lot of time in the casino and was going to be a part of the blackjack tournament. His name is Glen."

"Very good," Officer Jareg said as he wrote some notes. "I will see if I can find them."

"If I see either of them, I'll tell them to contact you."

"That would be helpful. Thank you."

"Of course," Sadie said as she stood. They shook hands across the desk, and she left the security office feeling as though the air was clearer and the sun was brighter, even though the cloud cover made it impossible to see the sun. She barely missed a step when she came around the corner and saw the door to Tanice's room, but reassured herself with the knowledge that she may never need to see that door again.

With a little luck, she was done with the security department on this ship.

CHAPTER 37

♥

Sadie felt the need to take a little time to meditate on all that had happened, and since Pete was probably still in the casino, she made her way through all the levels until she found an area off deck five that was empty. She hurried back inside long enough to call Pete's room and leave him a message about what had happened and where he could find her if she didn't answer her cabin phone, then she returned to her little corner and let the beauty of the shoreline wash over her.

It was colder here in the bay than it had been anywhere else, but she had her new pink "Alaska" jacket on and gloves for her hands. Knowing that her kids were okay and would rejoin her in the morning gave her an entirely new outlook and made the chill of the air less noticeable.

During the therapy sessions she'd taken after her emotional breakdown last year, Sadie had learned a powerful imagery exercise that she found helpful in letting go of things. With the mountains around her and the worst of this trip behind her, she was in a perfect position to purge the yucky things from her mind and rediscover a foundation of peace.

She began by spending a few minutes thinking about Shawn and all the hard things associated with him this week: knowing he had a secret, feeling hurt by his distance, and learning about Lorraina and the fact that he'd told Sadie nothing about the journey he'd taken to find her, let alone that he'd shared Christmas with her. He'd told Breanna. He had planned to tell her the truth on this trip, and when he did, the surprise had nearly ruined everything. He hadn't been very nice to Maggie. She listed everything she could think of that she'd been unhappy about—he was eating too much at the buffet; she really didn't like the Afro look and wished he'd grow out of it—every little thing.

When she'd thought through everything, she imagined all those thoughts being surrounded in a huge bubble. The bubble trapped all the negative energy she'd put into those thoughts, containing it. She closed her eyes and pictured the bubble floating in the air just in front of her. Then she took a deep breath and blew the bubble away. She took another breath and blew it even farther from her. She imagined the bubble getting farther and farther away with each breath from her lungs. Eventually she could imagine having blown it out of sight, up into the atmosphere, through the ozone, and into space where it kept going and going until it became a star somewhere within that sea of stars she could only see at night. She could never know which star were those thoughts.

As silly as the practice seemed when she'd first learned it, she'd found it to be very helpful since then. All those negative things with Shawn were beyond fixing, and holding onto them would just weigh her down.

When she finished the negative bubble, she thought of all the wonderful things about Shawn: he was loving, he was compassionate, he was two classes away from finishing his degree. He worked hard, he gave the best hugs, he and Breanna were good friends, he respected Pete, he appreciated truth. He was attractive and strong. He was ambitious and kind. He had an entrancing smile. That list went on and on and on until she felt on the verge of tears at how wonderful her son was.

She closed her eyes and surrounded all those things with a bubble—a pink bubble because for her pink had always been a happy color. She pictured this bubble hovering over her head where it popped, raining down all that wonderful goodness about her son where it was absorbed into her skin and hair and heart.

She wiped at her eyes as the feelings overcame her. Shawn was *her* son and had been since the day she brought him home, and perhaps even before that if one believed in a world before this one where families were formed in advance. Shawn loved her and, even through this hard experience, their relationship was okay. That was impressive.

She went through the bubble exercise with Breanna, who hadn't been as connected to Sadie in recent years. Sadie processed all the hard feelings left over from the separation. She let go of her fears for Breanna's future, and her dual disappointment that Breanna would likely live the rest of her life on another continent and that she wouldn't have a wedding that would show Sadie's stamp of "Mother of the Bride."

Sadie sent that bubble way up into the stratosphere, then worked through all the wonderful things about Breanna and let those seep within herself. There were bubbles for Pete and Maggie too, leaving Sadie grateful for them both and determined to make things better with Maggie as soon as she had the chance. Then Sadie had to process through the last pair of bubbles—Lorraina.

"She *is* Shawn's birth mother," she said out loud. "She is Shawn's *birth* mother. *She* is Shawn's birth mother."

No one doubted that anymore. Lorraina shared something with Shawn that Sadie did not and never would. Sadie hated that. But it was the truth. And if not for Lorraina, Shawn would never be here. Lorraina could have terminated her pregnancy, or she could have kept him, or she could have even waited a few extra days to put him up for adoption, which may not have sent him to Neil and Sadie's home.

But Lorraina gave Sadie a son, and regardless of the difficulties her reconnecting with Shawn had created, she was the same then-anonymous woman Sadie had thanked God for in her prayers for years. All those years, she'd been praying for Lorraina. Did she want to take those prayers back? Was the impact Lorraina had made on Sadie's life up until these last few days diminished by what Sadie had learned since then? That was an easy question to answer.

Sadie filled a bubble full of all the insecurity, anger, resentment, and jealousy Lorraina's presence had triggered. Then she blew it away, up, up, up until it became a star far away in the heavens. The pink bubble for Lorraina then filled up, and that one made Sadie cry more than any of the others had, because without the ugly thoughts, the good that Lorraina had done was so very good.

Sadie filled up that bubble and then burst it over her head, putting her arms out and her face up so that the feelings cascaded over her like a waterfall. She didn't want to miss a single one.

Who was to say that the heart-wrenching decision sixteen-year-old Lorraina had made to give her child up for adoption hadn't haunted her? Learning she was dying despite being barely forty years old, being taken off the medications that gave her a stable mind, feeling that her only child, whom she hadn't been able to raise, didn't care enough to save her life—those were heavy burdens for anyone to carry. And the ending was not written yet and might not be a happy one. Lorraina deserved Sadie's gratitude and forgiveness. She deserved the acknowledgment of greatness for the part she had played in *Sadie's* happiness.

"Everything okay?"

Sadie turned, her arms still outstretched, and saw Pete standing a few feet away with his hands in his coat pockets, looking at her with concern. She smiled and closed the few steps between them. She wrapped her arms around his neck and give him a big kiss smack-dab on the lips.

"Everything is wonderful," she said after squeezing him tight and taking a step back. "Did you have a good time in the casino?"

He eyed her curiously. "Not as good a time as you've had, it seems. What exactly did the nurse give you for pain control?"

Sadie hooked her arm through his elbow. "Who needs medication when you know your kids are okay and you have a dashing man at your side?"

"You talked to Shawn and Breanna?"

"I did," Sadie said and happily filled him in on all the details. What had been a fifteen-minute conversation took almost twenty minutes to relate because she had to add all her thoughts along the way.

"What a relief," Pete said. They had left Sadie's little hiding spot and were strolling along the deck.

"And I helped Tanice turn herself in."

Pete did a double take. "What?"

It took another twenty minutes to explain how all of that had happened. Pete was impressed, and Sadie gave his arm a squeeze. "So, how was the casino?"

"Good. I made almost two hundred dollars, which sounds paltry compared with everything you accomplished in the last two hours."

"Oh, stop it," Sadie said with a playful slap, though she liked the praise. "Did you really win two hundred dollars?"

"I did," he said with a nod. "Which is why I made reservations for us to eat at the Bistro."

"Isn't that the one with the $30 cover charge?"

Pete grinned. "Seeing as how I'm rolling in the dough, and we apparently have a lot to celebrate, it seemed only appropriate to ignore my frugal ways—which balk at the idea of buying a meal when I can eat for free—and spend my winnings on the best meal available and to share it with the most beautiful woman on this ship."

Sadie blushed but grinned widely. Had she started this day feeling frumpy and old? Pish-posh. This was the best day ever!

They had a fabulous dinner of lemon-zucchini fettuccine, which Sadie was determined to replicate once she returned home, and all the crusty French bread and tangy tossed salad they could eat. They were going to order dessert, but Sadie remembered the chocolate-covered strawberries waiting in her room; she had to have limits somewhere. They went to the show—another Broadway review—which was very good, and after the show, she and Pete returned to their spot on deck thirteen-aft and ate every one of those strawberries.

It was super-cold, but a little snogging now and then helped keep them from hypothermia, at least for a while.

Lemon-Zucchini Fettuccine

2 large boneless, skinless chicken breasts
2 lemons, divided

¹/₄ cup plus 3 tablespoons olive oil, divided
2 tablespoons red wine vinegar
1 tablespoon kosher salt
2 medium zucchini
Salt and pepper
5 to 6 cloves garlic
8 ounces fettuccine
Fresh basil (about ¹/₂ cup)
Fresh oregano (about ¹/₄ cup) or about 1 tablespoon dried oregano
1 cup grated Parmesan cheese

Prepare grill. You could also do this on the stove top in a skillet or a grill pan.

Place chicken in a zip-top bag with the juice of one lemon, 2 tablespoons of olive oil, and the red wine vinegar. Seal the bag and gently squish the bag to make sure the ingredients are incorporated and surrounding the chicken. Set aside for 15 to 30 minutes.

In a large pot, bring water with about 1 tablespoon of kosher salt to a boil. While waiting for the water to boil, slice the zucchini in half lengthwise. Drizzle with 1 tablespoon olive oil and sprinkle with salt and pepper.

Press or finely mince garlic cloves. In a small saucepan on the stove, place ¹/₄ cup olive oil and add garlic. Turn the burner to medium-low heat. It shouldn't be popping and frying, the oil should just slowly warm, infusing the oil with the garlic and removing that zing fresh garlic has.

When the water is boiling, add the pasta.

Remove the chicken from the bag, and salt and pepper both sides. Place the chicken and zucchini on grill.

While the chicken and zucchini are grilling and pasta is boiling, chop herbs and prepare the cheese. Zest both lemons and juice the one that hasn't been juiced.

When the zucchini and chicken are done, remove them from the grill. Allow the chicken to stand for 5 minutes and then chop the zucchini and chicken.

Reserve about $1/2$ cup of pasta water. Drain the pasta and immediately place in a big bowl. Place the chopped zucchini and chicken on top. Add lemon zest, lemon juice, cheese, herbs, and the garlic-olive oil mixture.

Now take some tongs and give everything a big toss. If you feel it needs more moisture, add a little of the pasta water or a little more olive oil.

Garnish with a little more Parmesan on top and another squeeze of lemon if you have any left.

Serves 4 to 6.

Tip: When cooking garlic, it's important to keep an eye on it to make sure it's not getting brown and crispy because it cooks very quickly and can become bitter.

Serving Suggestion: Chop any leftover oregano, basil, and garlic and add them to softened butter to serve with crusty sourdough bread. Add a tossed green salad.

CHAPTER 38

🍓

On the way back to their rooms around 10:40 that evening, they passed several passengers carrying plates heaped with chocolate desserts, reminding Sadie that tonight was the famous Chocolate Fiesta on deck twelve.

Sadie had just eaten half a dozen chocolate-covered strawberries and she had a stomachache, but miss something like this? Never.

The lights were low when they entered the buffet; lucky for them, the fiesta was wrapping up. Sadie could only imagine the mob that had descended when the buffet first opened. A few of the featured items, like the triple chocolate mousse and the black forest cake, were gone, but there were still cream puffs and fudge and a Baked Alaska with a chocolate cake base.

Sadie had never made Baked Alaska, and had only had it when it was made in a pie crust, which she hadn't loved, but after sharing a slice of the cake-based treat with Pete, she changed her opinion of the dessert. The way the textures and flavors of the different parts blended together was delicious and unique. She wondered how the recipe would work as a cupcake; since working with Lois in her cupcake shop in New Mexico, Sadie had experimented with several new and interesting cupcake recipes. A Baked Alaska cupcake could be fun. Lois would love it!

"I guess we don't dock in Ketchikan until one o'clock tomorrow afternoon," Sadie said when they waddled out of the buffet half an hour later. "Is there anything you'd like to do in the morning?"

"When I was in the casino, they announced a final qualifying round for the blackjack tournament tomorrow morning. I was thinking about signing up."

Sadie thought of Mary Anne's husband who seemed to spend all his free time in the casino and tried to hide her frown. Glen was likely a gambling addict, and yet Pete had spent a good portion of his free time—of which Sadie admitted there had been very little—doing the same thing. Should she be worried?

"Sadie?" Pete asked. "You don't like that I'm gambling?"

"My mother thought face cards were evil."

"And your father taught you to play with M&M's instead of money."

Sadie whipped her head around to look at him. "How did you know that?"

"Breanna told me when we went to the casino together the other day. Your brother taught her and Shawn to play, you know. She's pretty good, and I think she left with an extra twenty bucks in her pocket."

"Jack taught them how to play?" Sadie shook her head. "What a sneak."

"I know when to quit, and I've never had a problem with it."

Sadie nodded, feeling silly. "Can I watch? Just to make sure I can stage an intervention if you need it."

Pete chuckled and leaned in to kiss her cheek. "You can be my good luck charm."

"I'm surprised they're still doing qualifying rounds. The tournament must be coming up quick; the cruise is almost over." Maybe Sadie would see Mary Anne there and could relay the fact that Officer Jareg wanted to talk with her, assuming he hadn't caught up with her before then.

"I guess one of the winners dropped out so they opened up another round at ten tomorrow morning, which is when the tournament was originally scheduled. The tournament itself was pushed back to eleven."

They'd reached deck eight, where Sadie's cabin was located. Without her children around, they had no chaperones—no one to keep them honest with what they did or where they slept—but the very idea made Sadie blush. It was just a few more months until Breanna's wedding, then she and Pete could start their future knowing they hadn't compromised their values during the long, and often arduous, wait to be together.

"What's the tournament prize?" she asked Pete.

"Five hundred dollars *and* a mug with a picture of the ship on it."

Sadie gasped and put a hand to her chest. "A mug? You're kidding me, right?"

"No, ma'am," Pete said with a slow shake of his head. "A *mug*. For real."

"Well, I don't know how you would ever live with yourself if you *didn't* play in that qualifying round. I just hope your heart isn't broken if you don't win that mug."

"I'm so glad you can see things my way."

Baked Alaska

1 quart of ice cream, softened (strawberry is traditional)
1 egg
2 tablespoons water
⅓ cup sugar
¼ cup all-purpose flour
¼ cup unsweetened cocoa powder
⅛ teaspoon baking powder
Dash of salt

Line a 1-quart round bowl with plastic wrap, allowing some to hang over the edge of bowl. Spoon softened ice cream into bowl, spreading until level. Freeze overnight (or at least 4 hours, until firm).

To make the cake, preheat oven to 350 degrees. Grease a pie pan with nonstick cooking spray. Cut a round of waxed paper to fit bottom of pan and place in pan, then spray with nonstick spray again.

In a medium-sized mixing bowl, beat egg, water, and sugar together for 3 to 5 minutes, until sugar is dissolved. Mix remaining dry ingredients in a small bowl with a whisk. Sprinkle dry mixture over egg-sugar mixture and fold together until just combined. Pour mixture into prepared pie pan and bake for 12 to 18 minutes or until cake begins to pull away from the side of pan. Invert onto cooling rack to cool and remove the wax paper.

Once the cake has cooled completely, increase oven temperature to 475 degrees.

To assemble the dessert, return cooled cake layer to pie pan. Remove ice cream from freezer and invert onto cake layer (if the ice cream is sticking to the bowl, press a warm kitchen towel against bottom of bowl). Remove plastic wrap. Cover ice cream and cake with meringue, swirling decoratively, being sure to cover ice cream completely.

Bake for 4 minutes or until lightly browned. Slice into wedges and serve immediately. Cover and return any leftover slices to freezer.

Serves 8.

Meringue

4 egg whites
½ teaspoon vanilla extract
½ cup sugar

Whip egg whites until frothy. Add sugar and vanilla. Continue beating, adding sugar slowly, until whites are stiff and glossy.

Baked Alaska Cupcakes

2½ cups all-purpose flour
3 teaspoons baking powder
½ teaspoon salt
¾ cup shortening
1½ cups sugar
3 eggs
2 teaspoons vanilla
1¼ cups milk
2 quarts ice cream, softened

Preheat oven to 350 degrees. Place paper baking cups into 2 muffin pans (48 cups). Spray paper cups with nonstick cooking spray. (Be sure to use liners on this recipe!)

To make cupcakes, mix flour, baking powder, and salt in medium bowl; set aside. In large bowl, beat shortening with electric mixer on medium speed 30 seconds until smooth. Gradually add sugar, scraping bowl occasionally until well combined. Add eggs, one at a time, beating well after each addition. Add vanilla. On low speed, alternately add flour mixture, about ⅓ cup at a time, and milk, about ½ cup at a time, beating just until blended.

Divide batter evenly among muffin cups, filling only ¼ full. Bake 10 to 14 minutes or until toothpick inserted in center comes out clean. Cool 5 minutes in pan, then 15 minutes on cooling rack.

Spread 2 heaping tablespoons of softened ice cream on each cupcake—it should reach the top of the cupcake liner. Cover. Freeze at least 2 hours or overnight, until ice cream is hardened.

When ice cream is solid, preheat oven to 450 degrees.

Spread meringue over ice-cream-topped cupcakes, covering surface of ice cream completely. Place finished cupcakes on cookie sheet.

Bake 2 to 3 minutes or until meringue is lightly browned. Serve immediately.

Makes 48 cupcakes.

CHAPTER 39

🍓

The next morning, they finished breakfast then headed to the casino to get Pete signed up for the qualifying round. Hopefully it wasn't already full.

"I'd like to play a few practice hands," he said after they learned there were still a few open spots. "Do you mind signing me up?"

"Not at all," Sadie said. She headed over to the table under the sign "Tournament" and asked for an entry form.

"Passenger or Seaboard Club member?"

Sadie's mind jumped to the paper she'd taken from Officer Jareg's office and the list of English words written at the bottom. Seaboard had been the first word in the list. Could it be a reference to the Seaboard Club?

"Ma'am?" the staff member asked, bringing her back to the moment.

"Sorry, um, I'm not a member of the Seaboard Club." Were the other words or names on that list something similar—programs or groups? She'd have to ask Pete what he thought.

"This is the form you want then," the staff member said, handing her one of the forms. "And here is some information about the

Seaboard Club; it's our frequent cruisers program and membership gives you substantial discounts for many on-ship amenities."

"Thank you," Sadie said as she took both papers and then scanned the room for somewhere to sit. The scan stopped when she saw Mary Anne sitting at one of the window seats on the starboard side. Sadie made her way toward the older woman and said hello.

"Oh, hello," Mary Anne said, standing up to give Sadie a hug. She still had that silly purse, and yet somehow it fit her personality. She was wearing a turquoise top with wispy purple flowers attached to it along with a pair of khaki pants. She wore a sun visor on her head despite the fact that the onboard paper had warned them about rain. "What are you doing here?" Mary Anne asked when she pulled back.

"Pete's going to compete in the blackjack tournament, or well, the final qualifying round, I guess."

"Really? Is he any good?"

"He seems to be," Sadie said. Was it her imagination that Mary Anne's smile fell just a little bit? "He made a couple hundred dollars yesterday and took me to the Bistro for dinner."

Mary Anne's smile returned full force. "Glen has made over twelve hundred dollars," she said proudly. "I think they would ban him from the casino if they could, but they can't—we checked."

"Wow," Sadie said, feeling defensive of Pete's winnings, which Mary Anne had just pooh-poohed. Pete wasn't spending twelve hours a day in the casino like Glen was, either. "Isn't Glen already qualified for the tournament?"

"Of course. That's why I'm here. I never miss a tournament," Mary Anne said. "He's the top winner with over eight thousand dollars."

"He won eight thousand dollars!" Hadn't she just said it was $1,200?

"No, no, no," Mary Anne said, shaking her head but seemingly pleased to be able to explain. "In the tournaments you play with the casino's money. The person with the highest total in each qualifying round gets to compete in the final tournament, but they don't get to keep the winnings."

"Oh, right," Sadie said. She wished she'd asked Pete how it all worked so she wouldn't have felt foolish.

The final qualifying round was announced—it would start in fifteen minutes—and Sadie remembered the entry form in her hand. "I better hurry and fill this out, then," she said, reaching for her shoulder bag only to realize she'd left it in her room that morning and simply put her ship-card in her back pocket. She turned toward the tournament table where she remembered seeing a whole container of pens. "I'll be right back, I need to get a pen."

"I have a pen right here, dear," Mary Anne said, opening her purse. "I always keep one in my pocketbook." She pulled out her rectangular wallet and shifted her purse so she could pull open the snapped closure. Then she flipped open her wallet and pulled the pen out of the leather strap that held it in place. It probably would have been faster for Sadie to get a pen from the tournament desk.

In the process of retrieving the pen, however, Mary Anne fumbled the wallet and dropped it. Sadie immediately bent down to pick it up. As she was standing back up, she glanced at Mary Anne's driver's license, then did a double take. It read "Mary Anne Parkinson Rydell." As Sadie read the name a second time, she pictured the notepaper she'd taken from Officer Jareg's office yesterday:

SEABOARD

RYDELL

BAKER

JENSKOWSKI

She had thought "Seaboard" was part of the list when she'd seen it two days ago, but what if, instead, it was the *title* of the list and simply missing the proper punctuation? The other words on the list could be last names; and Mary Anne's was on it. By the time Sadie was fully upright, she'd been able to repair her expression.

"Your last name is Rydell?" she asked as she handed the wallet back. "Isn't that the name of the high school in the movie *Grease?*"

Mary Anne took her pocketbook back. "I don't care for that film," she said. "I was in high school in the '60s and that show made us all look like a bunch of sex-crazed ninnies. We had values back then, not like the young people today."

Sadie forced a smile while Mary Anne put the pocketbook back into her purse and handed over the pen. For a moment, Sadie couldn't remember why she needed the pen because her thoughts were back in Officer Jareg's office, pondering on that note. She snapped out of it and went about filling in the information on the form while her head spun with more questions. Her eye fell on the brochure for the Seaboard Club the tournament attendant had given her. "So, you were saying the other day that this is your second cruise of the year. You don't belong to the frequent cruiser club, do you?"

"Oh, yes," Mary Anne said. She sat down on the bench and moved her purse onto her lap. "Glen and I have been a member of the Seaboard Club for two years now. We've cruised four times a year since then."

"Oh," Sadie said. What she wouldn't give to be able to read

Filipino and therefore know the context of the note. A quick glance at the staff members in the casino, however, told her that there were plenty of people on the ship who could tell her what the other words of that note said. Assuming she could find someone she could trust not to turn her in for stealing the information in the first place.

"Um, what are the benefits of belonging to the club?"

"Well, you get free upgrades on your rooms," Mary Anne said. "And a flat ten percent discount in all the shops on board the ship, plus all kinds of other perks, like discounted shore excursions. And some of those on-ship tours regular passengers have to pay for are free for us to go on, though not all of them. And then, of course, each trip we get twenty free tokens to get started on the slot machines and half price on the tournament entries—that's Glen's favorite part."

"Oh, I was meaning to tell you," Sadie said as though she'd just remembered, when in truth she was curious to see Mary Anne's reaction. If she had something to hide, she wouldn't like hearing that Sadie had talked to Officer Jareg about her, right? "The security department would like to talk to you about the conversation we had about the guy who died at the buffet."

"Oh, they already did," Mary Anne said, waving it away. "I pretended I couldn't understand their accent. They should have native English speakers in those kinds of positions anyway."

"Oh," Sadie said. Mary Anne didn't seem the least bit worried. "Is that all they talked to you about, then?"

"How should I know? I couldn't understand a word they said." She laughed while Sadie tried to keep her own smile in place.

A voice came over the intercom. "The final qualifying round will start in ten minutes. There are still three spots left. Please sign up at the tournament desk."

"I need to hand this in," Sadie said before she filled out the last portion of the paper, then hurried back to the registration table and gave the attendant her ship-card so he could charge the entry fee to her room. He gave her a paper with the number five written in black marker and told her to put it on the table.

Mary Anne had walked over to Glen, who was already sitting at the table reserved for the qualifying rounds. He was playing even though he was already the top qualifier from another round? Why?

Sadie headed toward the table on the far side of the casino and stood behind Pete's chair. He was up $75 but stood as soon as the round was finished, thanked the dealer, and put his chips in his pocket.

"Thanks for signing me up," he said to Sadie as they moved toward the qualifying table.

"Sure thing," Sadie said. "Um, just as a reminder, you're an attorney whenever Mary Anne is around. Have you met Mary Anne?"

Pete shook his head and so Sadie took a few moments when they arrived at the table to introduce him to Mary Anne, who, in turn, introduced both of them to Glen.

Glen was bald on top, with glasses and jowls and a white button-up shirt a shade brighter than the undershirt beneath it. He hardly looked the part of a card shark, but perhaps that was the secret of his success. Luckily, no one asked about Pete's occupation during the exchange. Pete wished Glen good luck, but Glen didn't say it back; he was watching intently as the dealer shuffled the decks of cards that would be used in the game.

"Glen already qualified," Mary Anne bragged, her hands on Glen's shoulders since he hadn't stood up for the introductions. "But we'd love for him to beat his score—the *high* score, by the way. Glen's a master blackjack player."

"Well, then, it will be a pleasure to play with someone with such skill," Pete said, offering his hand to Glen. It took a few seconds for Glen to notice Pete's hand there at all, but Pete just smiled and waited.

When Glen took his hand, he jumped slightly, then looked up at Pete with a little more interest.

"Good luck to you," Pete said before letting go of Glen's hand.

Glen mumbled, "Good luck," and flexed his hand slightly—the way Sadie did after encountering someone with an extremely firm handshake.

"What was that about?" she whispered to Pete as they returned to his seat.

"Just a little friendly intimidation," Pete said. He took his seat and smiled when Mary Anne glanced his way—as though they were best friends.

"Wow," Sadie said. "I didn't realize you were so competitive."

"I'm not," Pete said. "But neither do I like to be deemed an easy win. Trying to beat his own high score and can't even be bothered to be gracious to his wife's friend? That's obnoxious."

"Remind me never to be ungracious," Sadie said.

Pete winked at her. "Consider yourself warned."

"By the way," Sadie said a moment later, leaning down so she could whisper in his ear. "Remember that paper I took from Officer Jareg's desk with the list of English words at the bottom? I think it's a list of last names of people who all belong to the Seaboard Club. Glen and Mary Anne's last name is Rydell, which was the first of the three names on the list."

Pete understood the significance of that right away. "Really?"

Sadie nodded and explained about Mary Anne's retelling of how she'd responded to the questions security had asked her. "Weird, right?" she said when she finished.

Pete looked down the table at Glen and Mary Anne.

"Players, please take your seats," the announcer said into a microphone. "We will begin the final qualifying round as soon as everyone is in position."

There was no time to discuss it. Mary Anne was standing behind Glen, who sat in the seat second from the end, while Sadie straightened behind Pete, who was in the fifth position of the six players. The sixth seat was taken by a lanky young man who Sadie wasn't convinced met the age requirement.

Sadie found herself focusing on Glen as the dealer continued to prepare the table. He was incredibly focused, and the game hadn't even started yet. Sadie put a hand on Pete's shoulder, and he gave the backs of her fingers a kiss before taking her hand in his and holding it. Sadie continued to watch Glen and Mary Anne while pondering what the list could mean and at the same time reminding herself of what she'd thought when she'd first taken it—that the information on that paper could have nothing at all to do with her interests. And yet, what if it did? She hoped she wasn't becoming some kind of masochist who was subconsciously addicted to the drama of chaos.

The announcer explained the rules: each player would start with $500 in chips, the dealer stayed at seventeen, splits and double downs were allowed, no touching any other players or spectators during the game. Sadie let go of Pete's hand and took half a step back. Though Sadie had never gambled as an adult and wasn't a fan of the gambling industry as a whole, she was glad to know enough about the game to be able to follow along.

The players placed their bets and then the dealer dealt each player their first card, facedown. He dealt his second card faceup—the queen of hearts—and then went around the table, tapping in front of each player who then signaled whether they wanted another card or not. Pete stayed on sixteen, and it turned out to be a good move, since the dealer busted a minute later. Only Pete and Glen doubled their chips on that round.

The cards were cleared and another hand was dealt. This time, Pete split eights, busted on one but got a twenty on the other one—a tie with the dealer, which meant he didn't lose his second bet, but he didn't win anything either. One other player also got a stay, but everyone else lost their bets.

Two more rounds, both of which Pete won, put him above the rest of the players.

Sadie was impressed with how well he was doing, but continued thinking about the significance of Mary Anne's last name being on that note. Maybe she'd won some kind of promotion? Maybe she owed some dues? Sadie needed someone to read that note so she could put her thoughts to rest, if nothing else.

She glanced over at the dealer—his name tag indicated he was from Indonesia. He wouldn't be able to read the note, not that Sadie had the note with her; she'd left it back in her room. She looked toward the registration table. The staff member who had helped her with Pete's paperwork was idly tapping his pen and didn't seem very into the game. He could be Filipino.

It was risky to ask, and Sadie didn't want to miss watching Pete play so she gave up on the idea for the moment and turned back to the blackjack table.

Pete's stack of chips was twice the size of anyone else at the table. One of the players was already out, and two of the remaining five players were down to half a dozen chips or less. During the next three rounds, both of those players busted out, leaving Pete, Glen, and the young man next to Pete who didn't look old enough to play.

Pete seemed to be the least intent of the three, but was clearly winning. Glen looked downright angry, which Sadie found somewhat amusing until she looked at Mary Anne, who stood behind him. Her eyes were narrowed behind her glasses as she watched every move of the dealer just as intently as any of the players did. It was an unexpected reaction. From everything Mary Anne had said about Glen's gambling, she'd never insinuated that she was into the game much. Seeing her now, however, had Sadie questioning that impression. There were no players in the chairs between Glen and Pete, though quite a crowd had formed around the table.

Sadie moved around the spectators between them in order to get close to Mary Anne. "Do you ever play?" she asked.

Mary Anne didn't seem to realize Sadie was talking to her for a few moments, then she glanced up. "No," she said, keeping her attention squarely on the game. "And I thought your boyfriend didn't play much."

"He doesn't," Sadie said. The older woman's hands were clenched in fists as she watched both Glen and Pete place their bets. Pete slid half his chips into the betting circle; he was obviously feeling confident.

The dealer dealt the first card—a ten of hearts—and Sadie held her breath. He went around the table to see who wanted additional cards. Pete's cards totaled twelve—a jack and a two—so he tapped the table to indicate he wanted another card. He got the nine of spades, and Sadie clapped with the spectators. It looked pretty well decided that Pete would win this round.

Within two more hands, only Glen and Pete were left, but Glen was down to ten chips and he looked angry to the point of having flushed cheeks.

Glen was all in with his next bet. Pete matched his bet chip for chip, but compared to how much he could have bet, Pete's wager was conservative. They both lost, which meant that Glen busted out of the game and Pete was the winner of the round despite holding a losing hand.

The announcer came over and counted out Pete's chips. "Eight thousand five hundred dollars for Mister Peter Cunningham, who now takes the number-one spot in the tournament, which will start in twenty-five minutes."

The spectators cheered. Well, everyone but Mary Anne and Glen, who were already walking away. Sadie felt bad that they were disappointed, but their behavior struck her as very poor sportsmanship.

Since there was a twenty-five minute wait until the final tournament, Sadie wondered if now was the best time to find someone to read that note. She really wanted to stop worrying about what it said. If the names had been chosen at random from all the Seaboard Club members and would be featured in some article for the next magazine put out by the cruise line, Sadie would feel bad for all her concerns regarding the Rydells' inclusion on the list.

The announcer handed Pete a clipboard and asked him to write his name in one box and sign his name in the box beside it. Pete took the pen and entered the information.

Sadie glanced over his shoulder as he was finishing and then grabbed the clipboard out of Pete's hands.

"Sorry," Sadie said, her eyes trained on the paper on the clipboard. "But does that say Benjamin Jefferies?" Sadie pointed. The top name on the list had been crossed out with a single line. She had to make sure her eyes weren't playing tricks on her.

"I'm sorry, ma'am," the announcer said, taking the clipboard from Sadie, who had to let go.

Pete had said the casino was holding another qualifying round because someone dropped out. But Ben Jefferies didn't drop out—he'd dropped dead.

"Make sure you are in your seat on time for the tournament at eleven," the announcer said to Pete before turning away.

Pete thanked her, then took Sadie's hand and steered her toward the exit. "What was that all about?" he asked as they left the casino.

Sadie had been counting the seconds for the opportunity to tell him.

CHAPTER 40

S adie explained about Benjamin Jefferies's name on the clipboard,
then about how intense Glen and Mary Anne had been about
the game. She also voiced her suspicions that they may have known
Ben Jefferies had had a heart attack even though they shouldn't
have—Sadie couldn't remember for sure what Mary Anne had said
that morning when she first told Sadie about it. She should check
her notes.

"So what are you saying?" Pete asked when she finished.

Sadie sighed. "I don't know. That everyone I meet is a homicidal
maniac, I guess. I'm seeing too much in things, aren't I?"

They reached the stairs, and Pete let go of Sadie's hand and put
his hand on the small of her back instead, guiding her up the stairs.
"I don't know, there have been a lot of questions about people having
been on other cruises. Maybe there's a pattern that the cruise line is
seeing that we don't know anything about. Maybe the list is about
that. Maybe there's more going on than a poisoned bottle of wine
and a cheating husband."

Having Pete support Sadie's vague theories gave her confidence.

"There's got to be someone on this ship who will read the note for us," Pete continued. "That would at least tell us where to start, though I suppose we should probably go to Jareg with it."

"What about your contact on the medical staff?"

"He's from the Netherlands; he wouldn't be any help."

"Your tournament starts in twenty minutes," Sadie reminded him. "And shouldn't someone keep an eye on the Rydells, just in case? Oh, wait!" Sadie came to a stop on the stairs as she remembered Henry from the computer center. She suspected he was already breaking a rule by studying during his shifts, and he worked alone in an isolated area. No one would see him talking to them. "I didn't bring the note with me, but I think I know who to take it to."

After getting the note out of her room, they headed to deck five, and Sadie held her breath as she opened the door to the computer center. Prior to today, she'd been concerned about the long hours the staff seemed to work, but this time she was grateful to see Henry behind the desk, just as he'd been when she'd met him the first time.

"Hello, again," Henry said when she entered. There was a woman at one of the computers and Sadie eyed her carefully as she and Pete approached the desk. She didn't want anyone to overhear their conversation.

"Hi, Henry," Sadie said, smiling. "This is Pete." The two men nodded in greeting, but Pete stayed a half a step behind Sadie, giving her the lead. "I was wondering if I could ask a favor." She spoke quietly enough that he had to lean forward to hear her.

"If I can help you I will be happy to."

Sadie pulled the note from her pocket and slid it toward him. "Could you translate this for me?"

He scanned it, and she watched an expression of concern grow on his face. After a moment he looked up at her. "Where did you get this?"

"You can read it?" Pete asked.

"It's Tagalog," he said, looking between them with a nervous expression. "But yes, I can read it."

"Please," Sadie said. "It's important."

The other woman in the center logged off of her computer and stood. "Thank you," she said, giving Henry a little wave. Henry told her she was welcome. They all breathed a sigh of relief when the door shut behind her.

"I could get into big trouble. The rules are very strict on the ship."

"No one will know you helped us," Sadie assured him. "But it's important that we learn what this says."

Henry looked at the note, but wasn't softening.

"Would it help if we told you what we think it says?" Pete offered.

That was a good idea. Henry nodded, relaxing a little bit.

"I think it says that someone with one of the last names on this list"— she pointed at the names on the paper—"is a member of the Seaboard Club and is suspicious somehow, or needs to be watched or something like that."

Henry looked at the paper again. "Yes, it does say that, but it says more." He looked toward the door and then up at her. "I can lose my job for this. It is . . . sensitive information."

"A man died two nights ago—" Sadie began, knowing she was taking a risk by sharing the information, but stopped when Henry's eyebrows went up.

"Someone died? On the ship?"

"You didn't know that?" Sadie asked. "I assumed the staff would know."

"We know what we need to know for our positions," he said, keeping his voice low.

Sadie considered that, and then continued. "I'm sorry, but it's really important that we know what this note says. I won't tell anyone you helped me."

Pete spoke up as soon as Sadie finished. "We think the note talks about other cruises these people were on and that there might be some kind of pattern—perhaps other deaths."

Henry looked between her and Pete, then back at the paper as his expression changed to one of surrender. "It says there have been some deaths on other cruises and that the company has investigated and found that these persons"—he pointed to the list of names— "were on every cruise where someone died. And they all belong to the Seaboard Club. It says to wait for more information before speaking with anyone, but to watch these persons, specifically when they get on and off the ship. More information will be provided before the cruise ends so that the persons can be secured if necessary when the ship returns to Seattle."

Sadie could feel her heart rate increasing.

"Does it say how many deaths?" Pete asked.

"No, just that there are others—more than two."

Sadie pictured Glen and Mary Anne's intensity at the qualifying round earlier. She thought of how angry Mary Anne had been when Pete had won. She felt the blood drain from her face as she spun around to face him. "Ben was the top winner in the tournament before he died," Sadie said, grabbing Pete's shirt. "But now *you're* the top winner in the tournament. You're beating Glen!"

Pete took her hand and gently pried her fingers off his shirt. He smiled slightly, remained perfectly calm, then looked past her to Henry. "Henry, could you do some research for us?"

"What kind of research?" he asked carefully, but the fact that he was asking at all showed some willingness.

"Can you find more information on the other deaths this note is referring to? It would be on other Seven Sea cruise ships, probably over the last few years."

"Two years," Sadie said, remembering the detail Mary Anne had mentioned offhandedly. "That's when the Rydells joined the Seaboard Club."

Henry pulled open a drawer and grabbed a pen and paper. He wrote down some details, then looked up at Pete for more instructions.

"We need to find out, specifically, if the people who died on the other cruises spent much time in the casinos."

Henry furrowed his brow, and Pete nodded. "I know, it's a detail that might be hard to find, but can you try? If we're right about this, you'll be helping to capture a serial killer."

CHAPTER 41

●

"Steer clear of them," Sadie said to Pete as they entered the casino. She'd tried to convince him to drop out of the tournament, but he insisted on keeping his spot in order to keep an eye on Glen and Mary Anne. The final round would start in just five minutes. "Don't drink anything, don't sit next to him—nothing. And make sure you lose—the sooner the better."

"I know," Pete said. "You'll check with Officer Jareg first, right?"

Sadie nodded. Their plan was for Sadie to call Officer Jareg, but if he wasn't available, she would try to get into Mary Anne's room to see what might be in there. Mary Anne's distraction with the tournament provided a unique opportunity. When else would they be certain she wouldn't come to the room?

"And you're sure you can get Mary Anne's room key?"

"She keeps it in the cell phone pocket of that horrible purse. I don't think it will be difficult."

"And if you can't get it, or if anything goes wrong, we meet back at the security office. Deal?"

"Deal."

They approached the table and with a final look, parted ways.

Sadie found Mary Anne at the same window seat they'd sat at before. Her expression was relaxed again, and she looked more like the Mary Anne Sadie had first met. Once Mary Anne saw Sadie approaching, her smile got wide, and she pointed a finger at Sadie, narrowing her eyes behind her glasses.

"He won't win again," she decreed playfully. "Glen never loses."

Sadie had to force a smile. "May the best man win."

"Oh, he will," Mary Anne said with a nod. "I can promise you that."

Sadie's mouth went dry, and she took a deep breath. "Could I borrow your pen again? Pete wants to sign up for the player's card they have on the ship."

"Sure," Mary Anne said. She put her purse on her lap and pulled it open.

Sadie stared at the pocket where Mary Anne's ship-card was stored. She glanced to her right and saw a couple walking toward her. As soon as the couple was behind her, Sadie stumbled forward, landing practically in Mary Anne's lap as though she'd been tripped.

Mary Anne let out a small scream of surprise while Sadie attempted to right herself. In the process, she *accidentally* snagged the strap of Mary Anne's purse and flung it to the ground where she also landed beside it in a very unladylike—and uncomfortable—heap. She reached for the bag and picked it up from the bottom so that all the contents spilled out. If something suspicious were there, it was now on the floor and could save Sadie from having to take things further.

"Oh, I'm so sorry," Sadie said after the contents of Mary Anne's purse were sufficiently dumped. She got to her knees and started picking up everything she'd spilled. She moved fast and kept her back to Mary Anne, who was just getting up from the window seat.

Sadie used one hand to put Mary Anne's pocketbook back into the purse while she fished in the front pocket for the card with her other hand. She made sure to block Mary Anne's view with her body. Her fingers felt the smooth surface of the card, and she slid it out of the pocket and under one knee before she reached for the other items scattered across the floor.

A few other passengers bent down to help her clean up, which Sadie was grateful for because it kept Mary Anne at a distance long enough for Sadie to slide the card from under her knee and into the side of her sock. She watched all the items going back into the purse, looking for anything suspicious, but nothing stood out other than the fact that there was so much stuff. The purse could hold an entire medicine cabinet and still leave room for a twelve-pack of soda.

When the last items were put into the purse, Sadie thanked the people who'd stopped to help and then stood, watching to make sure the cuff of her pant leg fell over the card hidden in her sock. She turned to hand Mary Anne her purse. "I'm so sorry."

"Are you alright?" Mary Anne asked, sweetly enough that Sadie almost felt bad for the deception. Almost.

"I think I twisted my knee," Sadie said. She attempted to take a step, but added an exaggerated limp.

"Oh, you better not walk on it, then," Mary Anne said, reaching out for Sadie's arm to steady her. "Maybe you should go to the clinic. Would you like me to go with you?"

"I think I just need to walk around, maybe put some ice on it." She glanced toward the tables on the far side of the casino. "I hate to miss the competition, but, ooooh, yeah, I need to get some ice on this. You stay, though. I'm fine."

Mary Anne patted her arm. "I'll keep an eye on that man of yours—don't you worry."

That was precisely what Sadie *was* worried about. "That's very sweet of you. I'll take a few turns around the ship and see if it loosens up."

"I thought you were going to put ice on it."

"Right, a few turns, then I'll bring the ice back with me."

"Before you go," Mary Anne said, putting a restraining hand on Sadie's arm. It was all Sadie could do not to shake it off. "I had a message from the head security guy on my phone a minute ago. He has more questions for me and said he'll ask someone to interpret for me. What exactly did you tell him I said about the man in the buffet?"

"Um, I just said you were the first to tell me about it. I really don't know why they are so interested in talking to you about it. They're talking to Jen, too, since she was the one who knew the man's name."

"So, they think I know too much? Is that what they are going to ask me about? Glen's the one who told me about the man; I only told you what Glen said to me."

"Oh," Sadie said with a nod, "then you have nothing to worry about."

"But Glen does," Mary Anne said. "It's really *him* they want to talk to, right? Since he's the one who told me. Remember what I told you about him, about his . . . problems?"

"Right. You should tell security about that, then," Sadie said, shrugging. "Honesty is always the best policy. If there's nothing to hide, then there's nothing to worry about."

"Well, I have nothing to hide," Mary Anne said, looking across the casino toward her husband. "But sometimes Glen really worries me." She turned back to Sadie. "Maybe you should come with me when I talk to them; you could tell them how strange Glen's been acting."

"I only met Glen an hour ago, Mary Anne."

"But I've told you all about him. You're like a character witness."

Sadie was becoming increasingly uncomfortable with whatever agenda Mary Anne was trying to pin onto Sadie. "Oh, I don't know. I better get moving on this knee before it stiffens up too much. I really want to get back for the end of the tournament."

Mary Anne pursed her lips together and looked toward the windows, thoughtful and not pleased, though she nodded.

"I'll be back in a bit," Sadie said, taking a limping step toward the casino's entrance.

Mary Anne offered to come with her again, but it was half-hearted, and Sadie insisted Mary Anne stay. Finally, Sadie hobbled out of the casino, and Mary Anne headed toward the tables. Sadie waited until she was out of view, then experienced a miraculous healing and took long strides up the stairs to the reception area where there was a courtesy phone.

"Security," Hazel said after picking up the phone. "Is this an emergency?"

"No, or, well, I don't know. Can I speak with Officer Jareg, please?"

"I'm afraid he isn't available. I can send a security officer to meet you."

Sadie shook her head. "No, I need to talk to Officer Jareg." What should she do? She could talk to someone else, but they might not know the context of the entire situation. And Sadie did have that room key . . . "Would you tell him that Sadie Hoffmiller called and that I have information regarding Glen and Mary Anne Rydell.

Tell him I'll be in the casino along with Pete Cunningham and that he should come as soon as he can."

Hazel wrote down the message and read it back to Sadie. By the time Sadie finished the phone call, her anticipation levels were causing her hands and feet to tingle.

Sadie headed for the stairs again. Should she have said this was an emergency? No, that might have brought more security guards and a medical team. She didn't want that, she just needed to pass on some information.

When she reached the stairs, she stopped long enough to remove the ship-card from her sock and check for the room number. It was on deck six, the same level as the casino—convenient for gambling-addicted Glen.

"Room 616," she muttered when she got back to deck six. Glen and Mary Anne's cabin should be on the aft end of the ship. Room numbers started on starboard aft, then increased as the cabins moved forward.

The steward's cart was a few doors down from 616 when Sadie got to that portion of the hallway, but she didn't see the steward himself. When she arrived at the door, she slid the card into the slot and let herself into the room. The steward had already made up the bed, which meant she didn't have to worry about him coming back while she looked around.

The room had the same layout as the one Sadie shared with Breanna, except that there was one bed in the center of the room rather than twin beds against the walls with an aisle in between. The bed frames were flush against the floor, which meant Sadie didn't have to check underneath them.

Glen and Mary Anne would know the stewards would be in and out of their room all day, so they would have to hide whatever it was they had used to induce Ben's heart attack somewhere that wouldn't be readily discovered. She checked the drawers carefully enough not to mess them up but thoroughly enough to be sure she hadn't missed anything. She then pulled the suitcases out of the closet and opened them, checking all the pockets—nothing. She put them back exactly as she'd found them—they filled the entire space—then shut the closet and found herself staring at the safe. Of course! The best place to hide something was in the safe . . . which Sadie couldn't access. Why hadn't she thought of that possibility when she first came up with this idea?

Just in case, though, she examined the safe and realized it hadn't been used. The door was open, and the safe was empty. That seemed to indicate that whatever they had to hide either wasn't in the room or it wasn't obviously suspect. She turned to look at the room again. Could there have been something in Mary Anne's purse after all and Sadie just didn't know enough to recognize its purpose?

Sadie had no idea how long she'd been in the room, but it felt like at least five or six minutes. She needed to get out of there soon. She entered the bathroom and immediately spotted several prescription bottles. Could one of them be what caused Ben's heart attack? She pulled out her phone and took a picture of each bottle so that she could look up the labels later.

She was putting them back in a row when she noticed another bottle set behind them. It was bright yellow with a label that included a tropical fish; it looked completely out of place. Next to it was a small, clear travel bottle, the size that could pass through security in a carry-on bag at the airport. It was filled with a bluish liquid. Was it shampoo? Mouthwash? She took a picture of it and the fish bottle, just in case.

There was a makeup bag and a shaving kit on one of the shelves.

The makeup bag didn't have anything of interest, but there were a few hypodermic syringes wrapped up in a plastic baggie in the shaving kit. That got Sadie's heart racing. Were either Mary Anne or Glen diabetic? Why else would they have syringes? There were different types of syringes for insulin than were used for other medications, but Sadie didn't know how to tell the difference.

Sadie was digging through Glen's collection of hotel soaps and Q-tips in search of anything else when she heard voices outside the cabin door. She paused, then leaned back out of the bathroom. Surely they weren't voices she needed to worry about, right? There were three thousand passengers on this ship, at least five hundred of them had cabins on this floor.

"Steward!"

It was Mary Anne, and Sadie felt the blood drain from her face. Mary Anne couldn't get into her room without her ship-card—which Sadie had—but Glen would have a ship-card for the room too. Had Mary Anne realized hers was missing and borrowed Glen's? Why wasn't Mary Anne at the game? Had she suspected Sadie's deception?

Sadie crept out of the bathroom and walked to the door in time to hear the end of what the steward, presumably, said, " . . . without your ship-to-shore card."

"But you've seen me here for the last five days. Surely you can let me in. I've talked to you every day."

Sadie's heart rate took off so fast she could barely breathe. She didn't even need to look around to know there was nowhere in this room to hide. The closet was the obvious choice, but it was full of empty luggage.

Don't let her in, Sadie thought to the steward, as though he could hear her. *Stick to the rules, Mr. Steward, and make her go to reception for a new ship-card.*

"I can't find my ship-card, and I don't have time to get my husband's key. It's an emergency. And if you don't let me in, I'll sue this company. Believe you me, they don't need another lawsuit."

Panic filled Sadie as she turned to face the tiny room as though another hiding place had become available in the last ten seconds. What she wouldn't do for a Room of Requirement or an invisibility cloak like they had in the Harry Potter books.

She stepped back into the bathroom—hoping Mary Anne's emergency didn't include the bathroom—and pulled the door closed while formulating a completely elementary plan. The shower had a frosted glass door which *might* provide her some kind of cover. She reached above the sink and fumbled with the light fixture. She'd expected to have to unscrew the lightbulb but found the fixture to be plugged into an electrical outlet instead. She pulled out the plug, cutting half the light in the room, just as she heard the cabin door open.

Her mouth was so dry she couldn't swallow. She quickly stepped inside the shower and reached up to unscrew the recessed lightbulb there. On the third twist, the room was plunged into darkness. She tried sliding part of the shower door closed, but it made a scratching noise she couldn't afford. She crouched down as low as she could and pressed herself as far into the corner as possible.

The bathroom door opened. Sadie held her breath and heard the click of the light switch located outside the bathroom. Of course no lights turned on.

"What the—?" Mary Anne said out loud. She clicked the switch twice more. "For heaven's sakes," she said, then louder added, "Steward!"

Sadie heard a muffled answer.

"The light in my bathroom is not working." The switch clicked some more. "This is unacceptable. I don't have perfect vision, you know. This is a hazard!"

"I am sorry, ma'am. I will have maintenance see to it immediately."

"I need my husband's medication right now. Don't you have a flashlight or something?"

Medication? That was the emergency? That meant Mary Anne would be coming into the bathroom. *Please don't have a flashlight.*

"Yes, one moment."

Mary Anne muttered a racial slur, and Sadie visualized herself becoming smaller and smaller in the corner. She was hidden behind two layers of frosted glass and the room was dark except for the light coming in through the doorway. If no one peeked into the shower or shined a light right at her, she might get out of this. She could feel her lungs compressing, the earliest sign of a panic attack coming on, and she clenched her eyes closed harder than ever while forcing herself to breathe as deep as she could and trying to convince herself that she was okay. For now, at least. Her face was hot, and her hands started to shake. She clasped them more tightly together around her knees.

She opened her eyes in time to see a beam of light cross the bathroom floor. The light looked hazy through the panes of glass, and she hoped it wouldn't show the shape of her hiding in the shower. *They aren't looking in your direction. They just want the pills.* Still, she couldn't breathe while Mary Anne was rummaging around.

"Okay, I have what I need," Mary Anne said. Sadie was still trying not to lose it. "You better make sure that light is fixed before I get back or I'll be asking for a discount on my room."

"Yes, ma'am," the steward said as the bathroom door shut. A few seconds later the cabin door clicked shut as well, but it was nearly a minute before Sadie stopped shaking. She hadn't been caught. Once the adrenaline faded, she unfolded herself from the corner of the shower and stood carefully, her muscles protesting as she straightened up on shaky legs.

It wasn't until she was standing that she realized the bottom of the shower had been wet, and since she'd sat on it, her backside was now wet too. There were worse things, she told herself. Take it in stride.

She reached above her head and screwed in the lightbulb, then stepped out of the shower and into the bathroom to plug the light fixture back in as well, further illuminating the small space. She looked at the bottles of pills, consulting the pictures she'd taken in order to see what, if anything, was missing. All the prescription bottles were there.

She checked the shaving kit and confirmed pretty quickly that the needles were missing. She looked back at the shelf of medications. She moved the bottles out of the way and realized that while the tropical fish bottle was still there, the plastic bottle of blue mouthwash was missing.

What was happening here? Was Mary Anne involved instead of Glen? Or was it both of them?

Sadie let herself out of the bathroom, feeling another rush of adrenaline that sent her out the cabin door and into the hall where she came face-to-face with the steward before she'd had the chance to consider the possibility he'd still be there. He blinked at her in confusion as the door snapped closed behind her.

"The bathroom lights are fixed," she said.

He looked at her in confusion, but then smiled and shrugged. "I won't tell," he said.

"Thank you," Sadie said. She stepped around him, but he grabbed her arm. She instinctively pulled out of his grip, leaving him blinking again, his arm extended but holding nothing. "Sorry," she said. "Um, I'm in a hurry."

His extended hand turned into a point. "I was going to say that . . . uh, your bottom . . ."

Sadie put her hands on her bum and felt the wetness from the shower again. Shoot. She didn't have time to change. Khakis were the wrong pants to wear when hiding in a wet shower.

"Here," he said, handing her a staff uniform shirt that he pulled out of the cleaning cart. It was mustard yellow, not her color, but it would save her from embarrassing notice. She took the shirt and smiled. "Thank you so much." She put her arms through the sleeves, checking to make sure the hem hung low enough to cover her bum.

Pete was in the casino with Glen and Mary Anne and probably wondering what happened to her. Within a minute, Sadie was in the casino and halfway to the tournament table. Mary Anne stood behind Glen at the far left end of the table. Sadie remembered the limp a split second before Mary Anne looked over her shoulder and gave her a rather tight smile.

Sadie forced an equally tight smile in return while noticing one of the casino staff looking at her strangely, or rather, looking at the shirt. She worried he would say something and gave him a pleading look he seemed to understand. He smiled at her and went back to cleaning out the ashtrays. Maybe wearing the shirt gave her some kind of inclusion, like a secret handshake or something. She caught a glimpse of the back of Pete's head and felt as though she could breathe again. Wait, was he sitting down?

"Madam?"

She turned and was surprised to see Henry not far away. He beckoned her out of the casino with a nod, but left before seeing if she was following.

Sadie was torn between following Henry and going to Pete, but knowing Henry wouldn't have risked coming up here if it weren't important made the decision for her.

CHAPTER 42

She was only a few steps behind Henry as he left the casino, following him out one of the side doors that led to the outside decks. Sadie immediately felt the cold through her wet pants. She didn't have a jacket and there were still chunks of ice in the water. Henry stepped into the space between where two lifeboats hung, and Sadie followed.

"You found something?" Sadie asked. They weren't really hidden. Anyone walking on deck would see them and probably wonder what they were doing. But they would be harder to spot by someone not directly in front of them.

Henry nodded and handed Sadie a piece of notebook paper.

"Three cruises have had men die on board in the last sixteen months," Henry summarized, pointing at the name of each boat and the date of the deaths. "I couldn't find if the men spent time in the casino, but I will keep looking. The three names from the list you showed me were on all three cruises."

"Did the men die of heart attacks?" Sadie asked. She needed something specific to tie these deaths to Ben's.

Henry pointed to the second one that had taken place in May

of the previous year. "This one had a full autopsy and was ruled foul play. He was injected with a combination of two elements." He pointed to a line farther down the paper and Sadie read the words there: digoxin and calcium hydroxide.

"Digoxin is a heart medication," Sadie said. Was it one of the prescriptions in Glen and Mary Anne's bathroom? "I've never heard of calcium hydroxide. But you said he was injected with something? You're sure?"

Henry nodded, and pulled another paper out of his pocket. "I looked up both elements."

Sadie took the paper and scanned through the definition of digoxin, then read through the explanation of calcium hydroxide. "Commonly used to increase the calcium levels in salt-water aquariums. Oh my gosh!" *The bottle with the fish on it from Mary Anne's room!*

"This means something to you?"

"Yes," Sadie said. She looked up at Henry as several things that needed to be done ran through her head. She needed to get this information to Officer Jareg, she needed to get Mary Anne and Glen removed from the casino, and she needed to find Pete. But she couldn't do all those things at the same time.

"Madam?" Henry said, worried. He must have seen the growing look of concern on her face.

Her eyes moved from his face to the pocket of his jacket where the top of a pen peeked out. She grabbed the pen, turned over the paper Henry had given her, and wrote a short, quick note to Officer Jareg.

Rydells are in the casino; needles in her purse! Come ASAP.

"Henry," Sadie said. "I know this is a horrible thing to ask you, and I will do everything on your behalf I can to make this right should there be any fallout, but I need you to find Officer Jareg and give him this paper. It's a matter of life or death."

A look of fear crossed Henry's face. Sadie knew that if Henry handed over the paper to Officer Jareg, it could implicate him in this whole mess; he could lose his job. But to his credit, he nodded. Sadie gave him a quick hug. "I need to get back to the casino. Thank you so much!"

She ran back to the casino, scanning for Pete as soon as she entered the smoke-filled room. There were buzzers and dings from all the slot machines, and people laughing all around her. It made her dizzy.

Sadie was almost to the table when she saw Pete. Startled, she came to a stop as her neck flushed with heat. Why was he still at the table? He was supposed to lose quickly.

She walked a few steps closer and saw that he was neck and neck with Glen. Only four of the original six contestants were still in the game. *What was he doing?*

CHAPTER 43

Sadie's heart was in her throat as the fourth man busted and pushed away from the table. Sadie navigated through the crowd in order to stand behind Pete's chair. Weak applause accompanied the player's exit—now there were only three.

Pete, as the final qualifier, sat in the far right seat, while Glen, as the first qualified—after Ben was removed, anyway—sat in the far left position. Sadie didn't know what to do. Should she interrupt the game? Was anyone other than Pete in immediate danger? She looked around in hopes of seeing Officer Jareg marching toward the table. He wasn't; in fact there wasn't a single security officer in view. Shouldn't one be in the casino at all times? Anywhere that had booze and money mingled together should have some kind of security presence, right?

The players placed their bets; Pete went conservative. The third player was down to his last five chips and put three in his betting circle. Glen put in a huge stack of chips, almost twenty-five percent of his winnings. Sadie glanced at him, this possible killer, and noticed he was sweating profusely. He sent a sidelong glance toward Pete—an angry, sidelong glance—and Sadie stepped closer to the back of Pete's chair. She felt protective and wished they could take a time-out so she could tell Pete what she and Henry had found and get his help on figuring out what it meant. *And* ask why in the world he was still playing!

"No touching the players," the announcer said.

Sadie looked around before realizing the comment was directed toward her.

"I'm not touching him," she said.

"Back up, please," the woman said.

Pete looked over his shoulder at her and smiled slightly, clearly asking her to back up. Why was he still at the table? It was not difficult to lose everything at the blackjack table; people did it every day. And that was when their lives *weren't* on the line.

Sadie backed up, however, and tried to breathe normally.

"He's sure doing well."

Sadie jumped. When had Mary Anne come up beside her? "Yeah," she said as calmly as possible while taking a casual step farther away from Mary Anne. The blue solution in the bottle must have been the medication and calcium stuff dissolved into some kind of injectable solution. Henry had said only one of the three victims from other cruises had had a full autopsy—perhaps the other two were older? Maybe they had a medical history of some kind?

When Sadie spoke again she raised her voice to make sure Pete could hear her. "But you know how luck is—it can *run out at any time.*"

The dealer won that round, and everyone lost their money, including Glen, who looked pale as the dealer slid his chips away from him. The players placed their next round of bets, and again, Pete went conservative. The next guy put one of his two chips in the circle, then added the last chip with an "oh well" shrug. Sadie watched Glen push *half* of his chips into his betting circle.

"A fool and his money," Mary Anne said under her breath. "I guess I better go cheer him on. This is going to kill him."

She moved away and Sadie breathed easier, but she still wanted to wrap her arms around Pete and drag him out of this place. The curve of the table gave Sadie a good view of Glen and Mary Anne at the other end. Glen looked terrible; the game was really getting to him. He coughed into the back of his hand, and Sadie hoped that his physical reaction to losing would buy Pete some time. Mary Anne had told the steward her husband needed his medication, maybe she meant it. Could Mary Anne have retrieved any of the medication from the bathroom without taking the entire bottle? But why take the syringes and the blue stuff?

The next round was in motion. Pete had a three and a jack. Rough start. He vacillated for a minute, then tapped the table for a new card. He got another jack and busted. Both Glen and Mary Anne watched Pete's chips be taken back by the dealer with intense looks on their faces. Glen wiped his hairy forearm across his forehead. If not for Sadie's suspicions that one—or both—of the Rydells was a serial killer, she'd be worried about Glen's gambling addiction, which was taking a severe toll. Obviously he needed help. Maybe they had programs for that in prison.

The player in between Glen and Pete stayed at eighteen. Glen had fourteen showing. He tapped for a new card, got an eight, and went even paler as the dealer took his chips. Pete now had nearly double the winnings Glen had. The announcer signaled five more minutes before they would call the game. Glen picked up his drink and took a long swig. Pete absently restacked his chips, and when the table was open for bets, he put the whole stack in the betting circle.

The crowd gasped in unison. Mary Anne and Glen stared at the tower of chips in Pete's circle, and Mary Anne leaned down to say something in her husband's ear as the player between Pete and Glen put in a few chips as his bet.

"No touching the players, ma'am," the announcer called out. Mary Anne continued to speak.

"Ma'am, he will be disqualified."

Mary Anne lifted her hands in the air dramatically and stepped away. "Sorry," she said, not sounding the least bit apologetic. "Just wishing him luck."

The pit boss nodded, and Mary Anne lowered her arms to her side.

Glen took another drink, wiped his forehead, and coughed again before pushing all his chips into the betting area. The crowd gasped again. Two players were putting everything in? They could both lose it all. Then what?

Sadie could see the sweat rings under Glen's arms. Was he okay?

The dealer dealt the cards. Pete ended up with two sevens, the second player had eighteen again, while Glen had a five of hearts and a six of clubs—he was set for a twenty-one. The dealer had a ten of spades showing, but when he checked his cards, he didn't flip them over, which meant he didn't have an ace under there. The tension of the crowd was getting thicker by the minute. Pete held at the two sevens, eliciting another gasp from the crowd. He was holding at fourteen?

Sadie looked around for Officer Jareg again. Where was he? What could be more important for him to be doing right now than stopping the Rydells from striking again? She couldn't keep her eyes off the game for long. The temperature of the room seemed to be rising in conjunction with the tension in the air.

The middle player held. Glen asked for a hit, and everyone watched eagerly. He got a two of clubs. He asked for another hit— the king of spades. The entire room moaned in commiseration for his loss. Glen froze and watched with wide eyes as the dealer pulled the entire stack of chips away from his betting circle, mumbling an apology.

The crowd applauded Glen's participation, but Sadie watched to make sure Mary Anne wasn't coming their way. Had Ben been killed because he was competition against Glen, or because he'd beat Glen in that first round? Why kill him at all? The tournament winnings were only $500. Could it have something to do with the loss of the Rydells' pet store business? Was it a power trip? Mary Anne had said Glen was crazy, and yet even crazy people had motives. And it was Mary Anne who'd gone back to the room for the solution.

The dealer returned Glen's chips to the bank and every eye in the crowd was on the dealer's hand. Would he bust? Or would Pete lose too?

But Sadie kept watching Mary Anne as she leaned down to give Glen a hug from behind. It would have seemed a gesture of sweet affection if not for a flash of something in Mary Anne's hand as her arms wrapped around Glen's chest. Glen suddenly jerked and Sadie flinched.

A split second later, the room erupted into cheers. Someone stepped forward, blocking Sadie's view of Mary Anne. It took Sadie a moment to realize that the reason for the cheering was because the dealer had busted.

Pete had won. And won big.

All the spectators were cheering and laughing, clapping Pete on the back and saying how amazing he was. Sadie turned back toward Mary Anne and Glen, but she couldn't see them through the crowd that was pressing in around the table. Sadie started elbowing her way in their direction. What had she seen just before the crowd went crazy?

"Move," she said while pushing a man out of her way. The announcer was trying to regain control of the crowd as there were still two players in the game.

Mary Anne was suddenly in front of her, causing Sadie to come to an abrupt stop. "Congratulations," Mary Anne said, spreading her arms as though to give Sadie a hug. "You must be so proud. He's very good at the game."

Sadie backpedaled fast, but the wall of people behind her brought her up short.

Mary Anne kept coming. "I know when Glen wins, it's like everything's right with the world for a little bit. Everything's fair again."

Sadie looked at Mary Anne's hands; she didn't see anything in them, but she continued pushing backward. Where was Glen?

"No!" Sadie heard Pete say from behind her. By instinct or maybe some kind of telepathy, she ducked just as Pete lunged forward, catching Mary Anne in the chest and throwing her backward. Sadie was knocked toward the table as the crowd broke into screams and expletives. Sadie tried to get off the ground, but couldn't stand as mass confusion erupted all around her. She was going to get trampled.

Thinking fast, she crawled into the space between the chairs and the blackjack table and pulled her arms and legs close to keep from getting stepped on. She took a breath before rolling onto her hands and knees and crawling toward the end of the table. She needed to get to Pete as quickly as possible.

Within a few feet of making her escape, Sadie encountered a pair of black orthopedic shoes, toes pointed up and out. Her eyes traveled up the prone body and noted Dockers, and then the white button-up shirt a shade lighter than the undershirt beneath it.

"Glen," Sadie said, crawling over him until she was right above his pale blue eyes that stared up at the bottom of the table. His glasses were gone, and his mouth was open, a trail of drool slowly snaking down his chin. "Glen," she said louder, lightly slapping his cheeks before feeling for a pulse. Her own heartbeat was thundering in her ears so much that she couldn't feel if his heart was still beating. She glanced at the spot on his chest where she thought Mary Anne had injected him with the deadly solution, but nothing showed. It would only be a needle prick after all.

"Someone help me!" she screamed, scrambling over Glen. She lifted one arm and started pulling while still screaming for help a second time. A moment later, two sets of much stronger arms took hold and quickly pulled Glen clear of the table.

"Call security!" Sadie screamed, falling to her knees beside the body and digging in her memory banks for everything she remembered about CPR. She'd been certified every other year since she'd had children but had never actually used it. Mary Anne was screaming from somewhere behind her—a crying, horrible, scared, and angry scream.

"What's wrong with my Glen?"

"She did this!" Sadie yelled as loud as she could, pointing at Mary Anne.

Mary Anne looked shocked, and Sadie turned her attention to Pete, who was holding her back. "Check her purse for a needle and a bottle with blue liquid in it."

She saw just a flicker of a nod from Pete before she turned and started doing chest compressions on Glen. One and two and three and four and five . . .

CHAPTER 44

🍓

While it was announced to the passengers that pulling into the port of Ketchikan an hour late was due to delayed port clearance, the truth was that a federal officer and some local authorities had come on board to make sure that Mary Anne and Tanice were both secured before the gangways opened.

Sadie and Pete had given their statements to the investigators, who took down all of their contact information in order to get in touch with them later if needed. Because the second death on the cruise ship thirteen months earlier had already been under investigation, there was a basis to pattern this investigation around, and while the security team on the ship might not be trained to know exactly how to handle such an extreme situation, the federal officer commanded attention from the first word he uttered and everything from that point on was carried out with precision.

Mary Anne certainly had some explaining to do—chief of which, why kill Glen?

"Mary Anne's saying that Glen killed the others," Pete said after he'd met with Officer Jareg and Sadie had stopped by her room to change her clothes.

They were heading toward the gangways, and the closer they got to the exits, the more congested the hallways became as the unhappy passengers waited to leave the ship. "She claims that Glen told her about the murders only after Officer Jareg attempted to talk to her last night. She said she worried what he would do, so she killed him before he could hurt anyone else, hoping it would look like a natural cause in order to preserve her children's feelings. Apparently, she put the solution in his food at breakfast, hoping it would do the trick. She claims that she'd never used a needle before in her life, but felt desperate when the solution only seemed to make him sick."

"So, basically her version makes her into a hero."

Pete nodded. "Pretty much."

"And Tanice? Do you know what happens to her now?"

"She's still responsible for the wine, but will likely be able to plead the charges down—depending on what happens with Lorraina. I'm sure Tanice will get a good attorney."

Sadie shook her head. "Husbands sure didn't fare very well on this cruise, did they? Ben and Glen are dead, and Kirby got thrown in a river."

"Ben was a philanderer, Glen was a murderer—maybe—and Kirby, well, I talked to him at the river, remember? He was weird."

"So it doesn't bother you that the three marriages we saw up close on this cruise were unhappy ones?"

"I saw a whole lot of white-haired couples holding hands and taking pictures together. Three unhappy marriages don't dim my view of matrimony. Do they dim yours?"

"Of course not," Sadie said. "If anything, it convinces me that I've made the right decision in choosing a good man to . . . " She heard what she was saying and felt the blush creep up her neck. Suddenly the carpet beneath her feet was fascinating.

"A good man to marry?" Pete finished for her with a grin. "Is this when you tell me that you're leaving me for that attorney?"

"Stop it," Sadie said, still blushing. She didn't have to look at him to know he was smiling. "Look, I think the gangway's open." She was grateful that Pete didn't pursue the conversation. Nothing was formally finalized between them, and she was embarrassed to be jumping to such conclusions out loud.

Because of the wait before getting into port, the line for disembarkation was atrocious. Sadie would have thought she and Pete would have had some kind of priority, due to everything they'd done to help with the investigation, but it wasn't to be.

The wait did create an opportunity for Sadie to call Breanna. The flight that had brought her children from Skagway had landed a half an hour earlier.

"Wow, it sounds like we missed all the fun," Breanna said when Sadie finished explaining all that had happened.

Sadie didn't believe she meant a word of it. Standing guard at the dining room had been about Breanna's limit as far as investigative work went, and considering how ugly things had become there at the end, Sadie was relieved that her children hadn't been a part of it.

"How's Lorraina?" Sadie asked, glancing ahead at the crowd slowly making their way through the checkpoint.

"Good," Breanna said. "Shawn got a call this morning. The doctors want him to come to Anchorage after the ship docks in Seattle. The cruise line is even going to help change his ticket so it doesn't cost him extra. The doctors said they aren't sure when, or even if, Lorraina will be strong enough for the transplant, but she's made some improvements, I guess. Plus they want to finish the testing they need to do to see if Shawn is even a viable candidate. He'll be there a couple of days while they figure it out."

Sadie decided in an instant that she was going to Anchorage with him. Hopefully Shawn wouldn't fight her on that.

After agreeing to meet Breanna at the pier, Sadie finished the call. When she and Pete finally reached the computers that scanned their ship-to-shore cards, Sadie's phone chimed to indicate a text message. She assumed it was Breanna wanting the last word. It wasn't Breanna, though.

> **Sadie, it's Liam. Can you help me with something? It looks like your ship is finally unloading.**

Sadie blinked in confusion before reading the text again. "What?" Pete asked.

Sadie showed him her phone, and he pulled his eyebrows together. "Liam's here?"

"That's what it sounds like," Sadie said. "But . . . why?"

"Ask him," Pete said.

> *Sadie:* You're in Ketchikan?
>
> *Liam:* Yes. Can you help me?
>
> *Sadie:* Of course. With what?
>
> *Liam:* Can you bring Bre to Sweet Mermaids? It's a café on Front Street.
>
> *Sadie:* What's going on?
>
> *Liam:* We're getting married. Our way.

Sadie's hands froze, and she showed the phone to Pete again who read the text and then lifted his eyebrows in surprise. She got over the momentary shock and called the number. Liam answered on the second ring, and Pete and Sadie stepped out of line, allowing the passengers behind them to pass them up.

"Liam," she said by way of greeting. She plugged her other ear to make sure she didn't miss a word. "What are you talking about?"

By the time she and Pete reached the end of the gangplank ten minutes later, Sadie's phone was in her purse and she was vacillating between a silly grin and dissolving into a puddle of tears. Breanna and Shawn met them at the bottom and they all exchanged hugs.

"What's the matter?" Breanna asked when she pulled back from Sadie's embrace.

Sadie blinked quickly and wiped at her eyes. If she'd had any idea what this day had in store, she'd have worn her waterproof mascara. "Nothing," Sadie assured her, then looked around. "Where's Maggie?"

"We invited her to come but . . ." Breanna and Shawn shared a look, then Shawn looked back at Sadie but didn't answer. He didn't have to.

"She didn't know if she'd be welcome?" Sadie guessed.

Shawn nodded and put his hands in his pockets, looking at the ground.

"But she came to Ketchikan with you guys," Pete pointed out.

"Yeah," Breanna said, giving Shawn a sly look. "I think she might have some unfinished business with the Hoffmiller gang."

Sadie looked at Shawn in surprise, then didn't know what to think of the blush in his cheeks. She quickly reminded herself that Shawn and Maggie were not—and never had been—brother and sister.

"Where is she?" Sadie asked.

"Shopping," Shawn said. "Should I go get her?"

"Yes," Pete said, reaching for Sadie's hand and giving it a squeeze. "Then meet us at Sweet Mermaids. It's a café located at 340 Front Street."

"We just ate," Breanna said.

"Well, we're starving," Sadie said, which was true, but wasn't the reason why they were going to Sweet Mermaids. "We were told not to miss it." Were they ever.

"Okay," Shawn said. "I'll get Maggie and meet you there. You're sure you're okay with her coming along?"

"Tell Maggie that I can't wait to see her."

Shawn nodded and moved quickly toward a row of shops on the right side of the pier.

"We better get going," Pete said, moving toward the left. Sweet Mermaids was a small café, Liam had said, but owned by a talented friend of a friend who had agreed to help him pull this off in the middle of their busy season.

"You make it sound like we have an appointment," Breanna said.

Sadie and Pete shared a quick look, then Sadie asked about what happened in Skagway, hoping to change the subject. She knew the basics but wanted details.

Breanna was quick to fill in the blanks, and she didn't seem to notice the limo parked just around the corner from where Sweet Mermaids was located. Sadie had butterflies as they pushed through the front doors of the small bakery. Liam had said it was small, and he wasn't kidding, but front and center on top of the glass-fronted bakery case just inside the door was a beautiful wedding cake with pearl details at the edges of the three square layers and elegant scrollwork along the sides of each tier.

Breanna took one look at it and came to a stop, blinking at the white confection with big eyes and a completely confused expression.

"Breanna?" Pete prompted her when she said nothing. Sadie didn't dare open her mouth for fear she'd start bawling.

"That . . . looks just like my cake," Breanna said in a hush. She took a step forward. "It's a smaller version of the *exact* same cake I picked out . . . in London."

Sadie heard the door opening behind them and turned to see Liam sneak in. He looked absolutely terrified. Several faces appeared on the other side of the glass, including Liam's parents, which Sadie was glad to see. When Liam told her what he'd done, she worried his parents hadn't come with him. Sadie quickly stepped to the side of the bakery case, pulling Pete with her so that Liam would have room to come up next to Bre.

Breanna turned her head to look at Sadie, completely unaware that her fiancé and soon-to-be husband was standing two feet behind her. "What's going on?"

"Hey, Bre," Liam said quietly.

Breanna spun around and, as if on cue, all the employees who had been trying to make themselves look busy, moved forward from the back of the shop, their eyes bright as they watched what was happening. Sadie wondered if they had been up all night making this happen. Liam had explained on the phone that he'd chartered a flight not long after Breanna had given in to his mom's version of her wedding day; he must have worked hard to put this in place before leaving London.

"Liam?" Breanna squeaked, and then threw herself into his arms, clinging tightly to him and burying her face in his shoulder. "What are you doing here?" She pulled back and brushed the hair off her face. When his only answer was a smile, she glanced at Sadie. "What is he doing here?"

Sadie nodded toward Liam. "He has the answers, not me."

Breanna looked at Liam, and he smiled, so sweet and kind and full of goodness that the last of Sadie's reservations about this marriage melted away like whipping cream on a hot day. They were a good match. They would make this work.

"I had a long talk with my parents after we finished talking with you the other night," Liam said, still holding her hands. "And we've come to some agreements."

"Okay," Breanna said softly, still looking confused.

"Mom really wants a fancy reception. I tried to talk her out of it, but she's insistent that on October 19, the day we were to be married, she gets to throw a great big obnoxious party. I'll wear a suit of her choosing, and we'll feature that overdone cake she likes, but you can wear the dress you already picked out."

"The day we *were* to be married?" Breanna repeated.

"That's the other part," Liam said, his smile getting a little bit bigger. "We do the wedding how we want it, when we want it, and where we want it."

Breanna looked at him, still trying to figure things out, then looked at the cake again. A moment later, one of the employees at the bakery came around the counter holding a clear dress bag with an exquisite wedding dress inside. Sadie had already seen pictures of the dress from the day Breanna had tried it on in London. It had cap sleeves, delicate beading at the sweetheart neckline and waist, but no train, no veil, no bling. Liam's mother had deemed it unfit for a countess, but it was perfectly suited for Breanna's style, coloring, and shape.

Breanna started to cry as she reached out and touched the bag. "My dress," she whispered. She looked up at Liam. "My cake and my dress."

"The two things you cared about."

"And you," she said even softer.

He smiled wide and took both her hands in his. "We'll make this work, Bre, we will. I will never let things get so out of hand again and we'll live the life we want to live—the life we've planned. Can you believe me when I promise you that?"

Breanna nodded and let go of one of his hands to wipe at her eyes. Someone handed her a napkin. Someone handed one to Sadie too.

"Today?" she said once she'd caught her breath.

"If that's what you want," Liam said with a nod.

"What do *you* want?" she asked, ever the diplomat.

He pulled on her hand that he was holding, bringing her closer to him. "I want you," he whispered so softly that Sadie could barely hear it. "All I've ever wanted is you."

CHAPTER 45

♥

Five hours later, Sadie held a hand over her mouth as the officiator read the marriage vows for Breanna and Liam. It was happening! Her daughter was getting married in a small pavilion set in the Tongass National Forest, not a cathedral. Instead of organ music, the patter of lightly falling raindrops and the chatter of birds and squirrels from the dense woods provided the only accompaniment. Across the small space, Liam's mother was also struggling to hold back her emotion.

After Breanna confirmed her vows, Liam took the wedding band from his pocket.

"I don't have your ring," Breanna whispered. Everyone laughed, except Sadie who was barely holding it together.

"It's okay," Liam said with a smile as he slid the band onto her finger until it was next to the diamond engagement ring she'd worn for only a few months.

"It's my honor," the officiator said, "to pronounce you husband and wife. You may kiss the bride."

Breanna stood on her toes before Liam had a chance to lean into her, but he quickly wrapped his arms around her and returned the kiss with a vigor that bordered on embarrassing. The small group erupted with applause as the kiss sealed the deal, completed the day, and verified that Breanna and Liam—the Viscount and Countess of Darling—had joined their lives together. From this day on, they belonged to one another. It was more than Sadie could handle, and she finally let loose the emotion she'd been holding in and sobbed and cried as everyone exchanged hugs.

Sweet Mermaids had not only made the cake—which, just as Sadie had suspected, they'd stayed up all night to replicate—they also catered the wedding luncheon with bagels and lox, crisp green salad, and the most delicious thing Sadie had eaten the entire week: their signature salmon and red potato chowder. Sadie had begged the owner for the recipe and, gem that she was, she gave Sadie a copy, which Sadie couldn't wait to put into her Little Black Recipe Book once she got home.

Sadie had cried off the rest of her makeup by the time she needed to help serve the cake to the fifteen members of the wedding party.

A photographer and videographer had been there to capture every moment, which Sadie found especially comforting since she wasn't sure any of them would remember much on their own, it had been such a whirlwind.

All too soon, and yet right on time, a touring Jeep pulled up. Liam had arranged for the two of them to stay in a cabin several miles from town for the next five days. The wedding party all hugged again, then waved and cheered as the Jeep drove away.

With the bride and groom gone and the party winding down, Liam's parents and friends said good-bye to the Hoffmillers and got in their prearranged taxis that would take them to their hotel rooms back in town while Pete, Sadie, Shawn, and Maggie took a taxi back to the pier. The ship would sail in an hour and a half, but the gangways closed in thirty minutes.

Just like that, Breanna was married, and Sadie was a mother-in-law. It would take some getting used to.

Half a block from the pier, Shawn asked the cab driver to pull over. "We want to do some quick shopping," he said, stepping out and holding the door open for Maggie.

"Why don't we walk back, too?" Pete suggested to Sadie.

Obviously, the others weren't as exhausted as Sadie was, but she agreed. With the wedding over, it would be nice to absorb the atmosphere of this cute village a little longer, and the sun was setting in a beautiful swirling mass of pink, gold, and purple amid the clouds overhead.

"We'll see you on the ship," Shawn said after they all stepped out of the cab.

Sadie and Maggie hadn't had a chance to talk, but Sadie had a feeling they would have plenty of time to work out whatever issues might be left between them. Maggie had been a wonderful help with the whirlwind wedding, doing anything that needed to be done without being asked. As Sadie watched Maggie and Shawn walk back to the ship side by side, she felt her heart do a little jump. People came together in the strangest ways sometimes. Maybe this was the purpose Maggie would find in all this heartache.

"They better hurry," Sadie said, realizing how few people were left on the pier and how quickly the dockworkers were moving to ready the ship for departure. "We'd better hurry, too." She took Pete's hand and tugged him toward the boat, but instead of following like she expected him to, he pulled her back, causing her to stumble into him. She didn't mind—what was one more minute?—and easily wrapped her arms around his neck. "Wasn't today amazing?" she said, going up on her toes to kiss him. It wasn't until she was once again flat-footed on the ground that she realized he seemed a little tense. "Are you okay?"

"I'm okay," he said, but he didn't sound okay.

Sadie took a step back. "What's wrong?"

"Nothing's wrong," he said with a laugh—a nervous laugh. He put one hand in his pocket.

"Pete," she said, taking his free hand in both of hers, "whatever it is, we'll—"

"Maybe you could just stop talking for a minute."

Sadie flinched. "You're telling me to shut up?"

Pete laughed again, a real laugh this time, and shook his head. "I'm asking you to let me say something."

"When have I ever not let you say something?"

He lifted his eyebrows, and she took a breath, pulled an invisible zipper across her lips and turned the invisible key. They really did need to hurry back, though. If she hadn't just zipped her lips shut, she'd have asked if they could continue this conversation on the ship.

But then she saw the excited glint in his eye, and the fact that he had just pulled something out of his pocket. Sadie's breath caught in her throat, and she put a hand over her mouth as Peter Cunningham sank down to one knee in front of her. Even if she'd wanted to speak at that moment, she couldn't have found a single word.

Pete reached for her left hand—a hand that hadn't worn a ring for a very long time. The setting sun caught the diamond on the ring he held, and Sadie's chest tightened even more.

"I knew if I waited to do this until after Breanna was married, you'd be expecting it and I couldn't have that." He looked up at her with those beautiful hazel eyes of his, and she didn't dare blink for fear she would miss an instant of this. "I'd hoped to find the perfect moment to say the words I've spent weeks planning to say, and now I've forgotten all those pretty words."

Sadie moved the hand still covering her mouth. "I don't need pretty—"

"Shhh, I'm not done."

She zipped her lips again and gave the key an extra turn.

Pete cleared his throat. "Since that first day when I helped you make applesauce in your kitchen, I've been inspired by your energy and impressed by the size of your heart. As we've grown together in the years since then, and as I've lived through adventures I never imagined could happen in real life, I find myself surprisingly hungry for more." He held the ring poised at the end of her ring finger. "You said that you didn't feel like I benefitted as much from our relationship as you did." He paused, and it was all Sadie could do to hold back the tears. "Sadie, you bring life into my living, and joy into my journey. I can no longer imagine a future without you in it, and I welcome whatever lies ahead for us. Sadie, will you marry me? Will you be my wife?"

The tears started to fall, and Sadie nodded several times.

"You can talk now," Pete said.

"Yes," Sadie said, pushing her finger through the ring Pete still held and falling to her knees on the pier in front of him. A jarring pain shot up her left leg, but she ignored it. "A million times, yes."

He took her face in his hands and kissed her so hard and deep that she felt it in every cell in her body.

When she finally pulled back, she looked into his eyes and could see the years ahead of them. They were a beautiful sight. "I love you, Pete. More than I can say."

"Oh, Sadie, Sadie, *almost* married lady, I love you, too."

Salmon and Red Potato Chowder

5-pound bag of small, unpeeled red potatoes, cut into 1-inch cubes
  (peel half, if desired)
3 to 4 bacon strips, diced
1 large onion, diced
4 celery ribs, diced
2 quarts milk
4 cups Knorr's Chicken Stock (or water/chicken-stock equivalent)
¼ cup dried parsley
1 teaspoon salt (optional)
½ teaspoon pepper (or to taste)
¾ cup butter
¾ cup flour
1 cup whipping cream
2 cups of cooked, flaked salmon (not smoked)

Place potatoes in a large pan, cover with salted water and bring
to a boil. Cook until potatoes are tender. Drain in colander and set
aside. (Do not return potatoes to original pot.)

In the pot you used for the potatoes, sauté bacon on medium-
high heat until it just begins to crisp. Add onion and celery and sauté
until vegetables are tender. Add milk, chicken broth, parsley, salt, and
pepper. Heat through, but do not boil after adding the milk.

In a medium saucepan, melt butter over medium heat. Add flour
and stir constantly for 1 minute, allowing to brown slightly. Add
whipping cream slowly and stir constantly until thickened. Do not burn.

Stir flour-cream mixture into soup, stirring constantly. Add
cooked potatoes and salmon. Let simmer 10 minutes, until soup is
thick. Keep on low heat.

Serves 20 (feel free to double as necessary).

Note: Substituting chicken, turkey, ham, or corn for the salmon
creates a variety of chowders.

Note: A touch of mustard brings out the flavor of the salmon—but just a touch.

Note: Don't tell Shirley or Debi, but canned salmon works in a pinch.

Enjoy this sneak peek of

ROCKY ROAD

Coming Fall 2013

CHAPTER 1

Bittersweet Anniversary

On the two-month anniversary of Dr. Trenton Hendricks' disappearance during a hiking trip in the Paradise Point area, his wife, Anita Hendricks, has announced a memorial service to be held in his honor on Thursday, June 20, at 2:00 at the Bloomington Funeral Home.

Dr. Hendricks was last seen on Saturday, April 8, when he set out on an overnight backpacking trip alone. "He is an experienced hiker," his wife said on April 12. "And he often takes to the backcountry in an attempt to clear his head following a busy work-week."

When Dr. Hendricks failed to return from the hike, Mrs. Hendricks contacted Search and Rescue on Monday afternoon. Dr. Hendricks' car was found at the Chuckwalla trailhead, but after six full days and thousands of man-hours, the official search was called off.

The memorial service will be held just one day prior to the Red Rock Cancer Walk, a Breast Cancer Awareness fundraising event that Dr. Hendricks and his business partner, Dr. Jacob Waters, began nine years ago. Though rumored to have been cancelled this year due to Dr. Hendricks' disappearance, Mrs. Hendricks has confirmed that the event will take place as it has in previous years. When asked about the decision to continue with the event, Mrs. Hendricks said, "It is what Trenton would have wanted. He was passionate about his work, and I take comfort in knowing that while the hole he has left in so many lives will never be filled, he left this world a better place than he found it."

In lieu of flowers, donations may be made to the Red Rock Cancer Fund, an organization which provides free breast cancer screenings to low-income women in Iron and Washington Counties.

Community members are invited to join the event this Friday at 7:00 p.m. The 12-hour Night Walk will begin at 7:30 and end with a pancake breakfast Saturday morning at 8:00 a.m. Entry for the walk is $25 per person. Each participant will receive a T-shirt and a gift bag containing contributions from local sponsors.

This paper would like to officially extend our condolences to the Hendricks family. The staff grieves for your loss—one that is shared by many in this community.

Sadie finished reading the article and looked up at Caro, Pete's cousin and Sadie's friend. She and Caro had just checked into their hotel room in St. George, Utah, as part of an extended girls' weekend they'd planned last month—before Sadie's unforgettable cruise and unexpected trip to Anchorage. If she'd felt she could have stayed home without hurting Caro's feelings, Sadie likely would have—she'd been traveling for most of the month of June—but she loved spending time with Caro and didn't know when she'd have another opportunity to visit with her like this.

Was it Sadie's imagination that Caro had been a little too excited to have her read this article as soon as they got into their room? And did Caro also seem too expectant of Sadie's response?

"That's too bad about Dr. Hendricks," she said, refolding the newspaper carefully and placing it beside her on the bed.

"It *is* too bad," Caro said from where she sat on the other double bed. "And weird, right?"

"Weird?" Sadie repeated, wondering at Caro's pointed interest. "Weird how?"

"He *disappeared*. . . . And everyone seems to be assuming he's dead, but there's no proof. I read some other articles about it, and no one has found anything. Not his pack, a shoe—nothing."

"Disappearances are always hard to deal with," Sadie said, ignoring what she feared was behind Caro's comments. Caro wanted to investigate; Sadie could feel it, but she didn't share her friend's anticipation. Sadie had come to St. George to enjoy a few days with her good friend, not to investigate the disappearance of a man she'd never met.

"He was Audrey's doctor, you know, when she found the lump. She said he was really great—sympathetic and up-to-date on the latest treatments. She and many of his other patients are really heartbroken over this."

Sadie put her hands in her lap and pondered a few seconds before speaking. "Please tell me this isn't why we're here," she said with a faltering smile. "Please tell me we came to attend some plays and eat yummy food and be part of the walkathon with your cousin?"

"Of course that's why we came," Caro said, looking sheepish. "Audrey and I have participated in this walkathon every year since she was first diagnosed, and I'm so excited that you're with us this year. You're going to love Audrey; she's so much fun." She looked at the newspaper still beside Sadie on the bed. "I didn't think much about Dr. Hendricks' disappearance when Audrey first told me about it either, but the more I read about it and talked with her, the more I thought . . . well, here, let me get the other articles for you. Audrey gave me a whole stack when I got here Monday."

Caro hurried for her suitcase by the door. Once her back was turned, Sadie let out a breath, wondering how best to tell her friend that her interest level in solving mysteries was at an all-time low. A glance at the diamond ring on her left hand initiated the familiar zing she felt every time she looked at it. She was engaged. Engaged! *To be married!* Though eager to seal the deal, planning the wedding required some flexibility on her and Pete's part if they wanted their families to be there—which they did. July 26 was chosen as the big day—but that was still five weeks away. For that reason, it was probably a good thing that Sadie had plenty to do between now and then, this trip with Caro being one of the things that would fill her days while she waited to become Mrs. Peter Cunningham.

"Sadie?"

Sadie blinked and looked up to meet Caro's bemused expression. "What?"

Caro was sitting on the bed across from Sadie again, holding a stack of papers in both hands—the articles, Sadie assumed. "I asked if Dr. Hendricks' disappearance seems strange to you. Have you dealt with anything like this before?"

"Not like this, no."

Caro nodded, but seemed disappointed in Sadie's response. Caro was a natural when it came to investigative work. She was detail-oriented, smart, and uninhibited when it came to sneaking around.

Plus, she found it all very exciting. When she'd helped Sadie with an investigation several months ago, Sadie had loved those qualities about Caro. But Sadie's head was in a different place now—she had a wedding to plan, a married life to prepare for.

"I wonder," Caro said, boldness coloring her words, "if you and I could look into things while we're here, ya know? Answer some of the as-yet-unanswered questions and figure out what happened to Dr. Hendricks."

"Search and Rescue looked for six days, Caro."

"I don't mean searching the backcountry. You and I both know that's only part of the mystery. I mean, why did he go out by himself? And why hasn't anyone found any of his gear? And what was his personal life like? Professional life? Was anyone angry with him? Did he have debts to hide from? St. George isn't a big city, and the people are nice. I bet we could gather a lot of information."

Sadie tamped down the curiosity that began to stir in response to Caro's questions. Her own investigative instincts were never far below the surface. Instead of giving into the tingle and pull, however, she shook her head and tried to think of what Pete would say. "I'm sure the police are investigating, and you're jumping to some pretty extreme conclusions with no evidence. Did Audrey put you up to this?"

"Not really," Caro said in a tone that clearly meant Audrey *was* part of this. She'd gathered all the articles and had given them to Caro for a reason. Did Audrey know about Caro's forays into investigation work?

"I'm happy to share my concerns with Audrey," Sadie said, "but if you're thinking of trying to investigate this disappearance, you'll have to count me out." She smiled in hopes of softening her words, though she meant every one of them. "Most people who know my history don't believe it, but I don't go looking for mysteries to solve—especially now. I have a wedding to plan, and you know what happened on that cruise. I realize that this is a difficult time for the people who cared about Dr. Hendricks, but I'm really not interested in pursuing this, Caro, I'm sorry."

Caro bit her lip while looking at the pile of papers in her lap; her disappointment was impossible to ignore. Sadie felt bad shooting Caro down, but she had told her the truth and so refrained from apologizing again.

"What if . . ." Caro started just as the silence was becoming awkward.

Sadie waited for her to continue, but Caro seemed to be thinking hard about what to say, or perhaps, whether to say it at all. Caro couldn't know what her delays did for Sadie's curiosity, which was growing by the moment. What if Dr. Hendricks *did* have a reason to disappear?

Sadie prompted Caro to finish her thought. "What if, *what?*"

Caro looked up from the articles she was holding tight in her hands and met Sadie's eyes, a distinctly guilty look on her face. "What if I already found something?"

Acknowledgments

🍓

In May 2012, I found a fabulous deal on an Alaskan cruise, I asked my husband if he wanted to go, and he said "Heck yeah!" We cruised the Inside Passage in June, and then I pretty much put this book off until September. The cruise made all the difference in helping this story come together, and Debi and Shirley, of Sweet Mermaids, made my day when they agreed to let me print their recipe for Salmon and Red Potato Chowder, which truly was the best meal I had that whole week; that is saying a lot since the cruise had fabulous food. Big thanks to them for inspiring the end of this story and for letting me share their recipe with my readers.

The other recipes were finely tuned by my amazing test kitchen: Danyelle Ferguson (Chef Ferguson's Stuffed Mushrooms), Don Carey, Katie Kennedy, Megan O'Neill, Lisa Swinton, Sandra Sorenson (Sandra's Sweet and Sour Sauce), Whit Larsen, Annie Funk, and Laree Ipson. These guys are simply amazing, and I owe them so much for making the recipe portion of this book possible. My sister, Crystal White, donated the caramel popcorn recipe, my friend Kara Monroe let me use her delicious bread pudding recipe, Becki Clayson gave me her recipe for glazed salmon, and Sara Wells and Kate Jones of *Our Best Bites* generously allowed me to use their recipe for Lemon-Zucchini Fettuccine. Thanks, ladies, I so appreciate your help.

I am so grateful for my writing group: Becki Clayson, Ronda Hinrichsen (*Betrayed*, Covenant, 2014), Jody Durfee (*Hadley, Hadley Bensen*, Covenant, 2013), and Nancy Campbell Allen (*The Grecian Princess*, book three in the Isabelle Webb series, Covenant, 2013). They are absolutely priceless both in the critique process as well as the necessary brainstorming that goes into each story. Thank you also to Crystal White and Jenny Moore for beta-reading this story. And a big thanks to Gregg Luke for giving me a method for murder.

Thanks goes to the staff at Shadow Mountain for all their hard work to turn my words into an actual book: Jana Erickson, product director; Lisa Mangum (*After Hello*, Shadow Mountain, 2012), editor; Malina Grigg and Rachael Ward, typesetters; and Shauna Gibby, designer. They make me look and sound so good.

Thank you to my friends and family who cheer me on, my readers who keep wanting more, and my writing networks that enhance the writing experience so much.

The foundation for my ability to do what I do is my amazing husband and fabulous children. Thank you for being nothing short of wonderful. Each one of you are such a blessing in my life. I thank God for you each day.

AUTHOR'S NOTE

Sweet Mermaids is an actual café located on Front Street in Ketchikan, Alaska, that opened for business on April 4, 2011. The owners, Debi Hanas and Shirley Solaas, were awarded the Rotary Club Business of the Year for Ketchikan 2012 for their Spirit of Entrepreneurship.

My husband and I ate at their cute café during our port stop in Ketchikan and got very close to embarrassing ourselves due to the "Mmm"s and "This is so good" that we kept batting back and forth across our bowls of their delicious chowder. Following the cruise, I contacted Debi and Shirley about the possibility of using that recipe, telling myself that the worst they could say was "No." Imagine my excitement when, instead, they said "Yes."

If you ever find yourself on the beautiful island of Ketchikan, I highly recommend stopping in at their establishment. They take great pride in what they do, and it shows in every bite.

You can find them on Facebook at www.facebook.com/pages /Sweet-Mermaids.

About the Author

Josi S. Kilpack began her first novel in 1998. Her seventh novel, *Sheep's Clothing*, won the 2007 Whitney Award for Mystery/Suspense, and *Lemon Tart*, her ninth novel, was a 2009 Whitney Award finalist. *Baked Alaska* is Josi's eighteenth novel and the ninth book in the Sadie Hoffmiller Culinary Mystery Series.

Josi currently lives in Willard, Utah, with her husband and children.

For more information about Josi, you can visit her website at www.josiskilpack.com, read her blog at www.josikilpack.blogspot.com, or contact her via e-mail at Kilpack@gmail.com.

IT'D BE A CRIME
TO MISS THE REST OF THE SERIES . . .

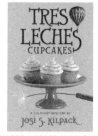

BY JOSI S. KILPACK

Available online and at a bookstore near you.

www.shadowmountain.com • www.josiskilpack.com

SHADOW
MOUNTAIN